Praise for
OATHS OF LEGACY

"Skrutskie sets her characters' competing political and personal motivations against stellar battle scenes. . . . An engaging narrative that should satisfy existing fans and new readers alike. Recommended for fans of anime-inspired space opera and readers looking for queer relationships in their sf sagas."

—*Booklist*

"Skrutskie's breathless, brilliantly written action sequences and tear-jerking quieter moments will keep readers enthralled. [*Oaths of Legacy*] is a knockout."

—*Publishers Weekly* (starred review)

"*Oaths of Legacy* is a wildly thrilling and fast-paced sci-fi adventure, and equal parts a heart-wrenching romance torn asunder by bloodrights and galactic war."

—*Your Money Geek*

"Skrutskie is a master of perspective."

—*But Why Tho?*

Praise for

BONDS OF BRASS

"A fast-paced space opera with heart and style, *Bonds of Brass* had me screaming KISS ALREADY on every page."

—Delilah S. Dawson, *New York Times* bestselling author of *Star Wars: Phasma*

"Fast ships, quick decisions, a new friend who likes to blow stuff up, and a love story with empires at stake: This story's got it all."

—Kevin Hearne, *New York Times* bestselling author of *A Plague of Giants* and the Iron Druid Chronicles

"Thrilling and unpredictable, this book kept me on the edge of my seat all the way to an end that I did not see coming. All I can say now is . . . wait for it . . . wait for it."

—Mindee Arnett, author of *Onyx & Ivory*

"*Bonds of Brass* is an action-packed, incisively clever, and unapologetically queer space opera."

—Tordotcom

"A gripping tale of romance and galactic intrigue that snared me from the first chapter and never released its hold . . . With lovable, memorable characters, an exciting web of empires and freedom fighters, and dangerous secrets, this book will keep you breathless to the last page!"

—S. J. Kincaid, *New York Times* bestselling author of *The Diabolic*

Also by
EMILY SKRUTSKIE

Bonds of Brass

Hullmetal Girls

The Abyss Surrounds Us

The Edge of the Abyss

OATHS OF LEGACY

OATHS OF LEGACY

BOOK TWO OF THE BLOODRIGHT TRILOGY

EMILY SKRUTSKIE

NEW YORK

Oaths of Legacy is a work of fiction.
Names, characters, places, and incidents either are the product of the author's imagination or are used fictitiously. Any resemblance to actual persons, living or dead, events, or locales is entirely coincidental.

2022 Del Rey Trade Paperback Edition

Published in the United States by Del Rey, an imprint of Random House, a division of Penguin Random House LLC, New York.

Del Rey and the Circle colophon are registered trademarks of Penguin Random House LLC.

Originally published in hardcover in the United States by Del Rey, an imprint of Random House, a division of Penguin Random House LLC, in 2021.

This book contains an excerpt from the forthcoming book *Vows of Empire* by Emily Skrutskie. This excerpt has been set for this edition only and may not reflect the final content of the forthcoming edition.

Library of Congress Cataloging-in-Publication Data
Names: Skrutskie, Emily, 1993– author.
Title: Oaths of legacy / Emily Skrutskie.
Description: First edition. | New York: Del Rey, [2021] |
Series: The bloodright trilogy; book two
Identifiers: LCCN 2021003365 (print) | LCCN 2021003366 (ebook) |
ISBN 9780593128947 (paperback) | ISBN 9780593128930 (ebook)
Subjects: CYAC: Kings, queens, rulers, etc.—Fiction. |
Inheritance and succession—Fiction. | Government, Resistance to—Fiction. |
Gays—Fiction. | Science fiction.
Classification: LCC PZ7.1.S584 Oat 2021 (print) |
LCC PZ7.1.S584 (ebook) | DDC [Fic]—dc23
LC record available at https://lccn.loc.gov/2021003365
LC ebook record available at https://lccn.loc.gov/2021003366

Printed in the United States of America on acid-free paper

randomhousebooks.com

1st Printing

Book design and title-page illustration by Edwin Vazquez

To Tina Guo's sick electric cello riffs on the *Wonder Woman* soundtrack, which fueled the most important parts of this book.

OATHS OF LEGACY

CHAPTER I

THERE'S A QUIET to captivity. Its monotony steals time. I can feel myself getting slower and duller to match it.

It's the exact opposite of what I should be doing. If all had gone according to plan, I'd be at the Umber Imperial Seat right now, preparing to take my crown. I'd be caught in a tumult of meetings designed to bring me up to speed on the seven-year handover process that would begin the day I turned eighteen. I'd be proving to my mother, Iva emp-Umber, that I deserve wholeheartedly to take up her mantle—that I *am* the perfect heir she raised. That's all gone to hell now.

All of this is to say that my guard is solidly *down* when the man comes crashing through the grate on the ceiling.

I'm lounging on an ostentatious couch that used to belong to Berr sys-Tosa, legs kicked up on a pillow, and for a moment I find myself locked in my messy repose as my body scrambles to inject the necessary adrenaline into my bloodstream. Two horrible, still seconds pass as the intruder locks his sights onto me.

Then he lunges.

I grab the pillow from behind my head and fling it at him, but it glances harmlessly off stealth-black tac armor. I barely manage to snag the pillow at my feet and jam it up between us before he's on me, his right hand swinging up with an obvious glint in it. The blade sinks into the pillow, the tip of it tearing free mere inches from my throat. The sight of it sparks something deep in my gut, a survival instinct so strong that for a moment my brain takes the copilot's chair. I twist my arms, yanking the knife away from my jugular as I brace one foot on the sofa beneath me and lunge upward.

The assassin staggers back a step, giving me the space I need to snatch his wrist and lever his arm up over his head. The whites of his eyes flare in surprise, and I jam the heel of my hand up against the hilt of his blade, popping it out of his grasp before he can counter. The clatter of metal against the stone floor sends a pulse of relief coursing down my spine.

Then the man's free hand latches around my throat.

He throws me down hard, nearly cracking my head open on the tiles. I've got one breath left in my lungs, and before he can tighten his grip, I holler, "*Help!*"

My brain slides back into the pilot's chair just in time to realize what a waste that is. There are guards stationed outside my room, but their only order is to prevent me from getting out. They don't care about anybody getting *in*—in fact, they'd probably welcome the death of the Umber heir with open arms. Most people in this palace are solidly on the side of cutting off the Umber line of succession.

I'm one of the few holding out on the other side. I squirm as my throat collapses under the assassin's weight, trying to wrench a knee up somewhere soft. All I find is more tactical weave, bruising me wherever I try to strike it. My hands scrabble fruitlessly at his wrists, a plea caught in my spasming windpipe. All my life, I've been surrounded by people who leap into action whenever someone tries to kill me. Bodyguards when I was a kid, growing up in the shadows of the Imperial Seat. Sleepers once I left its safety to study on Naberrie and train on Rana, in the heart of the former Archon Empire. And when that life and the secrets that propped it up shattered on a clear winter's day in the skies above the academy—

When a Corinthian mobster on a wiretram raised his gun with my heart in its sights—

When the great Archon general Maxo Iral, risen from the dead, victorious in his bid to reclaim the old empire's capital and have his vengeance on my parents for their conquest, held my fate in his hands—

Fury strikes like flint, and my blood ignites. My gaze flicks sideways and catches the end table perched next to the couch. *Within reach?*

It had better be. I lash out with one hand, knocking over the glass of sweetwine I've been nursing. It shatters with a sharp, clear noise that doesn't break the assassin's laserlike focus on watching the life drain from my face.

Pity. If he'd looked, he would have caught the moment my fingers closed around the stone coaster.

A thrill washes over me the moment I slam it into his temple. I feel myself come back to life in the *crunch*—all the way back, back from the languor that's lasted so long that I've nearly lost track of the time I've spent here. His hands spring free as he instinctively reaches up to guard his head against another blow, and I choke down the breath I sorely need. But the air has its price; the assassin is already lunging for the knife he dropped. I surge to my feet and hurl the coaster at him, striking him hard on the back of his skull. He falters enough that I have the opening I need to leap on top of him.

No one is rushing in to save my life now. For the first time in nearly eighteen years, I have to do the damn thing myself. My fists rain down on the man's head furiously, my stomach convulsing as I try to keep down the urge to gag long enough to stop him from killing me. I lose my rationality to the steady rhythm of beating him senseless, and for a moment I think I understand why Archon people like their drums so much.

It isn't until a second set of arms wraps around me from behind that I come back to my senses. I buck and thrash against the grip, but they pin me tightly, yanking me off my knees, up and away from the twitching, groaning man I've left lying on the floor.

The first clear thought lodges in my head when I spot the coaster next to him—*Should have used that to finish the job, would have done more damage.*

The next: *What the ever-loving* rut *is wrong with you, Gal emp-Umber?*

I'm half a second from throwing my head back into the nose of whoever's grappling me when I note the emerald-green stitching on their sleeves. Imperial-guard uniforms, which means this is one of the two useless louts who were posted outside my door. Confirming that suspicion, the second surges past me, tucking a blaster back in her belt as she drops on top of my would-be assassin and wrestles his arms behind his back.

"Oh good, you got him," I say flatly, and she fixes me with a thin-lipped look over her shoulder. I don't dare articulate the concern that gripped me earlier. If they were hoping the assassin would finish the job, I'm sorry to disappoint.

My guard pulls the poor man to his feet, giving me a good look at my handiwork. His nose is crooked, one eye swollen shut, the lower half of his face painted in blood from a split lip. The slickness on my hands apparently isn't just sweat. I reach back and wipe them on the uniform of the guard holding me.

A resigned sigh wheezes in my ear.

"Traitors," the assassin chokes, spattering blood in the face of his captor. "That Umber whelp should be beheaded at the seat for the galaxy to see. Not kept in this ruttin' jewelry box." He rolls his eyes at the lavish appointments around us.

"He has a point," I mutter, and the hands restraining me tighten painfully. My guards are well aware of the public opinion. The Archon people want to give the Umber imperials a taste of their own medicine. Justice for my mother's execution of Marc and Henrietta emp-Archon. They've been calling for my blood for weeks, but this is the first time anyone has had the gumption to take the matter into their own hands. I'm almost impressed, although that sentiment is dampened by the fact that he very nearly succeeded.

Probably on account of being kept in a ruttin' jewelry box. If I were in a normal cell with normal round-the-clock surveillance, there'd be no chance someone could get within striking distance. But instead I'm kept in comfort and nearly got my throat cut if not for a fancy embroidered pillow.

"I'll get this asshole to a cell and call in a perimeter check," the female guard says. "You take the prisoner to the emperor and report the incident."

I resist the urge to squirm out of the guard's grip, even though he releases me a second later. My blood heats back up to a simmer in a flash. *Cool it, hot shot,* I tell myself, rolling my head from side to side as I wring my hands, trying my best to wipe some of the slickness off my skin. Absentmindedly, I muss my hair, as if that's going to do anything to smooth it back from its unruly state. Probably shouldn't have done that. Getting the blood and spit out later is going to be hell.

But if I'm going to see the emperor, I gotta look my best. As the guard beckons me toward the door, the absent weight at my wrists reminds me that I'm forgetting something. "One second," I call to him, bustling to the other side of my suite.

The platinum cuffs are right where I left them. My reflection warps in them as I approach, turning me into a twisted facsimile that blows monstrously huge as I reach for one. The cool, solid weight of it slips around my wrist so easily that for a moment I let it be nothing but comforting.

These cuffs have been my constant companions in the weeks since General Iral ran down the *Ruttin' Hell* and dragged me out in front of the galactic eye. Wrought in the Archon Empire's metal, they mark me as a prisoner of the Crown, reassuring everyone I encounter of my status within the court. I wear them every time I leave my quarters—because of course otherwise it's a little difficult to tell where I fit in, given the way the emperor has chosen to imprison me.

I spare the room's decor another withering glance. It's neither my fault nor the Archon Crown's that I'm being kept in such perceived luxury—that honor goes entirely to Berr sys-Tosa, the governor whose abandoned mansion the Archon usurper has turned into his base. In fact, most of the trimmings in this room are still done in obsidian and brass, the stone and metal of my own empire.

The empire I stand little to no chance of inheriting, thanks to the cuffs around my wrists.

I rub one sleeve over the red-stained thumbprints I've left on them, then straighten my back. "Right then," I tell the guard. "Let's go see the emperor."

CHAPTER 2

THE FIRST TIME I entered the room that would become the Archon court, I was cuffed in brass and convinced I was about to die.

There wasn't much time to admire the majesty of it with its Umber trappings—the vaulted ceiling above, the geometric brass statues that not-at-all-subtly point the eye to the center of the room. General Iral's steady hand kept an iron grip on my shoulder as he marched me to the dais at the court's focal point and started barking orders. I stood at the eye of the regime change's storm, watching as the incoming Archon army installed itself firmly in the hole Berr sys-Tosa left when he ceded the planet to Iral and betrayed my identity.

They had been setting up cameras, and I knew I was about to be shot in front of them.

I'd almost made my peace with it when the faint strains of the Archon anthem echoed from the hall outside. Followed by boltfire. Followed by a senseless boy striding through the ornate doors, brandishing a platinum-and-emerald ring and declaring himself to be heir by bloodright to all of Maxo Iral's spoils.

A senseless boy I was in love with up until precisely that moment.

Now it's my turn to blow through those doors, my escort's grip locked firmly around one of my biceps as he slams them shut behind me and signals to the others guarding the room. Within seconds, every exit is sealed, trapping us under the cavernous vault of the court's high ceiling.

Trapping me in a room with *him*.

I keep my gaze averted as the guard marches me up to the dais, passing the officials who had been presenting to the emperor before our interruption. They throw glances my way that dance the line between hatred and amusement. I feel the weight of their attention hit my platinum cuffs the strongest. *Good,* I swear I hear them think. My humiliation is proof that all is right with the world. Doesn't even matter that I have blood on my knuckles that's not mine—as long as I'm cuffed, in their eyes I'm harmless.

And much like the guards posted outside my room, they don't give a shit if I come to harm. The only person in this palace who actually does is sitting on the throne ahead.

I can't look at him. I have to look at him. He's a black hole and a burning sun all at once, the gravitational center of everyone in the room. All I want is to escape him, but everything about him makes that impossible.

I pin my focus to the cuffs on my wrists and my twisted reflection within them, wishing the Archon occupation hadn't done away with the brass sculptures. I could have spent hours distracting myself in their geometries. Instead, all I have is my own image thrown back at me in the trappings of my imprisonment. Since the moment the emperor presented the cuffs to me, pleading with me to understand that it was just for the coronation ceremony—just for the cameras, just for the *galaxy* to see and know for sure that I was his prisoner—I haven't let the goddamn things out of my sight. If I'm going to be his prisoner, I'm going to rub it in his face as much as I can. Every moment he sees me in the cuffs is a reminder of what he's done to me, and I want that wound to bleed forever.

In the warped, silvery metal, I see him rise abruptly from his throne. "What," Ettian emp-Archon asks, "the ever-loving *rut* is going on?"

"Perimeter breach, Your Majesty," the guard dragging me says. "The intruder's been apprehended, but we're going on lockdown until we figure out exactly how he got in."

It's absolute agony to hold my tongue, but I bite down on the urge to butt in. Ever since Ettian burst through the doors of this room with that unforgivable signet ring on his finger, I haven't said a single word in his presence, and I'm not about to break that streak just to be pedantic. Instead I twist my wrists, knowing the glint of the cuffs will catch his eye and the sight of blood on my hands will keep it.

"What happened?" Ettian asks. In my warped periphery, I see the suggestion of him sweeping down from the dais. "What did you do this time?"

Don't you ruttin' dare react, I warn myself, even though it's taking a full-body effort just to keep myself from rolling my eyes. Over the past month, I've taken every opportunity possible to test the limits of my imprisonment. Knocking plates off tables and watching them shatter. Clicking my cuffs together over and over again until the guards' eyes start to twitch in time with the noise. If I had the means, I would have sent the bedsheets up in a blaze, but I haven't figured out how to start a fire yet. The aim of the game is petty annoyance—seeing just how much I can get away with in the confines Ettian has imposed, and showing off to the guards just how loose a leash he keeps on me.

"The intruder . . . got to him," my guard admits after an optimistic pause, no doubt hoping I'd answer for the hole he's dug himself in. "It seems to have been a targeted attempt on his life."

And I can't stop myself—my eyes give in at last, flicking where they're drawn just in time to catch Ettian's expression twisting into fury. A month ago, the sight would have warmed my heart. In a way, it still does, but it's a twisted sort of glee that takes over at the sight of his flared nostrils. The dipshit may have killed off any feelings I had for him, but from his reaction, it's clear his feelings for me are alive and well.

Which is continuing to bite him in the ass, if the tightening of the guard's grip on my arm is any indication. The emperor should know better than to express this kind of sentiment over an enemy captive when soldiers are out dying on his front lines. "Tell me again what happened," Ettian demands, authority dripping from his cool, lethal tone.

I don't understand how he's like this. I don't understand where this *came from*. He's explained this to me before—explained while I studiously ignored him in favor of scratching a button on my sleeve into the varnish of the table in front of me. The boy I knew as Ettian Nassun rose from the ashes of Trost, the Archon Empire's former seat, after Umber bombed it into submission and took the empire for themselves. He spent two years scrapping for his life as the city slowly put itself back together around him and another three in a foster system once such a thing had the decency to pluck him off the streets.

I met him at fifteen, when both of us enrolled at the Umber Imperial Academy on Rana. I was a prince in disguise, surrounded by sleeper agents posing as fellow cadets, meant to get an education out among the common people before duty called me to assume my bloodright and take the empire's reins from my parents.

He was a prince dethroned, desperately searching for purpose in a galaxy that no longer needed him.

But all I saw was a gaunt, gangly kid who looked just as terrified and out of place as I felt. As I got to know him, I learned that the war had left him scarred—so scarred that he wouldn't even talk about anything prior to the moment he got taken off the streets. And like any decent person, I didn't pry deeper. I took him at face value and slowly, inevitably fell in love with all that he was.

Now I've blown it, so I might as well look unflinchingly at all that he is. He's dressed in a suit that's been expertly trimmed to his lean, slender height, the jewel-green tones complementing his dark complexion and the platinum trim sparkling like stars. An ugly, twisted crown of platinum sits atop his close-cropped, wiry hair. I remember well the feeling of the weight of it leaving my hands as I set it atop his head before a screaming crowd. He seems tired under the load—the nonstop burden of being the sole carrier of the Archon bloodright, the weight of having to rule and win back his empire in the same breath.

And this situation probably isn't helping.

Good.

"The . . . prisoner was in his quarters," my guard starts. "We were posted in the hall outside. We heard a disturbance from the room, but assumed it was his usual antics. By the time we grew suspicious, he had already taken care of the attacker himself."

"Taken care of?"

"We had to pull him off the guy," my guard says.

It takes the faint rattle of metal on metal for me to realize that my hands are shaking. *Don't do it,* I scream at myself internally. This can't be the thing that breaks me. But I'm not about to let this asshole put the emperor's mind at ease, and I'm *certainly* not going to let him get away with a lie that'll get me killed if I'm not as lucky the next time someone makes it past him.

"I yelled for help," I announce.

The court falls silent. A second later, I hear the sharp hiss of Ettian's inhale as he realizes these are the first words I've spoken to him since the day I found out who he really was. His eyes lock on mine, and I fight the instinct to dodge his gaze.

"The man got in through a vent. He came at me with a knife. I yelled for help." I hold up my hands, flashing my bloody knuckles at him. "Two guards were posted outside the door, and I had to beat the assassin down myself."

"We didn't hear any—" the guard tries to insert.

"You clearly heard *something,*" I retort, jabbing one reddened finger under his chin. The guard snarls and twists my arm, wrenching me down into a contorted bow, and even though it barely hurts, I let out a pained yelp.

"*Stop,*" Ettian snaps, and the guard releases me, taking a step back.

I drop to my knees, trying to conceal my smirk. Once again, there he goes displaying an affection he's been advised to scorch out of himself, right in front of people whose loyalty he desperately needs. I tip my head back, baring my throat to the light. I haven't had a chance to appraise the marks my would-be assassin left there, but from the slight hitch in Ettian's breath, I know they've done what I need them to.

"You're relieved of duty," the emperor announces.

Oh, this is almost too easy. I can all but feel the room's opinion of their emperor crumbling away. Ettian emp-Archon's transition to power was slipshod at best, and ever since I set that crown on his head, it's been doing its best to wobble right off again. Originally the Archon invasion had planned to let their military lead while they hacked away at restoring their former holdings, then transition to a more democratic system of government with assistance from their Corinthian neighbors. Then Ettian waltzed in, brandishing his father's signet ring, and everything went to hell.

Much like Umber, the former Archon Empire believed strongly in the bloodright of its rulers. Power transitioned from generation to generation through clear-cut lines of succession, aided by the common practice of hiding one's offspring from the galactic eye until they were ready to step up and begin taking over their parents' reign. But when Umber conquered Archon and Marc and Henrietta emp-Archon were beheaded at the Imperial Seat, no heirs came tumbling out of the shadows to fill their place. Power transitioned easily over to Umber governors like Berr sys-Tosa, people who stepped in ready to oversee the effort it would take to sculpt the Archon territories back into their proper shapes. Archon pride withered away, aided by the defeat and apparent execution of Maxo Iral.

Now it has a new figurehead: my dumbass former roommate. The boy who once pancaked a Viper on a runway because he'd used his landing gear to literally glue himself to me is now the leader of a haphazard attempt to reclaim an empire. The Archon people saw his revelation as a sign, proof that bloodright reign will restore what they lost.

But the fact remains that they've handed governance of a revolution over to an eighteen-year-old whose last brush with imperial training happened when he was *ten*. Worse—at least from an Archon perspective—since then their heir has been raised by the Umber military machine. Now he's doing his damnedest to take the reins of one that's unflinchingly Archon, trying to scrape back what trust he can rebuild from the people he failed. I could rant in his face for hours and still not even scratch the surface of all the mistakes he's making.

I won't, though. Instead, I'm going to see just how many more missteps I can dance him through. Because if I'm doomed to be their pet princeling, I'm going to do my damnedest to topple his fledgling empire from the inside. I know what it feels like to lose all my faith in Ettian emp-Archon. Might as well see if I can get the rest of his people to follow my example.

And it starts with the slight scoffing noise my guard makes as he's relieved of his post at my side. It's a sound of disappointment, a sound of resignation, a sound that makes it clear the young emperor isn't doing anything to keep his people's faith. It's a crack I can dig my fingernails into and *peel*. A sort of hunger keens in my stomach, eager for the next opportunity to strike.

So strike I do.

"Seriously?" I ask, throwing my voice loud enough that it echoes off the cavernous ceiling overhead. I brace for another move from the guard, but he's already taking a long step backward, thrilled to be free of my orbit.

Ettian's incredulous gaze snaps to me, like he's not sure he's lucky enough to be hearing me speak twice in one day.

"You're letting this asshole *live*?" I ask, and point vehemently back at the guard. "He defied orders. He nearly let your most valuable hostage die to satisfy a personal vendetta. You're gonna reward that? Look at him—he's thrilled you're taking him off this assignment. He should be ruttin' terrified."

"That's not how we do things," Ettian replies, his voice soft but full of firm conviction.

"Why, because you think it's gonna win you people?" I scoff, resisting the urge to tuck my bloody hands into my armpits. "All it proves is that you're not really in charge here."

At least he's not stupid enough to rise to that bait—though I wasn't really counting on him doing it. Blustering about how he *is* in charge would have the opposite of its intended effect in the eyes of the room. But speaking those words aloud has its own kind of power, the kind of grain-of-sand irritation that grows pearls with enough time. If I can get him insecure, I can get him sloppy.

If I can get him sloppy, I might even achieve the second thing on my to-do list.

Because sure, toppling a regime from the inside would be impressive, but it also sounds tedious as hell. There's a throne waiting for me on the other end of the galactic arm, and three months until I'm old enough to start my own succession. If I'm wise about how I use them, there's a chance I might make it home and start my reign right on time.

Getting my guards fired is a damn good start. The more I can degrade the security around me, the better—especially since measures will probably increase in the wake of the assassination attempt. Ettian dismissing the guard is an opportunity, and I've got to figure out fast how I'll spend it before the snare closes around my legs again.

A sudden banging from the fore of the court wrenches me away from the churn of my thoughts. Ettian straightens, eyes narrowed, then relaxes when he glances down at the datapad in his hands. "Let her—" he starts.

With a shriek of boltfire and a puff of smoke, Wen Iffan kicks through the door.

". . . in," Ettian finishes flatly.

CHAPTER 3

A MONTH AS Ettian's rogue enforcer has been more than kind to Wen. She's traded ratty rags for a lightweight set of tac armor, and her wiry muscles have rounded out with good food and better work. Even her gait has changed, her light-footed, darting steps settled down into a confident stride that carries her through the massive brass doors at the court's entrance with her head held high.

She's also smoking slightly.

I've heard the stories that whisper through the usurped city that serves as the rebellion's haphazard Imperial Seat. Rumors of a girl the people have taken to calling the Flame Knight carving through any Umber dissidents left in Trost. I've seen the smirks on my guards' lips when they sight a plume on the outskirts of the city, the signal fire that lets the galaxy know that Wen Iffan is working.

I've also seen scowls. Wen's been effective at rooting out any attempts by the Umber-loyal to organize in the city, but that effectiveness comes at a steep cost paid in property damage. If Wen were native to Trost, maybe she'd be a little more careful about her work, but she left the lawless, rough-and-tumble city of her birth back in the Corinthian Empire and brought its philosophy along for the ride. For the people who call this place home, it's . . . grating, to say the least.

She waltzes across the room, her grin visible from a distance. "Good hunting today, boss," she calls as she approaches the dais. "Up until, of course, I heard we had a little kerfuffle back at home base. Hey, Gal."

I tip a sardonic wave at her, and she lifts her chin, tilting her face so I catch a full view of the burn scars that coat half of it. She wears them proudly, her hair pulled back and slicked down, a constant reminder that once upon a time in Corinth, a mobster stuck her face in the tailpipe of a starship.

That's all you really need to know about Wen Iffan. Some people are made of joy or love or hate. Wen, it seems, is made of trouble. She drags it wherever she goes like a kid pulling a favorite stuffed toy through the dirt. If she hadn't tethered herself to Ettian's ship, I might find her charming. Fun, even. But this is war, and the sides are clear. Something unshakable clicked into place between Wen and Ettian when they met, something I was right to resent.

Ettian has all the hate in my heart. But Wen just pisses me off.

"We've had an intruder, yes," Ettian says. There's an interesting note of consternation in his voice, and I find myself studying his face a little closer than I should. "Before that, though, I received a report of a crisis in the Hensi District. Something about a prewar building toppling."

Wen's grin gets wider. "Yeah, I didn't think it would work as well as it did, but—"

"You're saying this was on purpose?" Ettian asks tersely, eliminating any need for further study.

Wen didn't get this far by missing cues like this. The grin drops from her face, though the ghost of it stays tucked in one corner of her mouth. "My team cleared the area. Sims ran the demo—you know he always checks his work thoroughly. No civilians were harmed. And we took out an entire cell that might have been a threat—"

"You knocked over a building in the middle of a city."

"I dropped a building on some would-be terrorists. Technicalities."

Ettian huffs. "And meanwhile, there are assassins crawling through the vents of this very palace."

Wen's eyes go huge. "Someone tried to kill you?"

"Someone tried to kill *him*," Ettian corrects, and I have to force myself not to flinch at the weight that last word carries in his voice. If he's giving out gifts, though, I might as well worsen the implication, so I throw him a sly warning look—one I hope reads clearly as, *Babe, there are people watching.*

Ettian's too focused on Wen to catch it, but he seems to realize his misstep all the same—he straightens, lifting his chin as if that's going to make him look any more imperial. First he fires a guard over the safety of a prisoner, and now he's allowing a subordinate to openly defy him in the sight of his entire court. I smirk when his nervous gaze flits to me. *Go ahead. Show me how you salvage this.*

"I can't have you running wild in the capital—in *my* capital—"

"I'm half the reason it continues to *be* your capital—"

You have to appease her first, dipshit, I want to scream in his ear. Why I want to tell him how to lead more effectively is beyond me. Maybe it's some sick sense of self-preservation—after all, Ettian's proven himself to be the only person in the Archon territories who genuinely cares about my well-being. If he's ousted, I'm dead, most likely in a painful, public manner.

But if he lives, I'm still a prisoner. Kept in a cushiony cell, but a cell all the same. A pressure point to bend my parents where previously they were immovable. The fulcrum of his entire war.

If I topple his regime, I need an ejector seat primed and ready to get me out of the mess it'll leave in its wake.

I need a plan.

"If this revolution goes anywhere, it needs to do so with the trust of my people behind it," Ettian declares. "And you're damaging that. Until I know for sure you won't damage it further, I think it's best if you stick to applying your talents within the palace walls."

His gaze sneaks back over to me, and my stomach drops.

"Fortunately, a position's just opened up."

Oh no, I think.

"Oh no," Wen says out loud, settling her hands on her hips. "Ett—" She catches herself. The scrutiny of the court demands that she address him properly, even if to her he's still just the deserter she once tried to con into buying a ship with no engines. "Your Majesty," Wen continues, "I have work I can't just set aside. Leads I've been pursuing. The strike today was the culmination of weeks of dedicated effort, and it's only the beginning. If you want to win this war, you have to hold this city. And if you want to hold this city, you need—"

"The work can continue without you," Ettian says. "And continue it will." He steps forward off the dais, bending close to her ear in a way that has everyone else in the court craning to catch his words. "Work with me, Wen," he murmurs. "We can figure the rest out later."

She softens, but then her gaze skitters over to me and her jaw winds tight. "Someone gunned for him?" she asks, her eyes dropping to my hands.

"Got in through the vents," Ettian confirms. "Figured you're fit for the job since you've had some experience in that area."

Wen smirks, and the sight of it sends my stomach dropping back to the moment I was first dragged into this palace. She was at my side then, her hands cuffed in brass, her eyes wide and glazed in confusion. She knew she had been betrayed by me and Ettian when we tricked her into flying off-course and dropping our cargo of Archon soldiers directly on top of an Umber patrol. When I tried to convince her to fly me to the rendezvous we'd planned, she held course, demanding that I tell her exactly what was going on.

By then, the Archon fleet had been informed of my identity through Berr sys-Tosa's treachery. When they closed on us and bullied us out of the sky, I felt the tearing sensation of history repeating itself, doubled by her threatening to crash and kill us both if I didn't spit out the truth.

So I did.

Once again, it was too late to salvage anything. Wen was taken prisoner alongside me. We marched up the palace drive side by side, flanked by Archon soldiers and bound in matching chains. I kept glancing sidelong at her, but she'd—possibly deliberately—put me on her burnt side, leaving her expression inscrutable.

But I'd been through it all before, in the very same skies we'd just left. I told Ettian who I really was, shattering the illusion that had bound us together for two and a half years. And then I was taken away and locked in a cushy room that didn't *look* like a cell to await Berr sys-Tosa and, potentially, a lifetime spent as his pet prince. In desperation, I snuck a message out to Ettian, asking him to get me out of there.

And with that, I doomed him.

I wouldn't make the same mistake twice.

"Save yourself," I whispered to her. "Don't get dragged down with me."

At that, she smiled, and I caught the glint of the pick in her teeth.

The next time I saw her was on Ettian's heels as he burst through the doors of the court for the first time. It was a different kind of heartbreak I felt then, couched in the larger betrayal of Ettian's identity. Wen had done as I told her. One second she was there, and the next her cuffs were whipping into the head of the guard next to her, knocking open the formation just enough for her to bolt through. She didn't look back once. She saved her ass and left me to my fate.

Then she ran headlong into the chaos of Trost's turnover and found Ettian. She told him exactly how to get to me. She tried to come back for me, tried to fix this mess that she felt responsible for, tried to do right by both of us. In a way, she saved my life.

But in the same act, she tied herself irrevocably, unforgivably to Ettian's side. She, as I understand it, was the first he revealed his true identity to. Not me, the only other person in the galaxy who might understand his plight, the person he's so in love with that he would throw himself in the sights of my mother's wrath. No, Ettian emp-

Archon first pulled out that ring in front of a Corinthian gutter rat he'd known for a month. He gave her a choice, and she chose to follow him.

I still don't fully understand the bond that snapped into place between them barely a day after they'd met. Given that she nearly blew him up ten minutes after they first laid eyes on each other, it seems improbable. The Ettian I knew—or thought I knew—was always slow to trust. I slept in a bunk above him for two years and even though I knew him better than anyone, I also knew there was a vast ocean he kept walled away. I assumed it was because of the hell he'd lived through after the War of Expansion, the two years he spent surviving on the streets of Trost. And I didn't prod or pry at that barrier, because I was a good goddamn friend.

But Wen didn't either—she just swam in from the other side. She'd fought through her own hell, taken in and then cast out by the mobsters who killed her mother, burnt and scarred and unstoppable. And just by virtue of being herself, a connection sparked between them that I can't hold a candle to. I'm born to inherit the ruttin' galaxy, but I pale in the shadow of Wen Iffan.

With her guarding me, my chances of escaping have been all but crushed. She's ten times more savvy than any of the people Ettian has posted outside my door so far, and unlike most of them, she actually gives a damn about me—even if it's only for Ettian's sake.

But *there's* an interesting thought. My focus flicks back and forth between them, gauging Ettian's lifted chin against the way Wen's weight carries on the balls of her feet. She holds herself on guard like she's about to spring into action at any second. Or like she's about to run. Wen's whole body is a balancing act, and suddenly I find myself extremely interested in tipping it over.

Because if I know anything about revealing your imperial identity to someone, I know that it breaks something badly between you. I remember the fight Ettian and I boiled into after our escape from the academy, the things he accused me of. Those words and the fears they carried lodged in me like daggers—that I had been selfish in cultivating a friendship with him, that I'd *used* him as my ticket out of there, that nothing between us was genuine. And then there were all the things he didn't voice but I knew all the same. That my bloodline had been responsible for the conquest that had turned Trost into his personal hell. That he was scarred and traumatized and it was all for an empire I'd one day inherit. That he wasn't even sure if I was the person I'd promised to be or if I was secretly more like my mother than he could ever know.

I peer more intently at Wen, as if doing so will unearth the cracks in her armor. She's never explicitly expressed the kind of resentments Ettian did back when I first told him who I really was. But then, she's never really talked to me about anything of consequence. She was always Ettian's first.

Her gaze slides over to mine, and against my better judgment, I smirk at her.

Maybe it's time we do something about that.

CHAPTER 4

ABOVE ALL, BEING a political hostage is *boring*.

The assassination attempt put a decent dent in the monotony, so much so that I contemplate trying to send the guy a formal thank-you. Otherwise, my days are mostly spent staring out windows, fantasizing about breaking everything around me. Once, a guard had the presence of mind to ask if I was okay after she noticed me staring too hard at a houseplant. I'd been contemplating the most effective way of shredding it, but she didn't need to know that.

Now that the excitement's gone down, I'm back in my old routine, pacing my quarters, chewing the tough, starchy Archon food that an aide delivers to my rooms every morning and evening, and aimlessly plotting bloody revenge.

More exciting things are happening elsewhere in the galaxy, or so I hear whispered through the palace. Ettian currently holds Rana, the former capital planet of the Archon Empire. In the wake of his victory, fringe rebellions have boiled up all over the territories, though not all of them are in communication with Ettian's usurper regime. This entire region of the galaxy is teetering on a sliding scale between unrest and outright war.

Meanwhile, Berr sys-Tosa, the former governor—and the man

who betrayed my identity and got me taken hostage in the first place—has holed up at the core of the Tosa System on the inner world of Imre, amassing his forces. No assault has hit Archon-held Rana in over a month, which is causing all sorts of nervous speculation. There are some who insist the delay is because Iva emp-Umber has hauled Tosa to the Umber Citadel to make an example of him, but I know better. Even if he sold me out, Berr sys-Tosa and his intimate knowledge of the system remain an asset—one my mother won't waste in this war. She'll keep him alive long enough to milk his strategic value for all it's worth.

The rumor I buy is that he's holding back, hoping for reinforcements from the empress and her Imperial Fleet. A force of that size and skill takes longer to mobilize, but the results when they raze their way through this haphazard uprising will be glorious to behold. Even more glorious will be the reckoning coming for Tosa once I'm free to get my hands on him.

The main body of the rebel fleet is focused on rooting the system governor out of his exile, led by the Umber dreadnoughts that the Archon resistance managed to commandeer in their first strike. General Maxo Iral, the war hero once known as the Shield of Archon and thought to have been crucified before my parents at the Imperial Seat, leads the resistance forces.

A crop of interesting rumors has begun to sprout about the general's command, echoing through the halls with increasing frequency. Before Ettian marched into the court and demanded his bloodright, Iral was the clear leader of this rebellion. He was a figure with a storied history—the general who continued to fight for two entire years after the Archon imperials were beheaded. Calling the Archon people to his side was supposed to win hearts and minds so easily that taking back the empire would happen in a snap.

And then along came Ettian emp-Archon, whose very existence destroyed a plan half a decade in the making. While most of the Archon populace were overjoyed to see the legacy of Marc and Henrietta emp-Archon risen from the ashes, Ettian himself remains an unknown quantity to them. They know that he looks like their beloved imperials, but then there's the fact that he was schooled at an Umber military academy. The fact that he only saw fit to reveal himself when Archon had reclaimed ground for the first time since the War of Expansion.

And the fact that he was—and by all accounts appears to still be—in love with the Umber heir.

Our relationship wasn't a secret when we first joined up with the resistance on Delos—even though at that point, it was a ruse we maintained to give us a reason to constantly be off on our own, plotting and scheming and whispering in each other's ears. It served us well in that capacity, and then even better when Ettian decided to finally act on the feelings he'd resolved to bottle away for the sake of our mission.

Now that choice is biting him in the ass. Not in any way he can face—it's creeping through insidious back channels, building through gossip, eroding the foundations of his young rule. *Wouldn't it be better with Iral in charge?* the people whisper. *Isn't that how it was meant to be from the start? Shouldn't this fragile hope hang on the shoulders of a seasoned veteran, not on an eighteen-year-old whose heart's been corrupted by Umber rule?*

But gossip isn't enough to actually *do* anything right now. Which is part of the reason I've asked my newly appointed guard to see if she can't set up a moment alone between me and her emperor.

The other part is that I really, *really* need a break in the monotony that doesn't involve someone trying to kill me.

Wen was all too happy to facilitate, which is a nice change of pace from my old guards. I mentioned it to her as she swept in with breakfast this morning, and by lunch she told me to expect an afternoon coffee with the emperor. I spend the hours between fussing with my hair and clothes as if I'm genuinely preparing for a date, a fact that's not lost on Wen when she enters to escort me.

I decide the way she smirks as she looks me up and down means I'm doing *something* right.

She leads me to an observation deck in the palace's upper levels. It offers a sweeping view of downtown Trost, the early summer sun glimmering off the skyscrapers that surround us. I take a moment to absorb the strangeness of the city skyline as I've never seen it before. While the construction of the newer buildings is unquestionably Umber, the layout is far more cramped than any imperial city planner would ever allow. The testament to the city's Archon foundations chafes in an uncanny way. Maybe it's the product of captivity, maybe the fault of a lifetime of various confinements, but something about the sight leaves a yawning hole in my chest for all the places in the galaxy I've never gotten a chance to see.

A thick sheet of duroglass shields the open space from the outside world, and I'm fairly certain that light's only permitted to penetrate it in a single direction. Ettian awaits at a table in the center of the room, painted in the slightly orange glow that filters through the duroglass's tint. He watches as I approach, but makes no move to greet me—only passes a signal to Wen with a tip of his hand when I reach the chair at the other end of the table. Her bootsteps pause, then retreat after a moment of hesitation.

Leaving us completely alone.

I read it for the insult it is. Barely a week ago, I beat a man bloody, but now I'm meeting with the emperor in private as if I pose no threat at all. As if I don't toss and turn at night, consumed by fantasies of his throat collapsing under my hands. There's a part of me that desperately wants to prove I'm worth their caution, but I came to this meeting with higher goals—goals that get frustratingly difficult to remember with the usurper's eyes locked on mine.

"You wanted to speak to me?" Ettian's tone is laced with obvious disbelief. I've maintained both my silence and my utter disinterest in him steadfastly since he took me prisoner, and the fact that I've sought him out now is—while obviously welcome—suspicious as all hell.

"There are a lot of things I want to do to you," I reply, and he lets out a soft choking noise as his expression pinches. Not for the first time, I wonder how the blood of an imperial line managed to produce an heir as guileless as Ettian emp-Archon. Every day under his leadership is further justification for the fall of the Archon Empire and further evidence that his rebellion is doomed to fail. It wouldn't bother me so much if I weren't squarely within the blast radius of that failure.

Or maybe I'm the only thing shielding the Archon resistance from that blast. The thought has occurred to me, and I'm not entirely sure how that weight sits on my shoulders. If my mother rallies just right, if she successfully unites her system governors and all of their resources and rides in to save Berr sys-Tosa from his mess, she could wipe this system from the star charts. Every time I look to the skies, I hope to see an Umber dreadnought bearing down on Trost, but of course it's far too early for her to make a move like that when the war is just beginning to unfurl across the Archon territories.

After all, my mother unexpectedly lost track of an imperial heir the first time she bombed Trost. She's not about to do it again, not when this time, the heir in question is her own goddamn son. In a funny way, the only reason Ettian's rebellion is succeeding is because of me. My capture is forcing her to be more strategic, and as long as I'm tied to Ettian's side, she'll have to be a little more creative about getting him out of the way.

Which means I've got a bit of work to do myself.

"I have some unsolicited advice," I start, throwing myself down in the chair opposite Ettian. Without asking, I snatch a mug and pour myself a healthy dose of whatever's in the steaming carafe in front of him. I take a whiff of it and wrinkle my nose. "Ruttin' hell, you poor Archon bastards—where do you get these terrible beans?" Not waiting for a response, I grab a fistful of sugar from the pot and throw it into the drink, then brush my hands off, sending a spray of granules skittering over the table.

"Why are you like this?" Ettian asks, staring down at the mess I've made.

I clink my mug against the platinum cuffing my wrist, shrug, and then throw back a hefty swallow of my drink. My time in the Archon territories has acquainted me with the taste of their bitter coffee, but we've never been good friends and that certainly hasn't changed. I let out a foul cough. "Anyway, advice."

"I have advisers."

"None of whom want to see you in power, if the rumors are true."

He scoffs. "And so, what? I'm supposed to listen to you? I think apart from your mother, there's no one in the galaxy who wants me in power even less than you."

"And if you were smart, you'd see that for the advantage it is," I counter. "But you're not all that smart, so it seems my offer's wasted."

I take way too much pleasure in watching the barb land—so much so that it's a struggle to keep my own expression nonchalant. I'm missing six months of the education I was supposed to have before I was unveiled to the galaxy. Ettian is missing eight years. The way his lips twist in displeasure tells me that he's all too aware of this flaw—and fully aware that I meant this as a strike. I do have an actual objective here, and if I'm going to accomplish it, I need to stop insulting him and get to my point.

But it's just *so fun*.

I gather myself, closing my eyes and drawing a deep breath through my nostrils. I used to be known for being able to talk anyone into anything back at the academy, though it was a title I had to fight hard to maintain against the wiles of cadets like Hanji Iwam. She and I were always tangled in one battle of wits or another—or at least that was how we saw it. Those outside our little struggles probably thought we were the two biggest dumbasses the academy ever let past its doors. Here's hoping she prepared me enough for this conversation.

"Look, I've got no illusions about my situation. It's in my best interest that you stay in power. Iral would hang me on a crucifix the second he had clearance, and with the way you're governing, that moment isn't far off. Believe me when I say my advice serves both of us."

"I don't, but go on," Ettian says, taking a slow sip of his coffee. He's probably enjoying it, the bastard—both the taste of that wretched blend and the sound of my voice after too long without it.

That notion has me reluctant to give him any more than he's getting, but I remind myself that there are greater stakes here. "I get the instinct. You've spent eight years just surviving, and it seems harder than ever now that the galaxy knows who you really are. I know a little of what that's like."

He nearly spits his coffee across the table on a laugh, but I press onward.

"The very first thing you learn when you're born into bloodright is that protecting yourself is always your priority. And so the first thing you did when you came to power was hole up in your palace. When's the last time you went beyond its walls?"

"That's definitely above your security clearance," Ettian scoffs.

I shrug, flicking a grain of sugar across the table and smirking when it plunges into his lap. Ettian stiffens. "What I'm really saying," I continue, "is that the people don't know you. The most remarkable thing you've done so far is reveal yourself to the galaxy. Since then, all the great deeds I've been hearing about come from Maxo Iral."

Ettian's expression grows surprisingly grim, and for a moment, I think I've hit the mark. I press on. "Just last week, I heard one of my guards bragging that her cousin pulled the trigger that struck the decisive blow in the Sparza maneuver Iral ordered that shattered Tosa's most recent attempt to regain ground."

"Iral has been holding the front admirably," Ettian says, his voice low and steady. "I'm glad his achievements are getting the praise they deserve. But the battles he's winning are built on foundations I've been working myself to the bone to lay, which you might have some awareness of if you'd ever governed a day in your life."

I scowl—let him think his dig has landed squarely in my pride. "Maybe you've governed, but I learned from the woman who broke your empire over her knee, and I know for sure my mother would never stand for a military leader overstepping the scope of his narrative the way Iral has."

"I don't remember much of my father's lessons," Ettian starts softly.

I tense. Apart from his loud declaration in the court, I've never heard him talk about his parents—not even in vague terms during our years at the academy together. I know Marc emp-Archon was the carrier of the imperial line. I know he was the first to fall to my mother's ax. But I've never seen him through Ettian's eyes, and I'm not sure if I'm ready to.

"He didn't have much time to impart them on me, and I was too young for most of the important stuff," Ettian continues. "But one thing he made sure I knew from the moment my tiny brain could first comprehend it, was that a ruler who measures himself through notoriety is a ruler who has lost his way."

"That doesn't . . . You don't . . ." I scrub my hands helplessly down my face. "How else are you going to prove that you're actually doing something?"

"Oh, I don't know, maybe by overseeing the *legion* of ministers it takes to usurp a government when ownership of a planet transfers in a single day? Maybe by making sure there's a plan in place for governing the next world we take that accounts for imperial rule? But of course, you haven't thought of that because only one person at this table has ever worn a crown."

"Ah, and there's something else my mother told me," I counter. "Bloodright can't be bought with the metal and stone on your head. It can only ever be seized. And yours is slipping through your fingers."

"So what would you have me do?" Ettian asks. His eyes fix on mine, unblinking, unbearable.

"Go to the front," I tell him.

It would be better if he laughed, and I spend the long moment where he just stares at me trying to process exactly why that is. Isn't this what I wanted? For him to take the suggestion, to seriously consider it, to eventually admit it's the only way forward. It's working, for gods' sakes. So why does the sight of it working fill me with dread?

In my head, it seemed so neat. The easiest way to get Wen to turn against Ettian is to separate them. Create a distance that forces them to keep secrets from each other. With Wen all but tied to my side, I can unravel her insecurities stitch by stitch, aligning them with everything she doesn't know about Ettian. And once she sees all the ways he's using her, all the ways he's trapped her in this life, all the ways he's going to get her killed—then I can convince her to free us both.

And as for Ettian, well. There's a risk that the front of the war might challenge him into becoming a leader to be reckoned with—one who can actually take his bloodright with more than a dinky ring. But the greater risk, the one I'm gambling on, is that it'll just kill him. I'd even be satisfied with some light maiming if it took him out of the picture long enough for his people to lose faith in him. Even if he manages to stay unscathed, throwing him in the same room as his army's senior staff is going to bring him head to head with General Iral, pitting him directly against the man who *could* probably take back these systems and restore the Archon Empire.

The convenient bonus being that it'll leave him with very little time to pay attention to me.

I didn't think I was particularly convincing in the lead-up to my suggestion, but Ettian's face says otherwise. His brow is furrowed, and the sight of him locked in concentration sends me rocketing back to days at the academy I spent staring at him out of the corner of my eye as he puzzled through a tactics essay, blinking guiltily away every time his focus lightened enough to realize he had an audience. He was never a master strategist—it never came to him as innately as to Hanji or Rhodes—but he wasn't scraping by, either, because he always thought long and hard about all angles of a problem.

Which, I'm fast realizing, is a problem for me. The more time I give him to think, the more time he has to rut me over.

I snap my fingers in front of his face, startling him enough that his knee knocks into the table and sends every liquid on it shuddering. "Sorry," Ettian murmurs. "It's just . . . You really do want me dead, don't you?"

I sputter. "Should I not?"

"You used to be different."

"Did I?"

"Gal, don't bullshit me. After we escaped the academy, you told me you'd spent your whole career there working out ways of dismantling your mother's violence. I followed you because I believed in that cause as much as you did. I thought you'd manage a rise to power that didn't involve you stepping over bodies—I put my own life on the line for the idea of an Umber imperial like that on the throne."

My fingers tighten around my cup, its heat searing against my skin. I was an idealist at the academy. I'd never been shot at, never had to fight back, and so I romanticized the notion of a subtle war that pulled the strings of my mother's rule until it unraveled. Ettian, who'd been fighting back all his life at that point, should have known better.

He should still know better.

And now there's a real war to reckon with. I'm no longer inheriting an empire where I could rule as a peaceful negotiator. When I take my crown—*when,* I swear to myself every goddamn night—I won't get a choice of whether to rule with violence. If I don't fight back, Ettian's rebellion will metastasize across the former Archon territories and leave them ravaged for generations to come. To save them, I have to stay vicious.

"It never would have worked," I tell him. "It took me a while to understand it, but . . . I got there."

I got there the moment he claimed his bloodright. There are no soft wars to be waged here. This ends in blood—his, mine, or maybe both of ours—and no other way will suffice.

"I turned you into this," Ettian says, staring into his cup. "And now you're trying to turn me into you."

"What, you think it's that easy? You think you're just going to show up at the front of the war and the proximity alone is going to unlock your dark side?" I pause, feeling the right words bubbling on the edge of my tongue, stained with bitter coffee. "Being a monster is a choice. You make it or you don't."

"You're not a monster, Gal."

I bare my teeth, feeling my heart constrict against my better judgment. "I could be. I will be." Those words sound pathetic. I regret them the second they leave my mouth, because I know they're empty threats. For rut's sake, I'm sitting across a table from my mortal enemy, unobserved, with several potential weapons within reach, and the worst I've done so far is flick some sugar into his lap. The monstrous thoughts don't mean anything if I can't act on them, and I *can't* act on them. I can all but hear my mother's voice whispering in my ear to grab the carafe and throw it at Ettian, to smash the ceramic mug and take a sharp edge to his throat.

But killing him doesn't win this war the way I need to, and I promise the throbbing ache in my chest that it's the only reason I'm staying my hand.

"I might be the only person in this palace who truly has your best interests at heart," I say after a long pause. "And I'm telling you: you need to go to the front."

A heavy, quiet moment passes, the two of us sitting in the truth of those words.

"Then I'll go," Ettian says at last.

I didn't expect to get this far, and I don't know what to do with the moment now that it's here. My eyes fix on Ettian's. His lock on mine. And though I'm still having trouble believing the words, there's no doubt about the conviction sparking through him.

It worked. It actually worked.

I think of all the times he berated me for not having a plan of my own and have to suppress the urge to smirk. *How's this for a plan, Ettian? You go off to lead your war and the painful, agonizing failure that will inevitably result, and in the meantime, I'll turn your most loyal follower against you and free myself from your ruttin' imperial—*

"And you're coming with."

Shock grips me like a squeeze toy, my eyes bulging and my stomach feeling like a dreadnought has just hit it at superluminal. "Excuse me?" My voice skips up a dignified half octave.

Ettian leans forward. "Did you expect otherwise? Did you think I'd abandon you here to the next assassin?"

"But I've got Wen looking out for me now—"

"I know it's hard to believe, but the Flame Knight does occasionally need to sleep. She's effective, but I'd never leave the task to her and her alone. And besides"—he rises, a smirk playing over his lips—"she's not the most effective protection in this palace. They may call Maxo Iral the Shield of Archon, but don't think I've missed that someone else deserves that title just as much."

I sputter. "I'm the reason my mother's gunning for you so hard. The Imperial Fleet—"

"You're the reason this city hasn't been blown off the map yet," Ettian says coolly. "And I think that confirms something else. You're an only child, aren't you?"

"There's no real way of knowing—"

"Nah, your mother's reaction tells me all I need to know. They don't have a backup. You're the only hope of the Umber imperial line continuing."

He has the audacity to lean over the table, his eyes fixed on mine, confident and unblinking. I have to hold myself back, to keep myself from rising to meet him.

"And I'm not letting you out of my sight."

CHAPTER 5

IT'S THE DEAD of night, the palace has gone quiet around me, and I'm quickly discovering that the realities of an escape attempt are so much less fun than I'd originally imagined.

It's not like I haven't thought this through. I've had a solid month where the most strenuous demand on my faculties was a knock-down-drag-out fight for my life that lasted about a minute, tops, which has left me with more than enough free time to put together a couple options. But when Ettian declared that he's dragging me to the front with him, I realized I couldn't sit around and wait for him to ruin my life so thoroughly. There will be no hope of freedom once I'm aboard a dreadnought in his fleet.

Well, apart from the sweet release of death, but I'm aiming to avoid that outcome.

So I picked the most well-developed plan in my arsenal, one that was all but gift-wrapped by my would-be assailant. *If someone can get in through the vents,* I reasoned, *there's probably a way out in that direction too.* Over the span of my imprisonment, I've learned the interior of the estate well enough that I've put together some solid guesses about how the ducts wind between the rooms, and I committed that information to memory—sometimes encoded in mnemonic songs I'd make up and whistle at the guards just to irritate them. I paid close attention to the adjustments palace security made to my quarters in the wake of the assassination attempt, using them to deduce what options were still open to me.

All of this is to say that I *had* a plan. But I might have overestimated a few aspects of this when I managed to pry the screws loose from one of the cooling vents tucked in the back of my suite's bedroom and stuff myself into the awaiting maw. How was I supposed to know how *hard* it is to squirm through an enclosed space barely wider than the span of your shoulders? Or how noisy the whole affair would be—which has slowed my progress to a miserable, inching crawl in an effort to keep half the palace from realizing what I'm up to. My confidence in which turns to take withers by the third intersection, when it truly settles in for the first time how little of this palace I've actually seen.

It's almost a relief when a shadow falls over the spill of light from one of the vents. "Had enough yet?" Wen asks.

There's a panicked animal part of my brain that considers bolting—damn the noise, damn the fact that she can probably keep pace at an easy stroll. I want *out,* and I'll go kicking and screaming if I have to. I already lost all my dignity when I knelt before Iral. There's nowhere lower I can go.

But all that's going to lead to is Wen dragging me out of here by my ankles, and I'm not in the mood for more bruises. I let out a long sigh, going limp. "Yeah, I'm done," I groan, the duct's metallic echo rattling my words back at me.

The shadow shifts, and I can easily picture Wen setting her hands on her hips. "Over a month in chains, and *this* is what you try for your first escape attempt?"

I take a moment to consider my retort. If I'm not going to be able to make an exit tonight, I've got to make the most of this attempt at one. Wen thinks she's got me. I'm stuck in a vent, completely at her mercy. She won't be anticipating my strike.

"Has he told you yet?" I ask, the tremor I push into my voice aided by the duct's acoustics. "Oh no, of course he's already told you."

"Told me what?"

I let the silence settle, let her doubts seed in it. Just as she's drawing breath to ask again, I say at last, "He's going to the front. And he's taking us with him."

Wen gives me an equally measured silence in return, one that makes me resent the fact that I'm pinned in the blackness of the vents with no access to the expressions that could be chewing their way across her half-burnt face. And like me, she waits for the second I'm about to break before snapping, "What the hell do you think you're playing at?"

"Not dying by dreadnought," I sigh, "but apparently we can't get everything we want."

Wen's shadow looms over the grate as she crouches next to it, and through its slivers I catch the flash of bared teeth. "As far as I know, this morning Ettian had absolutely no designs on the war front. He's told me repeatedly that he's leaving the war to Iral and focusing solely on governing what we've managed to secure—for the good of his people, for the stability of the region, for a thousand other reasons that make plenty of sense to me. What makes *no* sense whatsoever is him suddenly deciding to catapult off to the ragged edge of this empire—unless you talked him into it on your little date this afternoon."

I nearly blurt an ill-advised excuse, but Wen saves me from it by diving into the next part of her tirade.

"But if you talked him into it, and you got what you wanted, then why the rust are you making a run for it now?"

"Like I said," I snarl between my teeth. "Not interested in dying by dreadnought."

"Then why—"

"Because I didn't think he'd drag us along with him," I snap, loud enough that Wen rocks back on her heels. I remember a time—a more innocent time, a more ignorant time—when I talked her nails out of Ettian's throat by reminding her that he'd never put us in danger. Clearly that's all been proven to be bullshit, but if the way she's been single-mindedly devoted to his cause is any indication, Wen still seems to believe it.

So that's the first fissure I'll delve into.

"I thought I knew him," I murmur, pouring a healthy dose of some genuine shame into the words. "I never thought he'd . . . well, maybe he'd risk me. I'd get it if he risked me. But *you*?"

I dose that *you* with a healthy amount of truth too. All my furious resentment for the girl who threw me into this situation, the girl who's now been tasked with keeping me in it. I don't envy her for being Ettian's new best friend—I don't envy anyone in that position after what he did to me—but I wouldn't mind if she thought that venom in my voice came from jealousy.

"*Ettian*'s not the one risking me," Wen says in a tone of voice that makes me grateful for the wall standing solidly between us. "I've chosen this. I chose him."

"I thought I'd chosen him too," I remind her. "But I wasn't careful to make sure he'd really chosen me back. He said he did. Made all the pretty promises a boy can make. But if he'd *really* chosen either of us, I wouldn't be in this ruttin' air duct and you wouldn't be waiting for me to crawl out of it."

This time I don't give her the breath to think. "Is this really what you'd pick for yourself if you could go anywhere in the galaxy? Be anyone you wanted to be? Do anything you'd sworn to do?" I lay heavy on those last words, certain I'm pressing exactly where it hurts.

Because Wen's already told us exactly what she wants—confessed it to us on the very night we met her. She latched herself to our coattails to escape the Corinthian mob that killed her mother and took her in as its ward, and she's out for their blood. This whole affair with the Archon Empire is just a long, protracted detour, and I'm hoping to hitch my own wagon to her realization of just how far she's strayed from her goal.

The silence on the other side of the grate tells me it's working.

"Look at yourself," I say, glad she can't look at me instead. This horrible girl who got Ettian's secrets out of him before he ever bothered to tell me any of the important ones. I want her feeling as small as I do, pinned inside this narrow metal cage. "You let him gas you up with fantasies of being his knight, told yourself it was something you wanted, forced yourself into the shape of his expectations. I've seen the way you dress—all that armor, all that platinum, all that green. Like you're trying to convince yourself you belong in his world."

The dark of the night, I'm certain, is doing half my work for me. I've spent enough sleepless hours staring at the ceiling's distant detail to know how easily your fears and doubts expand to fit the amorphous shape of the blackness around you.

There's just one final twist of the knife I need to land this. "And none of it mattered. None of it worked—that's the worst part, isn't it? You gave up your dreams, you jammed yourself into new ones that didn't quite fit right, and Ettian tore you away from them all the same, all supposedly because you're the only one he trusts to keep me alive. And yet he's dragging us to the front with him. You know what that says to me?"

"What does it say to you?" Wen asks. I can't tell if her tone is weary or wary.

"Says it was never about keeping me alive. He tied you down in the palace just to keep you from burning his city to the ground. He's never wanted to see you in shining armor. We're all just pieces on his board."

"Rust off," she mutters.

"Wen," I urge, dropping the contempt from my voice. I know she's been leaning on it, using its solidity as an excuse to dismiss what I'm saying as the words of a vicious prisoner looking for an out—or the ravings of a dumbass stuck in an air duct. Without the reliability of my hatred, she won't have her guideposts for how to process the next words I hit her with. "Ettian told you about the history of knights in Archon, right?"

"Told me enough. Told me they wore powersuits and fought for justice throughout the empire. Told me one once cleaved a fighter in half with a vibrosword, one once rode a ship through an atmospheric burn, one once . . . I dunno, wild stuff like that." I hear a soft smile on her lips, and I wonder whether it's for the thought of her one day achieving feats like the suited knights or the memory of Ettian telling her their stories.

"And he told you what happened to them all in the end, right?"

I swear her eyes find mine through the grate, even in the darkness. "You mean what your mother did?"

I sneer. Not too long ago, my feelings about the slaughter of the Archon knights would have been more mixed. I remember noticing the way Ettian tensed every time one of our fellow academy cadets made a joke about the "tin can idiots" and deciding I didn't have to make those jokes too. I submitted essays in tactics classes that made snide references to the overt cruelty of Knightfall and felt a shiver of illicit thrill at the thought of those words falling into my mother's hands.

But once I got a taste of war firsthand, my perspective began to shift. I imagined myself in the cockpit of that fighter, pinned in equal parts by centrifugal force and fear, just trying to keep a bird in the sky. I imagined the sight of a human figure keeping pace, a vibrosword shuddering in their hand. I imagined the cold inevitability of the moment the knight made their move, the sight of that sword plunging through my cockpit window being the last thing I ever saw. Imperial decree restricted most archival footage of the suited knights, but my own mind was all too happy to reconstruct the terror of them from the stories I'd heard. They were dangerous maniacs, ripping through battlefields without oversight, and the Archon people ruttin' *worshipped* them.

Of course they had to die.

"My mother did what she had to," I tell Wen. "You've worked as an operative clearing out resistance from this city. You know that the right person's death at the right time can do more work than the unnecessary deaths of hundreds." I pause, savoring how perfectly ripe my next words will be. "I just thought you were smart enough not to become one of those people."

Wen's shoulders stiffen. In the safety of the shadows, I allow myself a triumphant grin.

After a long moment, she speaks. "Everything I do could get me killed, and nothing's killed me yet." Her voice is firm, but she's laying on the bravado thick enough that I know I've done the work I need to.

"Whatever you say," I tell her, making sure no part of me sounds convinced by her posturing. "Now, on to the important stuff. Does that vent open from the other side?"

"No," she replies, shoving herself abruptly to her feet. I manage to clap my hands over my ears just as she unclips her blaster.

When the ringing clears from my hearing and the smoke clears from my lungs, I worm forward, picking my way over the white-hot edges of the hole she's cleared in the metal grate. "You didn't even check if I was far enough back," I whine as I spill onto the ornately tiled floor. I splay flat on my back and lie there for a second to appreciate the chill of the hall's open air and the fact that my limbs are free to move any direction I so choose.

Wen looms over me, looking ready to snap me in half over her knee. I blow a stray dust bunny up at her, then glance at our surroundings. "Oh wow." I laugh around a cough. "I have no ruttin' idea where we are."

CHAPTER 6

I WAIT FOR the repercussions of my escape attempt to catch up to me. It's almost disappointing when I realize they aren't coming. I slouch back into the drudgery of my routine—I eat, I sleep, I get a lovely bit of pacing in when the morning sun streams into my quarters just right. I wait for my inescapable doom. After the attempt in the vents, I'm out of ideas for escape plans that won't make me look like a total buffoon. One way or another, Ettian's dragging me to the front.

But first things first, he drags me in front of a crowd.

I stand on the dais at the center of the imperial court in what I've come to think of as *my* spot—which probably isn't healthy at all—two paces behind Ettian and two to the left. He's dressed in his best, a sleek suit in a deep shade of green, with clean lines that smooth over his lanky frame. The ceremonial crown I first placed on his head at his coronation is perched upon his brow, a spiraling, twisting, ugly thing that I have to physically restrain myself from smacking off his head every time my gaze lands on it. Platinum chains cascade from his shoulders and connect at his elbows. If I were bored enough, I could count every single link of them. Better than listening to Ettian drone on about how much he appreciates the support of everyone in this room.

But I know what that would look like on camera, and so I keep my eyes fixed on the distant wall instead. I swear I can feel the prick of a bevy of lenses—all of them focused on Ettian, of course, but all of them making sure to keep me in the shot. My every move will be documented, the barest flickers of my facial muscles analyzed to attempt to unravel my mental state. This broadcast will make it all the way to the Umber Core.

My parents will see it.

The first time I realized this, I was tempted to do something dramatic. To start twitching my jaw muscles in military code or at the very least flash subtle, rude hand gestures while pretending to scratch an itch. But I quickly realized just how little valuable information I possessed and how pathetic it would make me look to use this as a venue for petty revenge. I wanted to have a little more goddamn pride than that. So I stand rigid and try to project strength. To communicate that I haven't broken, that I won't *ever* break.

And no matter what, no matter how tempting, no matter what he says, I can't look at Ettian.

Too many people knew us as a couple on the Archon base. That common knowledge mutated to a vicious rumor the second our identities were revealed and Ettian took me captive. I can play into the implications in the privacy of his administration, where only *he* has to manage the fallout, but here, where I'm visible not only to his people but to mine, I have to tread carefully. Any move of mine in his direction in the public eye will only feed the fire, and I understand with horrifying clarity that if I'm ever going to take my throne, I'll have to kill off this line of thinking with impunity.

I have to be a statue. I can't react to any of the words coming out of his mouth—which is one reason I've tried my best to tune out what he's spewing completely—and I've trained my body to immediately pick any focal point but him the second I'm brought into a room with a camera.

This room has far too many. Ettian has gathered the rebellion's senior staff and the fledgling government he's set up on Rana in a glittering sea of hopeful, upturned faces. Some are new installations, lifted from the ranks. Some are refugees of the prior Archon administration who fled Umber rule and found their way back when Ettian ascended to his throne. The worst of them—the ones I've marked for the day I get free and take my crown—are the traitors. The Umber turncoats who helped lay the foundations for my mother's rule here, then swore fealty to Ettian at the first opportunity. Bottom-feeders, latching themselves to the most powerful thing they see, unable to *conceive* of how rutted they'll be when Umber puts the rebellion down for good. I haven't been in front of this many people since Ettian's coronation, although the crowds on that day spilled over the lawn of the palace, the skin drums pounded so fiercely that I feared my teeth might shatter, and most people weren't nearly as well dressed as they are tonight.

This is a much more restrained affair, with good reason. Ettian's trying to shore up support and make sure his hold on Rana stays firm when he departs for the front. Most of the people in this room don't know that he's planning on leaving the planet, but he has to inspire their confidence so that when he does, it doesn't look like he's running away.

He seems to be doing . . . passably, so far. Though I've all but turned his words to radio static, I can't ignore the sudden upswells of noise in the room every time he says something particularly rousing. Glasses raise, boisterous voices interject from the back, and by the time Ettian finally shuts up, the applause that washes over the crowd is all but universal. I stay rigidly still until the lights on the dais dim and every last one of the camera operators swings their lenses elsewhere.

Then I continue standing, unmoving, because I'm not sure what I'm supposed to do next. I glance to my right, where Wen seems to be working through a similar confusion. Ettian has already stepped forward off the dais, plunging into the welcoming embrace of the crowd and leaving the two of us without assignment. Her eyes catch on mine.

I lift my eyebrows. "Want me to get you a drink?"

Wen doesn't put nearly as much thought into schooling her expressions as I do—her face drops into a scowl without a moment of hesitation.

And since the cameras are off and everyone's busy swarming the emperor, I loose a smirk of my own. "That a yes or a no?" I ask, sidling over to her. "I can guarantee your more precious prince is a little too busy to make the same offer."

Wen's lips remain rigid, unbent.

I soften, knowing it'll unbalance her. "Look, if there are two people who belong less at this party, I'd desperately like to meet them."

"One drink," Wen says after an extra minute of consideration. Her eyes flick warily to the crowd, and it hits me how rigidly she holds herself—almost as rigidly as I was just a few moments ago. But my performance ends when the cameras go dark. Wen has to keep up her Archon act every waking moment she's in public.

She's dressed the part too—almost garishly so. She can't have done the elegant crown of braids that sweeps her hair up herself—not with the delicate threads of platinum twisting through them. She wears a collar inset with emeralds that winks and glitters in the low light, and her armor tonight is flimsy and lightweight enough that I highly doubt it'll stop any attempts on her life.

The only part of her she doesn't bother to cover—has never bothered to cover, to be fair—is her burn. I consider asking her why she doesn't try to even it out with makeup, but there are far more worthwhile things I could get punched over. "You look nice," I say instead, and wrestle back my smile as I watch her struggle not to swing.

We step down from the dais, and the crowd that came rushing in to greet Ettian swells ten feet back for us. It seems no one wants to risk damaging the emperor's most precious asset. Or maybe they're more worried about his loose-cannon Corinthian taking an arm off. Rumors of Wen's unpredictable approach to establishing order in the city have given her a reputation that certainly justifies the safe distance people seem to be keeping.

I'm surprised I'm being allowed anywhere near these people, but I'm going to push that luck as far as it goes. These are the rebellion's officers, the new government's rising stars, and some of the most wealthy people in the city willing to back Ettian's war. I want them to be as suspicious of my freedoms as possible. So I set my shoulders back, let an easy smile break over my face, and saunter to the bar at Wen's side as if she's my date, not my guard.

Look at the prisoner, they'll think. *So favored by the emperor. So free to do whatever he wants. How can we trust our leadership when it's in the thrall of our enemies?*

The bartender offers us two flutes of the evening's choice bottle with a surprisingly impassive expression. I take them off his hands and eye him, clinking the glasses together and lifting an eyebrow when they chime like the real, breakable stuff. The bartender eyes me back, then nods unambiguously to my escort. The message is clear: *You try anything and my money's on her handing you your ass before the last shard hits the ground.* I scowl and pass one flute off to Wen, who looks at it dubiously. "Probably local," I remark as I take a sniff. "At the academy cantina, we only drank imported polish thanks to the officers. None of them would dare try *Archon swill.*"

I take a sip and immediately develop an alternative theory. None of the polish I guzzled in my time as a cadet was anywhere near this strong. Gods of all systems, the Archon people must like getting drunk fast. Makes a bit of sense, I suppose, when you factor in how bland and efficient their food is.

I glance sidelong at Wen to find her downing the dregs of her glass. She eyes me with a challenging tilt of her eyebrow, and I follow suit. It benefits no one but me for both of us to get sloppy tonight.

Unless someone tries to kill me again, but hopefully enough polish will put that out of my mind.

I lean over to Wen's ear, trying to look as friendly and familiar as I can. "Sure looks like you need more than one drink. Rough week with His Highness?"

"That's above your clearance level," she mutters, and for a moment I'm seized by the delightful image of a file in some Archon database that outlines what I'm allowed to know and what I'm not. I imagine it's not much more descriptive than a picture of my face and the word "NO" stamped in declarative red text.

"Worth a shot." I take her glass and gesture to the bartender, whom I've decided is going to be my new best friend when he tops off both with a generous pour. Apparently he's interested in seeing what happens when the Archon emperor's right-hand operative and his old flame turned prisoner get sloshed.

Already a bit of warmth is seeping into my fingertips, the sensation rocketing me back to hazy nights in the academy cantina with condensation slicking my hands and Hanji Iwam muttering encouraging nonsense in my ear as I tried not to let Ettian catch me staring at him. An uncanny twist of longing catches me before I can quash it, aching for the simplicity of the days when I was just a boy with a crush on his roommate and a secret that might tear the galaxy in half—and the former seemed more important than the latter.

The heady rush of it hits my body before my brain can do anything to stop it. And in that moment of confusion, I can't stop myself from breaking the one rule I'm not supposed to break.

My gaze flicks across the court, homing in on Ettian like he's magnetized.

And the emperor is looking back.

But before the panic can seep in, a realization hits me. I'm not the only one misstepping here. And maybe I can afford to break the rules if Ettian is too. After all, I'm not getting any more powerless.

Ettian, on the other hand, has an entire empire to lose.

So I let myself tumble headfirst into the horrific thrill, holding the eye contact like it's a lifeline. I bring my glass to my lips and take a long, slow sip. Ettian mirrors the gulp. My heart quickens to a snare rattle, and I barely manage the control it takes to make my glance away a slow, sly affair, rather than the desperate escape I'm longing for.

It's even harder to keep myself from checking the sight lines of every single person around me to see if anyone caught my slip. But even a casual survey of my surroundings reveals what might be a sadder truth: No one's paying attention to me at all. The party guests have given a wide berth and placed their backs to us, worried about the consequences of seeming too interested in me.

There's only one person who genuinely *should* be paying attention to me, and I glance to my left to find her regarding me with narrowed eyes over another hefty sip from her glass. "What?" I ask Wen.

She shrugs. "Seem to remember some nonsense about how you *weren't* still—"

"A person with eyes?"

Wen fixes me with a stare so embittered that I'm almost tempted to wash it away with another hearty swig of my polish.

"I . . . You really don't get it, do you? For rut's sake, weren't you a hostage to that Korsa guy?"

Wen now looks like she might dump the dregs of her drink on me. "In a manner of speaking. No cuffs, could come and go as I pleased, as long as I reported in at the right times."

"Then you know what it's like when your life's not your own. You know what it's like to not be able to trust your own thoughts and feelings because of the way they've been manipulated by the man holding your keys. And in the end, what did you do? What did you vow?"

Her fury simmers, but I swear I see the glass warping slightly under her grip.

"You were supposed to burn him to the ground, Wen. You should know by now what I'm supposed to do here too."

"But you won't," she says, far too confidently for my liking. "Not with the way you look at him now. It's true—I said I'd reduce Dago Korsa to ash. And then I found a world beyond that kernel of hate I'd formed myself around." She takes a step closer, close enough that I can see the rough geography of her face in perfect detail even in the low light. "I'm still trying to figure out who I am without it. What about you?"

I shouldn't let the question get its claws in me. For gods' sakes, I was *raised* to let this kind of thought roll off my back like water, especially when it's coming from a Corinthian barely three months removed from the rough streets that raised her. But if I could shatter the layers of contexts that surround me and Ettian, what would I do? If we were two strangers with no titles tied to our names meeting for the first time, what would happen?

I don't know the shape of the answer to that question, but I know the dryness it leaves in my throat all too well. Wen nods, smirking with a smugness I hate seeing on her. "All that big talk, acting like you know me. Well, I know you too, asshole, and I know you won't. And you're gonna prove it." She downs the rest of her drink, sets her glass on the bar, and pulls out her datapad. After a few seconds of furious typing, she shoves it back in her pocket and grabs me by the elbow.

I slosh my own drink haphazardly down my throat as we go, certain that wherever she's taking me, I'm going to need the polish in my system. We wind our way through the Archon elite, past heroes of the last war and financiers of the new one, past would-be governors waiting for Ettian to reclaim their destined seats and officers who will be on the front lines of the effort to do so. Some of their curious gazes stick on us as we move, their expressions ranging from relatable confusion to smug satisfaction that at last the Umber prisoner is leaving and now the party can really begin. I offer them a sly smile in return, partly because I hope it'll confuse them, but mostly because I hope it'll mask just how confused I feel too.

The hall outside the court is a dark, looming expanse that feels at odds with the polish sparking through my system. It makes me want to duck into the cozy alcove we pass that houses a massive vase, though I usually prefer to do that sort of thing with company and I wouldn't particularly enjoy it with Wen. Her grip on my arm is unrelenting, a constant reminder that while I've been losing my academy muscles, she's been doing nothing but gaining.

I have enough of a buzz going that it takes me almost a full minute of walking to realize we're headed toward an unfamiliar area of the palace. "Wen?" I hazard.

She lets out a hiss, glancing warily back over our shoulders. Two guards are posted at the doors of the court, and the wink of familiar security-camera lenses glitters overhead. We're far from unobserved, and our exit wasn't subtle, so I'm not sure what kind of secrecy she's trying to preserve here. She tugs me around a corner, her other hand running along the wall until her fingers pause in a catch I barely even saw.

She crimps into it, and a door swings inward, letting out a soft sigh of cool air and revealing a darkened passage.

"Close the door behind you, turn left, and start walking," Wen says, her voice low enough that the words barely go farther than my ear. I put a steadying hand on the edge of the door, peering into the blackness. It seems to be some sort of servant corridor inside the walls. Useful intel, if ever there was any—wish I'd known about this before I tried to crawl through the vents. A part of me prickles with wariness, but the polish settling into my bloodstream is quick to soothe it away. Whatever Wen wants me to prove, I'm game.

I step into the darkness, grab the edge of the door, and heave. Wen's pleased smirk is the last thing I see before the last sliver of light from the hall disappears.

It takes me a minute to adjust and realize that I'm not completely in the dark. Two dim orange strips run along the floor, casting a soft flush against the walls. I reach out, spanning the corridor to steady myself as I turn left. My fingers curl tighter around the stem of my glass.

Maybe this wasn't the best idea. This could be the place someone kills me and gets away with it. There aren't cameras. Wen's on the other side of the wall, and if she matched me drink for drink, she's well on her way to becoming just as useless as I am sober. Panic creeps up my throat.

I swallow it back with another gulp from my glass and start walking.

There's something familiar about these corridors, something that reminds me of the hidden chambers of the Imperial Seat on Lucia. I grew up in the core of a labyrinth of servants' passages and locked doors, a secret so protected that I didn't see daylight until nearly a decade into my life. My parents were on such rigid schedules that my time with them was sparse, their visitations always accompanied by a timer ticking down and a complicated security scheme that left me far too anxious to do anything but nod along to whatever hasty lesson they were trying to impart.

I remember that time as comfortable—maybe because I didn't know any better comforts—but teetering back toward the feeling of those narrow halls feels downright claustrophobic.

What am I doing? Why am I going along with this? I lean close to the wall, trying to spot the hinges of a door that might let me out of here, feeling for cracks that might lead to an exit.

A shuffling noise from farther down the hall doubles my heartbeat's force. A shadow looms in the low light.

Someone's in here with me.

A familiar raw impulse overtakes me, the same heady feeling that sang through my blood when the assassin dropped out of my ceiling. My wrist flicks, smashing the glass in my hand against the wall. The bulb shatters, leaving a wreath of sharp ends attached to a stem. "I'm armed," I call out into the darkness.

"Gal, it's me," a far-too-familiar voice calls back.

The shadows resolve into a lean form that slips closer, feeling along the wall. He's discarded his crown, and the sight of his bare head takes me by surprise, dragging me back to the boy I loved, not the emperor I hate with every fiber of my being.

"There's uh . . . broken glass," I tell him flatly when he gets close enough for me to make out his eyes. His gaze drops to the makeshift weapon in my hand, and I suppress the urge to grimace. We're too comfortable with each other, a fact that the tabloids are all too happy to point out, but it's never really sunk in how instinctive it is to treat him as a friend, how naturally my body wants to slip into it. *Hold the line,* I tell myself, my grip on the glass stem tightening.

And now I feel Wen's amorphous dare slip into its true form.

I could kill him right now. He's standing mere feet away, I have the weapon in my hand, and there's no guard around to stop me or retaliate. This secret passage probably has a convenient exit somewhere, one that'll leave me with far more options than my mad scramble through the vents a week ago. I can feel the possibilities branching inside me, sprouting like an unruly bramble patch.

But killing him does nothing—I've paid too much attention to ignore that fact. Killing him just hands the reins to General Iral, a far more competent leader. It removes the internal tension that might be the only thing preventing Archon from excising Umber completely from these territories. I want to believe it's the logical choice not to kill him. I want that logic to absolve me completely from the reason Wen shoved me into this passageway in the first place.

But something inside me knows I couldn't. All the hate in my heart, all the good it would do the galaxy to remove the Archon bloodline—and still, it isn't enough to outweigh the force that's keeping my hand from raising the jagged shard of glass and plunging it into his jugular.

Ettian eases closer, his hands drifting up warily as he takes another step that falls with a splintering crunch under the heel of his shoes. "Wen pinged me. Told me you wanted to meet," he says, his eyes fixed on the glass in my hand. But still, he leans closer, drawn by a gravity that fear can't outweigh.

Of course she said I "wanted to meet." Of course that's all it would take for him to abandon a critical night, a party that could decide the scope of his campaign, his last chance to cement his status among his elite before he deserts his post on Rana for the glory of the front. One mention that I wanted to see him, and he rushes right in like the vast fool he is. And yet, he's the one crowned, the one who gets to live in his bloodright, the one who doesn't have to live each day in *ruttin' chains*.

As Ettian teeters closer, I rise to meet him.

Not with lips but with glass.

I feel the soft pulse of his breath on my cheek and the steady thrum of his racing heartbeat in my fingertips, conducted through the shard I've laid against his throat. He freezes in place.

He could pull back, but he doesn't. I may not know Ettian as well as I used to believe. But he knows me just as well as ever, and he knows I go no further than this.

It's hard to suppress the flicker of indignation that sparks to life in me. Shame rides in on the heels of that spark. I could end him with a flick of my wrist. His bloodright is pulsing below my makeshift blade. He's giving me the opening, not even making it difficult. A true Umber imperial would carve his throat open without hesitation and then move right along to solving the next problem. My mother did it with her sister to claim the throne, and I can feel the echo of the history in my blood trembling through my hand.

And yet.

Ettian's lips twitch into a slight smile.

Maybe it's the dark, I tell myself as his hand curves up to ghost along my wrist—still not pulling me away, still trusting that I won't press down. Maybe it feels like I can get away with this because no one will see, least of all me. Maybe I'm just drunk, and that's excuse enough.

Maybe in the dark, I can fool myself into believing that no part of my emotions is involved in this.

The soft brush of his fingertips sends a jolt through me more powerful than a Viper's engines. Sweat prickles on the back of my neck, and I feel my pulse rise to meet the thrum I feel through the stem of my shattered flute. I don't know how my brain could have possibly strayed to death when all I can feel between us is life. And all that vital instinct is pushing me to do is tilt my head back, rise on my toes, and seal my lips over his.

Ettian inhales sharply. For a moment, I think it's because he's surprised, but then I feel a faint wetness slip down my blade. Without breaking the kiss, I let the glass tumble from my fingers and press my hand carefully against his neck. A scratch—nothing more—but the warmth of his blood on my skin feels downright sinful mixed with the warmth of his mouth on mine.

I want more. I want to take this boy, who's taken everything from me, for everything he has. I want him to pour himself into me, to fall victim to the relentless gravity of the raging star I am. I want him obsessed. I want him confused. I may not be a killer yet, but I can claim his life in other ways.

He presses me back, my spine rolling straight against the wall of the passage. His thigh slips between mine, and I buck against the heat of it, seizing his bottom lip between my teeth. I could bite down hard and spill more blood, but I only tease it with a tug, and he comes away smiling.

That's right, I think. Let him enjoy this. Let him get his every desire. Let him think he can hold both me and his corner of the galaxy at the same time. Let him forget every rumor about the two of us for some drunken fun in a dark corner. Let him lose the repercussions in his happiness.

And let me never forget them. Let me always remember that every stroke of my tongue against his confirms a thousand vicious theories spinning around the two of us. Let me remember the cost of the heavy ache stiffening against his leg.

Let me never forget that this isn't real.

But for a dangerous second, I do. There's a moment when my hand slips around the nape of his neck and cradles the base of his skull just like I used to, and in that moment I'm in love with him again. It hits me so hard that I almost lose my feet, forcing me to cling even tighter to him—all of the joy, all of the terror, all of the feelings that made me understand why he likes flying so much.

And on the heels of that, I realize something so glaring that I can't believe I never considered it before I rose to Wen's inane challenge. I've been treating the love I had for Ettian like this fake thing—an illusion that shattered when I learned his real name.

But he's in my blood, and I haven't flushed him yet. The familiar patterns his lips press against mine, the familiar shape of his hands on my hips—they're all feeding a fire I thought I doused. I could stand encouraging the rumors that I'm down on my knees for the emperor every night if I knew they didn't brush close to a truth deep inside me.

And that truth means I don't stand a chance of pulling this off.

I shove Ettian off me so forcefully that he staggers back, catching himself on the opposite wall. "Gal, what . . ." he murmurs, his eyes widening in the low light.

"You've got more important things to be doing, don't you?" I reply, trying to disguise my breathlessness as I nod to the empty spot on his brow.

"Can we at least talk about this?"

"There's nothing to talk about. Your precious little knight insinuated we might enjoy some time alone, I was drunk enough to think it might be fun, and, well . . . Now I've had my fun." I shrug. And learned a few things he *definitely* doesn't need to know—for purely tactical reasons, or at least that's what I'm telling myself. "You probably don't have time for anything else," I add with a wicked tilt of my eyebrows I learned from Hanji.

"Gal," he says again, and the sound of my name on his lips tugs like a fishhook in my gut so much that I feel myself leaning back against the pull of it.

"I think it'd be best for all parties involved if this little incident never happened," I tell him. "Wouldn't want anyone wondering why you let an Umber prince put a knife to your throat. Might want to get that thing cleaned up before you go back to the party, by the way," I add, wiggling my bloodied fingers at the nick on his neck.

Ettian lifts a hand to his wound, looking somewhat stunned that it comes away wet. I'll give myself credit where it's due if he completely forgot he was bleeding. I give him a different grin as his eyes lock on mine again. One that I learned from his rogue knight. One that should remind him of the fact he keeps forgetting.

I'm dangerous, and they all keep missing it.

Just not as dangerous as I'm supposed to be.

His lips slip open like he's about to try one more line, some last desperate attempt to convince me to have a real conversation. But for once this night, Ettian emp-Archon follows his better inclinations and simply turns on one heel, feeling his way back into the gloom of the corridor and leaving me wondering how the hell I'm going to get myself out of here.

CHAPTER 7

By some miracle and a lot of panicked fumbling, I manage to find an exit from the passage. It seems like Wen must have cleared a path for me, because I'm able to sneak unnoticed through the emptied halls of the palace and collapse in my own bed before the adrenaline high comes crashing back down. My mind's been caught in that eternal, buzzed circling around the drain of sleep for what feels like hours when three heavy knocks pound on my chamber door.

Terror swipes up the back of my neck before my rationality can swat it back, and I'm halfway out of bed before I remember that anyone who wants to kill me wouldn't knock. Somehow the sheets get wrapped around my legs, and I flop gracelessly, kicking and floundering.

The pounding repeats. I wriggle free of the sheets and make my way out into my antechamber. I have no idea how I managed to seal the complicated lock on my door behind me, but it takes me three tries to pry it open again, wondering all the while who could be knocking when anyone with any reason to visit me already has the clearance to access my rooms.

When the door swings open, Wen Iffan tumbles face-first into me. I'm too startled to catch her properly, and she goes down hard with a sharp, short laugh. "Rocks and rust," she mutters, lurching to her feet and listing sideways into a table. "Hold on—"

"Take it you didn't stick to two drinks either?"

She snorts. She's barefoot, her fancy chest piece askew. Her eyes are fringed with ruby streaks, and she seems to be having a hard time focusing them on anything. The table creaks under her weight, and I take a step forward with far less caution than she deserves, catching her by the elbow. "Bed or couch?" I ask as she leans into me.

"Didn't even . . . tried to stay out of the way and I didn't even . . ."

"Couch's closer." I yank her forward, and she digs her heels in.

"No," she mutters, her eyes lighting up with cold focus.

"Wen, you need to get off your feet before you hurt yourself."

She stills, as if to prove to me that if she can just hold herself rigidly upright, she's good to go. But even that's too hard to maintain for more than a second, and with a resigned wheeze she allows me to guide her to the anteroom's sprawling couch and collapses face-first onto it.

I double-check that the door's locks have reset, then set myself next to her, rubbing my hands down my face. "Why am I the prince who gets to deal with all your drunken fun?" I groan.

Wen's voice is muffled and small. "I thought I was doing well. Thought everything was good. *I* was good—I tried to be, but . . . but I'm not good enough." She rolls on her side, plucking halfheartedly at the snaps that lock her chest piece into place. "Can't even get this rusted thing off."

I consider helping her—a weird impulse I don't fully understand, although this is already a weird night—but Wen tends to ask for the help she wants and trying to help her get undressed is asking to lose a hand. "What happened?" I ask, a little firmer this time.

Wen pauses her fumbling. "Emperor found me after your little rendezvous. Tried to tell him I thought it was for the best that you get . . . whatever's between you still out of your systems. He didn't like that." She scowls, her head lolling backward. "Betting I'm about to get the same from you."

I'm strongly considering it, but I know it'd just go in one ear and out the other in her current state, and that robs me of all the satisfaction. Yes, I'm a little pissed that she pulled a move straight out of an academy cadet playbook, taking two people who obviously have some unresolved tension between them and throwing them in an enclosed space to let it out. Even more pissed that it went exactly how it was supposed to. Ruttin' *furious* that my weakness humiliated me so badly, even if Wen and Ettian were the only witnesses. I scrub one hand self-consciously over my lips, battling against the memory of what happened just hours ago.

Luckily I've sobered up a little since then. Enough to push down the mortifying emotions urging me to snap at her just like Ettian did and realize that the dipshit emperor has given me exactly the opening I need.

"I can't say it wasn't . . . fun. More fun than that stupid party ever could have been."

"Yeah, I'll bet," Wen says with a bubbly snort. "Was it fun when you put a sharp edge to his throat too? I'll give you credit—didn't think you'd go *that* far."

"He told you about that, huh?"

"Showed me the nick and everything. Tried to explain to him that I knew you wouldn't actually kill him, but . . ."

I sit with that for a minute, letting my own head drop back to stare at the brass filigree lining the ceiling. "How did you know I wouldn't?"

Wen's bare toes squirm on the couch next to me. "'Cause you don't have nothing to lose yet," she says after a long pause.

I sneak a sidelong glance at her, wondering if she's actually drunk. She's still bleary-eyed, her scar smushed flat against the couch cushion, but I guess there are some parts of her that never dull. And as long as she's being honest . . .

"So he's pissed at you for setting him up like that? He told me you told *him* that I wanted to meet. Sounds like he's blaming you for his own poor choices."

"Told him exactly that. Not a good idea, turns out."

"Please tell me you weren't out in the open."

Wen sighs. "Might as well have been. Enough people saw. And now that he's got me guarding you instead of doing real work, they're probably gonna start rumors that I'm out of favor."

"I mean, you're guarding the empire's most precious asset," I reassure her sarcastically, gesturing grandly up and down my body. "But don't let anyone hear you call me that or Ettian's gonna find himself yanked off that stupid chair at superluminal."

The tautness of her smirk tells me my words are working their magic. I've just reminded her that if her job has the worth Ettian wants for it, her emperor isn't fit to rule. And given what she just enabled between the two of us, Ettian definitely values me as more than just a prisoner. The vector from that line of thought should be painfully clear. She's caught in the middle of something doomed to fail—enabling it, even—and with Ettian ducking into dark corners for a chance to meet with me, that failure's not far off.

"Y'know, you're right," I continue, staring down at my own bare feet. "You guys haven't managed to kill off my hope yet. My throne still awaits. I'm not even of age to begin my succession. And the fact that we haven't been scorched off this planet yet means my parents haven't disavowed me. If my mother didn't expect me to inherit her crown, she'd have torn through this system with the Imperial Fleet a month ago."

Under other circumstances, this confession would be downright dangerous. Even though any rational person would assume my goals, the apathy I've been carefully presenting has scored me a few freedoms my guards have been taking for granted. Explicitly stating that I'm aiming to make it back home to the Imperial Seat would probably result in a security lockdown—or at least more scrutiny that would make it even more difficult for me to put shards of glass against the Archon emperor's throat or have unsupervised, inebriated talks with the head of my security staff.

But Wen's drunk and vulnerable, and I'm taking whatever advantage I can get in this war.

"You told me about your mother once," I confess to the dark, letting my head drop between my knees. "You told me she raised you to inherit her throne." Granted, it was a shitty mobster throne, but a throne all the same—and for my purposes, I let the word glow off my tongue like it's the most precious thing in the galaxy.

And a glance tells me it works. I catch the way Wen's glassy eyes sharpen, the way her brow furrows.

"I guess I used to think you'd understand me because of that, but now I'm not so sure. Don't you feel . . . I dunno, guilty? For abandoning your purpose?"

"I didn't abandon it," Wen hiccups. "I'm just . . . I need to be *more*. And I've found *more* here."

I shake my head. "That's the point of bloodright though. What's in your veins is already enough. Your mother passed that essence on to you and raised you to hold on to it."

Wen might be a little too intoxicated to process the philosophy I'm laying on her. She makes a low grumbling noise, her fingers tightening on the cushion beneath her. "Spoken like a true princeling who's never had to deal with the logistics involved in seizing power," she retorts, the words spilling out like she's just spent the past minute formulating them. Honestly I'm a little proud of her for making that valid of a point while drunk. "I started this year with nothing. I barely knew what I was doing. Now I'm . . ."

"You're what?" I ask, trying not to grin at the trap she's just stumbled into. Wen may be colloquially known as the Flame Knight, but Ettian's never granted her an official rank. I'm almost certain she isn't even considered a citizen in the eyes of the people for whom she's been toppling buildings, the people whose colors she wears with her head held high. She's utterly devoted to Ettian, and in return she has . . . nothing, still. No status. No protection. No ejector seat for when this all blows up in her face.

"I'm building," she finally decides. "I'm laying foundations."

"You're laying foundations for a war that's going to trap you here forever. A war that's going to kill you before it's done with you." I sigh, and I'm surprised to find there's a real weight behind it. "Look, believe me, I don't even want to know what the Umber empress thinks of me right now. Guess we're both failing our mothers."

Wen rolls her face off the pillows. A spill of moonlight from the windows overhead traces over the topography of her burns. "Sometimes I think she wouldn't even recognize me," she confesses. "And sometimes I think that's for the best."

"You've told me what she did, but never really what she was like." I don't turn it into a question, just a hanging statement begging for her to complete it. I can't have her feeling like I'm prying. I just want her to feel like there's something missing.

"She was kind to me and terrible to everyone else," Wen admits. "As a mother, she was perfect. As a gang boss, she was also perfect. But she was never cruel for no reason. Her terribleness always had a purpose, whether it was gunning down a young upstart where he stood or throwing a snitch on an impossible mission. She didn't have love from her people—she had respect. Honestly sometimes I wonder if she used your mother for inspiration. But I'd like to think she improved upon the model," Wen says with a sly glance.

So maybe she's not completely out of the game yet. I can't ignore the sting of the barb, the implication that my mother could ever possibly misstep. Her way is paved by the right in her blood. When I was small, she'd tuck me in the crook of her arm during her brief visitations, running her fingers carefully through my hair as she spun stories of Umber achievement. Those stories were promises of the greatness I'd one day inherit, the greatness that only our bloodline was capable of wielding. In my memories she looms as large and unimpeachable as a goddess.

"A bold notion," I scoff, playing exactly the jumped-up princeling Wen wants to see, "that a Corinthian mobster who never rose above the north side of Ikar could outdo the Umber empress."

Wen shrugs. "My mother always had the benefit of hindsight. In the heat of the moment, maybe yours has better gut reactions. But, for example, if there was even the slightest chance of someone carrying on the Archon line, my mother would have rooted him out and taken him in instead of letting him slip through her fingers to wreak his vengeance on her."

"Well, that doesn't sound like your mother. That sounds like

Dago Korsa." She flinches, and to soften the blow I add, "And you slipped through his fingers in the end anyway."

I have to be careful in this particular minefield. Wen's sketched out the details of how the Cutter boss killed her mother and adopted her into his organization, how she fought to survive under his eye until the day a lieutenant snapped on her and threw her into the tailpipe of his speeder. She's vowed to burn him to the ground one day, but I'm not sure what kind of emotions she has tied to that goal. And with what sounds like a little too much polish in her system, those mystery feelings are riding close to the surface. If I touch a topic wrong, she might shut down completely, rendering all my efforts wasted.

But I may never get another opportunity like this again.

"What makes you think you aren't enough to take on Korsa?" I ask. I drop my voice low, the words quivering out of me like I'm terrified someone else might hear. "You've been pulling Trost up like a rug and beating your opposition out of it as if you were born to do it. You've gotta be an expert in the kind of warfare that would take him down by now."

Wen snorts. "Think you're the only one who'd call what I'm doing *expert*. And I'm losing my edge every day I'm stuck babysitting you."

"So, what? You're scared you'll botch it?" The notion's outrageous. Sure, she might have been a little sloppy in her methods—which was plenty worrisome when she was working for the Crown. But on her own, in a city that raised her, beholden to no one but the reason she was born? She'd burn him to the ground and walk through the fire.

And that's the thing that's genuinely going to sell this—I *do* believe in her. I believe she's more than capable of doing the exact thing she was born to do, just as much as I believe in my own bloodright. I think it's bullshit that she's abandoned her purpose to ride in Ettian's wake, and I'm hoping the weeks of being my guard have reinforced the pointlessness of her presence here. She might suspect I'm trying to drive a wedge between her and the emperor, but I don't think she suspects that I truly think she's capable of crushing Korsa—only that I'm trying to sway her by arguing that it's for her own good.

Maybe she can't be convinced to betray Ettian, but I'm betting I can convince her to be true to herself.

"I'm not scared I'll botch it," Wen grumbles.

"You're gonna botch it if you keep giving him more time to dig in his roots," I mutter, trying for disapproving but landing squarely in condescending.

"Might as well say the same about you," Wen replies snidely. "And I didn't have a knife at Korsa's throat two hours ago."

The temptation to reach over and muss her hair for that is both overwhelming and startling. Is it just because in this moment she's a drunk teenager with her shoes off? Because I can't see the knife on her, even though I'm sure she's got one tucked away somewhere? This is the Flame Knight, the scourge of Trost, who drops buildings on the people trying to hold the city for my empire.

But this is also the girl I need on my side. And despite everything, I think I might be genuinely starting to like her. "You're rooting for me, huh?" I chuckle.

Wen stills, and I can all but feel the careful bricks I've built tumbling down. I pushed it too far. There's not enough distance between suggesting she's in my corner and reminding her that means siding with a man who wants to annihilate Ettian and everything he stands for. There's not enough between us to put her in my corner anyway. I've just reminded her that I benefit immensely from driving the two of them apart. She's not drunk enough—might never be drunk enough—to let that slide.

"I'm rooting for you," I admit, and the truth behind those words hits me like another glass of polish. "Which is more than Ettian can say."

I watch the moment it saves me play out in the pale moonlight, watch her stabilize like a building adjacent to a blast. Her lips purse inward, her brows drop, her eyes shutter. Maybe what I said isn't a fact, but it's rooted in an all-too-real fear for her. Being Ettian's rogue operative might be a worthwhile endeavor if he were as invested in her goals, but from the look on Wen's face, he isn't and she knows it.

She needs real allies.

She needs *me*.

Obviously I'm not going to suggest we run away together tonight. All I want is for her to wonder what might happen if we did.

CHAPTER 8

The next morning, my usual pacing session is interrupted by a squad of five soldiers in full tac armor storming into my quarters. They're blacked out with helmets and cowls, but when a sixth figure enters the room on their heels, I recognize Wen's stride immediately.

"Surprised you're not bent over a toilet somewhere," I remark with a smirk, quirking an eyebrow her way. I smother the panic trying to seize me. Do they know about my little rendezvous last night?

"Shut up," the squad's leader snaps in Killian Arso's unmistakable harsh-edged voice. On closer examination, one of the other soldiers matches Tarsi in build, and from there my brain finally connects that this is half of the people we flew to Rana in the *Ruttin' Hell*'s hold. In the time since Archon took the planet, they've been working for Ettian's administration as a lightly supervised task force. Wen did her best, most destructive work with them, though I've heard plenty of rumors suggesting they're getting on just fine—possibly even better—without her.

"Are we clear?" Arso asks.

"Room's secure," one of the other soldiers replies, tapping their goggles.

"Red Two, Red Six, secure the package."

"What do you mean pa—" I manage before two of them are on me, one pulling my arms together in front of me as the other snaps a set of cuffs—real cuffs, chained together, not the ceremonial platinum nonsense I've gotten used to wearing in public—around my wrists with practiced fluidity. The panic I've been holding at arm's length breaks free and coils around my neck as I remember all too well the feeling of being bound and marched to what I thought would be my execution.

I'm not well dressed enough to be killed in public right now. I almost open my mouth to announce that fact, but then Arso flips a hand signal and I find myself yanked bodily out of the room before I have a chance to say anything.

Wen moves in to flank my other side as we rush through the halls, her head bent low and one arm braced against my back. "What the rut is going on?" I mutter, leaning over to her ear.

She draws a breath to answer, but before she gets a word out, the shriek of air-raid sirens blares through the palace.

There was a feeling of muddled tension before, but the piercing howl carves it into perfect clarity. Trost is under attack. And even though I've only lived on Archon soil for a little under three years, I understand the visceral fear these people feel, a fear rooted in the sight of a dreadnought in their skies seven years ago, in the rumble of boltfire pummeling into the ground, in the acrid smell wafting from the brand-new crater blasted just north of the city. The Warning Shot was a reminder of just how frail Trost is against a dreadnought's guns, and if any of those ships have broken through to our skies, annihilation is certain to follow.

The hall collapses into a flurry of activity, doors opening and slamming, people slinging datapads back and forth as they shout and beckon. My escort closes tight around me, packing me between their shoulders. I'm not sure if I'm meant to be seen. I'm still trying to puzzle out why they're blacked out and I'm not when an abrupt yank on my elbow veers me into a recess in the corridor where one of them jams a hand into a crack in the wall.

A door swings open into a familiar orange-tinted darkness.

I balk like I've never seen it before, forcing the soldiers escorting me to tighten their grips. Better to act like I don't know this place—and on the assumption that only one other person here knows what went down in these tunnels last night. That person wheezes a consternated sigh that fogs her goggles and shoves me forward into the dark.

The tunnels seem a thousand times tighter with seven people hustling through them. I lose track of the turns and nearly trip over my own feet when they pack me down a staircase. The temperature drops as we descend, the walls going from the smooth, refined concrete and steel of the palace to rough-cut bedrock. Down here appears to be storerooms and facilities for the palace's support staff, but it's eerily empty. We storm past the machines and shelving without a second glance, set on a vector for an ancient-looking boiler.

Two of the soldiers disappear improbably behind it. One of them hollers, "All clear!" and I find myself stuffed forward into a narrow slit in the crumbled stone.

I tumble out into a surprisingly open passage that seems to have been bored through the bedrock. It's lit by harsh floodlights that skim over the outline of three agile-looking transporters—Kinos, I think. Similar capacity to an Umber Beamer, but much sleeker and a little toothier thanks to the pair of guns they sport on the top and bottom of the ship.

I glance back at the crack in the rock as the rest of the squadron worms their way through. Am I dreaming? Am I getting out of here? My knees go a little weak at the thought that I'm outside the palace for the first time since I put that ruttin' crown on Ettian's head. *Keep it together,* I warn myself. I'm just getting moved somewhere less predictable due to the inbound attack.

But if *I'm* getting moved, then—

I turn to find six more people waiting for us at the hatch of the nearest Kino. All of them are dressed to match the squad that escorted me here, but a few have their helmets off—including Ettian emp-Archon. He regards me with a surprisingly composed look. You'd never guess that just last night he was trying to stuff his tongue down my throat.

I'll grudgingly admit—*grudgingly*—that the tac armor looks good on him. Or maybe my standards have dropped significantly to the point that "anything not Archon colors" gets me going. I'm not going to unpack that.

"You people aren't boarded yet?" Arso snaps as she shoulders through her squad. "We're on a tight schedule, you bricks. The engines should be hot already—let's go, go, *go*!"

The soldiers scatter like rats—four to the first ship in the lineup, four to the second. The two escorting me pull me up the ramp of the third, tailed by Ettian and Wen. At first, I feel the impulse to object to traveling with Ettian. It's better strategy to divide your assets if you have to fly a risky mission, and I can't think of anything riskier than moving the emperor and his most valuable prisoner together while an enemy attack hits the city.

Then I remember my other role in this administration. Ideally, these ships will make a clean break and get us to . . . wherever we're going, but in the event someone locks onto our tail and we can't shake them, we can reveal that Gal emp-Umber is aboard and all but guarantee our escape. If there weren't a fear of me strangling him, they would have probably handcuffed me to Ettian already.

"Get him in the cockpit," one of my escorts tells Wen in a voice I recognize as Tarsi's. She's the squad's sniper, and unsurprisingly she starts climbing to the topside gunner nest as soon as she's handed me off. My other escort ducks down the ladder to the one beneath us, leaving Wen to drag me to the fore of the ship and set me in a chair positioned behind the pilot's.

"Buckle him in," she tells Ettian, bending over the ship's controls.

A deep rumble starts up somewhere behind us, which is advantageous—it conceals the way the thump of my heart kicks into overdrive as Ettian bends over me. He pulls the straps down over my shoulders, nudging my cuffed hands out of my lap so he can buckle them between my legs. I should do something. Wink. Smirk. Make a sly comment. But all I find myself doing is tilting my head back and tracking him with wide eyes and my lips slightly parted. Maybe that has the same effect, but it doesn't feel like one I controlled. I don't get the same sense of satisfaction when it takes Ettian three tries to latch the buckle.

It could have nothing to do with me. Ettian's whole expression is shuttered, and not in the way I expect. This isn't the forced stoicism of an academy cadet after a particularly successful night. There's no hint of smug pride for what he got away with in the corridors' dark. There's only fear and stress.

It occurs to me that we may have left the noise of the air-raid sirens behind, but Ettian hasn't. Umber forces could be in the skies of Trost, and for the young emperor, that dredges up a host of bad memories.

He shoves up off my chair and slides himself into the copilot's seat, pulling down his own straps and fumbling them into place. "Ready when you are," he mutters to Wen, straightening his back as if he's bracing for impact. His dark, serious eyes stare unflinchingly into the tunnel's maw—until he pulls the helmet over his head, blacking himself out like the rest of the soldiers.

"Green Three, all passengers are secure," Wen announces into her comm as she secures a headset over her ears. "Preflight checks are good. Ready to roll."

She tilts her head at some response, then drops her hands to the ship's controls. Ahead of us, the other two ships launch down the tunnel with an earsplitting roar. I mimic Ettian's posture a second before Wen throws the engines hot, sending us careening after them.

Any doubts I had about Wen flying after last night's overindulgence are quickly put to bed as we tail the rest of the squadron. The clearance in these tunnels has me clutching my knees—in the cuffs, I can't reach my armrests to brace for impact the way I want to—but Wen guides us through them with a steady hand. I have no idea where they lead, but they seem to go on for eons. Just when I'm about to lean forward and ask an annoying question, a shard of daylight appears ahead.

Wen throws our nose skyward the second we're clear of the tunnel, jamming us hard into our seats as the Kino's engines scream. I squeeze my eyes shut against the harsh glare of the sun, but I can't resist cracking them open as soon as it feels like they aren't about to be scorched out of my head.

In the corner of the cockpit window, I catch the fast-fading shape of Trost's downtown. No pillars of smoke are rising, and the post-reconstruction skyscrapers still stand tall. The air traffic scatters in a familiar pattern. I remember descending into this city a month and a half ago with Iral's hand on my shoulder, watching as my people fled in droves. Now, once again, people are running from the assault descending on their planet.

At least, I think it must be an assault. Could an Umber dreadnought have broken through? I switch my gaze skyward. In the early-afternoon sun, it's difficult to pick out objects in orbit, but the flash of boltfire is unmissable. Something's going on up there.

Something we're on a direct vector for.

"I know I'm not really consulted for any of this," I announce, leaning forward as much as the acceleration allows me to, "but why are we heading *toward* the battle with Archon's most valuable asset? And the emperor too?"

Both of them pretend not to hear me. It takes me back to the last time the three of us flew into battle together—me and Ettian at the helm of the *Ruttin' Hell* with a plan that relied on a secret Wen wasn't privy to. When she realized something wasn't right, she tried to choke answers out of Ettian. As we get closer and closer to the boltfire ahead, I strongly consider repaying her the favor, but I'm cuffed and strapped down and certain Ettian will stop me before I lay a finger on Wen.

And that reminds me of the words I told Wen while trying to wrench her hands out of Ettian's trachea. *We're in the ship with him,* I snapped at her. Ettian would never fly us into deliberate harm.

But that was before he revealed himself as the Archon heir. Before he stepped into a role that demands he rise above his personal ties for the sake of his empire. Before he told me he was going to the front and dragging both of us along with him. If I add all of that up, it tells me the boy I thought I knew back then is not the man in the copilot's seat.

My gaze slips to him, watching the play of the distant boltfire flickering against the impenetrable glossy black of his helmet. His face is inscrutable, but even with the doubts rattling through me, I still know him well enough to know he's utterly calm about our vector. Is that enough? My feelings for him have changed since that last frantic flight in the *Ruttin' Hell*. But his feelings for me?

If last night's run-in is any illustration, this little fighter careening into battle is the safest place in the galaxy.

And besides, Wen's in here too. She flies steadily—surprising, now that she has free rein to sway and loop and play with the ship all she likes. But then I spot the other two Kinos up ahead and realize she's holding our place in a formation, flying to blend in with the others. Our position at the rear is a gamble, attempting to disguise the importance of this ship, but I notice that the gunner nests ahead have angled themselves as if their center exists squarely on top of this ship. As we streak for the melee, the squadron is making sure the emperor—and his human shield—is as protected as they can manage.

"Are we going to engage?" I mutter under my breath, not expecting an answer from either of them. Now that we're drawing closer, I lean forward against the straps of my harness to peer at the ship's console over Wen's shoulder. There's no sign of a dreadnought—Umber or Archon—only a fleet of ships stamped with brass sigils and the scrambled Archon fighters weaving between them, trying to beat them back. Far below, larger Archon ships are heaving their way out of the atmosphere, but the Umber attackers have the advantage of Rana's gravity on their side. The field ahead is a mess, Archon fighters whipping through the oncoming forces in sloppy vectors as they try to beat back the Umber ships long enough for the reinforcements to arrive.

And for all intents and purposes, we look like we're about to join the fight.

Both Ettian and Wen probably have earpieces in, cluing them in on the strategy behind whatever this maneuver is. I've got nothing but sweaty palms getting sweatier. *Ettian wouldn't kill the three of us,* I try to reassure myself.

But what makes him—and Wen, and every other soldier flying this run—think that it's all going to turn out fine?

"Got a few bogeys that might nibble at us," Ettian says, tapping the console in front of him to highlight the ships for the rest of our formation. It's strange to see him flying shotgun to someone else. Ettian, to me, belongs in a pilot's chair. For as long as I knew him as Ettian Nassun, that was the only thing he ever wanted. He once told me that the helm of a fighter was the one place in the galaxy where he felt like he was fully in control of his life. I laughed at him then, thinking of the chaos that tended to ensue whenever *I* had to fly. Now I wonder how he looks so comfortable calling shots from the copilot's chair without a single hand on the controls. Have a few months of governing changed him so easily?

"Bogeys on their way," Wen says through what sounds like gritted teeth.

"Steady," Ettian replies, then tilts his head. "Sorry, Green One. Yes, the con is yours."

I smirk. So he's not so comfortable in his place after all. Ettian spent the more recent end of his academy career leading formations. He's a bit shitty at sitting back and letting one act without his directive.

The reassurance I find in his weakness washes away when I remember what's about to happen. How the rut did every single one of the soldiers we're flying with today tolerate this back when we first flew combat together? All ten of them were belted down in the hold of the *Ruttin' Hell,* completely helpless as we sent the scrappy little Beamer careening through an active field. My hands itch for something to do, something that'll make me feel like I have at least a little control over my fate, but I can't even grip the arms of my seat properly. I fight the panic building inside me, trying to take steadying breaths, but any sense of rhythm I've established is yanked away the second Wen wrenches our nose into a spiraling evasive maneuver that crushes the air out of my chest.

Twin howls echo from the gunner nests behind us as the soldiers are flung into the webbing that keeps them strapped upright and agile enough to whip their mounts around. One of them fires, a rapid staccato burst rattling the back of my seat, and the edge of the cockpit window glows from a steady stream of boltfire. The other starts slamming another kind of rhythm into the bulkhead of their nest.

My stomach drops at the familiar rudiment. Ettian once tried to teach me the meanings embedded in different Archon drum patterns, hoping it would help keep me from tensing up every time I heard one. I dig my fingers into my kneecaps, trying to dislodge the sensation of his hands, sitting cross-legged across from him, my palms flat on the floor, as he tapped each beat into my bones until I was able to mimic it too.

This rudiment is one of their calls to arms, meant to encourage a fellow soldier in an act of valor. In the copilot's seat, Ettian picks up the rhythm with his free hand as the other dances over readouts, clumsily trying to coordinate this ship's place in our formation as the incoming Umber fighters do their best to dislodge us. "Y'know, I could probably do that better," I wheeze over another wild twist from Wen.

"Not really the time, Gal."

"You're not trained for that position," I snap. "Only one person in this cockpit has actually flown combat in the copilot's chair, and neither of the people at the controls are that guy!"

"Okay, 'flown combat' is a *loose* approximation at best—"

"Ettian!" Wen yelps, yanking hard on the controls as the readouts flare with a proximity warning he should have flagged seconds ago. "Rocks and rust, you're gonna get us all killed."

"Do you really need much more instruction than 'fly evasive'?" Ettian asks, tapping frantically at his side of the dashboard.

"*Yes!*" Wen and I shout simultaneously.

"Bogey's coming wide around our rear, trying to get on top of us," I mutter a second later, straining up against my harness to get a better look.

"Noted," Wen replies. She tilts us forward with a decisive spin of the Kino's gyros, reorienting so that both gunner nests have clear shots at the incoming fighter. The steady chug of boltfire rattles the ship, and a second later, the bogey peels away. "Locking back in formation now," Wen announces, throwing us back on course and spurring the engines with a kick that knocks me back in my seat.

Ettian shoots me a look over his shoulder, and even with the glossy helmet covering his face, I can picture the furious, frustrated glare he's sending my way with perfect clarity. "Eyes on the sky, asshole," I tell him with a smirk.

"Rut off," I think I hear him mutter.

"Seriously though," I add after another minute of skirting the edge of the battlefield. "Where are we going? What's the plan? What the rut is an *emperor* doing in an active—"

When an object comes out of superluminal, it feels like there should be some sort of noise. Or some sort of explosion. *Something* to indicate that where once there was a vacuum and maybe a few Umber war barges hanging back to hold the rear, there is now a rut-all massive dreadnought blotting out the light of this system's star.

With no warning, it's impossible to process. Your brain scrambles for a foothold, but when confronted with miles of starship, it feels like the meat in your head shuts down completely. I notice an odd, glittering dust flaring up against the dreadnought's metal and it takes me what feels like a full minute to comprehend that those plumes are all that remain of the Umber barges. From that shaky foundation, I make the next logical leap.

This dreadnought isn't one of ours. It started that way most certainly, but with a wily ex-Umber pirate in command, the Archon forces have mastered the art of commandeering the cityships and turning them against us.

I blink, and then blink again, and finally I recognize the ship. It's not just any Archon-claimed dreadnought.

It's the first.

"Hail *Torrent*," Wen says, smug satisfaction curling through every note in her voice as she wheels our nose toward it. "Green Squadron's coming home to roost."

CHAPTER 9

"So the attack was a cover," I say conversationally, kicking my feet up on the headrest of Wen's chair. I stopped peering over their shoulders at the console when the *Torrent*'s guns opened fire. Everything after that point was a foregone conclusion.

A foregone conclusion that feels like a black hole inside me. I can't help but teeter through the maw of its implication. Those were my people flying those ships.

Those plumes against the *Torrent*'s hull were my people.

There are too many things I'm trying to conceptualize at once, and it's shutting me down. And so I've slipped back into the safest persona I have, the detached aloofness that's kept me from pulling my hair out every single day of my captivity.

But my knuckles are still pale in my lap, and there's a telltale tremor in the glimmer of my cuffs.

There was nothing I could have done, I try to tell myself. Nothing in a single person's power can stop the vector of a dreadnought. Those fighters died for the glory of the Umber Empire. Their fearless service is my bloodright, part of the unquestionable power I'll wield when I'm crowned. I try to hear the thoughts in my mother's voice, but my own keeps intruding, telling me that the most honest emotion I've felt in a month is the relief that flushed through me when the dreadnought dropped onto the field.

The squadron of Kinos is back in formation and bound for an access point on the *Torrent*'s hull. If any Umber ships managed to track our vector and inferred that we started from the tunnels beneath the palace, the Archon forces have long since taken care of them. For all intents and purposes, this looks like an attack on Trost gone wrong, annihilated when a dreadnought took an intrasystem superluminal leap to enter the fray.

But I'm sure if I traced the logs of the Umber fleet, I'd discover a moment when they should have been stopped, long before they ever reached Rana. A moment where the Archon defenses had them in their sights and let them slip by anyway. There was no easy way to get Ettian to the front without a series of unavoidable vulnerabilities—moments that Umber would have exploited the second we saw them coming.

Now Ettian flies for the safety of a dreadnought, human shield in tow and Umber none the wiser.

Credit where credit's due—it even had me fooled up until the very end.

The process of entering a dreadnought is like being eaten alive. As we nose up to the great ship's hull, a hatch winches open like a gaping maw, admitting us through the outer layer of armor. I tense in my seat as we slip into the shadow and search the darkness for the pinpoint lights that stripe along the miles of blackness, marking the tram routes and flight decks stacked along the inner wall of the cityship. If not for the uniformity of the lights, it would look like distant stars. Up ahead, there's only more blackness. Somewhere within it lurks the dreadnought's command core, cloaked by both the outer hull and the shadows the metal wraps around it. Even dreadnought crews themselves are rarely privy to the exact positioning of the core relative to the outer hull at any given moment.

The disorienting entry is only worsening the panic building inside me. I didn't know this would be happening today—if I had, I would have been scrabbling at the walls last night, looking for any spare hatch that could turn into an escape route. Boarding the *Torrent* is, in essence, starting over. Or dooming me completely, because I'm not confident in my prospects of finding a way off this ship once we're all the way down its gullet.

Wen flies carefully in the wake of the other two ships, her helmet stripped off for better visibility, navigating by the sight of the beacons glowing at their wingtips. She's never flown a dreadnought entry run before, and even though I know she's got the skills to stick it, I understand her caution. The distant glimmering lights along the cityship's inner walls unmoor more than guide when you're this far away from them, and the core can only ever sneak up on you.

At a command I hear faintly from her earpiece, she flips our gyros, reversing the ship's orientation along its vector. My stomach flips along with them, and rather than leaning over to watch her instruments, I close my eyes and brace against the deceleration of the main engines firing, waiting for the telltale jolt of the docking arm.

I open them in time to catch the friendly clap Ettian lays on her shoulder and the quiet, proud smile she gives him in return. A twinge of jealousy snaps through my heart. I try to mold the desire into something more appropriate—*I wish I had that with someone on my side, I miss my academy friends, I wonder where Ollins, Rin, Rhodes, and Hanji are right now*—but every sentiment resonates false against the truth still shuddering in my flesh.

I miss intimacy. A weird thought for a guy who made out with someone less than a day ago, but I'm not about to fool myself into thinking a few brisk minutes in a darkened passage make up for a long, lonely month and a half. Being Ettian's captive has stripped away the camaraderie that used to sustain me, and the rate at which it chips away at me doubles whenever I see what I'm missing out on.

The rear of the ship rattles with the noise of Tarsi and the other gunner extracting themselves from their nests, pulling me out of the funk threatening to pin me in my seat. I pluck halfheartedly at the buckles keeping me strapped down, but with my hands still cuffed, I can't do much. Ettian clambers over to help me, and I keep my gaze firmly pinned on the metal binding my wrists together this time. I'm not about to let him see that he's gotten to me—that he did it without even trying.

"We have a seal," Wen confirms, springing up from the pilot's seat as she finalizes the tiedown. The Kino quiets around us, settling into its berth. I duck into Wen's wake as she sweeps down the hall after Ettian, tempted to latch onto her belt just to keep her close. I don't know what good it could possibly do, but in the palace, I was mostly surrounded by the court and a few guards.

On the *Torrent,* it'll all be soldiers. People who don't just want me dead—people who have the skills and tools to make it so.

I seize the reins of myself, hauling my brain away from the panic winding around my throat. Later. I can break later. I can think about how I'm about to step onto a ruttin' Archon dreadnought bound for the front later, when I have . . . already stepped onto the ruttin' Archon dreadnought. My desperation hardens into reckless resolve, because it feels like it's the only thing that's going to save me from cracking. I *will* survive this. The doors open to me on Rana have closed, but I can find new ones. I've made it this far already. I have to keep fighting, or else the blood in my veins is worthless.

We arrange ourselves at the rear ramp, waiting for the last security clearances to pass and unlock it. Ettian leads the party, his helmet tucked neatly under one arm and his posture poised and princely. The snipers flank him, still blacked out. Wen and I bring up the rear—she takes a step back and slips a gentle hand around my biceps as if she senses the fears rocketing around my head.

"You could have said," I mutter to her.

"You're the enemy, Gal," she reminds me. Maybe I'm imagining things, but it almost sounds like she's joking.

A klaxon sounds, announcing the ramp's descent. There's a slight hiss as it cracks open, the air pressure between the Kino's cabin and the dreadnought core equalizing in an instant. The sound triggers an instinctive response in me, stalling my next breath in my lungs. A flicker of childish shame teases the skin on the back of my neck. I was scolded once for the habit, the first time I shipped from the Umber Imperial Seat on Lucia to Naberrie, the world where I began my schooling when I was ten.

It's not going to make a difference whether you've got air or not if there's nothing on the other side of that door. I can barely remember the guard's face, but her words have stuck with me for years.

But there's more than air on the other side of this door. As the ramp descends, I get my first good look at our welcoming party over Ettian's shoulder.

"Commodore," the emperor says warmly. "I'm thrilled you could join us."

Adela Esperza holds her salute, but a wry smirk pulls up the corner of her lips. "Pleasure's all mine, Your Majesty. Welcome aboard the *Torrent*." Ettian inclines his head to her, and she drops her glimmering metal hand, stepping forward to offer a shake. The officers surrounding her let down their own salutes, but none of them can share the same degree of familiarity.

When we first met this woman, she wasn't a commodore and neither of us were calling ourselves princes. Ettian and I were desperate to get a stolen ship off our hands, and out of the shadows of a Corinthian borderworld city slunk Adela Esperza, driving a hard bargain that softened just enough for her to send us on our way with a cheap room to hide us.

Imagine our surprise when we arrived at an Archon base to find her in uniform. Turns out the Esperza we'd met in Isla was a half-truth—and an enigma to boot. She'd apparently spent her youth as a pirate on the Umber fringes having adventures that ranged from sacking cargo ships to getting her right hand blown off. Then she ran into an Archon knight, got entangled in the affairs of an empire she had nothing to do with, and somehow ended up a ranking officer in General Iral's resistance movement.

Her ex-pirate tricks paid off in a major way when they started hijacking dreadnoughts, and now she wears a commodore's platinum and answers only to Iral and the emperor.

Her gaze slips past Ettian and lands on me, and I see the immediate hardening of something deep inside her. "Well, hello there, kiddo," Esperza says. Even in uniform, dressed to meet an emperor, she's still got a bit of pirate swagger clinging to her as she saunters forward. "Believe we haven't been properly introduced."

I glance down at the metal hand offered to me, whirling through the calculation it sets off in my head: *Don't take it—show fear, give her the satisfaction, confirm to everyone around you just how weak you are. Take it—look stupid, unthinking, and snap go your bones.*

After a breath of hesitation, I slide my hand into hers, squeeze firmly, and shake, trying not to flinch as the cuffs rattle obviously. "Gal emp-Umber," I tell her, my voice miraculously even. "Congratulations on your promotion, Commodore."

She returns my squeeze with just enough force to remind me who's in charge here, but she lets me go with all my fingers intact. I'll take whatever victory I can get. "Credit where credit's due—I'm not surprised often, but you kids managed to pull off a good one," Esperza says. Her eyes flick to Wen. "What about you? You got anything up your sleeve?"

Wen's got a bit of a starstruck glint in her eye, and it takes a jostle from me for her to realize the commodore's just asked her a question. "N-nothing you need to know at the moment," she stammers, flashing a nervous grin. I struggle to keep my jaw from dropping—I've never seen the famous Flame Knight so flustered.

Esperza meets her with an earnest, steady smile. "I like this one," she tells Ettian over her shoulder, and Wen's fingers crimp hard into my biceps. I nudge her in the ribs once the commodore's turned back around, genuinely delighted. Wen getting all moon-eyed over Esperza is material—I just need to figure out how to hone it into a weapon.

"How soon until we're moving?" Ettian asks. The longer this ship sits so close to Rana, the sooner suspicions might arise that it's got ulterior motives beyond putting a decisive end to the Umber attack.

"As soon as we get tiedown confirmation from every ship coming aboard, we go superluminal," Esperza replies, beckoning him to fall in step with her as she sets off down the hall. The rest of us follow in their wake. I take advantage of Wen's eagerness, lengthening my strides so that the two of us keep pace directly behind the emperor and commodore.

"Thank you," Ettian murmurs to Esperza, low enough that most of our escort couldn't possibly hear it. "I know the general has his doubts, but the extraction worked as smoothly as we could hope for."

It isn't exactly surprising to hear, but it warms me all the same to know that Iral and Ettian are still at odds—and to know that Ettian defied him on my suggestion alone. Of course the general would try to stall any concrete plan that would ferry the emperor to the front. As soon as Ettian commands by presence instead of proxy, he'll scatter Iral's best-laid plans with overrides the general can't counter. And the fact that the *Torrent*—and more important, the commodore herself—ended up at Rana anyway has interesting implications for where her loyalties lie.

Or maybe Esperza is just a pirate through and through, happy to buck the rigidity of military command when it suits her. She looked pleased enough with herself when she greeted us.

For a treacherous second, my thoughts stray to the Umber soldiers she pulverized with her maneuver.

Only a second. I blink them away with my mother's practiced poise, my stride never faltering. This is the heart of the Archon operation. To show weakness is to draw attention, and the last thing I need them to notice is how easily they've just welcomed me into their command core.

Esperza walks us through a security checkpoint, where I'm aggressively scanned and patted down, rolling my eyes all the while. They practically yanked me out of bed on Rana—what business would I have trying to smuggle something in? The patrols that conduct our search are noticeably armed. At first blush, it seems ridiculous that anyone would need to carry a weapon when you're protected by miles of dreadnought on all sides.

But then you remember how these dreadnoughts fell into Archon hands in the first place, and it all starts making sense. Esperza knows that it isn't enough to have a trick up your sleeve—you've got to make sure the same trick won't ever work again once you've played it. If an enemy force makes it this deep into the *Torrent,* intent on overtaking the cityship, they're gonna find themselves roasted by the boltfire these patrols are packing.

I try to lift my chin, try not to let my eye be drawn. I have to appear aware, but not focused. Confident, but not overly so. These are new people, people who haven't had a chance to form an assumption about what my captivity looks like. If I play this right, they become assets.

If I rut it up, they become obstacles.

From the checkpoint, Esperza guides us through the maze of honeycombing corridors. "We've set up quarters for you adjacent to the bridge. Recreation, dining, and most other facilities are on the outer edge of the core, but we have the essentials stocked within every siege-able ring, just in case," she says with a reassuring shrug.

I have an academic knowledge of dreadnought structure, but seeing a command core in the flesh is another thing entirely. The term "cityship" should really tell you all you need to know—and yet, there's something about seeing it function up close and personal that grounds it in a reality you can't ignore. People spend their entire lives on these things. I'm pretty sure I spot a sign for a nursery around a corner. To get to the bridge, we summon an elevator that moves laterally as well as up and down, shunting us up and over until at last it releases us at the innermost ring of the core.

"Emperor on deck!" Esperza calls out as she strides off the elevator. A ripple goes off across the massive room as techies and sector captains rise from their stations and salute. The bridge is built around the same principles as the dreadnought itself, arranged in concentric circles that trickle down to the most important position. At the center of the room sits a massive circular command station, visible only because of the layers of clear screens flowering around it. Perched in the middle of it is a woman with deep midnight skin and captain's platinum decorating her shoulders.

She rises from her chair and salutes like the rest of her crew, but while everyone else fixates on Ettian, her eyes immediately drift to Esperza and a slight frown creases the edge of her lips. "Your Majesty," Esperza says as we approach the captain's station. "Allow me to introduce Captain Deidra con-Silon."

I grit my teeth. When Archon commandeered this dreadnought, it was under the command of a woman named Nita con-Silon—not a relation to the current captain but a member of a bloodline Umber installed to a continental governorship on Rana. With Rana now under Archon control, it seems Silon's reverted to the people who once laid claim to it, and one of those people went ahead and staked her claim on this ship while she was at it.

"A pleasure to meet you," Ettian says smoothly. He should shake her hand, but the screens ensconcing her stand in his way, and she doesn't show any signs of letting them down. At his nod, Silon drops her salute.

Then her eyes slip to me, and her frown deepens. "Your Majesty," she says, her voice smooth and melodic. "I can't help but notice that an enemy agent seems to have infiltrated my bridge. I hope you won't hold it against me."

The veneer of her diplomacy is as thin as an onion skin, but with her pleasant tone and the vague deference she paid to the chain of command, there's nothing to call her on outright. I hold my breath, waiting for Ettian's response.

"Excuse my subordinate," Esperza says, putting a hefty emphasis on the last word as she steps between the emperor and the captain. "Silon here likes things to be in their proper places."

"Like dreadnoughts in their positions on the warfront," Silon retorts mildly. "Prisoners in the brig. That sort of thing. Call me organized."

"And when your meticulous organization slows this ship down so much that it gets you vaporized, I'll be sure to divvy your remaining electrons into neat little boxes," Esperza replies with an exasperated smirk.

"Captain," Ettian says, neatly sidestepping Esperza. "I greatly appreciate this ship's assistance. I understand it may be frustrating to be pulled from the fight, and I'm just as eager as you to set a vector back to where the *Torrent* is needed most."

"Unfortunately 'where' is an ever-shifting quantity that depends on '*when*,'" Silon says with a sniff, settling back in her command chair, which swivels slightly as it takes her full weight. With the pivot, she's able to access every screen surrounding her—which she does, almost absentmindedly, one hand tapping away at the display as her eyes flick back and forth between it and Ettian. "The *Torrent*'s whens and wheres are usually up to the general's strategy."

She says "the general" with an interesting note of reverence, one I'm sure Ettian doesn't miss either. Seems the *Torrent*'s loyalties are . . . skeptical, at best, of where the emperor really belongs in the chain of command.

Silon glances over to another screen on the opposite side of her station, letting out a long-suffering sigh. "Looks like the last ship finally logged a tiedown. Navigation?"

"Ready," an officer across the room replies.

"Ship is clear for departure. Get us oriented on a heading. Engineering?"

"Ready."

"Confirm our superluminal drives are ready to fire. Communications?"

"Ready."

"Send our Intent of Arrival ansible to the fleet's main body with target coordinates attached. Then put out an unencrypted broadcast for ships in the area alerting them that we're about to jump to superluminal."

As Silon spirals further into the preparations for our superluminal leap, she all but melts into the helm. On a smaller starship like the Beamer we flew to Delos, jumping to superluminal was as easy as jamming down a button. But the complexity of coordinating a jump increases exponentially with the scale of your craft, and for the miles and miles of the *Torrent*, the process is almost too intricate for a single mind to grasp.

Back at the academy, we'd run dreadnought command sims designed to push our teamwork to the limit. I found that I got a bit of a thrill from disappearing so entirely into the operation of a starship that it started to feel like an extension of my body. I'd fantasized that it'd be something like running an empire—at least up until the moments when Hanji would stick her finger in my ear to see if I was "still in there."

But nothing I achieved at the academy is anywhere near watching Silon work. Trying to keep up with the commands she rattles off is hopeless for us onlookers, but her bridge crew picks up each order and socks it down the correct channel on reflex. She's a weaver at a loom, gathering together every color of thread and running her shuttle effortlessly through the steps she needs to achieve her goal.

"Confirmed for jump to superluminal," Silon announces at last, and only then do I realize that at some point I stopped breathing. For the first time she hesitates, a flicker of consternation passing over her features. "Commodore," she grinds out. "At your mark."

Esperza shrugs, glancing sidelong at Ettian. "You ready, Your Majesty?"

Ettian squares his shoulders—just a tad, just enough that for a moment, in his well-fitted tac armor, with his chin lifted just-so, he looks like a little bit more than a kid dressing up as a soldier. "Punch it," the emperor says.

The synapse of command fires, his words snapping through Silon's orders and branching through her subordinates. A great inhale goes up around the room as a vibration pulses through the floor, everyone bracing for a massive acceleration that never comes.

And just like that, we're past the speed of light. From the interior of the *Torrent*'s core, it's like nothing's changed at all. If we had some sort of window through the armor of the hull, we'd see that the blackness of space has bled to gray around us. But with no other reference, the only confirmation we get is the engineering chief straightening in her chair and announcing, "Course confirmed. Ten seconds to arrival."

The *Torrent*'s path isn't an average superluminal journey. Instead of spanning the galaxy in a long, restless week, we're leaping across the Tosa System. Usually superluminal travel within a star system is banned, but wartime makes exceptions and dreadnoughts eat excuses for breakfast. They do their best to calculate a clean path, but there's always a small risk they might run someone down streaking through the black so recklessly.

A small price to pay, it seems, when the *Torrent* has places to be.

"Dropping from superluminal in three. Two. One. Mark," Engineering announces.

Once again, there's no noise or snap or change in the air. We drop like a stone back into sublight, and the screens around us flicker as they start absorbing every last drop of data about the ship's surroundings as fast as possible.

"We've exited superluminal on target," Navigation calls across the bridge. Silon pulls up the readings they hand off, the sector map spilling over the screens of her command station. I feel my buried panic start to simmer and clench my hands, trying my damnedest to keep the cuffs from rattling. I fix my eyes on Ettian's square shoulders and the sprawl of ships visible over them—the mantle of his command, now at his fingertips.

The emperor has arrived at the battlefront.

CHAPTER 10

WITHIN A MINUTE of our arrival, logistics rear their ugly head. "Now that all that's settled," Silon says, rising from her chair, "we can finally get the prisoner set up in his cell."

And oh, the panic kicks up to a boil now, reaching back around my throat like an old friend. I've gotten so used to people forgetting to treat me like a proper captive that I'd almost forgotten myself how I really should be treated. I hadn't even factored that in when Ettian announced his intention to bring me to the front with him. How much of my grandiose vision of tearing the Archon rebellion apart from the inside have I hung on the outrageous degree of freedom the emperor has granted me so far?

Fortunately it's the emperor who comes to my rescue. "Absolutely not," Ettian says firmly. I try to keep myself from looking too pleased about it. Not only is he favoring me, he's doing so against the express wishes of a critical subordinate. As captain of the *Torrent,* Silon has an entire cityship under her sway, and if she's not thrilled with the emperor's decisions, that resentment will no doubt trickle down to the people under her command.

"I'm concerned for the prisoner's safety," Ettian continues.

"There have been attempts on his life already. Worse than that, the people I've entrusted to guard him have not done their due diligence—sometimes to a suspicious degree. At present, Wen Iffan is the only person who I'm certain can guard him competently."

Silon's suspicious eyes find a new target. "Ah yes, the famous Flame Knight. Not an official title, or so I've heard. But I've heard plenty of other interesting things about this one."

"Good things, I hope?" Wen asks—maybe because Ettian's praise has bolstered her confidence. I catch her stopping herself from glancing sidelong at Esperza.

"*Interesting* things," Silon repeats after a noticeable pause. "Remind me what her rank is again, Your Majesty?"

Ettian's jaw tightens. Esperza's brows knit together. A hint of a blush creeps into Wen's unburnt cheek. "She doesn't hold one," Ettian admits after a too-long beat.

"Like I said. Interesting."

Okay, I like Silon. She's doing my job for me, and being extremely smart about it. She can't insult the emperor directly, but she can do the next best thing, running her critical fingers through his most questionable policy decisions. On Rana, it seemed like cleverness to let Wen operate rogue, but now he's brought her to a dreadnought—and of all dreadnoughts, one run by a woman who seems to thrive on formality and order.

The fact that Silon seems to hold a continental bloodright is just the icing on top of the cake. It means Ettian can't replace her with a more compliant captain, not when he risks offending members of his own frail gentry. I remember the upturned faces that filled the Archon court at the party last night, all the people he was trying so desperately to impress. If they're anything like Umber governors, they want assurances that he'll serve them well. One persnickety captain with continental bloodright might erode all the goodwill he's built so far.

But before I can get too pleased with myself, Commodore Esperza steps in. "Now, hold on. You're telling me that this girl's not ranked?"

"Well, why should she be?" Silon shrugs. Wen's spine goes a notch stiffer.

"For starters, she just flew that mission. In fact, she just flew the *linchpin* of that mission," Esperza says, a hint of fury showing in the tightness of her jaw. "Which isn't even the first mission she's flown in the service of this resistance. She's been working as the emperor's operative for over a month now—and from the reports I've gotten, she's been pretty damn good at it. She's a hell of a pilot, enough so that she's entrusted with the emperor's life when it comes to secreting him out of his capital. That role should go to a ranking officer. And given how committed this kid seems to be to our mission, it's . . ."

Esperza catches herself mid-rant, flicking a guilty glance sidelong at Ettian. She knows he's been under attack since the moment he stepped onto Silon's bridge, and she'd clearly meant to ally herself with him against her disgruntled subordinate.

But I also realize the nerve this must have struck with her. Adela Esperza wasn't Archon-born and had no stake in the future of the Archon Empire until she had the misfortune of befriending one of its knights and getting swept up in its bullshit. Now she's not only a ranking officer, but she holds the reins of an entire fleet of commandeered dreadnoughts flying in the name of Ettian emp-Archon. That glimmer of idolatry I saw when Wen reunited with Esperza is a two-way channel. Esperza sees herself in Wen Iffan.

And now she's found out that a girl who's given so much to the Archon resistance already hasn't received so much as a title in return.

The commodore draws herself tall with a deep breath, squaring up into a military stance that looks a tad ridiculous on someone so unconcerned with formality. "Your Majesty," Esperza says. "With your permission, I'd like to grant Wen Iffan the rank of lieutenant. I *understand* she hasn't received formal military training," the commodore admits, cutting off Silon's attempt to object with a dismissive gesture, "but I would be willing to take her under my wing on my own time to fill in the gaps."

I catch Silon grumbling something that sounds like "With *what* time?" but it doesn't seem to reach Ettian's ears. Wen's fixed the emperor with a sweetheart-at-a-carnival-game look, begging him with her eyes to accept the commodore's offer.

But Ettian's focus has landed on me. "I'm not sure that will be possible, given the situation with our prisoner."

Silon takes an eager step forward. "Your Majesty, I assure you that the *Torrent*'s brig will be more than adequate to contain the prisoner while Iffan goes about her duties. We have facilities that—"

Ettian cuts her off with a hand gesture, and Silon is enough of a stickler for formalities that it works. "Gal emp-Umber is not some common prisoner. We can't afford to toss him into a cell and call it a day. And as I've said already, Wen Iffan is the only one I trust to guard him. Perhaps if you earn that trust, we can reach a new arrangement."

"I apologize, Your Majesty, but I try to run a tight ship, and I need not mention that this is *wartime*. I can't tolerate an Umber agent running free on the *Torrent*."

"If I could interject," I say at last, and everyone's surprised enough that I dive haphazardly into the space I've carved in the conversation. "If the emperor wants to be reassured that I'm looked after at all times, perhaps he should be the one looking after me."

I know in an instant that I've rutted up royally. I thought the absurdity of my suggestion would help frame how ridiculous Ettian's stipulations for my safety are, but Esperza immediately gets a look in her eye that I don't like. "A high-priority prisoner shadowing the emperor is about the most ridiculous thing I've ever heard, but I suppose the fact that you made that suggestion means you're probably witless enough that you won't be too much trouble." The commodore's gaze shifts between me and Wen. "Iffan alone bearing the weight of guarding this kid seems only a few ticks less stupid. There are better ways she can use her time. And as long as the Umber heir is aboard my ship, I want to have eyes on him."

Silon shoots her a look that *begs* her not to say what Esperza is almost certainly about to say.

"How about this? The prisoner sticks with Iffan. Iffan trains under me. I'll be able to directly monitor both his whereabouts and what information he has access to at all times."

"I can't even begin to list how many security codes that could violate," Silon mutters, pinching her brow.

But I already know her objection has come too late. Ettian's nodding, Wen's smirking, Esperza's got a look of sly satisfaction, and I'm stuck glancing between the three of them and wondering how I just managed to effectively quash any plans I'd begun to formulate.

In the palace, I had Wen's ear, and with Ettian's attention too scattered by the war, I had a chance of pulling her away from his side. But now she's got Esperza's attention, which means I've got Esperza's attention, which means I'm not going to get away with *shit*. I have no illusions about being able to pull any shenanigans under the nose of that ex-pirate, especially not with her imprinting so strongly on Ettian's precious Flame Knight.

Instead of slipping a step closer to the emperor, instead of chaining myself to the hand that will shape the course of this war, I've effectively doubled my guard.

I catch my new best friend Deidra con-Silon's pained gaze, and I can't help but mirror it.

The question of where I'm going to sleep is an entirely different protracted argument that I sulk through, stubbornly silent. This ship wasn't built to hold prisoners anywhere *but* the brig, and it takes an entire team of Silon's security officers to confirm that one of the suites built for the *Torrent*'s more esteemed guests has adequate locks on the doors and nothing dangerous hidden in any of the drawers. I'm installed in one room of the suite, with Wen set up in the other.

My new digs are sparse but sleek, clearly designed for a visiting dignitary or a high-level officer. No decorations—nothing for me to smash or hurt myself with, I suppose. I guess I'll just have to take my impulses out on other people.

Good thing Wen's next door.

The core security team has disabled my door's functionality so I can't lock myself in. Wen gets to keep hers, a decision I understand but resent all the same. I have to jam myself against the sliding mechanism just to wrestle the thing open, and I'm in the midst of doing so when I nearly topple headlong into the emperor himself.

Ettian takes a startled step backward, then regains his princely composure. "I came to see how you were settling in," he says, though he sounds unsure about whether that was his real motivation or not.

I spread my arms, gesturing to the vast expanse of my empty room. "Just finished unpacking, as you can see."

He looks pained. I'm glad of it. "I'm sorry—"

"Careful. Anyone could be listening."

Now he looks like he's about to grab me by the throat, and I hate that I'm a little into it. "I'm sorry it caught you off-guard," Ettian continues, apparently heedless of anyone who might catch him groveling to his prisoner. "I know it must have been terrifying."

"Not the first time I thought I was about to be marched to my execution. Probably not the last either." I shrug, brushing past him and throwing myself down on a couch in the suite's common area. "At least I was dressed, unlike the last time someone snatched me from my rooms." I pass him a coy look that dares him to get swept up in the memory of that haphazard night—the one where he set off a mob of streakers and plucked me from the academy head's private quarters. He'd shown up like some sort of action hero, busting through the window in an ascension rig and no shirt.

I'd been dressed in a robe and slippers, caught completely off-guard. I'd asked for a rescue and received an unholy reckoning of chaos descending upon the walls that dared to trap me. Maybe I should have noticed then—Ettian emp-Archon never did anything small.

"I was hoping we could talk," Ettian says, blatantly ignoring the way I've draped myself over the furniture.

"Oh, *now*? *Now* you want to talk?" I wave a hand in a gesture I hope captures the enormity of the *Torrent* around us. "These walls are probably bugged. That delightful dreadnought captain—she's my new favorite person, by the way—is probably listening to every word we say."

Ettian shakes his head. "These rooms are meant for governors and imperials. It would be a massive security risk to have them under surveillance."

Interesting. Excellent to know. I really ought to thank him for it—how easily he spills this useful information at the slightest nudge. "So the next person who decides it might be fun to try their hand at killing me is going to get away with it, huh?"

"Wen and I are the only ones with access to the outside door of this suite."

So if I get myself past that door, Wen or the emperor himself are the only people who can get me back through it. Also good to know. "Fine," I mutter, making a valiant effort to maintain the ruse of my consternation.

Ettian casts an uneasy glance over at Wen's sealed door. She locked herself in there as soon as security finished briefing her about our setup, muttering about how her head was about to break in half. It seems that between the drunken late night and the early call time for this mission, she's been running with about an hour of sleep in the tank. The fact that she flew the mission flawlessly—apart from the issues with her copilot—is . . . well, terrifying, to be honest.

The only thing more terrifying is what she'd do to us if we woke her up. Pity, because I'm both completely certain what Ettian wants to discuss and absolutely sure I won't be able to have a levelheaded conversation about it.

"Last night," he starts, and just those two words transform him. He's not the young ruler who squared his shoulders against the fleet unfurled before him, not the princely diplomat wrangling support at his gala with a glittering crown perched on his brow. He's just a boy with an uncertain hope.

And a nick on his neck, barely visible over his collar, where less than a day ago I pressed a piece of glass to his throat.

Ettian takes a deep breath and starts over. "I'm sorry about last night," he says. His eyes are locked on mine, unwavering, as if he's daring himself to see how long he can hold my gaze.

"I'm not," I blurt, regretting it instantly. I only meant to rile him, but the moment it leaves my mouth, I hear the exact reason I shoved him away in the tunnels laced through the words. I should regret last night. I do, in some ways. But it's less that I regret what happened, more that I regret what it revealed about me.

What happened proved I can't use him like that, just as much as it proved how much I'd love to use him like that.

"I mean, look, I was drunk," I continue, trying to salvage this conversation before it even begins. "I shouldn't have . . . Well, *you* shouldn't have, since you're my ruttin' jailer and all. Well, not my *ruttin'* jailer. Good thing this room isn't bugged, huh?"

Ettian looks about two seconds from steam starting to leak from his ears. *Say something,* I dare him with my eyes. *Yell at me. Full volume. Wake Wen up.*

Because I need *something* to get between the two of them after the debacle on the bridge. Last night, I thought I finally had her coming around. I did everything right—reminded her of her mother and the mission she left behind, put her in my shoes, living with a similar failure. But all of that progress hinged on her insecurity about her role in Ettian's administration, an insecurity all but codified by her lack of a title.

And now—or at least once the paperwork clears—she's Lieutenant Iffan, reporting directly to Commodore Esperza herself. I'm not sure Ettian even realized how close he was to losing her until Silon highlighted how ridiculous it was that Wen had no title and the commodore started taking him to task over it. But the crux of the matter is that he could give her a title. He could give her the galaxy if he wanted.

What do I have to give?

The answer hits me a second later like a glint in the smithereens of my former plans. Ettian may have saved himself for the time being, but time is just the thing he lacks. Now that he's arrived at the war front, he'll be swallowed into the mechanics of running his campaign, most likely while butting heads with General Iral and the rest of his staff. I've known this for ages: no gift in the galaxy is enough to replace his genuine attention.

And Ettian's just made sure I'm tethered to Wen at all times.

There's one step further I can take this. I glance up at Ettian, letting tension wind my joints tight, dissolving my comfort and making it look like it's entirely his fault. "It'd be better for both of us if we try to cultivate some distance. For your image. For my . . . peace of mind."

There was no lie in the way he kissed me last night. Ettian cares for me beyond reason. He did even when he knew who I was and who he was. He . . . well, he was once very clear about his feelings, long after he found out about my identity, and it doesn't seem like they've changed since then. So when I tell him to back off, he does the only thing anyone who truly cares for me would do.

"Of course," he says without hesitation. "Whatever you need. Just promise me you'll reach out if anything happens or anyone tries to give you trouble. You can trust Wen to get a message to me. And I swear these rooms are the safest on the ship for you."

I catch his gaze and hold it for just a second too long. Let him sit in just how much he's confessed out loud with those words alone. "Yeah, like I said, real good thing these rooms aren't bugged," I mutter.

His lips falter into a frown. *Were you expecting anything else for your goodwill?* I wonder. He has to realize how utterly stupid it is to express his wishes for my well-being out loud on this ship. After a long beat where he seems to be chewing on a retort, Ettian turns on a heel and leaves without another word.

The moment the door hisses closed, the tension in my chest unspools. I tip my head back against the sofa, staring at the smooth metal of the ceiling overhead. I try to visualize the dreadnought beyond it—the layers and layers of the command core wrapped around me, the miles of darkness, the impenetrable outer hull. The Archon fleet outside it, and the war that awaits. The high of running circles around Ettian can't offset the bitter truth.

The hole I've dug myself in just keeps getting deeper and deeper.

CHAPTER 11

WHEN ESPERZA OFFERED to train Wen, I assumed it would be a sparing thing. There's a war going on, after all, and she's supposed to be commodore of the entire Archon dreadnought fleet. Worse, Wen's stuck with me, and there are only so many security loopholes the commodore can slip through to accommodate the both of us. I thought Wen's education would be fed on Esperza's table scraps.

Instead she's feasting.

Every day she yanks me out of bed well before the morning round of drums sounds through the command core and drags me down to the nearest gym. I doze on a weight bench close enough to her that she can keep an eye on me until she's finished, then follow her dutifully back to the room to shower and change for the day. In any other situation I'd be complaining my ass off the entire time, but I'm committed to winning her back, and that means I'm committed to making sure her mornings go as smoothly as possible.

I dress in Archon fatigues, leaving my cuffs in the drawers. Back on Rana, I wore the platinum to stand out and rub my imprisonment in Ettian's face, but here aboard the *Torrent*, I need to blend in to the best of my ability. I've even started carrying myself like a soldier, keeping my back straight and my strides measured as I trail Wen from our quarters to Esperza's offices.

The commodore is always there before us, no matter how early we come. I suspect the steaming mug her aide keeps constantly warm and filled on her desk—but after my last brush with Archon roasts, I don't envy it at all. Esperza's come a long way since her days of raiding ships, loath as I am to admit it. She's got a surprisingly functional staff under her, managing the requests for her attention that seem to crop up faster than weeds.

On the first few days of Wen's apprenticeship, the commodore had one of her secretaries brief her on the scope of the war. Wen's spent practically all of it on Rana with her focus on the city, so she's just as unaware as I am of the front's layout.

I'm handed a pair of noise-canceling headphones and told to turn my back and stare at the wall when it's presented to her. I nearly laugh out loud at the suggestion, but the secretary fixes me with a look so sour that it's almost preferable to clamp the headphones on and turn away. I make a show of fussing with the way they rest on my unruly hair, knowing full well I'll be written off as a vain little princeling.

Which is all I need, because it disguises the moment I tuck a thick twist of my curls into one of the cups, lifting it just enough to break the seal and let me hear what the room is saying.

At present, the Archon rebellion is fighting to regain control of the Tosa System, the former heart of the conquered empire. The system is comprised of three habitable rocky worlds, an asteroid belt that's been strip-mined since the conquest, and a gas giant standing sentinel in the farthest orbit with a few occupied moons scattered around it. Rana is the outermost rocky world, the former capital of the former empire, and the only planet the rebellion currently holds.

The next closest world is Ellit, both by orbital circumference and by the planet's current position relative to the capital. The innermost world, Imre, is currently on the other side of the star, and it's there that Berr sys-Tosa, the Umber-appointed system governor, has rallied his forces and built up a stronghold for himself. The gas giant, Dasun, is even farther, its long orbit currently wheeling it around on the opposite side of the system.

Ellit is our current target, from the sound of this briefing. The planetary governor has shored up its defenses with what I'm assuming is a six-point standard dreadnought blockade that will prove difficult to break. The Archon fleet sits at a safe distance, ready to make a superluminal skip over at a moment's notice. At present, it seems like General Iral and his leadership are debating the best way to break the blockade without taking a toll on the planet's population, most of whom are former Archon citizens they're counting on to welcome their liberation. Dreadnought-to-dreadnought combat that close to a planet is all but impossible to execute humanely. One stray shot from an inbound Archon ship could wipe a city off the map, a fact the Umber forces are relying upon to keep the Archon fleet at bay.

I sneak a glance over my shoulder to watch Wen trying to ingest this information and can't help but feel a little bad for her. She was orphaned at eight, worked as a runner for the mob, and eventually found her way into a placement at a chop shop. I'm pretty sure she can read, but I don't think she can read fast enough to keep up with everything Esperza's staff is trying to pack into her brain. She'll nod along to what's said, but her eyes seem stuck on the diagram in front of her, rather than parsing through the words next to it.

It doesn't affect her enthusiasm, much as I wish it were otherwise. By the third week, I strongly consider stuffing a pillow over my head and groaning, *How can you possibly enjoy this?* when she fetches me for her morning gym trip. Maybe watching me suffer is fueling her.

I'm trying not to suffer though. Even though it's exhausting to go through these motions every day and painful to keep myself constantly alert and aware around the soldiers, I recognize the wealth of opportunity I've been given. I'm at the heart of Archon operations, and even if they're being wary about what information I have access to, I'm in the commodore's office with shocking regularity. I'm learning the layout of the *Torrent*'s core a little better every day. As long as I never seem *too* interested in the happenings around me, I'm able to absorb a remarkable amount of it.

I also have to make sure I never let myself think too hard about how difficult it's gonna be to get out of here, or else the panic starts to creep back in. When Esperza drags Wen out of the core for a tour of the *Torrent*'s outer decks, I nearly lose all hope staring into the black pit of the dreadnought's hollow interior on the shuttle ride over. No rescue could possibly come for me as long as I'm aboard, and I'm not naïve enough to believe I can extract myself from this hellhole either.

It's agony to walk past the rows of launch tubes, to see the Vipers and other light fighters staged along the deck. Back in my academy days, I never would have imagined a situation where I longed to be at the helm of a ship, but now I find myself taunted by the grim, bitter knowledge that even if I got myself into one of those ships, I'm not skilled enough to pull off the kind of escape run it would take to get me free of the *Torrent*'s clutches.

The only way I'm getting off this ship is if Ettian says so.

The emperor's been keeping his distance as promised. I know he must still be aboard—no one would let him get too far away from his human shield, and I'm not sure he'd dare leave me and Wen completely alone here. But I haven't even seen him in passing for weeks.

I don't *miss* him. But I feel his absence. It's the longest we've been apart in nearly three years, and even though I don't want it to affect me, the lack of his presence is . . . grating. I keep catching myself glancing sidelong as if hoping to catch his eye and finding nothing but empty space beside me. Marking funny little things I observe to tell him later and then realizing I'm not supposed to be talking to him at all.

Sometimes it even feels too quiet in the middle of the night. Those are the times I hate myself the most.

Maybe I was handling it better when I saw him almost every day, when the sight of the crown on his head and the impulse to slap it off could remind me that he's my sworn enemy, that he's fighting to destroy my legacy, that he betrayed me so thoroughly that I still haven't gotten used to the shape of the hole it ripped in my chest. Now he's just a whisper between soldiers that quiets when they notice I'm listening, a slot in the commodore's schedule that I'm never present for.

And the emperor of a goddamn uprising, but I don't think I'll ever forget that.

"Have you ever been on a dreadnought flight deck before?" Wen asks, startling me from my teeth-grinding. She's staring at the grand machinery around us with a bit too much of that touristy wonder that makes the other soldiers crack cruel smiles behind her back. On the one hand, I feel like I ought to warn her about how she looks.

But on the other, that's directly aiding Archon. Even if I'm aiding the only person in my life who still talks to me like I'm a human being. Everything that alienates her from the military rank she's finally managed to achieve is a kernel of hope for me, as long as I'm not the one doing the alienating.

Because I may not be able to fly the escape run that would clear me from the *Torrent*, but Wen sure as hell can.

Unfortunately I think she's a little too enamored with the ship to ever leave it. Every time Esperza's tours introduce us to some new feature of the dreadnought that Wen's never encountered, she gets this goofy grin that reminds me she used to work as a mechanic long before she got swept up in this Archon nonsense. She's endlessly fascinated by the engineering that makes these ships possible, and within days of starting under Esperza, she'd already charmed her way into a copy of the *Torrent*'s schematics that I catch her studying on her datapad at odd hours.

"They brought us up for a tour of one while I was at the academy," I tell her with a nervous glance at Esperza's back. The commodore doesn't seem to mind the slips of conversation that pass between me and her new lieutenant, but I worry all the same that she's going to whirl around one day and snap at me to get away from her. Once I'm certain today isn't the day, I continue. "We weren't cleared for the command core, of course, but we got to see the flight decks, the batteries, and a good portion of the engine subsystems."

"That's my next goal," Wen says, nodding vaguely in the direction of the dreadnought's engines. I'm surprised she's certain enough to point to them without hesitation—I'm still not used to this place, and the disorienting ride out here from the core did nothing to help with that. "I want to see the reactors for myself."

I bite my tongue to keep from pointing out that most people with a good head on their shoulders would rather go a lifetime without getting close to an active reactor like the ones that power dreadnoughts. "I'm sure your new boss could arrange a tour sometime," I mutter. *I need her on my side, I need her on my side, I need her on my side,* I remind myself.

Before I lose my ironclad grip on my tongue, said boss waves her over. Esperza's just greeted this deck's commander, and expects her new lieutenant to log the report.

I brace myself for the inevitable disaster as Wen pulls out her datapad and starts recording both an audio log of the conversation and her own scrawled handwritten notes. I once asked her why she doesn't try other forms of input, but she claims that her handwriting is the fastest.

It's also indecipherable. I've seen the tight-lipped smiles of Esperza's aides as Wen hands off her notes to them and the dead-eyed look they get when they realize they're going to have to listen to the entire recording to decipher what she's trying to communicate.

My mental litany shifts. *She's the enemy, I can't help her. She's the enemy, I can't help her.* But I feel like the longer I watch her flounder, the more inevitable it'll be that she realizes I could be more than dead weight. I've snuck looks over her shoulder at what she's writing down. And really, she doesn't need a tutor for her penmanship—she just needs someone who can teach her what to listen for, what's relevant enough to log and what's chaff. It's every skill I learned at the academy put into practice. It's the stuff I was supposed to apply toward being a good emperor.

But she's the enemy.

I can't help her.

But if I *were* to help her—

The thought plagues me through cycles and cycles of the same routine. The incomplete equation rattles at the back of my brain. Wen could save me from the *Torrent*'s maw. Wen needs my help if she hopes to keep pace with Esperza's training. If I want my ticket out of here, I need to sway her to my side—I need to get her to value me more than Ettian. And I *have* something she'd value.

I just need to figure out how to make her ask for it.

During the first portion of my captivity, one of the few mercies was the relief that I didn't have to exercise. Now I can't help but feel left out—and inadequate among the ranks of jacked soldiers that surround me on a daily basis. So one morning I startle Wen by slouching off the gym wall and stepping up onto the next treadmill over. She's running at a furious enough rate that she doesn't have the breath to question what I'm doing, so I take that lead and run with it, quite literally.

When she finally spins back down to a walk, I match my speed to hers. Before she can get a breath in to challenge me, I announce, "I think you could get a lot more out of your gym time with a partner."

Her brows furrow quizzically, and rather than dignify me with a response, she grabs a towel and buries her half-burnt face in it. When she surfaces, she stares directly at the mirror ahead of us, as if she's trying to find the right reaction in her own sweaty, winded reflection. "I . . . have never had a gym buddy before," she finally says with what I'd agree is the appropriate amount of caution.

"I need something to do around here," I continue. "I was never a morning-drill enthusiast at the academy, but it's downright tedious to have to be up at this hour and not have anything to show for it. But I need supervision, or so I'm told, which means if I want to exercise, I'll have to buddy up with you. Seems to me like it could be mutually beneficial anyway." I let just a hint of cruelty into my smile. "And I get the feeling you're not getting similar offers from the other Archon soldiers."

Wen gives me a look that clearly reads as, *Asshole, you know that I haven't.*

"Can I—no, never mind, I don't need permission. Personal question: why do you want to be in the Archon military?"

"Why, you thinking of enlisting?" She snorts.

"Look, you dragged me to the gym so much that you got me to actually *want* to exercise. Not too far of a stretch for me to want to know why we're doing this."

Wen's in the perfect state: frazzled, post-workout, and already worn to the bone by all the days before this one. She smooths down some of the hairs that have escaped her plait, making a careful study of her reflection and sparing me from any attention whatsoever.

I slip into the opening of her hesitation. "Every day we're surrounded by people caught up in something that seems to me like a grand delusion. And for most of them, it can be explained away by patriotism, but you—*you*. The War of Expansion doesn't matter to you. It never has. So what is it that makes you look at a ship like this and think, *Yeah, I wanna be a part of that machine*? What makes you wake up every morning and decide you're going to bust your ass for a lost cause?"

That gets me teeth. Wen's lip curls, her eyes narrowing. "The restoration of this empire isn't a lost cause. In case you haven't noticed, Archon's been doing nothing but making gains since this campaign started."

I flap a hand, my strides still long and nonchalant. "You can keep telling yourself that until the Imperial Fleet shows up, but I still don't get why *you* have decided that playing soldier's the most valuable use of your time right now."

"Why do you need to know?" Wen fires back. She ticks her speed up, setting into a brisker walk, as if she's got something to prove.

"Because Esperza's going to ask eventually, and I don't want to be in the blast radius of the secondhand embarrassment when you don't have a good answer. Or maybe because it's kicking your ass, and I don't get why it's worth all *this,*" I snap.

"It's not kicking my ass," Wen mutters venomously, but I know

I've got my claws in her by the sullen silence she lets tag onto the heels of that lie.

"You don't even know half of the codes Ettian and I had drilled into us by the end of our first semester at the academy. You couldn't fly in a thirty-ship formation, much less direct it on the battlefield. And you're not learning fast enough to be of any use to Ettian, which—yeah, that's it, isn't it?" I leer as she fixes her furious stare downward. "That's why you've thrown yourself into this, and now that it's not coming naturally, you're having second thoughts."

"Rust off, jackass," she spits. "Not all of us are born princes and chained to a bloodright until we die. I want to be more than Ettian's rogue knight. More than what the rest of the administration seems to think I'm capable of. I've spent so long being small. Being nothing. Being an afterthought. I want to be the biggest thing in the galaxy, if I can manage it. You're telling me you don't ever wonder if there's more that you can be?"

Disdain verging on boiling insult courses through my veins. "There is, quite literally, nothing in the *galaxy* more than I am already," I retort. "I was born with the blood that rules the stars, and when Umber razes this system and takes me home, I'll rule the largest empire history has ever seen."

The look she's throwing me just worsens the furious heat rising in my face. It walks the fine line between genuine concern and bald-faced pity, as if Wen—who can't even pass muster in this sham of a military—thinks I'm not capable of everything my blood has fated me for. But then, confusingly, she lets out a sigh, her eyes go soft, and she says, "Ah, Gal. You'll figure it out eventually."

Wen turns off her treadmill, leaving me uselessly spinning on mine as I try to process what cleverness she thinks she's just pulled off. As she retreats for the showers, I catch her eyes in the mirror, and she lifts her chin. "I'll trade you. If you want a gym buddy, you'll have to help me learn all that shit they drilled into you at the academy. Sound good?"

I nearly trip off the treadmill mid-stride from shock, but I recover just enough to give her a firm nod in reply. I should be holding back a grin—she's just handed me exactly what I came here for.

But there's something in her knowing smirk that makes me worry. Something that makes me feel like I've just given her an upper hand.

The change is almost instantaneous. At first, I'm arrogant enough to take sole credit for it, but the more I work with Wen, the more I realize that it's something that rests almost entirely on her shoulders. Given the proper supplemental material and a dedicated tutor, Wen is learning at a truly prodigious—and somewhat frightening—rate.

She would have been an unholy terror at the academy, a thought that has me wondering what that could have been like. Aboard the *Torrent,* Wen has no company her own age apart from me. How would she have meshed with our peer group? Clearly she and Ettian would have been neck and neck for the top of the class in flight sims, but I already knew that. Her engineering knowledge would have her fitting right in with Rin and Rhodes, her mischievous spirit would definitely endear her to Ollins, and watching her help direct a flight drill from one of the *Torrent*'s outer command decks, it's clear she and Hanji would have been split complementaries.

The ships Wen's conducting are barely glimmers against the stars in the massive window that sweeps along one wall of the deck. I keep getting distracted trying to pick them out from the blackness when I should be paying attention to the readouts on her station, which paint a much clearer picture of the formations weaving and twisting together. The lieutenants running the drill are laid out in a row of command stations, with the higher-level officers lined up on the tier behind.

"Group One, execute third maneuver," Wen announces into her comm, moderating her volume so she's loud enough for the colonel supervising her to know she's called the next stage of the drill but not loud enough to be picked up on the mics of the subordinates in her bank running the other segments. I watch the result of her call play out on the readouts, resisting the urge to nudge her when one of her pilots overshoots the turn's arc by a few degrees.

"Black Eight," I murmur through my teeth instead. I've been given a seat next to her, my hands properly cuffed for peace of mind—though really, there isn't much mischief I could manage from here. I spare the room a quick glance as Wen corrals the errant pilot, checking to make sure no one's noticed.

My eyes meet Adela Esperza's. I've been so focused on the drill that I failed to notice the commodore has slipped in to observe her protégée in action. A flush of paranoia washes through me as the corners of her lips tilt into a smirk. *She could be smirking for any number of reasons,* I try to remind myself. *She smirks a lot.*

But I can't shake the feeling that she's noticed what I've been up to. Esperza's certainly seen the effects of my tutoring in Wen's rapid improvement, and I wouldn't put it past her to immediately divine the source of her sudden upswing. And instead of yanking me out of reach, she's meeting my eyes. She's smiling about it.

If one of the most shrewd strategists in the uprising is endorsing my behavior, what does that say about my strategy? Have I gotten away with anything, or am I just genuinely helping Archon? Or maybe this is her plan: instead of confronting me directly about what may very well be my corruption of her apprentice, she's just going to make me doubt myself until I stop all on my own.

I drop my focus back to Wen's readouts, trying to quell my misgivings. Whatever Esperza thinks is happening here, I've come too far to tear it all down and start over. Being Wen's tutor has given me a way into Archon operations, and I'll be damned if I give up that ground.

Even if it'd be damning me anyway, to help the Archon cause.

CHAPTER 12

It becomes easy, after months of captivity, to mistake complacency for patience. To mistake a few calm weeks positioned at the rear of the front for the experience of war.

To mistake the frantic drums pounding through the halls of the *Torrent* for the usual morning round.

I nearly sleep through it—a minor miracle, given how I used to tense up every time I heard drums beating when we stayed at the Archon resistance base on Delos. I awaken not to the harsh snares rattling through the corridors but to the clatter of Wen storming through our quarters as she scrambles to dress herself.

"Whasshappening?" I groan, flopping halfway off my bed.

"The rust do you think is happening?" Wen shouts, slamming another drawer closed. "We're under attack."

But I'm *here,* I almost protest, as if that's going to turn around an Umber assault. That excuse works for when they're toting me around in a small craft, where one well-aimed bolt can take out the ship and everyone inside it. Safe inside a dreadnought command core, I'm all but untouchable, even if they manage to tear the outer layer of the ship to shreds.

I consider not bothering with dressing—just staggering onto the bridge in bare feet and sleep pants. But I've spent the past weeks carefully trying to blend into the background for the soldiers surrounding me. I'm not about to undo that on a day this dire. Wen's hurry and her significant head start means I have no time to tie my boot laces and barely enough to tuck in my shirt. I scramble after her as she blows out the door of the suite, trying my damnedest to get the collar of my jacket to lie flat.

The corridors of the command core are choked with soldiers all moving in the same direction. I stick as close as I can to Wen without tripping her, nervous about the proximity of so many people who might want to take a swing at me. Even if they have more pressing matters at hand, I'm not letting my guard slip for one second.

The pressing dread seeping into my blood only gets worse when we pack into an elevator that speeds us toward the bridge. Usually a dreadnought sleeps in three eight-hour shifts, so my perception of the population is cut by a third. Seeing absolutely everyone up and about—and packing into a crowded elevator with them—just drives home how *wrong* all of this is.

If it were a more minor skirmish, we could probably let the outer layers of the ship handle it and sleep soundly through the night. The fact that the whole ship is snapping into action means the threat is dire.

So it's no surprise when I step onto the bridge and see another dreadnought laid out in enemy orange over the captain's screens. Deidra con-Silon sits in the strange cradle of her chair, muttering a steady stream of orders that she doesn't bother projecting. Her directives must contain a header and footer phrase that will get them channeled to the correct sector of her bridge, a measure that maximizes the capacity of her voice and therefore her ability to maintain command throughout the coming engagement. Even with an officer who outranks her on the ship, Silon remains the only one qualified to helm the *Torrent* in a time of crisis. Watching her work, it's clear how much training it would take for any other person to step into her shoes. Wen's expression matches my awe as we approach. At the academy, I saw footage of these kinds of moments, but seeing someone performing the feat in person is once again stunning.

I spot Esperza a second later, though Wen's already set a direct vector to her. The commodore's been relegated to a desk space adjacent to the captain's, where she's feverishly sorting through communications from the rest of the fleet. I peer over Wen's shoulder at her screens, tuning out the unnecessary chatter of her report for duty.

The *Torrent*'s position at the rear of the fleet formation has us distant enough that we're not easily defensible by the other dreadnoughts. It seems the Umber assault calculated our position and dropped from superluminal at our rear. This dreadnought has a battery back there, but it's also the position of our most powerful engines, and maneuvering a cityship like this into a complete turn is going to take time that we might not be able to spare.

In this moment, I understand Ettian a little bit more. He once told me that he'd rather fly than take a command position, and I saw genuine panic in his eyes when I tried to keep him from fleeing the academy with the suggestion he was bound for a dreadnought's helm. Even though Silon's calling the shots in every department, essentially treating the *Torrent* as one massive extension of her body, her fate is committed into the hands of her subordinates. We live and die by the choices made by others, by their reaction times and their skill at their posts. When you're in a Viper, it's you and you alone who decides.

And if we're up against another dreadnought, the command core is nowhere near as safe as I first assumed. The forward batteries of this incoming ship could punch clear through the outer hull. It hasn't identified itself yet, but it bears the telltale signs of a newer ship—one likely constructed from the belts mined out in the Archon territories.

That in itself carries a heavy implication, one that hits so hard that for a second I feel like I need to grab on to something. It's been months since the rebellion started. Months since Maxo Iral revealed my capture to the galaxy. More than long enough for the Imperial Fleet to move into the Archon Core.

But no reckoning has come from my mother.

I don't understand. We're on the warfront now, where the majority of Archon's military assets are concentrated. Wouldn't she set out to decisively crush them? Could it be that she's holding back? Maybe she's running the newer ships up against Archon first, keeping the true treasures of her war fleet in reserve. Letting Berr sys-Tosa's assets take the heavy damage to punish the governor for his betrayal and then sweeping in to pick up the pieces.

The thought leaves me feeling a rising, difficult-to-quash panic. The Imperial Fleet would work with precision to extract me—of that I'm certain. But I'm not certain that this dreadnought is even *aware* I'm on board the *Torrent*. Even if they were, Berr sys-Tosa's never been particularly careful with my life before—what if he's happy to let me get caught in the crossfire?

And my concerns don't stop with just my own safety. My whole life I've been told that power means nothing if you don't wield it. That the proper way to confront a problem is to strike and strike hard. Knightfall. The whole War of Expansion. Why is now any different?

But the second that question comes to mind, the answer arrives just as readily. At the heart of the Archon war machine, I can see it for the organized rebellion it is, founded on both a bloodright claim that will win the hearts and minds of the people and the military prowess necessary to reclaim the systems we conquered. I'm surrounded, day in and day out, by the way these Archon soldiers see themselves. But what does Iva emp-Umber see from the outside?

She sees a scrappy force of refugees who've managed to commandeer a dreadnought through tricks that won't work now that the rest of the Umber fleet expects them. A leadership that isn't sure whether it should be taking cues from a seasoned general or the blood-proven heir to these systems. Limited resources spread across already depleted worlds. Why send a fleet when Berr sys-Tosa should have no problem uprooting the infestation in a matter of months?

It's like using a war hammer to kill a fly—it just makes you look like you're overcompensating.

And if she rushes in like a weepy parent trying to snatch her son back from the jaws of danger, well, she wouldn't be the fearsome Umber empress who's bent the galaxy to her rule.

I'm still trying to decide what that means for me when the drums switch to a new rudiment. This one I know—I heard it pounded into the bulkheads of the *Ruttin' Hell* as we turned our nose and plunged headfirst into the terror of an active field on the day the Archon resistance stole the *Torrent*. This is the rhythm that spurs ships down launch tubes and into the black, that gunners chug their clips to match. This is the Archon call to battle.

Once again, I search for something to hold on to.

On Silon's displays, a matrix of green-lit Archon craft spew from the *Torrent*'s rear decks. A precise layer of covering fire cuts between them from the adjacent batteries, preventing any nasty surprises from slipping down the launch tubes before they have an opportunity to seal again. The sight of the battle sketched out in miniature unmoors me, and for a moment I tense, forgetting that all of this is happening miles away. It's only the sharp jab of Wen's fingers in my side that brings me back to the bridge. She gives me a significant look, one I interpret to mean *Stay close,* then steps up to Esperza's station.

The commodore glances up, passing Wen a tense smile. "Looks like Umber's finally decided to take a swing at us," she says, her fingers flying over her workstation as she sorts through communications. "Well timed on their part—they caught us inert with our backs turned." She points at the fleet's formation, tapping the engines of each Archon dreadnought tersely.

All of them are pointed away from us, making them nigh impossible to maneuver onto a vector in time to address the attack. One of them seems to be trying, though it's almost impossible to distinguish its rotation. Turning a miles-long spaceship under pressure is an agonizing affair.

"We've got twenty corvettes inbound, with a hundred in reserve,"

Esperza continues. "Half of those are standing by for evac if things get dire around here, but given that this fellow hasn't punched a hole in us yet, I'm optimistic about our chances against a single 'nottie."

"Where's Ettian?" Wen asks, and I glance sidelong at her in warning. This is a habit Esperza's been trying to break her from with little success. A habit that might be partially my fault. An obstinate prisoner with the same title can call the emperor by his first name. A lieutenant most certainly cannot.

"The emperor," Esperza replies firmly, "is secured. I need you to handle comms from the incoming reinforcements. Pull up a chair."

Wen sets herself next to Esperza's workstation with nervous stiffness. Her hands falter over the displays, fumbling as she pulls up the data she's supposed to be managing. I stand behind her, gritting my teeth.

Over the past month, our system has settled into place. After the moment I'm certain Esperza caught me, I try my best not to openly advise Wen in the sight of her superiors—even if it's occasionally agonizing to watch. Instead I build up a list of every grievance I register during the day, and at night we review them in the privacy of our rooms.

It's been a mess, for the most part. Often we find ourselves arguing because I'm approaching something from a pragmatic point of view, which she flags as being so Umber-minded that her mentor will immediately call her out on it. Or because she's interpreting something with a degree of leniency that's almost laughably Corinthian and has no place in any military, Umber or Archon. Occasionally we'll get stuck in an argument only to realize that neither side we've chosen is one that meshes with the Archon values she's meant to be upholding. At the end of those, I've taken to giving her a look she knows well, one that all but screams, *Why are you even doing this?*

That system worked fine for her training. Better than fine—she was improving like a prodigy. But now the war's gone hot around us, and Wen, whom I've seen fly gleefully in a ship that might as well be held together by prayer, is unsteady at the conn. This *matters* to her so much that it's got her hands shaking.

And I can't be caught helping her again.

I'm not sure what else to do with myself. I want to do something to help make sure I don't get incinerated by that ship, but this isn't like helping with flight drills. Any action I take here would aid Archon directly, to the detriment of my own empire. Then again, if I don't survive this engagement, it's an Umber loss either way. I have to do *something,* but I don't even have a place to sit on this bridge. I'm sure I'd get snapped at the second I tried to plant my ass anywhere, so I take a cautious step up behind Wen, just enough to brush her shoulder in warning.

She stills, stealing a glance at me. "Not a good time, Gal."

"I'd say it's as good a time as ever," I mutter, pitching my voice low enough that it falls beneath the general chatter flying back and forth across the bridge. "Sort your comm lines by auxiliaries and attack ships," I tell her, resisting the urge to reach over and do it for her.

"I know which is which."

"It's not about knowing—it's about being able to reach over and grab your auxes all at once."

An incoming message flares on the screen. Wen taps it, selecting the option to transcribe the communication, and leans forward to read it. *Don't let them see you mouthing along,* I almost snap at her, but now is not the time. With my life on the line, I've got to let her do whatever helps. "Ma'am, C-32 is detecting targeting coming from the 'nottie."

Esperza nods sharply. "Give all corvettes clearance for superluminal evasive."

I gulp. I'd forgotten this old standby of Archon battle strategy, deemed too dangerous by Umber to ever put in use. It's one of the only effective ways of getting out of a dreadnought's path, and relies on an engineering team that can react on a hair trigger. The ships cruise with the superluminal drives hot and a secure escape vector keyed in. The instant they detect a dreadnought about to fire, the captain punches in the jump. It catapults the ship to safety a few light-seconds away, but that's far enough to take them out of the battle completely until the drives cool enough to safely fire again. I was always taught that it's too drastic and too risky. A short-range superluminal jump is a nightmare of physics I don't even want to think about, to say nothing of the shitshow that'd ensue if a ship with a spun-up drive took a direct hit from a dreadnought battery. Or what might happen if they miscalculated their escape vector and tore clean through another ship in their formation. On top of that, it's a serious blow to the forces you have out on the field.

By the Umber playbook, it's always better to just take the hit. Sure, you'll lose people, but they'll die with honor, and there's a chance you'll still be flying enough of a ship to do some good in the battle. But Archon's fleet is cobbled together from hijacked dreadnoughts and Corinthian salvage. They have to save whatever ships they can.

"I need 'vettes in range for an attack run," Esperza announces suddenly, with a beckoning gesture toward Wen's workstation. Wen fumbles to grab the data and toss it over to her, and I nearly speak out again when I notice she's left one of the ships in range out of her packet.

Nearly, but don't, because Esperza's looking right at us. Or because I want to see what happens to that one ship. I feel the snarl of the tangled emotions inside me like a fishhook in my gut. That corvette is part of a system that's keeping me alive. At the moment, its goals align with my own.

But it's an enemy ship, my mother's voice croons. It may be a little blow I can strike against Archon, but little blows are better than the months of nothing I've sustained so far.

And yet. My life is important. It's a fact my entire existence has been sculpted around. From the moment I was born, I've been surrounded by people prepared to risk their own lives for the sake of mine. To die for me, even.

Ettian was one of those people—but I shove that thought aside before it can derail where I was going with this.

I was supposed to do some goddamn good in the galaxy when I took my throne. Billions of lives depend on the Umber Empire, which means that billions of lives depend on me securing my rule. Next to that, the Umber soldiers who might be taken out by that corvette are all but inconsequential.

In this moment, I'm finally starting to understand how my mother thinks.

So I point to Wen's screen urgently and announce, "Don't miss C-57."

I feel the disaster strike the instant the words leave my mouth. It's in the way Wen tenses suddenly, both because her mistake's been called out and because I forgot to moderate my volume. It's in the sudden prickle at the back of my neck as I feel the weight of Esperza's gaze bore into me like boltfire.

And it's in the sudden silence from the captain's chair as Silon freezes mid-litany, drawing a breath that seems to suck all of the air out of the bridge at once. The far-off battle drops from mind, and all that rises to take its place is a blazing intensity I don't even want to name. "What," the captain asks, her tone deceptively even, "is *he* doing on my bridge?"

Across the room, Engineering shouts, "Awaiting confirmation to fire engines for the about-face. Do we have—"

"Yes, *fire,*" Silon says with a flippant hand gesture. I realize with a sinking dismay that the captain's gaze isn't on Esperza. Of course it isn't—Esperza doesn't answer to her, and if it were Esperza's decision to bring me onto the bridge, she wouldn't be able to counter it. And it's not locked on me, either, even though I'm the one she has an issue with.

No, she's staring straight at Wen and waiting for an answer.

"The commodore summoned me to the bridge," Wen says, with a surprising degree of iron in her voice. I'm almost impressed—where was this nerve a minute ago?

"The commodore summoned *you* to the bridge. Not the prisoner," Silon says. Her voice is still even, but I've decided it's more terrifying that way. "Get him out of here."

Wen throws a panicked glance to Esperza. "Ma'am, I—"

If it were any other circumstance, I'm almost certain the commodore would overrule the captain. Esperza hasn't done anything to keep me from coaching Wen yet, and she'd be delighted to keep that splinter under Silon's skin, to remind her that her command's not the final say on this ship. Over our past weeks training under her, I've watched the commodore do it over and over again in a thousand small ways designed to grate on the captain's nerves without ever affecting the successful function of the *Torrent*.

But this is war, and Esperza's not stupid. This is boltfire and impulse decisions. This is fear and a dreadnought on our tail. The *Torrent*'s survival is dependent on Silon's focus. Already the bridge is full of panicked mutters at the interruption in the captain's orders, everyone unsure of whether to keep on the vector they've set or try to demand her attention for their issues.

Wen's not stupid either. The moment she realizes Esperza's going to prioritize the captain's calm over her obligation to guard me, she shoves abruptly up from the workstation. "C'mon," she mutters. "Let's—"

Her voice catches as her eyes snag on the frantic flash of C-57's message alert. The corvette captain's been trying to hail us, unsure why the other ships in their formation have suddenly begun a maneuver they weren't included in. And before Wen can reach down and shove the ship over into Esperza's comms bank, a neon LOSS OF SIGNAL message wipes over it.

For a brief moment, I hope it's because they've done the damnfool superluminal maneuver. But I hear the words "confirmed discharge" drift over from Telemetry. I see the blood drain from the unburnt half of Wen's face. I remember that the captain was too busy trying to hail the *Torrent* and confirm that they were being left out of the maneuver. I realize Esperza was too embroiled in the sudden issue of my presence on the bridge to address that a ship had been dropped from the ranks she was commanding. And now where once there was a corvette, there can only be twisted bits of metal cooling and blood flashing to vapor in the blink of an eye.

Esperza's seasoned. She takes the loss without so much as a blink, already diving into the next set of maneuvers for the ships she has in hand, making ready to retaliate against the Umber dreadnought. And Silon might not even register the loss—she's back deep in the workings of her own ship, reciting her commands so smoothly it might as well be poetry.

Only Wen is left to process what just happened.

To understand that it falls completely on her shoulders.

CHAPTER 13

WE END UP in the *Torrent*'s engines. It's almost too easy. With the rest of the ship caught up in the fury of battle, no one cares that Wen grabs one of the shuttles and fords the vast emptiness between the command core and the rear of the dreadnought. She uses some security clearance of Esperza's to get a confirmed tiedown, and muscles past the receiving crew that greets us with a curt nod and a few mutters about the commodore's orders.

I keep quiet the whole way, certain I'll lose my head if I dare say anything. I don't know if there's anything to say. We've both been in battles before, but neither of us have ever been responsible for something like this. A corvette's crew numbers in the hundreds. All of the people aboard C-57 are dead because of us.

I keep squirming away from the blame as if there's some perfect angle I can capture it from that will rid me of it. It's the corvette captain's fault, I argue. The captain got distracted and wasn't able to pull the ship out of the Umber dreadnought's sights in time. But who caused the captain's distraction? It's Esperza's fault for not noticing that she was short a ship. But who forgot the ship in the first place? It's Silon's fault for letting my presence usurp her duty and her attention.

That last one's almost too easy to counter.

My mistake got people killed. *Our* mistake got people killed. I don't know how that sits on Wen's shoulders, but for me it's a first. Hundreds of lives, gone, all because I was on the bridge and pointed out Wen's slipup. Hundreds of lives gone because she slipped up in the first place.

Hundreds of lives—Archon lives—that I tried to save. I'm still too raw and shaken to unpack the way that hits me.

It occurs to me as we plunge down the engineering levels toward the *Torrent*'s main reactor that this little escapade is putting us squarely in what has to be the most dangerous possible place on the ship. If our defensive array fails, the engines will be the first thing the Umber dreadnought targets. The closer we get to the reactor, the more I worry that's exactly what Wen intends. She wears a taut expression I can't quite parse—all I really know is that the look on her face scares me.

Finally, after a few more badge swipes and brush-offs, we emerge into a vast, cavernous vault. In the center of it hovers the reactor, suspended by wires that look spiderweb-thin from a distance—and only from a distance. Pipes drip from its spheroid body, each funneling its power away to a separate thruster. The heat hits us the moment we step into the room, and I have to squint against the force of it. We're still in the midst of the turning maneuver, desperately trying to swing our rear to a more defensible position, and the engines are blasting as hot as they'll go.

Wen stares up at the furious power of the reactor unblinkingly, and after a long moment, that scary intensity on her face melts into a soft smile. "Well, if they throw me off this ship, at least I'll have seen that," she says, leaning forward against the guardrail as if she's trying to get even closer to it.

"They're not gonna throw you off this ship," I mutter, reluctantly joining her. Even with the padded sleeves of my jacket, the rail feels like it's about to scorch right through me, and I'm not sure how she can rest so comfortably against it. "It was your first time running comms in a battle. Mistakes were bound to happen."

Wen's eyes stay locked on the reactor. Her expression shifts to a familiar focused squint. No doubt she's studying the machinery before her, picking it apart to figure out how it works. Hell if I know anything about that—I leave that shit to the engineers. "I'm glad I'm seeing it now anyway," Wen says. "In action, firing like this. Every piece of it serving its function."

"Yeah," I reply flatly, pulling on my collar. I'm pretty sure most people who work down here wear coolant suits to do it. "Neat. But seriously—they're not going to throw you out for losing a ship, and you can't get too hung up on it. That's the real failure, and that's the one they're going to notice."

"Pretty sure they also noticed when that 'vette got vaporized," Wen grumbles, her eyes tracing the length of one of the pipes that drops from the reactor down to the lowermost engine on the *Torrent*. "Even if they don't kick me out entirely, I don't think Esperza's going to keep me training with her. Losing a corvette isn't as big of an issue as the fact that I'm stuck with your delightful company, and Silon will never tolerate you on the bridge. Even if Ettian or Esperza made it an order, it would probably impact her performance so much that . . . well, neither of us can outweigh that kind of priority, y'know?"

I nod, unsure what more I can do beyond agreeing with her. I always knew our arrangement was going to backfire on her ambitions, but it's another thing to see it play out on a battlefield. To see it cost lives. Today's incident made it utterly clear that Wen can't serve in her full capacity if she always has me tailing around after her.

And despite the fact that she dragged me into a sweatbox just for the sake of her own curiosity, I feel an alarming urge to comfort her. Wen and I are far from allies, but—and I can't believe I'm thinking this—we've built a strange little friendship in our proximity. "You used to lock me in my rooms back on Rana," I offer. "I could always stay in our quarters when you're called to duty like that."

Wen's expression twists. "Yeah, but *you* were the one who noticed C-57. If it weren't for you, well. You almost saved them. You . . .

tried to save them," she realizes aloud, casting a suspicious glance over to me. "Why?"

"Sure is hot in here, isn't it?" I say with another tug on my collar.

"Gal, come on."

"You're asking me to make sense of a mid-battle decision. I can spool back and tell you what I was thinking when I decided to open my mouth, but—"

"No, yeah, that's exactly what I want you to do. Your turn for a little grilling."

I shrug. "I don't want to die. That's what all heat-of-the-moment choices come down to, isn't it? I looked at that field and I decided the thing that would most likely kill me was that Umber dreadnought. And from there I got to the fact that I needed to make sure our defense against it was effective."

Now the reactor's lost her attention completely. I take the weight of her gaze with a deliberate shift against the uncomfortable railing, hoping it'll scald away whatever reaction she seems to be searching for in my face. At last she lets out a faint, judgmental hum, barely audible over the ship's workings.

"What?"

"Well, for a second there, I thought you might have done it because you wanted to help me. But no, that'd be ridiculous, wouldn't it?"

"Ridiculous, yeah," I reply stiffly, pointedly ignoring the wry smile tugging on the burnt corner of her mouth. "Shouldn't we be somewhere else? Anywhere but this ruttin' oven?"

"I've studied the schematics. The shielding on this reactor is built so strong that it'd take multiple rounds from a dreadnought battery to penetrate it. The only way to get to it is through the engines themselves, and a direct shot straight through those vents is . . . well, let's just say unlikely until the day someone figures out how to curve boltfire. We're in the safest place on this ship." She glances sidelong at me, her half-smile out in full force. "Look, if I'm gonna fail at one job, I'm gonna succeed spectacularly at my other one. Nothing's gonna happen to you unless they shred the ship around us."

"And nothing's going to happen to you until they find you down here," I note with a significant glance back at the way we came. I expect her to snap at me, and I'm surprised when she doesn't.

"Yeah," she says, her eyes shifting back to the core. "I have no illusions about the fact that there's gonna be consequences. But this is the best rustin' place on the *Torrent* to wait for them to roll around."

So we let the battle outside drop away and quietly watch the machinery that fuels it.

In the end, it takes hours for the fight to wind down. We only realize it's over when the core finally starts to cool, the *Torrent* locking into a stable position once more. The sweet feeling of the heat in the chamber ebbing away melts like relief down my spine—and I don't allow that relief to get any more complicated by the fact that this means the Umber assault has failed. For now, I'm just happy to be alive and glad I'm finally going to be free of this sweatbox.

I'm less glad when Wen pulls out her datapad and starts sharing the report. The dreadnought and its forces managed to deal a significant blow to the Archon fleet, destroying more than two dozen carriers and hundreds of fighters. On top of that, it spooked off fifty-three ships, which are now waiting for their drives to cool enough to make a safe leap back to the fleet's position, leaving Archon even weaker. There's already chatter about delaying the assault on Ellit and retreating to Rana to lick our wounds.

But before that happens, a guest is approaching the *Torrent*. And we're on our way to receive him right now.

I spend the entire shuttle ride to the dreadnought's outer decks with my fists clenched tight at my sides, rehearsing my most inscrutable stone faces. Wen's my opposite, fidgety in her seat, her anxiety no doubt fueled by the way I've clammed up. She can usually count on me to pull faces behind the officers' backs, and the fact that I've shut up completely must read as foreboding.

Good. It's justified.

Because General Iral is coming aboard.

Unlike the emperor's arrival, this is no secret affair. The general's making his approach in his flagship cruiser, a war machine that's pushing the limits of its athleticism with its sheer size. Summons went out across the *Torrent* for the upper ranks to report to his entry deck—including Wen, for her connection to the commodore, which means I'm along for the ride as well.

I should be thrilled about this. The emperor had to be secreted aboard the *Torrent,* but Iral gets to board with a show of force. It'll chum the waters between their competing authorities, further weakening the prospects of Archon's supposed bloodright.

Unfortunately I can't seem to shake the sensation of Iral's hand on my shoulder, forcing me to my knees before the galaxy. It's been *months,* but every time I brush up against the shame of that moment, I feel the nausea roiling in my gut all over again. Iral had me completely at his mercy. I've torn through active fields in two Vipers strapped together, escaped converging missiles in a Beamer, and flown combat with Wen at the helm, but nothing's ever terrified me more than that moment. I can feel the echoes of it rattling my bones—or maybe that's just the drums greeting the general as we step off the shuttle and onto the deck.

The flagship has already docked, the seal so enormous that it takes up the entry deck's wall. Several transports have been shunted out of the way, surrounded by the shouts of the deck crews towing them. The drums momentarily succumb to the whine of pistons as airlock doors as long as six Beamers end to end winch open to admit the flagship's descending ramp.

Esperza and Silon have beat us here. They stand side by side at attention just behind the markings where the ramp touches down. Silon's pose is prim and perfect; Esperza's is slightly canted, like she can't resist adding a bit of piratical flair, even in front of the general himself. Their staffs fan out beside them on each side. Wen hesitates as if she's unsure where to position herself.

Time for me to teach by example. I march up directly behind

Silon, spread my feet, and drop into a perfect parade rest. To restore symmetry, there's only one place left for Wen to go—directly behind the commodore.

Under the thunder of the welcoming drums, I hear the slight whistle of her sighing between her teeth. But Wen steps into place, making it look as deliberate as possible, even though she doesn't spare me a consternated sidelong glare.

She'll thank me later. The commodore needs to see that this mistake doesn't rattle Wen, and the easiest way to show she's still got her fire is to keep making bold choices like this. Wen can't shrink to the back of the line—she can't afford to. If one mistake knocks her off the game, it's clear she's not cut out for this kind of work.

I don't realize *my* mistake until the general's already at the top of the ramp.

Maxo Iral cuts a striking figure. I've always thought the Archon general was either lifted from the pages of a storybook or grown in a lab to meet the exact mental image one conjures when told of a great general. He's built tall and broad, his skin a rich olive tone and his long hair bound back in a series of intricate, loose braids. He wears a decorative set of armor trimmed in light threads of platinum, though he's traded the usual Archon emerald for combat black. The sight of him sends a fresh thrill of fear coursing down my spine. My mind runs wild with the possibilities of what this man could order. If he phrased it in the right way, he could probably get these people to skin me alive.

But at present, he just strides down the ramp, flanked by his retinue, every step leaching pure confidence. This man has known the most harrowing defeat in the galaxy and still kept his head high.

And that makes him even more terrifying. Against Iral, I feel like a worm. What good is anything I've done in the universe when this man has resurrected a dead empire almost single-handedly? If it weren't for Ettian, I'm almost certain Iral would have had an ax in my neck, captured from a thousand different angles, just a few hours after he found out my identity. For all I know, he's still keeping an open slot in his extremely busy schedule, just for my execution.

I haven't faced him in person since the day of Ettian's coronation. On that day, I'm certain he saw me as nothing more than a prop meant to further legitimize the new Archon heir. Now I'm not sure what he'll think when he sees me again. One thing I know for sure—Maxo Iral is a keen strategist, and he'll play whatever hand he's dealt to maximum effect.

So I strengthen the angle of my spine, praying I present enough of a challenge that the general will be having second thoughts. I dare myself to look him in the eye as he reaches the bottom of the ramp and dismisses both Esperza and Silon with a cordial nod. "Commodore, Captain," he says, his voice a low rumble that carries over the deck—or maybe it's just the hush his presence inspires. "Congratulations are in order, I believe."

Silon jumps on the thread of conversation before Esperza even has a chance to inhale. "It was hard-fought, general, but we won the day in the end."

"No doubt the general noticed," Esperza says pleasantly, and Silon's expression twitches. "Sir, we're pleased to have you aboard."

Wise words—probably the only thing both she and Silon can agree on.

"Thank you for accommodating my arrival on such short notice," Iral replies. "Truly, I don't warrant these kind of formalities, but I appreciate them." His gaze slips over Silon's shoulder and finds me. "Well, most of them," the general says, his expression darkening.

Stand tall and look your enemy in the eye, my mother's voice orders in my head. I brace myself with the years of training it took to turn me into a practiced actor, capable of sustaining the long con of shadowing in an Archon territory. But even with all of that, I feel like the general can see right through me. No blank expression I wear against him can make up for the fear he saw in my eyes on the day his soldiers dragged me out of the *Ruttin' Hell*. Iral has seen the heart of me and known my lowest moment in a way few other people in the galaxy have.

And the look he gives me is impossible to mistranslate. Two years after the War of Expansion ended, my mother hung his twin brother on an electrified crucifix before the Imperial Seat. From the steely glint in his eyes and the slight sneer he gives me, Iral is biding his time until the moment he can finally pay her back in kind.

Silon's and Esperza's composure slips when they follow the line of the general's gaze and discover me standing behind them. The captain's full lips pucker just a little bit tighter. The commodore's metal hand twitches toward a fist. It's Esperza who jumps on the recovery when she realizes I'm flanked by her protégée. "General, I'd like to officially introduce Lieutenant Iffan," she says.

Wen steps forward to clasp Iral's hand, and I pay careful attention to the way he greets her. Iral's spent five years being touted as Archon's savior by everyone around him. I think it throws him a little bit, to face someone who barely understands that context. For the commodore, Wen has stammering idolatry. For the general, she's almost underwhelmed.

It bolsters me. My shoulders loosen, and I can feel the edges of a smile twinging in my cheeks. Iral nods curtly, but there's a slight crease in his brow that speaks volumes. "The famous Flame Knight," he says. "I'm honored you've decided to take an official rank."

Now it's Wen's turn to be slightly thrown. If she objects to the general's use of the word "decided" like she so clearly wants to, she's going to be left struggling to explain her whole situation in front of not only her boss but also her boss's boss—neither of whom really need the explanation. "Knighthood's just a hobby on the side," she offers casually.

At that, I catch at least three sharp inhales from the people surrounding and fight against my own intake of breath. I'm guessing Ettian never explained Iral's history with the Archon suited knights to Wen. Or maybe he did, and she just forgot how seriously the people around her take the notion of knighthood. Maxo Iral was once the lover of Torrance con-Rafe, a young knight stationed on one of the Archon borderworlds up until Knightfall.

Sometimes I wonder how much less brutal his campaigns against Umber would be if he had never lost her.

Iral's forehead crease deepens. "Well, I'm not sure the concept of a hobbyist knight will take particularly well in this empire, but I appreciate whatever effort you manage to devote to it."

Wen knows it's too far gone to salvage. She steps back, ducking her head and muttering a faint "Sir." Fortunately Silon sweeps in to fill the space she left, prattling some meaningless fluff as she leads the general toward the shuttles bound for the command core. The rest of the aides move with her, but when Wen makes to follow, a metal hand latches onto her upper arm.

"Iffan, if you would hang back a moment," Esperza says. The threads of steel in her voice could weave a suit of armor. "You might as well stick around, too, Your Highness."

I freeze, astonished that I'm being addressed directly. Ever since I've taken up my gig as Wen's shadow, Esperza's treated me like a patch of dead space, for the most part. She's caught my eye from time to time—scaring the hell out of me in every instance—but she's never bothered to say anything.

The commodore notes my surprise as she releases Wen's arm and recognizes it for what it is with a shrug. "As today has made abundantly clear, ignoring you doesn't make you go away."

"Ma'am, I'm sorry," Wen says. "Bringing him to the bridge in a battle was a mistake. I was focused on my orders and missed the damage it would cause."

Esperza nods. Her eyes are locked on a vector for Silon's retreating back, her lips slightly pursed. "I will, of course, also be speaking to my subordinate about how she allowed herself to be distracted. A good captain should be able to notice a security threat like that and *delegate*, not make it her own personal problem. This falls on her shoulders just as much as it does yours. But you're the one who could have prevented it all in the first place."

"Understood. It won't happen again."

Esperza pulls Wen around to face her. Wen stiffens in the commodore's grasp, immediately tilting her head to give her superior more of the inscrutable burn. But Esperza's gaze holds steady on her protégée, seeing through any attempt Wen makes to avoid it. "You lost lives today. So did I. That's a reality of command. Look me in the eye and tell me you understand that."

Wen's eyes steady on her commander's. "I do."

Esperza gives a short nod, patting her firmly on the shoulder. Then she hitches a chrome-plated thumb at me. "Now, tell me why *this one* had the nerve to call your shots."

Pinned under the commodore's gaze, Wen has no way of dodging the order. "I . . . He wasn't . . ." she stammers.

"She's smart enough to take the help she needs, no matter the source," I interject, and Esperza's eyes snap to me, narrowing.

The commodore's grip on Wen's shoulder tightens a little, a gesture I'd find almost adorably protective if I weren't facing down Esperza's wrath. "Your calls were good, princeling," she says. "At least from what I heard. You were clearly trained well at your academy, and it seems Iffan is lucky you've chosen to pass on what you've learned. Don't think I haven't noticed that you've decided she would benefit just as much from your tutoring as she has from mine."

"The prince is an asset," Wen says, straightening her spine and looking Esperza dead in the eye. "If no one else is gonna utilize him, I will."

"That's fine for your personal edification," Esperza replies firmly. "In fact, I think it's produced a marked improvement—which is why I've allowed it. He's clearly done you some good. But there has to be a line, and that line is a direct engagement with his people. On the bridge, in battle, he does *not* get a say." The commodore lets out a long breath, glancing between us. "At any point during today's engagement, did you ask yourself how much of what you were doing was because he wants you to do it?"

"I'm not sure what you mean—"

"If he's influencing your decision-making in battle, it must be serving his motivations somehow. Imagine yourself in his shoes. Imagine what he wants from you. Now ask yourself if he's getting it."

"My motivations are my own," Wen says firmly.

Esperza gives her a weighty, considering look. "And what *are* your motivations?"

I throw Wen a warning glance. The moment's come—and this time she can't spur her treadmill a little faster and try to literally run away from the question. I warned her this would happen. I hope she's thought about it since then.

"I'm here because Et—because the emperor needs me. I'm here to fight for him the same way he's fought for me."

Esperza takes Wen's reply like a weight on her shoulders, a flicker of disappointment in her features. If Wen had run that answer by me, I could have warned her this would happen. "An empire is more than its leader," the commodore says, a warning edge in her tone. "And as a soldier, you serve the empire above all else. Single-minded devotion to one person is for friends and lovers. What inspires your devotion to all of Archon's people?"

"Bullshit," I groan—partly because it is, and partly because Wen looks like she's on the verge of tears. "A leader *is* the empire. The empire's the machinery that spins around him at his whims."

Esperza rolls her eyes. "Please don't tell me he's been feeding you that Umber-minded garbage." After a beat, her expression softens. "Look, I get it. I didn't start out with Archon drums in my heart either. It took me a while. It took . . ."

Wen's focus sharpens abruptly, and I feel myself leaning in despite myself. I've always been curious about Esperza's history—I know part of it involves a knight, and even though I swear I'm not one of those Archon kids who gets swept away in knight stories, the prospect of one fills me with a sort of dreaded thrill.

Esperza stares off across the deck, scanning the array of ships berthed here. "I grew up in petty crime on an Umber borderworld called Jobal. By the age of fifteen, I was out on my own, stealing ships and making as much trouble as I could muster. I felt like my whole life was a kind of dare—to see how much shit I could get away with before a reckoning kicked in. I just wasn't expecting my reckoning to come in a powersuit."

The commodore pauses, drawing a deep breath as she closes her eyes. When she opens them again, there's a slight glint I didn't notice before.

"I was eighteen years old. Had just gotten myself a slick new hand that I was still kinda getting used to, and it had a few trick components I was very eager to try out on some patrol ships. There were rumors that a well-appointed system governor's kid from the interior had been exiled to command one such patrol for a little character building, and I was keen on finding out what kind of luxuries the bastard had packed for the trip.

"Unfortunately, I didn't look too closely into his command's activities. Didn't know his ship was doing a little bit more than patrol at the border. I chased him into Archon space and didn't even realize it. I'd just boarded when the knight came to call."

I catch myself bracing for the turn most Umber stories take at this part. The knight comes aboard, the vibrosword snarls to life, and the bloodbath starts. All of it aboveboard according to the Archon administration that sponsored them.

But this isn't an Umber story.

"As I was tearing my way through the ship at one end, she was doing the same from the other. Imagine my surprise when I met her in the middle—Lietta Omoe, the Nova Knight, in all her shining glory. And then—gods, it still feels like a whirlwind—all of a sudden we were back to back as the rest of the ship came charging in to avenge themselves on us."

I try to picture it, but all I can think about is the terror of those people. They gave no quarter, even against the inevitability of a suited knight. The only mercy they could have received was an honorable death.

"We took the ship in record time. Of course, then we had to sort out the reasons our paths crossed in the first place. I'll never forget the look on her face when she realized I only had eyes for the captain's lockbox. Started going on about noble purposes and the greater good and the worrisome Umber encroachment that had been happening with greater and greater frequency. I told her to cram it up her ass and thank me for the assist. I think she took a shine to my irreverence—she swapped contacts with me, and who was I to argue with that? I told her I'd call her if I ever needed some help with pirate business.

"Turns out she needed my help more. Less than a month later, she met me at a borderworld bar—this time on the Archon side of things—and told me she was running a mission that would go a lot easier if they had a pirate to pin it on."

It shouldn't surprise me as much as it does. The suited knights were icons in part because they were able to maintain an uncomplicated public identity. Their deeds were always noble and heroic. It makes perfect sense that they outsourced their dirty work to maintain that image.

"I took the gig, of course. We had a mutual interest in knocking the Umber military presence in the borderworlds down a peg, and having five hundred pounds of powersuited muscle to back me up if things went south was the best insurance policy I'd ever had. Lietta was . . . Well, she started out difficult to work with, but I came to rely on that difficulty. There was nothing better than kicking back in a seedy bar with an honest-to-gods knight, bickering over multiple glasses of polish about the jarring gaps in our world views."

Esperza takes a long pause, her eyes tracing over the intricacies of her metal hand.

"She was always trying to convince me to go straight. To take up an official role in the Archon military, where I'd have both the resources and the legitimacy to do more. Tensions were brewing at the border—in hindsight, war seemed inevitable, but back then there was a consistent hope that the unrest in Umber wouldn't spill over as drastically as it did. I guess Lietta might have seen it coming. Her hopes for me never made any sense—my *utility* to her lay in the fact that I was a complete scoundrel. But without fail, every time we met up, she'd raise that subject. Every time, I'd shut her down. For two years it was almost a joke between us.

"Then Knightfall struck. And it turns out the persistent wish of a dead woman is a whole lot more difficult to ignore."

Wen frowns at that. "Are you saying someone has to die to give me some convictions?"

Esperza chuckles softly. "I'm saying don't wait like I did. It took me far too long to see the value of the Archon Empire—to understand why it was something worth fighting for. If I had joined up for Lietta alone, I wouldn't have lasted a month in the ranks. To this day, I wonder if there was something I could have done—if I had gotten to that point sooner, if maybe I had been there, fully outfitted like she'd always wanted . . . Well, I suppose the point of Knightfall was that it was impossible to stop. Props to your mother, of course," the commodore says with a bitter nod in my direction.

I resist the urge to snap that Omoe had it coming. I'm not keen on finding out what it feels like to get punched with Esperza's prosthetic.

Wen doesn't seem entirely convinced either. She looks like she's biting the inside of her cheek to keep her doubts from spilling out in plain sight of her commanding officer. "I'm here because I want to learn, ma'am. I *have* been learning, in part thanks to bunking with the emperor's pet prince. And helping Ettian *is* helping the Archon Empire. I don't think Gal's too far off the mark when he says they're one and the same."

Esperza's eyes darken, and I feel a prickle of shame run through me for how happy I am to see Wen's misstep play out in real time. "I'm begging you to be smart about this," the commodore says in a low, level voice. "Especially now that the general is aboard. The rebellion's been in the works for *years*—Ettian emp-Archon only became a part of it recently. Think hard about what that means for the people you serve with. And be strategic about where your education is coming from. That's all." With a curt nod and a stiff squeeze of Wen's shoulder, she strides past us, following the rest of the general's retinue.

Wen's eyes meet mine, and I feel myself torn in two. One side pulls with the urge to comfort her—to say, "See, the corvettes didn't even matter." The other is a tangled, wrathful monster of shame and indignation that started simmering in the *Torrent*'s core and is only now coming to boil.

I'm weak. Weak for wanting to help her, for setting up a snare for her and falling right into it, for *rooting* for something so far from any of my own objectives that I think my mother would disown me on the spot if she knew about it. Weak for letting Iral's appearance rattle me, as if a general with no bloodright to his name at all has any sort of dominion over the prince of a ruttin' empire. Weak for my failure on the bridge, weak for the way my heart stutters at the mere mention of the emperor, weak for plenty of other reasons I'm sure I could enumerate if my self-pity spiral weren't happening while Wen's staring at me, no doubt wondering why I haven't started talking already.

And when she realizes I'm not going to say anything, her mouth hardens to a resolute line. "Maybe it's best if we both take some time to examine our motivations, then," she says, cementing what I hope is my final failure of the day. My greatest failure of the day—the one that knocks me back all the way to where I started, with no foothold toward getting my ass out of this wretched rebellion.

But it's not the one that hurts the worst, which only deepens my humiliation. Because the thing that aches, the thing that burns, the thing that makes me want to hop out the nearest airlock, is that I can't help Wen anymore.

CHAPTER 14

WITH IRAL ABOARD, everything changes. Gone are the long, slow days of trailing Wen through training exercise after training exercise. I can feel the temperature of the war rising around us. The strike against the *Torrent* was just the boiling point. Now everything is threatening to flash-cook.

And I'm pinned in place, locked in my quarters while Wen gets absorbed into the Archon strategy meetings. She won't tell me what goes on in them, and she seems hell-bent on not taking any more advice from me. I've tried to argue that Esperza actually endorsed my help, but Wen won't have any of it. She's determined to show the commodore that she's *truly* independently motivated.

After a week of having absolutely nothing to do but pace our quarters and fantasize about all the ways Iral could possibly have me killed, I finally cave. Wen may not listen to my advice anymore, but she's not cruel enough to deny my request once she hears it.

An hour later, Ettian appears at the door of our quarters.

"Wait outside," he tells his guards, and they take up posts in the hall. As he closes the door behind him, I catch the worried looks they pass each other.

They're right to worry.

"You wanted to see me?" Ettian says, with an unsurprising degree of surprise.

"I wanted to see you," I confirm, taking a good long look at him. He's dressed for war, ready for it to arrive at a moment's notice. Gone are the slick suits of his palace days—now he walks around in lightweight deflector armor emblazoned with platinum sigils. He wears a simple circlet of flattened, jointed platinum—which, as usual, I desperately want to knock off his skull—and his hair's still buzzed like a soldier's. I wonder if he wears it like that in the hopes that it'll make his subordinates respect him more.

I think it makes him look young. Far too young to be leading any army. I hope it's a sentiment shared by the rest of the *Torrent*'s population, but since I've been confined to quarters for the past week, I've fallen behind on the ship's gossip channels. That's part of the reason I've called him here. If I can't keep abreast of the rumors, I'm gonna create them.

A wicked hint of it must show in my eyes, because Ettian glances back at the door, no doubt wondering if he should call his guards in. I take a sudden step forward, throwing myself in front of him. "Shout for them and I drop to my knees," I murmur.

His lips peel back in distaste, and I swear I catch a flash of disappointment in his eyes. Did he think I'd thought things over and decided we *could* move forward in the precarious direction we were headed back on Rana? Was he carrying hopes about the things we could get up to in one of the few unmonitored rooms on the *Torrent*? I shouldn't be pleased that it's on his mind.

Or maybe I should, because it means I'm going to get exactly what I wanted.

"If you're only going to play games, I'm not sticking around," Ettian says. He stands resolute—not jumping back, not leaning in. He should be doing the former. I'd rather he did the—

No, I need to stay focused.

"Can you blame me for needing some ruttin' entertainment? Well, not *ruttin'* entertainment, though I wouldn't say no to—"

"*Gal*."

I hold up my hands. "Look, I don't know if word got back to you about Wen's run-in with the captain."

"You mean *your* run-in with the captain?"

"*Our* run-in with the captain, the end result of which was my expulsion from pretty much any excuse I've ever had to leave these rooms." I've spent so long practicing my invisible neutrality that it takes me an extra second to remember how to look pathetic. "I get it. I'm a tactical risk. But it's ruttin' torture sitting here doing nothing."

Ettian's eyebrows lift. "Doing nothing instead of tearing down my empire brick by brick?"

"Is that what you think I've been doing for the past month?"

"I don't know what you've been doing for the past month."

"Bullshit. Wen reports to you."

"Wen doesn't have *time* to report to me. Have you seen her schedules lately?"

"*No,*" I reply pointedly.

Ettian snorts despite himself.

"Well, then let me be the first to inform you that I've made myself useful around here." I spread my arms magnanimously, taking a step back. "I took your rogue knight and transformed her into a savvy young officer."

"Esperza—"

"Is a busy commodore with many important things to do. She's doing her damnedest, but she can't do everything. I, on the other hand, have had nothing but free time to follow Wen around and mercilessly criticize her. She's making outstanding strides already."

Ettian doesn't seem to be buying it—but do I really need him to? "And then that got taken away, and *now* you want to see me?"

"Well, if I can't mercilessly criticize *her* . . ."

He smirks, and the sight of it hits my heart like a kickdrum. And maybe I've loosened my expression too much, because suddenly Ettian freezes as if my face has given away every single thought rocketing around inside my skull. "I've—" He breaks off, grappling with the words for an extra second. "I've missed this."

I turn my back on him, even though I know exactly what that looks like. Let him see me wrestling my emotions back into place. Let him see how I have to physically wall myself off from him to process those words. For a moment there, everything felt normal. For a moment the war fell away and the walls of our old academy dorm rose to take its place—so much so that I could almost hear Hanji banging on the door, telling us to get our asses to the cantina.

For a moment, it almost felt like nothing's changed at all.

"I need something to do," I announce, flinching at both the hoarse notes in my voice and the abruptness of how quickly I've tried to move the conversation along. *Get it together,* I chide myself. It's like I've forgotten how to react to him entirely in the month we've been apart.

"I suggest taking up a craft," Ettian replies peevishly.

"I need something to do that feels *useful,*" I correct.

"I think your definition of useful is a little skewed compared to mine."

"See, but that's the thing." I turn on him, ready to make my big point, but the enormity of what I'm about to admit catches up to me all at once. *He just said he "missed this"—there's no way this is more embarrassing,* my brain screams, but what does my witless brain know? That's *feelings* feelings.

This is dread.

"I . . . The general is aboard."

Ettian's expression tightens. "And?"

"And the general was gonna kill me last time he was in charge. Doubt that's changed." My voice has gone soft—too soft, vulnerable on all sides, so much so that I beat a hasty retreat to the anteroom's couch and throw myself down on it.

"He's not in charge," Ettian says, but he can't quite make those words as firm as they need to be.

"How soon until that changes?" It's a good thing I sat down—I've gone from unsteady to properly shaky. I feel like I've grown numb to the way I've been holding myself together since I last saw Iral, and now it's all catching up to me at once.

Ettian fixes me with a look that lets me know I'm not the only one unraveling. In his eyes, I see the exact same stress that's been plaguing me for the past week. "It's my bloodright," he says, low and level. "He can never take that away from me."

"Since when have you given a rat's ass about bloodright?" I snap. "If that was something that mattered to you, you would have claimed it the second you walked onto that base back on Delos."

Ettian's nostrils flare. "You have no ruttin' idea what you're talking about."

"I'm the only other person in the *galaxy* who knows what you're—"

"*Gal.*" His whole body has gone taut like a wound-up spring, engines hot on the verge of ignition. "The war, the aftermath, the . . . *hell* I lived through—none of it went away when I walked onto that base. Don't tell me when my bloodright mattered to me and when it didn't. You never knew that then, and you certainly don't know it now."

I grimace, trying my damnedest not to concede the ground I've gained with my little outburst. I know what Ettian went through after the fall of Archon in broad strokes, but I don't know if I'll ever fully grasp the scope of it. I've never been so thoroughly abandoned, so destitute, so broken. Gods willing, I never will be. I don't know what I'd do if I went through the same things that molded Ettian emp-Archon—I just know that I'd probably never come through it as intact as he did.

"Circling back to the point," I say after what feels like far too much glowering eye contact. "The *Torrent* has been minding its own business for a month with you aboard. The second it lands its first victory with you in command, General Iral comes swooping in to insert himself in the ship's hierarchy. This is exactly what I warned you about when I said you needed to come to the front. He's going to do everything in his power to put your leadership into question." Ettian tries to open his mouth, but I cut him off with a hand gesture, a little thrill stealing through me when it works. "He's not gonna kill you. Probably won't even depose you. But if he turns you into a ceremonial puppet emperor, there's nothing that'll stop him from killing me."

I don't need to say any more than that—I see it all click into place in Ettian's head. "You want to make sure that doesn't happen," he says, though he doesn't quite sound like he believes all of the implications that come with it.

"Unfortunately, it's become something of a priority. Especially now that I'm being left unsupervised for long stretches," I say, sweeping my arms at the Wen-less room around me. "I need someone watching my back. You need someone watching yours."

Now Ettian definitely doesn't believe what he's hearing. "You put a *knife* to my throat a month ago."

"Yeah, but you liked it."

Ettian fumes, I smirk, and the inevitable conclusion I've just put forth solidifies in the air between us. "So, what?" Ettian finally says once he's collected himself. "You want to tag along with me instead of Wen?"

"That's a start. And while I can't be seen advising you directly, I can keep an eye on things and raise my concerns in private."

"I'm sure there will be many," Ettian says flatly.

"I'm good at this, okay? I've spent a month learning how to be invisible in a room full of Archon's top brass—er, platinum. If Silon didn't have it out for me, I'd still be doing it. And you can overrule Silon."

Ettian's eyes darken. "There's a cost to overruling Silon."

"Oh, come on, she's only got *continental* bloodright."

He points an accusing finger at me. "See, that shit right there. That's not going to fly if we're going to make this work."

I scoff. "She's no big fan of you—don't give her any credit she hasn't earned."

"That too," Ettian grumbles, holding up another finger.

"What?"

"All this Umber bullshit. Who outranks whom, who bows to whom—that's not how we do things." Ettian throws himself down in one of the chairs opposite me, managing to make even casual distress look damn good. "I respect Silon. She runs the *Torrent* like no one else can, and if I start overruling her too much, I lose not only her trust but the trust of all of the people who work underneath her. Same goes for Iral. He's been working with these people for five *years*. I haven't even made it five months yet."

I grit my teeth, trying to combat the rising tension wracking my chest. Ettian being bullheadedly Archon is ultimately good for my purposes. A government founded on those ideals is unstable—with no rigidity to their power structures, they're liable to tear themselves apart from the inside long before we have anything to do with it. But right now I need him to be a force. A fixed point, the center of his empire's gravity. I don't know any other way we can possibly hold out against Maxo Iral. "I'm not going to stop telling you how to keep your empire just because it makes you uncomfortable," I grumble. "But I can't force you to take my advice either."

"Is it advice, or is it just you trying to get under my skin?"

"Can't it be both?"

Ettian smirks despite himself.

"Look, remember when I told you I was the only person in the palace who truly had your best interests at heart? I think it's . . . triply true for this ruttin' dreadnought." I stretch, folding my arms behind my head as I kick my feet up on the low stone table in front of me. "So ignore my advice all you want, but don't come crying to me when it turns out you should have been following it."

His smirk breaks into a laugh, and it hits me so hard I'm lucky I'm already sprawled back against the couch. I don't think I ever really believed I'd make him laugh again—in scorn, maybe, but not the genuine stuff that makes me feel like I've been tied to a Viper. And because he's laughing, all of a sudden I'm laughing. I never could keep it in once he got going.

The surrealism of the moment catches us like insects in amber, and for one golden moment, the happiness that glows through me isn't rooted in cruelty or vindictiveness—it's the real thing, founded in how good it feels to be my goddamn self. I don't have to couch my feelings with Ettian. I don't have to figure out how to make myself palatable to him. He knows the whole of me already, and there's no point disguising any of it for him.

Of course, it's then that the main door slides open and Wen steps through. She takes a second to ingest the room—me splayed back on the couch, Ettian perched in his chair, his body leaning toward me, the last echoes of our paired laughter still bouncing off the walls.

We blink back at her.

"Weird," she says, after a moment. Then, after a longer moment: "My sleep schedule's completely rusted. I'm going to bed." But she pauses at the threshold of her room, again looking like she's mulling something over. "Don't make too much noise," she announces, then shuts the door behind her.

Ettian and I exchange an uncertain glance. He rises out of the chair, looking like he's just had a bucket of cold water thrown on him. "I . . . will call for you. Tomorrow. Or next . . . cycle—gods, it's been over a month here and I'm still not used to the 'living in space' lingo. Anyway. Tomorrow. Ish."

I save my next bout of laughter until he's safely back in the hall outside.

CHAPTER 15

I ALMOST EXPECT to be shot on sight the next time I set foot on the *Torrent*'s bridge. I press close to Ettian's shadow as we step off the elevator, hoping to keep myself occluded from the captain's view. But Silon's locked in a hushed conversation with Esperza, her back turned. The only one who takes interest in my presence is Wen, who straightens abruptly in her seat at the commodore's station, her gaze tracing a nervous ricochet between the bridge's major powers.

I resist the urge to tip her a cheeky little wave as I trail Ettian to his station, positioned adjacent to Esperza's on the innermost ring surrounding Silon's command chair. I wouldn't be on the bridge if I didn't have a mission here, and I'm not about to jeopardize it by putting Wen on the offensive.

Our luck runs out within seconds. As Ettian and I reach his post, Silon's gaze snaps up abruptly, her eyes sharpening on me. Just as she's about to open her mouth, Ettian snaps his fingers in the corner of my vision, drawing my attention, then jabs his finger at the chair that's been set up next to his. Not an invitation. A command.

I lower myself into it without protest, hating the necessity of it. The last time I entered the bridge, I snuck by in Wen's wake. It made it look like a mistake when Silon "caught" me. It *was* a mistake—

one we're not intent on repeating. My presence on the bridge is by explicit command of the emperor. And I'm here to obey his commands unquestioningly.

At least, it has to look that way.

"Enjoying yourself?" I murmur as Ettian settles into his own chair.

"Don't push it," he replies out of the corner of his mouth. Seated this close, I can tell he's been up all night. The subtle darkness of the skin beneath his eyes makes their rich browns even starker. I'm hoping the rest of the bridge finds them just as magnetic as I do, because running on this little sleep, we need all the help we can get.

The adrenaline high of being on the bridge is the only thing keeping me grounded in the reality of this moment. Ettian offered to order me a shot of that horribly rich Archon coffee, but I was almost certain that adding caffeine jitters to my already anxious mental state would get me thrown out of here for no reason beyond *He's being way too twitchy*. If the plan we hatched is going to work, I can't get booted right away.

In my current state, I'm still coming to grips with the fact that last night *happened*. Ettian burst through my door with no warning, barely giving it time to swing shut between us and his guards before announcing that General Iral had laid out the plan for the Ellit offensive. *Tomorrow afternoon, he'll present it in a strategy session,* he said, brandishing his datapad as he dropped onto the anteroom couch.

Is it any good? I asked, before realizing that it barely mattered. With this plan, Iral takes the reins of the Archon rebellion. The leadership is primed by seven years of precedent to follow him. If Ettian wants to stand any chance of maintaining control of what's happening here, he has to break it.

And not only break it—he has to come in with a plan of his own, a plan that so clearly outdoes Iral's that the leadership will back it as the only strategy to mount against the blockade at Ellit.

A month ago, before the general came aboard, I would have laughed myself sick if Ettian had not only showed me the full plan of attack for Archon's next offensive but also begged me to help him come up with a *better* way to loosen my empire's hold in the Tosa System. But last night, I simply sat down at his side and got to work.

It felt like a night at the academy, like digging into a tactics assignment side by side with the desperation of students who've blown all three of the semester's extensions on earlier papers. I could almost picture the rest of our friends arrayed around us. Hanji sprawled artlessly over one of the sitting-room chairs with her glasses drooping down her nose. Rin flat on her back on the floor, her heels hooked up on the couch. Rhodes on his stomach next to her, chin propped on a ridiculously thick volume of paper records. Ollins pacing, always too full of energy to sit still, even in the middle of the night. That familiarity kept me grounded—kept me from spiraling into the heady knowledge that if we didn't crack this, didn't figure out a way to outmaneuver Archon's most celebrated general, I might be a dead man.

Even if I'd had time to sleep, I'm not sure I would have.

I sit up straighter as I hear the faint whine that precedes the bridge doors whooshing open. There's no opportunity for me to duck behind Ettian or turn my head away and hope for the best. I fix my eyes on certain doom and greet him head-on.

General Iral steps onto the bridge with slow, steady intention. His presence draws every eye, and he knows it, keeping his head held high and his gaze fixed on nothing but the station that's been set aside for him in the inner ring. He's a man sculpted from duty, a man who's so committed to the image of his own myth that even I, with my cynical, terrified eyes, can't see a single crack in it. He's flanked by a team of equally purposeful aides and support staff, who move with him like a well-oiled machine, a reminder that where Ettian and I have been playing at warfare in academy sims for a few years, the general has lived it for over a decade.

Improbably, I find myself suppressing a laugh. There's no way we pull this off. We're deluding ourselves, thinking that not only could we outmaneuver this man, we could also sway the rebellion he built away from following his orders. Everyone on this bridge—save for me, Ettian, and Wen—joined this uprising because they believe in his legend. This is the man who single-handedly sustained Archon's hope for two years after the execution of its imperials. The man whose death was supposed to be the final extinguishing of that hope. The man who resurrected himself with the very same broadcast where he forced me to my knees before the galaxy.

Before my urge to topple into a total meltdown gets out of hand, Iral's attention zeroes in on the one anomaly in his perfect war machine—me. And oh, there's the crack. It's just a wrinkle in his brow, but it's *there*, enough to let me know I've thrown him. As he steps up to his seat, his gaze slides to the emperor at my right. "Your Majesty," Iral says with a short bow. "I was under the impression we were scheduled for a strategy meeting, but it appears the bridge still has some security clearances to pass."

There's a faint choking noise from the *Torrent*'s saddle, and my fear of Iral does vicious battle with my desire to see Silon's expression as she hastily tamps down her humiliated fury. I keep my eyes on the general as in my periphery I hear the captain announce, "Apologies, I was still in the process of determining why the emperor brought the prisoner—"

Iral silences her with an understanding wave. "Perhaps the prisoner has some strategic information he'd like to contribute. Or perhaps the emperor's finally of a mind to . . . extract the little Umber's strategic value, shall we say?"

And now I can't keep my eyes on my true enemy, because *this* I have to see—the flash of steel in Ettian's gaze as he regards the general coolly. I feel my center of balance cant at the realization that this has been an argument between them, a debate that never touched me because all along, Ettian has been holding the line. Thus far, my imprisonment has been relatively comfortable—not without its bumps and hitches, but nowhere near what my mother would do to an Archon prisoner of my status. The only information they've gotten out of me has been information I've volunteered. No one has ever suggested it could be different within earshot. No one had the temerity until Iral.

Ettian rises slowly from his seat. "As I've repeatedly reminded you, the prisoner's strategic value lies in his importance to the enemy. Successfully extracting information from him would only serve to compromise that value. He remains an advantage as long as Umber wants him enough not to kill him to get to us."

"From where I sit, it's no advantage to have him on the bridge for this particular meeting," Silon says with a sniff. "All he's contributed to so far is an argument that's eaten into our time slot."

Precisely, I almost declare out loud, but I settle for exchanging a smug little look with Ettian. Iral expected to bluster onto the bridge with his bureaucratic maelstrom and take decisive command of the war. Instead, he's mired himself in the trap my presence sets, too distracted to dive right into his agenda.

But of course we're not going to own up to that. "The prisoner remains with me," Ettian says firmly. "This meeting can proceed with him in the room. If you think there's even the slightest chance that Gal emp-Umber can somehow compromise our strategy, then I'd encourage you to have more faith in Silon and her administration of the *Torrent*."

The captain looks like she's just taken a hearty swig of engine hooch.

Before the emperor's twisted praise has a chance to settle, he plows forward. "And beyond that, I've spent the night reviewing the plans the general has proposed. While it is certainly a battle plan that *will* leave Ellit in our hands at the end of the day, the methods it proposes will almost certainly halve our fleet in the process." Ettian draws himself up tall, tilting his chin just-so. He'll never have the stature or the frame to match Iral, but bloodright is more than that—and in this moment, he so clearly holds it that I feel a filthy twist of shame for allowing him any sort of legitimacy. "A victory that costs us half our holdings is not worth doubling the number of planets we can claim. That tips our war into an unsustainable position. I will not allow this fleet to move forward with a strategy that carries a risk that great."

"Your Majesty," Iral says, his tone veering dangerously close to one you'd use to explain the orbit of a planet to a small child. "Umber's attack on the rear of the fleet was only the beginning. This war has stagnated while Tosa licked his wounds after Rana, but all of our scouting indicates Umber is making ready to mobilize. If we're caught between the dreadnoughts stationed at Ellit and the forces they're massing at Imre, it won't just be a half loss. It will be total. If we're to survive, we must take Ellit."

"I'm not arguing that we shouldn't," Ettian replies. "All I'm saying is that we're in dire need of a strategy with less risk attached."

Esperza sinks back in her seat, folding her arms behind her head with a wicked glint in her eye. I resent how much she's enjoying this, but I'll be damned if I don't take at least some secret thrill in how much pissy discord has settled over the Archon leadership in so little time. "Sure, Your Majesty—every commander in this war would *love* to fight a riskless battle. But if we sit around waiting for the perfect strategy to fall into our laps, we'll be navel-gazing easy pickings for Tosa's fleet."

At this, Ettian leans forward—hungry, eager, his barely repressed grin almost wolfish. "Well, then we're in luck, Commodore, because—"

"Oh, for the love of every ruttin' god of every ruttin' system," I groan loudly, scrubbing a hand over my eyes. It takes everything in me not to outright cackle at the stunned silence my outburst leaves. In my periphery, I swear I catch a security officer's hand dropping to his sidearm in alarm. "You're really going to try this? *You*?"

I loll my head sideways to find Ettian staring at me, brows raised.

"You have a general who was leading campaigns while you were still cowering in your parents' bunker laying out a solid battle plan made to win you a whole ruttin' planet, and you're going to act like you've just thought of something better? I mean, seriously?"

"I haven't 'just thought' of something better—I've worked my ass off to come up with it," he replies with a venomous edge. "I am *emperor*. It may mean something different to you, but here in Archon, that means I am at my people's service. That means I won't sit idly by if I believe I can save them from a risky battle plan."

"You're delusional," I scoff. "I mean, my gods, you're eighteen. You didn't even *graduate* your academy training. What could you possibly think of that the general hasn't already?"

"He's fought his wars, and I respect him for that," Ettian says, lifting his eyes to Iral and giving him a slow nod. The general's got his fingers steepled together, a look of wary consideration wrinkling his brow. "But he hasn't fought this one, against these ships. I've reviewed the scouting reports of the six dreadnoughts Umber has positioned around Ellit. Every ship in that blockade was manufactured in the Dasun Yards less than seven years ago."

The shift that overtakes the bridge is subtle. There are no gasps, no claps, no sudden moves to draw up the data and verify Ettian's claim. But the flame beneath the simmering doubt is sputtering. "A dreadnought's a dreadnought," I fire back a half-second too late and with just a little too much forced flippancy. "The guns on the newer ships will vaporize your armies just as easily as the ones on the old ones that took down your upstart empire the first time."

"Captain, if you would be so kind." Ettian makes a few elegant swipes on his station that transfer the data he's prepared to Silon's. She draws it up onto the transparent displays that wreath her, splaying out a pair of dreadnought schematics. On the left is a pre–War of Expansion ship, breathtakingly massive and viciously armed. I've always liked the older war machines' aesthetics—those wrought in the Umber Core have a flattened, sharp, brutalist quality meant to align with the design of the Imperial Seat itself. This ship doesn't just look like it'll mow you down. It looks like it'll brush you off like a fly.

On the right is one of the newer models. One of the six in the blockade, in fact—a fellow named the *Reach*, whose hull looks fresh off the line. It's designed around the same principles as its older cousin, built to annihilate with impunity, but its shape trends a little sleeker, betraying a few engineering advancements that have slipped into the base framework. With another series of swipes, Ettian zooms in on one of those enhancements in particular—the massive engines set at the ship's rear.

"The older model of Umber dreadnought was made to be as versatile as possible—to justify the use of that much metal, of course. But once they came into a fresh belt to mine, they began to rethink their priorities. The new models are still floating fortresses, but they're built to be far more maneuverable than their predecessors. The *Torrent* itself is one of these, and we reaped the benefits in our last engagement."

Ettian throws up a rendering of our last fight, when the Umber dreadnought popped out of the black at our rear. We'd been forced to rely on the support of our corvettes as we executed a turn to bring our main batteries around for defense. But when he overlays a parallel model of how an older dreadnought would maneuver, the difference in turn speed is starkly clear.

Iral frowns. "All you're saying is that the dreadnoughts we'll face at Ellit will be more maneuverable than the ones we fought in the last war. Everyone in this room is already aware of the advances that have been made since the last war, and I'm having difficulty understanding how it benefits us."

Ettian nods, unconcerned. "There's another aspect of this new design I want to focus on." He pulls up the dreadnought model again and highlights the main batteries, which prickle from the ship's fore. "Because the old guard of dreadnoughts had less maneuverability, they had to be capable of attacking from all angles. The newer models focus their firing power where it's most easily swung around."

With another twist, he overlays swaths of color that arc out around each of the cityship's guns, illustrating their firing radius. The heaviest coverage—the true promise of annihilation—cuts a deep red arc from the fore of the ship. The rear's got enough firepower to keep it defended, but definitely not enough firepower to front an attack.

Ettian locks his gaze on Iral. "At present, those undergunned rears are pointed at Umber-held Ellit, while the fores are arranged looking outward, to defend from any incoming attack. But if we can force a turn . . ."

Every eye on the bridge lights up. Even the soldiers who aren't brilliant strategists like Iral or Esperza know enough to realize the implications of what Ettian has just highlighted. The general himself looks like he's battling to keep his consternation from showing as the certainty settles—we'll be throwing out his battle plan and starting all over again.

Ettian, on the other hand, is having a hard time keeping that prideful smirk off his face—or maybe I'm just way too used to reading him. He seems just a little too caught up in the moment, so I nudge my foot against his under the station, jerking him sharply back into the reality of our situation.

There's one more piece to our own little battle plan. After the disruption of my presence on the bridge, after the scripted argument that had *me*—the prisoner, the Umber prince, the enemy—voicing the skepticism we might face, after Ettian silenced every doubt with the elegantly staged projections—there's one more thing we have to do to seal in his unquestionable place at the head of his rebellion.

Ettian's focus drops to me, his spine straightening imperiously. "You," he says, his voice dripping with ice-cold authority. "Out."

"I'll need an escort," I reply. "Unless you're volunteering."

"Wen," he says, with his tone just a smidge more tempered. "If you'd be so kind."

She rises from her station, exchanging a quick look with Esperza, then beckons to me. "Let's make this fast."

I don't need telling twice—we didn't plan it that way. I rise obediently, the perfect prisoner brought to heel by Ettian's command, and let her slip an arm around my elbow as she pulls me toward the bridge doors.

When we're far enough from the rest of the command staff to be out of earshot, she leans in close. "You two have gotten better since the last time you ran that scam on Delos. I don't know what you're playing at," Wen murmurs. "But if it doesn't go exactly according to plan, I will put you out the airlock before any of these Archon assholes can tell me no."

CHAPTER 16

I SHOULDN'T BE AFRAID.

I sit in the hold of a Caster Model X, my back pressed against the padding built into the wall and my ass getting sore on the hard plastic bench. The hull around us is coated with an ultrablack wrap that will seamlessly disperse detection along any spectrum, and we cut the engines twenty minutes ago, leaving us a perfectly still, perfectly silent, perfectly invisible stone going cold against the vast dark of the universe. Thousands of miles away, the Ellit offensive is about to begin, but it can't touch us here.

Here we wait, far from any sort of harm—and yet, I can't stop shaking.

Ettian's up front with the pilots. Two of them, two of us, and that's it. No escort squadron to defend us if someone manages to pick us out as more than space trash. Nothing more than the guns on this ship and the superluminal drive with a vector for Rana preprogrammed into it. Anything more would draw attention or introduce more points of failure into the equation.

I'm trying not to think about points of failure. Trying not to think about how the strategy we concocted is about to go into motion, about how we're powerless to affect its execution, about how we—

"You good back here?"

I jerk my head up to find Ettian leaning out from the cockpit. He looks steady, or maybe it's just the comfort of finally being in a small craft again. They were always where he was most at home. Before I can answer, he slips fully into the hold and plunks himself down on the bench opposite me.

"Not gonna talk the pilots into letting you do a few loops?" I ask. My attempt at nonchalance rings false, but I plow ahead anyway. "Can't believe you got so close to a pilot's seat and didn't use that fancy imperial title to put your ass in it."

He quirks an eyebrow. "Maybe I thought about it, but I didn't want to leave you alone back here. No telling what you could get up to with no one watching you."

I roll my eyes, spreading my hands until the cuffs I've been bound in bite into my wrists—which isn't very far at all. Some bullshit security protocol has decided that in addition to being trapped in a small ship in the middle of nowhere while a battle that could decide my fate plays out, I need to be trussed up like a bird ready for the oven. On the one hand, I feel like the danger I pose is being properly respected for once.

On the other, it's putting me right up on the edge of a panic attack.

Ettian notes my predicament with a smile that's far too sympathetic for my liking. Everything about him in this moment is far too sympathetic to begin with. He has just as much riding on this moment as me, and just as little control. He can't even commandeer the shuttle from the soldiers—not when he's already tied up in the oh-so-thrilling task of babysitting me. "I wish those weren't necessary," he says, nodding to the cuffs with his voice pitched low as if he means to slip by the ears of any eavesdropping coming from the fore.

So I reply, loud as I please, "Oh come on. If you didn't like me tied up, we wouldn't be in this mess in the first place."

He gives me a tight, annoyed look, then pulls a datapad from the inner pocket of his jacket. "Work with me, asshole," he mutters. "We're five minutes out from the start of the operation."

I draw a deep breath, trying to still my shaking hands. With the cuffs, my tremors are obnoxiously obvious, the chattering of metal a dead giveaway. I'm better than this. I was *raised* better than this, raised to ruthlessly helm an empire—or maybe I've equated that with being so far above consequence that the prospect of it is reducing me to a nervous wreck.

Ettian tips the datapad my way, and I eye him warily. This feels like a mistake he's too smart to make, which means it's almost certainly a trap. But after a full five seconds of blank staring, he shoves it into my hands. "Look, I'm betting it's going to make you feel a lot better if you have something to do," he huffs. "So you tell me what's happening."

"If anyone in your administration saw this, no victory is going to save their respect for you," I warn him as I gingerly spin the datapad around on my knee.

"Then it's a good thing no one's seeing this," he replies, though his eyes dart briefly to the cockpit door to confirm both pilots are still on-task.

I shake my head, then pull up the model of the battlefield. A network of stealth satellites is keeping it up to date by the second, and the three points at which Archon dreadnoughts will drop from superluminal are highlighted in pale pink. "Thirty seconds to the jump," I murmur, zooming in on the *Reach,* the blockade dreadnought Archon has elected to claim as its primary target.

Its rear flirts with the edge of Ellit's atmosphere, its rows and rows of fore cannons arrayed toward the stars. It gives no sign it's aware of what's coming, but I wouldn't be surprised if it is. At minimum, Umber scouting must know that the fleet is mobilizing, that the superluminal drives of three dreadnoughts are preparing for an immediate jump, and that Ellit is the next logical target for the uprising. But the *Reach* remains silent, the guns watchful, the bay doors down.

"Three. Two. One. *Mark.*"

Three dreadnoughts blink from the black, lined up in perfect syzygy against the pinpoint of the *Reach*. They immediately swap from superluminal to reactor power, plunging forward while maintaining their alignment.

The mission clock has just hit two seconds when the *Reach* opens fire.

"Confirmed discharge," I announce through gritted teeth, and in my periphery, I see Ettian's shoulders wind a notch tenser. The first Archon dreadnought takes the fire with aplomb, its thick metal shielding flaring hot as heavy boltfire chips into it. Its own cannons—the lighter ones, the ones that can afford to miss—chug a silent, steady barrage in retort, targeting the *Reach*'s gun mounts.

The two cityships tucked in the first dreadnought's shadow wheel their guns for a more distant target—the *Valiant*, positioned over Ellit's north pole. At this angle, they don't risk making landfall with a missed shot, and so they fire their biggest guns freely, their potshots striking with a relatively low success rate. I zoom in on the *Valiant*, my breath caught in my chest.

This is the moment that decides the entire battle. The moment that our strategy hinges on. We have a fallback—Iral's plan, a bloody, brutal assault that will decimate Archon's fleet. It has its own art to it—I respect Iral's skill as a strategist too much to discount it entirely. But if we have to revert to the battle plan he concocted, Archon reverts to following their hallowed general.

And they'll follow him right into separating my head from my neck.

"Come on," I groan through my teeth, eyes fixed on the *Valiant*'s bulk. "*Turn,* damn you."

And like it's heard my command and bent to the will of its future emperor, the *Valiant* begins to pitch its guns toward the thick of the fighting.

I pump my free hand, nearly knocking the datapad off my knees, and Ettian startles. "The *Valiant*'s begun its rotation," I explain, lifting my eyes from the battle just long enough to catch the complicated expression he flinches into. I mirror it—equal parts joy, because we were *right*, because now the true battle can begin, because now Archon has its opening to take Ellit, and fear, because now that the fleet is bound to commit to our strategy, that strategy has to work.

"How long until the runners are go?" he asks, leaning in to peer at the datapad. The greater weight's been lifted from his shoulders at the news that the *Valiant* is behaving as expected, and it seems he's finally ready to actually *look* at what's happening.

If we make it through this, I'll try to unpack thoroughly, but for now I just tip the pad so he can see better and tell him, "Five minutes, at the current rate of rotation."

It feels like an eternity. For five minutes, the first in the trio of our advance dreadnoughts has to bear the *Reach*'s battery, shielding its two brethren with its sheer bulk. The rendering on the datapad can't possibly do it justice. I watch the destruction with bile in my throat, trying to come to grips with just how punishing the full force of dreadnought fire is. It seems a miracle that it's not punching a hole clean through the Archon cityship's structure.

Ettian watches steadily, and for a moment I wonder how he could possibly ingest the sight with so much calm. I shouldn't be the one more affected by this—he's the one whose ships are on the line here. But it dawns on me slowly that I am far less familiar with the destructive power of a dreadnought than Ettian. I was safe in the Umber Core at ten years old, shielded from the War of Expansion. Ettian survived it.

He's never really told me how much of it he saw, but now I think I don't have to ask.

At the one-minute mark, a lucky shot from the *Reach* tears through the bridge of the first Archon dreadnought. Their communications drop out, but the ship remains mostly intact, mostly effective at providing coverage for the rest of the advance team. The surviving Engineering crews throw it into a turn of its own, forsaking the potential of its main batteries to wheel its rear engines around to face Ellit. At its current momentum, it will take a full hour to reach a point of no return with the planet's gravity, but if it's allowed to fall, it would wipe out life on the planet entirely.

Ettian shifts uncomfortably, his hands clenching together. "Time?" he asks hoarsely.

I wrench my focus back to the *Valiant*, which has already opened fire on the three Archon dreadnoughts with its ancillary batteries. "Any second now. Any—shit, *now*."

On the screen, the blockade runners bloom at the *Valiant*'s rear, screaming out of superluminal as close to the planet's hard atmosphere as they dare. To its credit, the *Valiant* takes barely five seconds to open fire with its rear batteries, but the ships we've fronted here are the fastest in the fleet, and they pour past the blockade like iron rain. Their shielding hits the atmosphere, flaring bright—brighter still, where the *Valiant*'s boltfire strikes true. But it will take another five-minute turn for the *Valiant*'s main batteries to wheel back around, and at that point the blockade runners will be far too close to Ellit's surface for the dreadnought to risk firing.

Once, during the War of Expansion, a dreadnought that broke through the blockade on Rana fired what became known as the Warning Shot, punching a crater into the planet's surface just north of the capital at Trost. It choked the air with particulate for days, even with the winds sloughing off the nearby mountains to diffuse the fallout. That was short-term compared to what the *Valiant*'s boltfire could wreak on Ellit if it fires on the northern ice caps.

And it has me by the throat, the fear that it might. Being Umber means being ruthless—I've known this since birth. I've trained my whole life to bring that ruthlessness under my heel the same way my mother once did, but I've never faced it as an opponent like this. Never feared the decision of one of *my* dreadnought captains, not because it would be strategic, but because it would be cruel.

This is not the time for this, my brain rages at me, even as my mouth is halfway through blurting the words that betray me completely. "Bloodright's a funny thing, isn't it?"

Ettian's eyes snap up warily from the battle. No doubt he's been waiting all day for me to try something. No doubt he thinks the moment has finally come.

But no, this is apparently just me finally short circuiting, because

I carry on. "It's a seed we carry, but we only earn it when we bloom. Or at least, that's how my mother tried to explain it."

"How old were you when she explained how her particular seed came into bloom?" Ettian asks levelly.

"Doesn't matter." I shrug, though the true answer, *Seven,* might as well be written across my face. I was seven years old when my mother explained that she'd had an older sister named Ximena who stood between her and the crown, and that the seed of her own right to rule had bloomed with a blade across her sister's throat. It took years for me to fully grasp what that act had meant—at seven, my immediate concern was that my mother would one day expect me to kill her.

Dear one, it doesn't work like that, she'd explained, stroking my hair. In later years, she'd elaborate. *You are my bloodright's logical continuation. I've earned you your place on the throne. But you must be careful never to lose your people's faith that you hold the right to rule. Never let them think that they could possibly carve out their own portion of what is meant to be yours.*

An overwhelming prospect for a kid, but I was a kid who'd spent my entire life safe within the citadel walls, knowing only my mother's fierce promise to bring me into the same blossoming. Now I sit across from the very usurper who threatens to knock out that trust and supplant it, watching as he deals yet another blow to my future regime.

Watching and doing nothing to stop it. Watching the *Valiant* pick off runners one by one, each flare a twist in my gut. Watching, realizing that the critical moment has arrived and I have no idea which outcome I should be praying for.

The tremor's worked its way back into my hands. I'm helpless against it, the datapad jarring unreadably in my grip. My internal turmoil is rapidly becoming an external one, and the only thought I can manage outside of the panic is gratitude that no one but Ettian is here to see the moment I break.

But before I can tip over the precipice completely, a pair of warm, rough hands slide around mine, pinning them gently against my knees. I stare at them, because the alternative is to meet Ettian's eyes and confront the fact that he's just leaned across the hold to comfort me.

I should tear myself away. Should remind him that there are two pilots at the fore of this ship who could check in on us at any second. Should hold the line I drew when we first came to the front, the line I've been daring him to step over ever since Wen shut me out of the *Torrent*'s operations and I had to invite Ettian back into my orbit.

But in this moment, we're too much the same to do anything but hold on to each other. We're trapped in the uncertainty of watching this battle plan we devised unfold, unable to do anything to affect its outcome. The only assurance we have is our own reckless confidence that the strategy will work. So I let out a long breath and give myself over to the sensation of his hands pressed carefully against mine. I can still pick out the calluses he earned on the controls of a Viper, still remember the echoes of the fantasies I had about that rough skin against my own. I push beyond the hook-in-the-gut instinct to chase those wanton thoughts and instead focus on the thought of how steady he flies with those hands.

How impossible it always used to be for him to steer us wrong.

My eyes, against all odds, drop closed, and I feel Ettian's breath sync with my own. Slow. Steady. Unrushed by the pixelated flickers of violence that chime tantalizingly beyond my eyelids.

This will work. I nearly flinch, realizing the voice in my head is my mother's. Are my palms going damp under Ettian's? Does he feel the moment my thoughts skew out of alignment with his own? I've been so careful these past few days, playing the perfect victim, the perfect terrified little prisoner, so bent out of shape about the general that I was willing to help Ettian concoct a battle plan to usurp Iral's command. I figured out all the points where our goals aligned and built myself a careful lattice between them.

It's too late for it to crumble now. I peek at the datapad through half-closed eyes, watching as runner after runner confirms safe landing on the frigid ice below. Within a minute of stable touchdown, their holds split and peel back to reveal their cargo. Massive surface-to-atmo cannons wheel up from the darkness within them, prickling against the sky like the sharpened blades they are.

When those cannons go hot and the second front of this battle opens, the rest is inevitable. When the *Torrent* and the remainder of the rear guard wink out of the black at the *Valiant*'s exposed flank, it's already over.

We've won.

I've won.

Archon's victory here could never be the messy bloodbath Iral would have inevitably led them into. It had to be decisive, overwhelming, unquestionable. And it had to be credited to Ettian emp-Archon, to establish his bloodright claim as legitimate, to prove this rebellion might truly be capable of reclaiming not only the system but the entirety of the Archon territories, uniting them under his throne. Claiming Rana through Tosa's cowardice may have been a fluke, but this victory legitimizes them as a worthy opponent.

One my mother will *have* to mobilize the Imperial Fleet to stamp out.

And yet. The triumph just won't *stick* in my heart the way I thought it would. Ettian's hands are still pressed carefully around my own, reminding me that no matter how good this outcome is for my own plans, it's the one he's been hoping for too. We were joined in anticipation of this moment, but now that it's here, it's impossible to ignore that we're on opposite sides once again.

On opposite sides—and *he's* the one who gets to wear this openly as a victory. Meanwhile I've just condemned a planet that was supposed to be my inheritance to Archon occupation. *It was mine to do with as I pleased, and this is how Ellit best serves me.* The thought was easy to stomach in speculation, but now it sours so much that I feel a genuine pang in my stomach.

It's a feeling I should be above. A feeling that *has* to be the fault of spending too much time around Archon leadership philosophy. It's not my obligation to serve the people of Ellit—it's the other way around. Has Ettian corrupted me so thoroughly already?

The warmth of his hands on mine is unbearable. I jerk back, and he immediately flinches away, his deep brown eyes going wide with surprise. I toss the datapad into his lap, twisting my cuffed wrists so I can tuck my hands safely in the pits of my arms, far from his comfort and the unbearable confusion it brings. "There," I mutter. "Your planet, Your Majesty."

Let the Imperial Fleet come fast. Let them rip through the Archon forces, pluck me from the wreckage, and take me back to the citadel's safety, where I can wash my hands of everything I did to get there.

Ettian's mouth slips open, but I'm in no mood to enlighten him on what's boiling over inside my head. I turn my shoulder to him, burning my gaze into the rivets of the Caster's rear door. Ettian gives me a second to decide this is what I really want to do. When it's passed, he rises slowly from the bench and slips back into the cockpit without another word.

The cold creeps in not long after.

CHAPTER 17

IT'S BEEN DIFFICULT to lose time during my imprisonment. Every second in platinum cuffs seared into my memory at the beginning of it and every day felt like another tally mark scratched into my skin.

But after Ellit falls—after I betray it—it feels like I blink and find myself aboard an open-topped truck, swept through the streets of the planetary capital in the midst of Ettian's triumph parade.

The parade's route takes us down a wide avenue, flanked by skyscrapers built tall and clad in elegantly curved metal that surely should have been stripped for use in starship construction after the planet ceded to Umber in the War of Expansion. Archon's waste of its resources never ceases to amaze me, but there's something oddly pleasing about the sight of something so strange, so *impossible* where I come from. A now-familiar ache pangs in my chest at the thought of how large this galaxy is and how much of it could still be new to me.

It's my first time out in public since the coronation, and I've been cleaned up for the occasion. My hair's been trimmed at last, after months of wild growth, and a team of artisans have dulled my dark circles and brightened my cheeks to lessen the impression that I've been living in a fugue state since Ellit fell. I've been dressed in well-tailored shirtsleeves, which have been rolled up so that the platinum cuffs are stark against my skin. I'm a little ashamed of how familiar their weight feels—even after more than a month at the front, I always felt incomplete walking out the door each morning without them.

My teeth are rattling nonstop, both from the vibration of the deflector armor strapped underneath my shirt and from the sonorous rumble of the imperial skin drums on the truck behind us. To everyone we pass, the victory rudiment they play is a new, joyous sound. For me, it's getting to be the hundredth time. I could probably replicate the rhythm myself, and that's saying something.

In the vehicle ahead of me, Ettian stands tall and triumphant, waving to the crowd that screams his name. He wears a truly ostentatious amount of platinum, much of it twisting around emeralds set into the seams of his suit. It's extravagant, but I'm barely begrudging him for it because General Iral is somewhere back with the rest of the officers, leaving the emperor to lead the procession—and claim rightful credit for the victory.

Unlike our last semipublic appearance together, this time I try to keep my eyes focused on the emperor alone. I don't want to see the faces of the people cheering for this victory—the victory *I* helped engineer. These people are supposed to be *my* people, and now they're wholeheartedly applauding their separation from the Umber Empire. I'm sure there are dissidents out there preparing to strike back, but none of them are stupid enough to show up to a parade like this.

At least I'm not the only one who's a little sour about the occasion. Wen's been installed as my guard today, standing at attention at my elbow. Her lips jut into the slightest of pouts as she surveys the parade route. "I listen to you and I get torn down," she mutters, barely loud enough to be heard over the drums. "Ettian listens to you and . . . this happens."

"Careful," I warn her, trying to move my mouth as little as possible. "Ettian needs this win. Save the criticism for when you're not in front of several thousand people."

Mentally I kick myself for that. Rumors of Wen's resentment could do work that I couldn't possibly achieve on my own. If Archon's precious little rogue knight is losing faith, what does that say about the state of the administration? But I also need to keep Wen from stirring up shit. She's fully aware that I enabled this victory—that I *encouraged* it. I've narrowly avoided her threat to put me out of the airlock, but I have to keep reminding her that digging too deeply into why might destabilize Ettian's reign, something neither of us can afford right now.

We process into an open plaza at the center of the city, where a platform with a podium on it has been erected. The parade vehicles unload as they move past it—first the emperor, then me and Wen, then the rest of the Archon officers. The crowd's noise swells appreciatively when Ettian mounts the podium, drops to low boos and hisses as I follow, then swells again when Iral steps up after me. This, too, is a careful calculation—one of my suggestions, in fact. With the gap in the noise, it's difficult to determine whether the emperor or the general drew more cheers.

It's the emperor who steps forward to the podium, after that—the emperor who will greet the crowd and proclaim this city, this continent, this planet *free* in the name of the Archon Empire. Which in itself is another victory, one that will cement Ettian's standing in his administration against the formidable shadow of Iral's reputation. I try to remember that as I cast a withering glance sideways at the cadre of new administrators he's about to introduce to their overeager subjects. The new planetary governor, a slim, tall woman with red-brown skin, looks a little queasy at the prospect, her gaze moving fast over the crowd.

I all but roll my eyes. These people have had *months* to prepare. Gods of all systems, they've even had a perfect model of government turnover with the way Berr sys-Tosa swept through this system seven years ago. They should be rigid and hungry, not anxious wrecks.

But if the Imperial Fleet's about to mobilize, maybe they're right to worry. Archon has won Ellit, but there's no telling how long they'll keep it once my mother's forces enter the game. If I can just wait this out, it won't be long until this world will be unshakably mine.

I switch my gaze once more to Ettian's back as Wen and I fall into place behind him. *On the day I replace you,* I vow to myself, *I'll show them all what it's supposed to look like.*

It takes a full fifteen minutes to get everyone in position onstage, but at least the drums go quiet after that. The deflector armor's still rattling around me, and I try to take a surreptitious peek at the battery levels. I was wheedled into attending this outing rather than rag-dolling on the floor of my room because I was promised protection. I just didn't realize my protection might depend on nobody getting long-winded with their speeches.

Ettian clears his throat, and the crowd's noise drops to a low hum as the speakers around the square send the noise echoing off the nearby buildings. "People of Ellit," he says—for with the cameras lined up along the front row, he's speaking to more than just those gathered in the fresh spring air of the capital city. "I do not come before you today as a liberator; I come as a servant."

I muscle my facial expressions into order as he delves into the prepared remarks. I've heard him run the whole speech twice now, and both times I didn't hold back with my muttering about how senselessly ineffectual it is. He's dithering on about how he's at his people's service, about how his leadership will be one of trust and communication, and I want to scream in his ear, "THAT'S NOT HOW GALACTIC EMPIRES WORK!"

But I hold my tongue. I stand, back straight, betraying no distress, staring out over the crowd with hard eyes that I hope read as resolute to the people watching carefully.

"I leave you with hope," Ettian says at last. His voice pitches soft, but the crowd leans in to hear it. "It's not a word we're used to hearing. It's not something we're used to feeling. For ten years, the Umber Empire has cropped our hope at the stem. We've fought to grow it back from whatever they left us. And now we'll show them just how strong our roots are. Just how deep they go. And just how much these worlds are irrevocably *ours*!"

He throws a fist in the air, and the roar of the crowd swells as if to catch it. For a glorious second, he *does* look the part of an emperor—proud of his conquest, fierce before his people.

"I stand before you today as the face of that hope. And I promise—"

Ettian cuts off on a gurgle that rings confusingly through the sound system. He cants suddenly backward before curling in over his stomach. His wide eyes blink once as he raises a hand to the front of his suit.

It comes away painted red.

The crowd's panic revs up like a starship engine—zero to screaming in the space of a blink. The guards around us surge forward, closing to form a wall of bodies around the young emperor as Ettian pitches backward again. Wen darts in to break his fall, her arms locking around his torso as she drops to her knees under his weight. She clings to him as the guards tear open his shirt, revealing the deflector armor he's wearing and the hole punched clean through it, all of them trying to make sense of the bloody mess unfurling over his stomach as if somewhere in it they can pinpoint the moment this afternoon all went wrong.

I stand on the edge of the chaos, completely forgotten for what might be the first time in my entire life.

My brain can barely process what's happening. I'm caught up in a flurry of sound and color, swaying slightly as the crowd's commotion starts to rumble the stage beneath my feet. But when my gaze catches on what looks like a rifle barrel slipping back behind a curtain on the upper levels of one of the nearby buildings, all that chaos falls away.

I'm moving before I can really comprehend that I'm moving. The numbness has flushed from my veins like someone's doused me in ice water. And no one tries to stop me. As I rip the platinum cuffs off my wrists and cast them aside, a series of large bangs go off on the edges of the square, sending the crowd scrambling for cover. I leap off the stage, landing in a haphazard roll that picks up enough dirt from the ground to drown out the obvious flash of my clothing. There's no time to look back, to see if anyone's going to stop me. I plow forward, joining the confused rush of bodies, my eyes fixed on the landmark of that window at the edge of the square.

Fear nips at my heels, but it's nothing compared to the fury yanking me forward. I charge heedlessly through the crowd, betting—perhaps a bit too optimistically—that everyone's too panicked to realize that the Umber heir just sprinted past them. I join the throng of people rushing for the streets that exit the square, but before I can get swept away, I duck into the alley behind the building I sighted.

Just in time to see a hooded person with a sniper rifle slung across their back drop from the fire escape.

They unholster their gun, whirling for the nearest set of garbage bins, but before they can get the lid open, I'm on them. The first punch catches the sniper by surprise and they go down hard. I follow, dropping to my knees and swinging again. This time they catch my hand—painfully, grinding the bones of my wrist together, and I bring up my other arm to block the inevitable retaliation.

It doesn't come.

"Gal?" the person mutters, astonished. They release my wrist.

If fury got me through the crowd, it's nothing compared to what unlocks now. I've felt this once before—that vicious, primal state I fell haphazardly into when the assassin tried to break into my rooms on Rana. But this time I go willingly, embracing every crunch of my bare fists against the sniper's face.

Go until I feel their nose give. Go until I feel my skin break. Go, even when a dull crunch sends a snap of pain rattling through one of my fingers.

Through it all, the person beneath me has gone limp, as if welcoming the beating. As if unable to do a damn thing about it.

My brain doesn't catch up to my actions until someone drags me off the sniper. They pin my arms behind my back, and I spit into the dirt at my victim's feet, seething through my teeth as another member of the emperor's security detail hauls them upright.

My rage flickers to confusion as I finally take a good look at the face I was dead set on ruining. It's a bloody mess, but a bloody mess I'd recognize anywhere.

Though her lips are busted and I'm pretty sure one of her teeth is missing, Hanji Iwam flashes me a grin.

CHAPTER 18

IT DOESN'T REALLY hit me until I see him.

The emperor's finally come out of surgery, but he's still unconscious and no one but his doctors is allowed in the room with him. Wen, the rest of his guard, and I have to wait in an adjacent viewing room, where we've got a clear view of everything and anything that might happen.

Which, right now, is a whole lot of nothing. A whole lot of watching his chest rise and fall, a whole lot of trying to divine any variation from the faint chirp of his heart monitor, and a whole lot of wondering if I'm fooling myself into thinking the ashen pallor of his cheeks is improving.

Ettian looks dead, and all at once the realization drops hard and heavy in the hollows of my chest. I don't want this. I never could have actually wanted this. The fantasy of strangling him seems downright childish when Ettian emp-Archon lies on the other side of a sheet of duroglass, hooked to a dozen instruments with a mess of tubes and bandages twining around his midsection.

A careful hand slips onto my shoulder, and I glance left to find Wen's burnt side. Her lips are snarled into a taut scowl that her molten skin emphasizes. All of a sudden I wonder what kind of care she got after the Cutter lieutenant shoved her into a thruster. From the wary uncertainty in her gaze, I'm guessing it wasn't anywhere near the dedication Ettian's received, and my heart aches for her a little.

Or she might just be worried about her prospects. She threw her lot in with Ettian, body and soul. She staked everything on his reign. Now he might slip away on the whisper of a breath, leaving her with nothing but a court full of people who doubt her and no meaningful reason to stay. The moment Esperza warned her about is here. Her whole life balances on whether Ettian pulls through or not, and there's nothing she can do to sway the way her fate will fall.

I know how she feels.

"How are your hands?" Wen asks.

I glance down. Most of the abrasions have been wrapped, but ugly bruises peek out around the white bandages. If I flex my fingers, they ache dully, but it's nothing, all nothing compared to—

"Gal." She shakes me, and I realize my jaw has locked up.

"One minor fracture," I mumble, wriggling the splint on my left hand's ring finger. If we were back at the academy, Hanji would probably gloat for days about the fact that her face broke a bone. I can't reconcile that Hanji—the strapping, cheerful tower tech—was the girl who sniped the Archon emperor yesterday. I didn't even recognize her until after I'd beaten her to a pulp. I swear her eyes were different.

Her eyes were mine. Hollowed by betrayal, honed by anger. Ettian's doing—of that I'm certain, because I know the feeling all too well. He's turned us into these bitter, vengeful little monsters, sharpening us until the only thing we're capable of is destruction.

I hug my arms against my chest, closing my eyes. I miss softness. I miss being a soft person. At the academy, I wore a different name and lived a different life. Gal Veres wasn't the kind of guy who'd break his hands on his friend's face. Gal Veres laughed and smiled and played all sorts of stupid pranks. He lived as if the idea of taking his throne was a joke he was workshopping, one that wasn't quite ready for the light of day.

I'm not sure when he died—on the day the rogue Wraith Squadron tried to kill him, or the day Ettian emp-Archon took him prisoner?

My eighteenth birthday was three days ago. I was so deep in the haze of Ellit's fall that I didn't realize. I've passed the metric that was supposed to mark me ready to begin my succession, and all I can feel is the numb certainty that I never could have been prepared for that, much less for what I'm facing now.

"Come with me," Wen says abruptly. Her grip on my shoulder tightens, yanking me toward the door. I balk, and her eyes narrow, flicking to the observation window and the devastating sight beyond it. "He's not doing anything anytime soon, Gal," she hisses. "And I don't care how many system gods you're praying to—staring at him isn't going to move anything along. Now, *come on.*"

With one last look at the shallow-breathing emperor on the other side of the glass, I let Wen drag me out of the room. Orderlies and guards alike duck out of our way as she leads me through the wide, sterile halls. Rather than stride down the middle, Wen sticks close to the walls, her eyes darting to the shadows and gaps and alcoves. I haven't seen her like this since the day I met her, when her worst nightmare was breathing down her neck on the streets of Isla. Wen is spooked. She's on her toes.

I'm all but expecting it when she yanks me suddenly into an empty examination room and hisses, "We have to leave."

"Not until he wakes up," I groan, rubbing my wrist.

"Not the building, dumbass. We have to get off this planet, off this world, out of this *empire*. You were right, Gal. Rust it all, I thought . . . I tried . . . I didn't think—"

Gods of all systems, so *this* is what it takes to break her. Her breath overcomes her words, leaving her choking on air and spit as she slumps back against the counter. All of the distance we've cultivated between us since Esperza's scolding collapses all at once. I catch her by the shoulder and pull her against me before her legs give out entirely, and she clutches the front of my shirt and shrieks through her teeth. The noise is twisted and feral and so *her* that it nearly rips my heart in half to hear it.

"Wen," I murmur into her hair. Her braid is tangled and snarled in places—she hasn't had a chance to unwind it since the attempt on Ettian's life. "Wen, hey, in and out, okay? In, two, three, four, out, two, three, four." As I chant the words, I pull my less-damaged hand slowly up and down the shell protecting her back. I don't know if she can feel the touch through the armor, but her breathing slows by hiccupping increments until she's following my count.

I go quiet and just hug her, half expecting her to yank away from me. But maybe she needs this, or maybe she's missed this, or maybe she knows I need it, too, because Wen Iffan's arms wind around my torso as she buries her half-burnt face in my shoulder.

She starts muttering something unintelligible, but I don't ask her to repeat it. Slowly her words stumble toward coherence until at last I can grasp them. "Millions of miles, trillions, billions, rust it all, I don't know how I ended up here. Isn't in my blood, isn't in my head, can't do anything right. I should have seen it coming, should have stopped it, should have done something to protect him—it's never enough . . ."

"Hey, no—you don't get to take the blame for it."

"It's the whole reason I'm *here*. And I failed, and if he dies, I have *nothing*, Gal," she spits. "And so do you, if Iral starts calling the shots. The general hates me—if he gets the chance, he'll turn me out. He's probably already planning on it while Ettian's out of commission."

"I won't let—" I start, but all that does is yank an explosive laugh out of her.

"*You* can't do anything! We're . . . This isn't sustainable. You were right. We need to get ready to grab what we can and run."

"I . . ." But I can't muster a response in the wake of the horror that overtakes me as I feel how *viscerally* my body reacts to Wen's words. This is what I've wanted all along. What I've been working toward for *months*. I set up all of the pieces, whittling away the support struts that kept Wen feeling bound to Archon's fate. All it took was one bullet to send the whole thing crashing down at last.

But I haven't been paying enough attention to my own footing.

Haven't had a chance to truly breathe since I catapulted myself off that stage. Haven't fully come to grips with why I shot off into the crowd like boltfire and instead of trying to disappear, to run like hell, to get free of the imprisonment I've been scheming to escape since the day the cuffs closed around my wrists, I ran straight for Ettian's would-be assassin and tried to beat her until her face was concave.

Now Ettian emp-Archon is clinging to life by a few threads, and rut it all—I can't run from that. But if I can't get the panic sparking in Wen's eyes under control, I might not have a choice in the matter.

"Listen," I start, trying to keep my reeling head far, far away from my tone.

Her gaze is darting wildly about, and I reach up to cup her face, meaning to get her to focus on me. She swats my hand viciously away before I can make contact with her burn, and I yelp, cradling my fracture against my chest and squeezing to try to tamp down the pain. Paradoxically, it works. For a moment, she's distracted enough by the immediacy of my reaction that her breathing starts to slow.

"Wen," I try again. "He needs us. We can't leave him."

"When has that ever mattered to you?" she mutters.

I hold up my still-smarting hand, look her in the eye, and wait for her to realize what a stupid question that was.

"That doesn't prove anything!" she snaps, the panic starting to overwhelm her again. "One dumbass move doesn't counter your entire upbringing. It's not even the first time you tried to beat someone's face in."

"Last time was because I was fighting for my life," I reply evenly. "This time was . . ."

"Was because you were fighting for your life," Wen argues. "Because if Ettian goes, both of us go with him. Which is why we need to get ready to run *now*. Even if he pulls through—" Her voice cracks, and her lips purse as if she's trying to bite back the sudden swell of emotions at the thought of the alternative. "Even then, he's out of commission. He's lost his seat at the table, which means the steerage of the Archon rebellion will go to General Iral. And Iral will rusting *kill you.*"

"What if we could hold him off?" I blurt. The idea's half-baked, but it's all I have to cling to. "Ettian's not out if we're still here to fight for him."

"We?" Wen asks, with justifiable suspicion.

"*I punched Hanji's face in,*" I remind her forcefully. "Obviously we're going to have to be a little more subtle than the last time we worked together, but you have your seat on the bridge. You could represent Ettian's interests—get him to endorse you as his official mouthpiece."

"Because *that's* going to go over well. The Corinthian street rat spouting Ettian emp-Archon's orders."

I scoff. "The *Archon lieutenant,* first of all, and it's going to be more elaborate than that. Wen, come on. Why don't you want this to work? Why are you so eager to run?"

She takes a step back, running one hand over the tangles of her braid. A soft laugh bubbles out of her that can't possibly be voluntary. "Because I've been here before. Because I didn't run the first time. In Isla, when a boss falls, there's a reckoning and a purge of their people, and the smart thing to do—the thing I couldn't do when I lost my mother—is get clear of it. Why are *you* so eager to wait it out and see what happens?"

I sigh, slumping back against the wall and burying my face in my hands. I can't exactly tell her, *Because the Imperial Fleet is probably on its way. Because I don't want Ettian to die. Because I thought I could abandon him easily to the fate he's earned, and turns out I can't even let someone get away with shooting him.*

There's a sudden commotion in the hall outside—or at least as much of a commotion as a well-run hospital is capable of producing. Murmurs echo down the halls, feet following in their wake, all of it moving toward the emperor's room.

Wen's eyes meet mine, reflecting the same combination of terror and hope that I know I must be wearing. We're out the door in an instant, racing side by side. My broken finger throbs with every step, but I push past the pain, skidding into the observation room a half a second behind Wen.

There's too much bustle going on to parse. Too many people shouting into comm lines, too many bodies blocking my view of the observation window. It's not until Wen turns around, tears welling in her brilliant brown eyes, that I fully grasp what's happening.

"We're in business," Wen says, cuffing me on the shoulder. "The emperor is awake."

It takes more than an hour for Ettian to get his bearings and, I'm assuming, less than ten seconds after that for him to do something extremely stupid.

"He's asking for you," an aide at the door says. Wen and I both perk up, and she starts to rise from her chair.

"No," the aide says, shockingly dismissive of the Flame Knight's capricious reputation. "You," she clarifies, pointing to me.

Wen and I exchange a glance. "Let him have what he wants," she mutters after a second, slumping back down in her chair. "He's gut-shot and drugged—we shouldn't be trying to rile him."

Right, I think, trepidation creeping up my throat as I follow the aide through the door. *Because if there's anyone notorious for not riling him, it's me.*

I feel the change in the air as I step into the room, its cool dryness washing over me, the electric hum of the life-support machines settling into my bones. Ettian emp-Archon lies at the center of their tangled tubes and wires like an effigy on an altar. His face is still ashen, but there's a spark in his eyes that only gets brighter when they lock on mine. He tries to lift himself, but only makes it about a centimeter up off the pillows before he collapses back down against them.

The sight of it makes me want to storm out of this room, find wherever they locked up Hanji, and punch her some more. "I—"

"I know," Ettian mutters weakly as the door closes behind the aide, leaving us alone in the room—or at least as alone as we can be when every inch of this place, right down to the emperor's heartbeat, is monitored. "Shouldn't have been you first. Spare me the tirade."

"I thought you liked my tirades." That gets me the barest smile I've ever seen him raise, but it feels like a victory rudiment starts up in my heart at the sight. "I get that you're drugged and confused, but gods—have some decorum. Try for a little subtlety."

"Heard what you did to Hanji," Ettian replies. "That doesn't exactly sound subtle either."

"No." I sigh. "Guess it wasn't."

And suddenly it sinks in with a totality so unfair that I nearly scream. He almost died. He got shot through the gut. He was bleeding out. And now here lies Ettian emp-Archon, held together with tubes and stitches and glue, dragging me into rooms that I have no business being in. Weak from surgeries, from the cocktail of medications keeping him from writhing in agony, but trying his damnedest to smile at my stupid jokes. He's the emperor of the reclaimed Archon territories, one of the most powerful men in the galaxy, my sworn enemy and jailer and the black hole my worst thoughts orbit.

And he's . . .

He's . . .

Before I know it, I've sunken hard into the chair at his bedside, burying my head in my hands. The faint, omnipresent beeping that's soundtracked the room grows more insistent as Ettian tries to reach over to me. I catch his hand before it finds my cheeks and the wetness starting to trail down them. His eyes have slipped closed. He doesn't know—but then again, he knows me well enough that he probably does. My hands falter as he takes them both, running his fingers over the splint on my broken finger with more gentleness than I could ever deserve. His fingers twist, trying to find their way into the spaces between mine, but I pull back out of his grip with a soft hiss.

"Gal," he whispers. "I'm so sorry."

"No apologies," I reply, as easy as breathing.

And that's just the thing. The thing I've been grappling with for months slotting into place, the thing that's felt like it couldn't possibly work suddenly clicking in an instant. We've always traded those words without a thought—I don't even remember when we started saying them or why. To me, it's always been a smug little reminder. *You don't need to apologize to me,* on the surface, but deeper than that, *I already know who you are, and I'm not gonna hold it against you.*

That last part's been in contention for a while now, but as the words settle over us, bringing a faint shine to Ettian's already bleary eyes, I'm starting to realize that I'm coming around on the issue. I can't begrudge Ettian for being Ettian, even when that means he's also Ettian emp-Archon. As long as he's alive. As long as he's safe.

My eyes drop to the mess of equipment doing its damnedest to keep him alive. "What *is* all this shit?" I ask, squinting at the fluid dribbling out of one tube and deciding in that same instant that I'm probably better off not knowing. "I mean, is this . . . permanent?"

Ettian shakes his head slightly. "I've been warned not to get too optimistic, but most of the machinery is there to hold me over until they can do the actual repairs. Which is a terrifying ruttin' thing to say about my internal organs, but . . . yeah."

I see the time it will take sprawled out in front of me, overwritten by the war's inevitable progress. Ellit has fallen, but now that Archon has made another gain, Umber will be shoring up to keep the system under their control. Berr sys-Tosa's forces are still holing up on Imre and around the gas giant Dasun. Both of those worlds are currently far-flung in their orbits on the other side of the sun. Meanwhile, word of Ellit's fall must have made it back to the Umber Core, and I'm certain the Imperial Fleet is already mobilizing. To press their advantage before reinforcements arrive, Archon will have to strike again hard and fast.

It's the worst possible time for the emperor to be out of commission.

Ettian's mouth has settled into a grim line, no doubt because he's thinking the same thing. "They're still formulating an estimate for how long it will take," he says, his eyes slipping to the readouts from the instrumentation at his bedside. I watch him watch himself living. Watch him weigh his health against his goals. Watch the weight of his determination knit his brow and hitch his heartbeat a tick faster.

"Wen and I were talking about what happens next," I tell him, low and urgent. It's probably not quiet enough to slip past the room's monitors, but at this point I don't really give a rut. "Just because you're bedbound doesn't mean this empire stops taking your orders. Wen can sit in for you. Enforce for you. I'll advise her. She'll keep me honest to your wishes, and I'll make sure she learns the ropes of governing."

Ettian eyes me warily. "You've changed your tune a little, haven't you?"

"Anything to keep my neck out of Iral's hands." I shrug.

"Hmm," he mutters, sinking deeper into his pillows.

There's a part of me that wants to argue, but the smarter part of me realizes his energy is waning. Before he goes completely, I tap him on the back of the hand, and his eyes twitch open. "Want me to get her?"

He gives the slightest nod, and I can't help the little thrill I get from understanding him so completely.

My hand's barely brushed the knob when the door wrenches open to reveal Wen Iffan wearing a smile so soft and weak that even with the obvious, unmistakable burn scar, I have a hard time believing it's her. I step out of her way, biting back a quippy remark about how eager she must be to see *me*. She's been through the same hell as me today, and she hasn't had the balm of the last five minutes to relieve it.

Wen crosses the room silently, dropping into the same chair I've just been sitting in. I expect her eyes to catch on the medical equipment that wreaths Ettian's midsection. It seems like the kind of puzzle her mechanical mind would instinctively start trying to untangle. But instead Wen only has eyes for Ettian's. Her lips keep working like she's trying to say something but the words just don't come.

All at once I remember the moment after the bullet struck. The moment I should have run and instead flew to Ettian's defense. I didn't realize it at the time, but I wasn't the only one whose true feelings were exposed in the heart of those panicked seconds. Wen should have been charging into the square to help clear the civilians, putting the safety of the citizens over the emperor's life like a true Archon soldier. Or throwing herself into action to get the incoming Ellit governors to safety before another bullet could find them. Or grabbing me before I made it off the stage and Archon lost its best shield in the chaos of the crowd.

Instead she caught and cradled Ettian, soaking her hands in his blood. I heard whispers as I was being dragged back to a safe zone and he was being medevacked away—rumors that she'd had to be pried from the emperor's side by General Iral himself.

Wen was supposed to be proving to Esperza that she valued more than just the emperor. Instead she all but screamed that his life was the only thing that mattered to her.

From the way she's looking at him now, I'm not sure she regrets it. She's aware of what she's done. If she were interested in repairing the damage to her reputation, she'd be off doing that. Instead she's here, like me. We've both said, "Rut it," and planted our flags squarely on Ettian. It's a declaration of war against Iral—and I can't think of any better battle to fight. With me and Wen on the emperor's side, Ettian still stands a chance of keeping control of his empire, and I still stand a chance of keeping my head attached to my shoulders.

So, win-win.

I hesitate as the silence draws long in the room. I don't want to break up the moment, but I can feel a prickle of jealousy digging into my sides at the sight of Ettian and Wen so comfortably sharing space. She spares the observation window no anxious glances. Wen doesn't care who might see her like this. She belongs at his side.

I never could.

With a sigh so soft neither of them could possibly hear it, I turn my back and slip through the door.

CHAPTER 19

THE WEEK AFTER we transition our operation back aboard the *Torrent* is long and boring, but it's made abruptly less so by Wen skidding through the door of our quarters one afternoon to declare that I have a date.

She escorts me to one of the lower levels of the command core, and I get my first look at what my life on this ship could have been—and what it *will* be, if Iral manages to overrule Ettian. This is the famous brig Deidra con-Silon was so keen on tossing my ass in, a cold, sterile place overseen by people I'm assuming are the coldest, sterilest soldiers aboard this dreadnought. We're led past a bank of sparse cells with clear fronts that seem more fitting for animal enclosures at a zoo. About half of them are occupied, populated with people I'm guessing are higher-level political prisoners. I try not to meet eyes as I pass them, but the ones I accidentally clock all wear the same expression of shock that slides easily into anger when they realize I'm walking free around the ship.

The brig guards lead us to an interrogation room that, at first glance, has a similar layout to Ettian's hospital setup—though I'm sure this observation window isn't a two-way street. Through it, I can see Hanji Iwam already installed at an interrogation table. She's got the nerve to sit with her heels kicked up, her arms folded, her head tipped back at a downright rakish angle.

I look at her and I think of summer afternoons, sprawled on the edge of the tarmac by Runway Three, passing a bottle of polish back and forth and sketching a scoreboard in the dirt to empirically rank our fellow cadets' asses. I think of late nights in the tower, a group of us playing a card game on the floor while Hanji lounged like an empress over all of us, her feet kicked up just like they are now and her hands swatting us away every time we tried to change the playlist to something that wasn't thirty years old. She was always smiling, always quick to jump in on a joke or a prank.

Apparently she's requested to speak with me—she's told her guards that they'll get full cooperation if I'm her interrogator. The idea would have been laughable just a week ago, but my splinted finger is making a pretty solid argument against dismissing the notion entirely, and with Wen keeping an eye on me, I guess the situation is palatable enough to allow. After a nod from one of the guards, I move to the interrogation-room door.

As I step into the room, I feel Wen's hand take root in the back of my shirt. The Flame Knight knows what happened the last time I got close to Hanji. She's right to worry about it happening again.

"Your Highness," Ettian's would-be-assassin says, still staring at the ceiling.

"Hanji."

At the sound of her name, she tilts her chin down, and I can't help the sudden, sharp inhale that fills my lungs. Her face is a marbled mess of bruising, both eyes swollen so much that I barely recognize her. My hands tighten into fists, sending a spark of pain along my fracture and a sympathetic ache kneading its way into my knuckles. "And the Flame Knight—I'm honored," she continues. "From the rumors that float our way on Imre, you're just as much the usurper's pet as dear Gal here."

I throw out a hand just in time to catch Wen across the chest. "Easy," I mutter.

She bristles. "I'm starting to understand why you cut loose on her face," she murmurs back.

Hanji raises a stiff eyebrow at us. "When'd you two get so friendly? Would have thought the new empire's most valuable prisoner and its most valuable player were kind of on opposite ends of the spectrum."

"Long story," I grumble as I set myself in the seat opposite her.

Hanji shrugs. "I've got nowhere else to be. Unlike some of us, Ettian doesn't let me walk around freely."

I give her a withering look. "Probably has something to do with the fact that I haven't shot him through the gut."

Hanji's smile stays, as ever, but her features darken. "See, that's the crux of the thing I'm trying to understand. Why isn't he afraid of you? You were always the foolish one, not Ettian. So why's he letting your leash get so long?"

Wen steps up to the table. "This isn't a two-way street," she says, looming over Hanji—a feat possible only because our prisoner is seated and cuffed to the table. "You're here to answer questions, not ask them."

"Look at you." Hanji leers, squinting at Wen. Belatedly, I realize she must not be allowed to wear her glasses or any sort of corrective lenses. "Ettian's little firecracker. What's your story?"

Wen straightens, her muscles going taut with wrath. But she's smart enough not to take Hanji's bait and snap back with something like, *I said no more questions*. Coaxing her into cooperation is going to take a clever hand and more than just gut reactions.

Still, the look on Wen's face would have almost every cadet at the academy pissing their pants. Hanji just smirks, her gaze shifting slowly and deliberately back to me. "Cousin."

"Dream big," I spit back.

She scoffs. "I may not have a title to flash around, but I do have blood ties to the Gordan System. We've got a great grandparent in common, dipshit. But I've got an older sister who's taking the bloodright and four vicious younger sisters who're intent on taking it out from underneath her. All I wanted was a cushy officer's appointment that would get me clear of that mess and give me a few dreadnought batteries to point at any of the little monsters if they try to come for me. And do you know what I got because of you, *cousin*?"

I tilt my hands as I shrug, making sure she sees the glint of the platinum cuffs around my wrists.

"Did Ettian ever tell you how he made it to Trost from the academy during the invasion of Rana?"

I give her a flat stare, Umber imperial for *no*.

"Ettian used me and Rin. Tracked us down during evac operations and told us he needed to get to you and he needed a big distraction to do it. We set off Ollins's fireworks, which was . . . not appreciated in the middle of that particular situation, let's just say. And that bit of dumbassery came back to bite us in a big way when our mutual friend decided to drop the fact that he was the ruttin' Archon heir."

Hanji kicks the table, straightening abruptly. I startle, then scowl—first because it brings a merry spark to Hanji's eyes and then deeper because I realize Wen didn't even flinch.

"I went down," Hanji snarls. "Rin went down. Ollins went down just for welcoming Ettian on the base when he landed. Hell, Rhodes even got busted for helping us make those goddamn fireworks. Ettian Nassun—Ettian *emp-Archon*—rutted over everyone he called a friend. None more so than you, if I may be so bold as to point out. But unlike you, we got held accountable for our failures right away. The four of us got handed guns and thrown to the front while you've been sauntering around a stolen dreadnought like you own the ruttin' place—"

I snap my fingers. And startlingly enough, Hanji Iwam—the very same Hanji I once saw mouth off to the academy head when he made a comment about her refusing corrective surgery for her eyesight—falls immediately silent. Her smile takes on a bitter tilt, and next to me, Wen makes a small, surprised hum. "Enough of that," I say as lightly as I can manage. "So you've been on the front for the past several months. Made your way to Ellit. And what, just took it upon yourselves to assassinate the emperor? Why *you*?"

Hanji's expression darkens, her lips pursing as if she's just swallowed a sour candy. "Berr sys-Tosa is a coward, but the nice thing about being a coward is that it teaches you how to stretch your resources. There's always got to be someone left over to throw in front of you when shit goes sideways. So he saves the pros for when he needs the pros. And for jobs like this, there's dipshits like us."

"And where's the rest of 'us'?" I ask.

Her gaze slips past me to the mirror at my back. "I would like to tell you, Your Highness," she says carefully. "But I would rather discuss the matter in a black box where our enemies aren't listening in on all sides."

"Am I not your emperor?" I ask, letting a dangerous edge bleed into the words. She let herself be silenced with a snap. She let me beat her to a pulp and didn't raise a single hand against me. She should be tripping over herself to answer my questions.

"You're the Umber heir, jackass," Hanji says. "But from what I'm seeing here, you're compromised by the enemy. I can respect your station, but I don't have to give up my friends' lives just because you snap your fingers at me."

I glance sidelong at Wen. "How hard would it be to set up a black box for the two of us?"

"I believe it'd be a little bit easier to start chopping off fingers," Wen replies stonily.

"Oh, come on, where's that stodgy Archon honor?" Hanji jokes.

"I'm Corinthian, longshot," Wen replies. I swear Hanji's tan skin grays slightly. "And your rusting ass can fry for what you did to Ettian, for all I care." She grabs me roughly by the shoulder. "This interview is over."

But when she yanks me out of the interrogation room and slams the door forcefully behind us, Wen is wearing a triumphant smirk.

And I'm wearing one to match. Sure, Hanji sniped and grinned and prodded every single button we have. And sure, it looked like Wen stormed out in a huff, dragging me with her. But she did so right after Hanji named her terms—and after she divulged that more of our classmates are out there, still plotting against us. Not only do we have the condition under which Hanji will talk, we also have the motivation that will guarantee it's met.

"Black box?" Wen asks with a nod.

"Name the time and the place."

Sometimes it astonishes me how quickly Wen's picked up the *Torrent*'s system. She's memorized every tree of the command structure and the exact levers it takes to shuffle them to her will, all while flying under Silon's radar. I'd assumed when she set out to get a black-box interrogation room set up, it would take a few days to shunt the request through the narrow tunnels of dreadnought bureaucracy.

It takes three hours.

Hanji's brows furrow when I walk into the new room unescorted. As the door closes behind me and I set myself gingerly on the uncomfortable metal chair opposite her, she tenses up, pulling cautiously at the cuffs that thread her through the ring in the center of the bolted-down table.

"Wen's the one you should be scared of, not me," I tell her, tossing a datapad down on the table. "I've already had my shot at you. She's still waiting on her turn." I push it in range of her cuffed hands. "Black box is set. Nothing goes in, nothing comes out. They've given me this datapad with root permissions unlocked. I'm giving it to you. You get to choose how much of this conversation we record and how much we don't."

Hanji's eyes brighten with obvious interest, but she waits until I've leaned fully back in my chair to scoop up the datapad. She fiddles with it for a few silent minutes, her clever tower-tech fingers dancing rapidly over the interface as she checks the processes running on it and throws out a few quick pings to confirm that we're locked up tight in here. Once she's satisfied with the security, she tosses the datapad carelessly back on the table.

"Up to your standards?"

"Well, if you start beating the shit out of me again, no one's gonna know," she says with a shrug.

This isn't the Hanji I faced off against just a few hours earlier, the cavalier sniper with her feet up on the table. Sure, that move was one hundred percent *her,* but she presented us with a single face throughout the entire interrogation. This is a few shades closer to the Hanji I left behind at the academy. The Hanji I *knew* beyond the cocky facade.

And she's scared of me—with good reason.

"This was your proposal," I remind her. "You said you'd talk if it was you and me in a black box."

"And you put it together suspiciously fast," she notes.

"Blame Iffan, not me."

"A Corinthian street rat gets shit done faster than a guy our classmates literally nicknamed 'The Negotiator'?"

"An Archon lieutenant gets things done faster than a literal prisoner, you mean?"

"Prisoner," she snorts. "Right."

I suppress the urge to object outright to her dismissal. I may wear cuffs on my wrists, but I've never set foot in this brig before today. I have to respect that distance if I want to get anything useful out of her. "Hey, you could do it too," I say slyly. "You might be smart enough to pull all the right strings."

Her gaze sharpens, and for the first time since I entered the room, she leans forward. "Sounds like you've been busy."

I shrug. "It doesn't look like much from the outside, but then again, that's the point of it. Most people in this administration think I'm so ineffective that it hardly matters whether they put me in chains or not. Everything that's happened since Seely and his Wraith Squadron tried to kill me has been either me stumbling into trouble or Ettian yanking me out of it. All they bother with is these"—I clink my cuffs together—"so no one forgets for a second what I am."

I swear I see a flicker of pity in her eyes, but it's gone just as quickly as I register it. "And what have you been doing with all of your apparent ineffectiveness?" she asks.

"Pushing here. Prodding there. Making sure Ettian's doubts are well fed. Wen's too." And sacrificing entire planets in the name of baiting the Imperial Fleet into this fight, but I'm not bringing that up just yet. "They don't see me doing it. They never look at the friction in their administration and realize it traces back to me."

Hanji nods. "So you've been busier than I gave you credit for. I'll let you slide on that. But then there's . . . this." She points two fingers at the mottled mess of her face. "If I'm going to trust you to take the information I tell you here and *not* run it back up to the people holding your chains—if you're really on my side here—why the rut did you try to beat my face in?"

"A moment of weakness," I tell her, which is as honestly as I can frame it anyway. And because no one's watching, I sigh and slump in my chair and rest my head in my aching hands. "Remember that night in the cantina on Trisu? When you caught me looking and then needled me nonstop until I admitted my feelings for Ettian went a little deeper than 'roommate and best friend'?"

I peek up at her between my fingers. Hanji, too, has loosened a little bit, her stare gone somewhere far beyond me. I think for a second we're both propelled back into a galaxy where I wasn't a prince, neither of us had seen a war firsthand, and my feelings for Ettian were the fragile, hopeful, harmless beginning of something.

"You were the first person I ever told. You know how long this has been going on. And you put a bullet in him. Not even boltfire—a ruttin' bullet."

Hanji sits with that for several agonizing seconds, her tongue probing the inside of her cheek. *It's not enough,* my brain screams at me, and I have to force my expression to hold steady. Nothing gets done until she understands why I tried to beat her senseless—and decides that despite that, she can still trust me. "That whole day is a blur for me now," she says at last. "Which might be because of the head trauma, I dunno. But I look back at the moment I was lining up that shot and I wonder why I didn't go two feet higher with it. I wonder if I could have, and I just . . . didn't."

"Well, you almost got the job done anyway," I reply drily. And then, because I can't help my morbid curiosity—"You were a tower tech. You always said you were happiest directing the action from a distance. How'd *you* turn out to be the one who took that shot?"

"It's like I said." Hanji sighs. "After the academy head let Ettian slip through his fingers, he needed scapegoats. He found the four of us—me, Ollins, Rin, and Rhodes. I mean, we'd spent the past three years making as much trouble as we could humanly manage while still passing our classes. So the bastard was thrilled, of course, that he could set us up to take the fall."

It's hardly a surprise that they all fell together. The four of them operated as a single unit of mayhem throughout our time at the academy. If one was clearly complicit in something, it was always a safe assumption that blame fell equally on the other three.

"See, I meant what I said about Berr sys-Tosa being smart about his resources. He had four kids who knew the Archon usurper better than anyone else in his grasp, had nearly three years of academy training under their belts, and worked together like a pack of demons. So he put us under the supervision of a man we only ever knew as the Quartermaster. And the Quartermaster threw us into every single hell he could find at the warfront, waited for us to accomplish whatever task he'd set us to, and scooped up the pieces. But there were always two grander tasks—the reasons our little squad was put together in the first place. The first got me chained to this table. The second's staring me dead in the face."

It takes me a full second to realize what she's implying. "Well, this is some rescue," I scoff at last.

"Isn't it?" she asks, looking far too pleased with herself. "For months, no one could even get near you. And now we're in a black box together."

I force my eyes to brighten. Force myself to lean in just enough to make her ease back. Play it like I'm eager to get the rut out of here, like I didn't just talk Wen down from tucking me under her elbow and running barely a week ago. "And what's next?" I ask around the shape of a wolfish grin.

She beckons for the datapad, and I hand it over. "I'm going to tuck an extra line in the comments of one of your config files. Do you know what that means?"

"Come on, I sat next to you in comms tech."

"Yeah, and that class was right after morning drills. I remember your snores."

"Just stick it in and tell me what to do."

Hanji fixes me with a stare. For a second, I'm not sure what she means by it, but then she wiggles her eyebrows and I nearly smack her on the shoulder.

"Rut *right* off, Iwam," I grumble.

"Yeah you'd like that, wouldn't you?"

"I can't decide if I wish I was more related to you or less."

She snorts, and for my part I can feel the laugh building inside me—the release I've needed so badly ever since the bullet bent Ettian in half. The fact that I'm sharing it with the girl who shot him only makes me want to laugh harder at what a mess my life has become.

"Okay, but seriously," she says, tamping down her smile. "I'm encoding this with a Nazyalensky cipher. Decoding it will get you the frequency of my squad's secure line. It's up to you to figure out how you're going to broadcast, but if you need to talk through some options, well. You know where to find me. Once you make contact with them, I'm sure you can make all sorts of magic happen." She makes like she's going to pass the datapad back to me, then hesitates.

My heart stutters, certain I've just given something away.

"I . . . I get that I'm stuck here," Hanji says, staring down at the screen in her hands—or maybe at the cuffs rubbing red circles on her wrists. "I don't expect you to change that. Like I said, I came here with two missions. I'll settle for completing one."

With that, she slides the datapad back across the table. I take it, half expecting it to burst into flames in my hands.

All my life I've been told that my people exist to serve me—that my will is the gravitational center of their orbit. It's one thing to see it in action among the guards assigned to me at the academy, who entered the service knowing full well what it may entail. It's another thing entirely to see that sacrifice coming from a girl who was pressed into service by Berr sys-Tosa for her ties to Ettian. I once considered Hanji one of my closest confidantes, and now I have to watch her resign herself to Archon custody—a custody she might not survive, given that she put a bullet in their emperor—for the sake of my potential escape.

It weighs me down like a stone around the ankle even after I've exited the black box and handed the datapad off to Wen. "Nazyalensky, in one of the config files," I tell her, praying the words stick in my throat and hating myself when they don't.

CHAPTER 20

THERE USED TO be a precarious balance to the *Torrent*'s bridge. Iral's grandeur weighed against Ettian's greenness. Silon's prim, proper hand countered Esperza's improvisational whims. I snuck in for as long as I was allowed, and Wen sat on the fringes, watching and learning as best she could.

Now she's taken Ettian's place at his station, and she's doing her damnedest to hold the floor as the balance tips inexorably toward Iral.

"This empire cannot afford to wait for its ruler to heal," the general thunders. "We have a window—an opportunity to drive Umber out of the former core once and for all."

Wen grits her teeth. She *knows* that, but Ettian's made his expectations clear. "The emperor's orders are to hold the line until he's back on his feet—literally," she says with as much firmness as she can muster. Her gaze flicks down to me for backup, and I throw her back a wide-eyed *What do you expect me to do about it?* look. If she's looking for a better advocate for the emperor's wishes, she's not going to find one in me.

If it weren't for the political situation, I'd agree that, from an

Archon perspective, holding back the war for the sake of Ettian's recovery is stupid as hell. Every point Iral has raised in this debate is completely valid. The rebellion's next strike will be on Imre, Berr sys-Tosa's unofficial capital, the roots that hold him in this system. Knock them out and Tosa's reach is all but claimed for Archon, which means the Imperial Fleet must be screaming on its vector from the Umber Core to put a stop to all of this. The system governor's advantage only grows the longer Archon waits to launch the offensive. If it were a fleet under my command, I'd be on his heels already.

But we can't do that under Iral's leadership. At least, not without putting up a fight to remind him where true power lies.

"True power" lies in a hospital bed with a hole in his gut, I hear my mother snidely remark. I shut out the echoes of her voice in my head. I can't lose sight of the fact that I won't survive to see the Imperial Fleet arrive if Iral ousts Ettian from the seat of power.

That isn't true.

I don't want to think about how it isn't true—how I've been given two outs back to back and taken neither. First Wen tried to cut and run and I talked her down. Then Hanji gave me the line to the rest of her squad and I turned it over to Wen. I jam my thumb against my broken finger and try to center myself in the dull, throbbing pain. We need to focus on keeping Iral's power in check, which in turn keeps my head on my shoulders and keeps Archon from gaining any more ground in this war.

It would be easier if Esperza had our backs, but the commodore's stayed on the fringes of the argument, fidgeting disinterestedly with her metal fingers and contributing little. I suspect she falls more on Wen's side than on Iral's, but she doesn't want to undermine her standing in the general's eyes by appearing to favor her protégée.

Wen can't call her out on that and Iral won't. So I guess the task falls to me.

"Commodore, you've been quiet," I say, cutting through the cyclical prattle bouncing back and forth between Iral and Wen. "It's *your* fleet the general would be committing to this assault—surely you have some input."

Esperza glances up at me coolly, her prosthetic's fingers curling and uncurling with steady, practiced precision. "The 'nottie fleet under my command is resupplying after the Ellit offensive. We've lost one ship entirely in the initial attack, and sustained damage to the others that still needs to be repaired before they can be cleared for combat. We've also added two of the blockade dreadnoughts to our number, but converting and outfitting them is only adding to the strain. With more time, we'd be able to space out our depletion of our new acquisition's resources, which ultimately would be better for the cohesion of our reborn empire. On the other hand, I'm wary of an ill-planned strike. But for the battle strategy, of course, I defer to my general. If he believes it possible, I'm bound by rank to follow his orders."

Wen stiffens. "But the emperor—"

"Is not here," Iral replies, the harshness of his words ringing off the walls of the bridge. "And rather than consulting with his established leadership, he's shoved you forward to make his demands." He leans forward over his station, his eyes steady and intent on her. "Lieutenant Iffan, what is it *you* want here? What do you possibly have to gain from being Ettian emp-Archon's mouthpiece?"

And for the third time, I watch Wen grapple for an answer that isn't there. These past months, she's been scrabbling to gain just a shred of legitimacy in the eyes of the Archon administration. She thought the formal rank would help. Then she thought it would be enough to distance herself from me and prove she could stand on her own. But despite all that, she's crumbling—because the only thing she ever wanted to do was protect Ettian, and she couldn't even do that.

Now the reckoning of Iral's scrutiny has settled on her shoulders. So Wen draws herself up straight and says, "I'm a servant of the Archon people, same as you. I want to fight for their freedom from Umber tyranny, same as you."

"And yet you're obstructing that very goal, all so the emperor can feel like he's a part of it."

"What more can I do for this empire than what the emperor asks of me?"

To my surprise, Iral rocks back, ingesting those words with worrisome seriousness. He reaches down to his station, fingers skimming for some piece of data that he finds and, with a familiar motion, passes it over to Silon at the center of the bridge. The captain looks up at him in alarm the second she registers what he's sent, but Iral only gives her a steady nod.

A projection flares to life over her screens. But instead of a battlefield or a fleet layout, this offers only an image of a room that looks something like a lab. In its center stands—

No.

No, it's not possible. They're supposed to be *gone*. Eradicated. They were all destroyed at Knightfall.

But in the middle of this room, splayed out like it's just waiting for someone to step into its embrace, is a powersuit. A few technicians bustle around it, but the checks and tests they seem to be performing have a perfunctory air to them that locks in my terrible gut feeling. This thing is fully operational.

"If you want to protect our empire, do it the way you're best suited for," Iral says.

Did he say "empire" or "emperor"? Because I swear I heard the former, but Wen's face looks like she heard the latter, and it seems to be tearing her down the middle. I can all but hear the vicious line of thought carving through her mind. She sees the armor and immediately her memory goes back to that day on Ellit and the bullet that tore through Ettian's stomach. She remembers holding him in her arms as he bled out, powerless. She remembers the day she failed to protect him and the quiet vow she made to never fail like that again.

She imagines how easy it'd be to keep that vow in a suit like this.

And she knows. She knows exactly why Iral is laying it at her feet now—why he's clearly been *preparing* to lay it at her feet now when he's obviously had the suit for much, much longer. If she puts on the suit, she steps away from this bridge, this position, from all the things she's carefully built in the time since she came aboard the *Torrent*. She goes back to being the emperor's wildcard instead of Esperza's handpicked protégée. Wen tried to elevate herself in the eyes of Iral, to earn his respect as a leader.

Now he's telling her in no uncertain terms that her place isn't with the emperor's administration—it's out in the field, a sword in hand.

My mind goes a step further, to the inevitable end of every single suited knight Archon ever threw out onto the field. Knightfall came for them all. My *mother* came for them all.

I know what her answer will be a second before she makes it. I'm whisked back to a night not long ago, a night when I lay in a dusty vent and tried my best to pick her apart—and still couldn't break the longing in her voice as she danced around naming exactly what she craves.

I see the echo of that longing in the look she's giving the power-suit right now—like it's everything she's never dared to want out loud.

"I'll do it," the Flame Knight says.

It takes twenty minutes to get her into the suit. Even with the metal flexing around her with eerie intelligence—intelligence that speaks to how sophisticated these machines are and why they've never been replicated since Knightfall—she needs extra hands to build her into it. They say this process will get easier the more she does it. That the suit will learn to embrace her, and she'll learn to embrace it in turn.

I watch it slowly consume her, wishing I knew how to stop any of it. As each of its joints comes online, they wrap around Wen's body with a possessiveness I find absolutely nauseating. When her head disappears into the chest piece and the helm snaps down over it, my heart sinks. I've lost her. She had the nerve to go and become someone in my life worth protecting, and now that she's committing to reviving the legacy of the Archon knights, there's nothing I can do to save her. The moment she steps onto an active field, she'll be blown to dust.

But right now, I'll admit, it looks like nothing could possibly take her down. She wears the armor like a second skin, striding off the mounts in a fluid step that surprises her so much that she freezes. A few of the technicians reach up as if they could possibly steady her five-hundred-pound mass, but she waves them off, a muffled laugh echoing from somewhere in the suit's chest. Wen straightens and flexes her biceps, dancing along the thin line between looking like a kid puffing out her chest and a steel-wrapped god.

Esperza and Iral stand on the sidelines, and for once they both wear the same expression, torn between the grief of what's been lost and the awe of this moment where it seems like they could get it all back. Ten years after Knightfall, a suited knight stands before us. Ten years after he lost his lover and she lost her best friend, a new hope has risen to take their places. I'm sure it's touching for Archon. I might even be moved—if I wasn't certain the only way this ends is with Wen in smithereens.

She takes another couple of steps, her confidence blooming with each stride. I'm almost certain she's about to start skipping, but then she seems to remember something else. Wen halts in the middle of the room, turns her palm upward, and peers curiously at the mechanism situated there.

"Now, hold on," Iral says with a degree of panic I'd find laughable if it weren't for the way several of the techs ducked back just now. "The safest way to start using those things is in a zero-g environment. Not something for the lab—got it?"

The powersuit tilts its head in a way that so clearly reads as *Sure, Dad* that I have to hide my mouth behind my hand to keep from grinning. Before anyone else catches the gesture, Esperza steps forward and the room's attention swings to her. "With permission, sir, I'd like to be the one to take her out."

Iral looks Wen up and down, and for the first time I realize this goes even beyond seeing the suited knights resurrected again. This suit, as I understand it, was dug from the rubble of Torrance con-

Rafe's headquarters by the general himself. It's not just his lover's legacy that stands before him—Rafe was literally the last person to wear this powersuit. Iral is usually a stone wall, not a hint of softness in him, but now there's a sheen in his eyes that it looks like he might need time to process.

"Permission granted," he says with a stiff nod.

Less than ten minutes later, we're streaking out of the *Torrent*'s maw in a Beamer—Esperza at the helm, me in the copilot's seat, and Wen sealed in the back hold. I'm sitting rigid, strapped in with all my harnesses double-checked, mired in memories of the terrifying ride that ensued last time Esperza took me for a spin in a Beamer. Of course, that had been when she was trying to bully us into lowering the ship's price, but I'm still watching for the moment she tries to throw the blocky little shuttle into a loop it clearly wasn't designed for.

"All right, we're coming up on our designation," Esperza announces over the ship's comm. "How's your breach sealing?"

"Oxygen levels look good," Wen replies. I glance down at the camera feed from the hold to catch the thumbs-up she gives us. "The suit says I'm clear for vacuum."

"Suit's probably right," Esperza says with a smirk. "Okay, I'm giving you a three count and then dropping the ramp. Sound good?"

"Sounds good," Wen says. I'm not sure if the tremor in her voice is more nerves or excitement, but it's definitely some combination of the two. On the hold feed, she squares up, facing the rear, and leans forward slightly as Esperza flips our rotary thrusters around and starts decelerating the Beamer.

"Your Highness, if you would be so kind," Esperza mutters, nodding to the ramp controls on my side of the console. I didn't realize I was here as anything more than deadweight, but Esperza returns my bug-eyed stare with a look that tells me she's not asking twice. "Three. Two. One."

I consider not doing it. Putting my foot down and declaring that

I won't unleash her on the galaxy—and pointedly not mentioning that I won't unleash my mother on her. But I see the way Wen's poised to leap and I know that in the powersuit, she could blow clear through the hold's wall if anything tried to stop her.

I jam down the button, the ramp drops, and the audio feed from the hold goes silent as the vacuum rushes in. There's a pinch of a sharp inhale on Wen's line that shifts to a long, slow exhale as she realizes her suit's seal is holding.

"Ready when you are, kid," Esperza says as the Beamer's deceleration zeroes out.

On the video feed, Wen rocks back on her heels, then throws herself forward, diving straight out of the rear hatch. Certain by now that Esperza's not going to take my head off for acting like a proper copilot, I reach up again and switch our displays over to the camera streams from her helmet. Wen falls away from us, slowly turning end over end. The massive specter of the *Torrent* looms in and out of the corner of her vision, and the sight of it alone gets my stomach churning. But Wen's a pilot through and through—on the readouts I see her heart rate settle where mine would only be skyrocketing.

"All right, start with the palm thrusters," Esperza calls into her comm. "*Gently—*" she adds a second too late.

Wen pulls her triggers hard and sends herself spinning ass over teakettle as the miniaturized thrusters in her hands fire at full capacity. Her arms are wrenched up over her head, the suit stiffening dynamically to keep them from snapping off from the force that pirouettes her through the void.

"Gods of all systems, she's gonna black out," Esperza mutters, glancing helplessly down at the controls under her hands. I realize too late that I should have seen this coming—Ettian had a near-identical experience when he introduced Wen to flying in zero-G. They spun out, and he was barely able to wrench the ship out of it in time.

Now she's in a powersuit, completely untouchable, and spinning unstoppably away from us.

But just as I'm about to start yelling out suggestions, Wen twists one wrist, the suit's reinforcement reading the intention of her motion and lending its own power to help her wrench it around. With a series of quick bursts from the thrusters, she slows herself until she's turning pendulously, and—*gods, of course*—quietly chuckling to herself through the comm.

"Okay, very funny." Esperza sighs. "C'mon—if you've really got a feel for it, prove it to me."

Wen evens herself out with a few quick bursts from her palms. I pull up a feed from the Beamer's rear camera to get a wider view of her, finessing the controls until I've got her aligned in the frame.

A second later, she lowers her hands to her sides, pulls her triggers, and catapults out of the shot.

"*Iffan,*" Esperza yelps.

As if that's going to stop her. I whip the camera back and switch to infrared, zeroing in on her rapidly fading heat signature. She's streaking straight for the *Torrent,* her internal cameras pointed downward to catch the furious burn of the thrusters attached to her arms. From the look of it, she's trying to max out her acceleration—and doing quite well at it. There's just one massive, hulking, looming problem.

"Wen, look up." I sigh into my comm.

If I sounded like I was trying to give her an order, I doubt she would have paid me any attention. It's an old trick I learned from Hanji—a failsafe for wrangling even the most unruly pilots from the tower. It works like a charm. Her helmet cams whip forward to find the sheer, unyielding hullmetal of the *Torrent*'s flank approaching at a rate edging from worrisome into inevitable.

"Rocks," she chokes, wrenches her arms forward, and leans like she's pressing against an invisible wall to brake until her speed burns off. "Didn't think I was that close." She lets out a nervous chuckle.

"Think about it in terms of mass," Esperza says. "Those little engines in your hands were designed to shunt starships around—things that weigh tons. You weigh about five hundred pounds in that suit. But that thing is also engineered to keep you from feeling the impact of accelerating like that. I don't get the physics of the inertial dampening going on, but I'm sure you feel the end result."

"Barely feels like I'm moving at all," Wen murmurs wondrously. Her cameras shift down to her feet. "Gonna try the boot thrusters now."

This time she's careful to point herself away from the *Torrent,* using quick bursts from her palms to get her body oriented along the vector she wants to follow. Once she's aligned, she presses gently on the triggers. Twin flares ignite from her heels, and she sways unsteadily as she tries to settle herself on top of the force they produce.

The more comfortable she gets, the more I want to melt into the seat. Wen's shakiness is quick to bleed away. Once she's sure of the boot thrusters, she jams her triggers down harder, throwing herself as fast as they'll let her go. Then she tries to throw the palm thrusters into the mix, using them to push herself into long, curving arcs. There's a certain threshold she vaults over after a matter of minutes—the point when she goes from looking like a kid clomping around in her parents' shoes to a terrifying echo of the footage of Archon suited knights. She's moving at starship speeds with an agility that starships could never hope for, and even though she lacks the finesse of her priors, the sight of her gamboling against the stars is enough to chill my blood. I'm not sure what's worse—that Archon is about to field a new vigilante, one who's already built a reputation for reckless destruction, or that the newest suited knight, whom my mother will no doubt kill in an instant, is one of the few people in the galaxy I can call a genuine friend.

To make matters worse, a hail pops up from the *Torrent*. I ignore it, forcing Esperza to reach across me from the pilot's seat and open the line. I expect a voice, and startle a little when instead a frenetic drumbeat blasts out of the cockpit speakers.

I've spent months living in the Archon rebellion. In that time, I thought I'd grown familiar enough with the standard rudiments they use, from the triumphant rhythms pounded out on massive skin drums to the gentle pulse of the morning rounds. But this beat is completely unfamiliar—a thought my pilot, who's slumping back in her seat with a hand over her mouth, clearly doesn't share.

"I don't know this one," I say, pitching it halfway to a question.

"It's been ten years since anyone had reason to play it," Esperza replies, scrubbing her knuckles over her cheeks. She leans over me and patches the line through to Wen. "This rudiment is the herald of a suited knight."

All we get in return is a slight hitch of breath from her end of the line, but in that hitch I hear everything. Wen's hearing herself *recognized* for the first time in this administration—and recognized for something she did independent of Ettian emp-Archon. In that little intake of breath, I learn a truth that pile-drives me into my seat with the force of a Viper engine. Outside, Wen throws a pirouette into her vector, and I swear the drums beat louder for her.

Nothing I say or do, nothing I could ever offer her, could possibly get her out of that suit. This is the belonging Wen's been searching for. The spot she feels she's meant to fill in the rebellion. She wanted to be big—the biggest thing in the galaxy.

But all I can think of is how small she looks against the *Torrent*. How little that suit is going to protect her from the battle to come. And if Wen goes down, there's no one left who can keep me alive.

The dread inside me builds to a feverish pitch until the hammering of my heart matches the frantic rhythm of the Archon drums.

CHAPTER 21

"We're rutted," I announce, blowing into Ettian's hospital room like a ship dropping from superluminal. "We're completely and utterly—why are you up?"

He's not just up. He's *up* up, standing on two feet, braced against his hospital bed with one hand as he hastily tries to wrestle his robe shut with his other. Through it, I catch the brilliant white flash of a fresh bandage that encircles his midsection.

"The painkillers must be making you extra stupid," I snap, lunging across the room and grabbing him by the shoulder as gently as I can manage. He lets me pivot him so he can lean back on the bed, but only perches himself on the edge of it. "The rut are you thinking, trying to stand?"

I expect the glare he fixes me with to be glazed by medication, but it's sharp enough to cut. "Like you said, we're rutted. I'm not going to take that lying down."

"Yes, you rutting are," I reply with a steady but insistent push. Ettian cants back onto his elbows and raises his eyebrows. "You've got a goddamn *hole* in your gut."

He tries to sit up again, but the motion isn't kind to his wound. I can all but feel the spasm of pain that contorts his face. "I don't need you nannying me. I was *up,*" he groans, slumping back on the bed. A furious sigh wheezes out of his nostrils.

"You were about to kill yourself."

"I can't sit by. I can't wait and watch my empire go to war without me."

"Well, you're gonna have to, thanks to Hanji."

"Thanks to *you,*" he hisses venomously, hands flapping as if to illustrate his helpless state. His eyes pinch shut in frustration. "I'm missing it. I'm missing . . . *her*."

"You're missing Wen, who is *also* trying to kill herself on behalf of this rutting empire," I correct. "And you're not missing much. She's just doing loop-de-loops outside the *Torrent* and people are losing their minds."

"I saw the footage," he murmurs, holy reverence in his voice.

Briefly, I consider his perspective. He would have been seven years old at Knightfall—an all-too-impressionable age for that sort of thing. The fall of the Archon Empire was the greatest galactic tragedy of his lifetime, but Knightfall must have been the first to scar, the first he remembers in vivid detail. Combine that with the fact that Archon children seem to have been raised on a steady diet of ridiculous knight stories, and it's understandable how worked up he is over all of this.

Is it sympathetic?

Not in the slightest.

"Iral showed me the powersuit, you know," Ettian continues, relaxing more thoroughly into the hospital bed. "Back on Delos. He thought there wasn't enough faith in Archon heroes to ever field a suited knight again. And there was his personal history with that particular suit on top of that. I thought he'd never give it away—and *especially* never give it to Wen."

"Well, your orders went and made her enough of a nuisance that he decided to dupe her into painting the biggest target in the galaxy on her back."

"That's not what it—"

"And ruttin' Esperza's endorsed it too—she all but primed her for it, telling her all those stupid knight stories. I've never seen the general and the commodore agree on something so painlessly, and it's offering Wen Iffan up for my mother to shred, and you're *fine* with that?"

Ettian sighs, his lips pursing as he stares up at the ceiling.

"You wanted this for her?" I press.

"I wanted to be there for her when this happened," he murmurs at last, his eyes starting to glimmer softly in the low light. "We both knew it was the path she was on. I never told her about the suit, because I didn't want Iral to be her enemy and I didn't want him to feel like she was trying to wheedle the suit out of him."

I stop short of tearing my hair out, but only just barely. "Fine, setting aside the whole goddamn knight thing, you know why Iral gave her the powersuit, right? He did it to take away your voice at the table so he can advance this campaign on his terms alone. And you're just going to let him have that?"

"I was *going* to return to the table myself, but you seem oddly against that for someone so concerned about my capacity to run my empire adeptly."

"I'm . . ." I feel myself swerve abruptly away from the truth I was about to blurt out loud. It's a truth I've already expressed, a truth my broken finger's more than enough to testify. But still, speaking it—saying it to his face, these words I've expressed too well with actions—is too much for me.

I'm concerned about you. And now, with the Imperial Fleet almost certainly on its vector, I'm terrified of what's about to happen to this rebellion. If I can just get clear of the Archon fleet, get *Ettian* clear, let Iral burn like he should have years ago—

"I'm almost one hundred percent certain you wouldn't even make it to the table," I finish flatly.

"So then what? You want to run? Because as I'm sure you've observed, I'm in no shape to do that either." Ettian makes a low groaning noise, one hand drifting up to the edge of his bandages and fussing with it. It's only been three weeks since the doctors patched his insides back together. If he pushes himself too far in this stage of his recovery, he might set himself back even further. "I've seen the news cycle. There were plenty of cameras in that square. Everyone knows I'm weak—"

"Well, they knew that before," I mutter, forgetting for a second that the point is to calm him down, not rile him up again.

"Rut off—everyone knows I'm weak after the attempt, which means they won't be expecting me to return to the front with a show of force. If I can make *that* my image—"

"Not likely."

"*Gal.*" He sighs.

"Which one of us has been trained from birth to lead an empire?" I ask. If I can't jab him in his physical wound, I'll lance right through the emotional one. Ettian started out on the same path as me. Though we've never sat down and hashed out exactly where our childhoods aligned, it's a fair assumption that his secret upbringing was shaped by the same sort of education. But where mine ran its course successfully—at least for the first seventeen and a half years of it—Ettian's was cut short at ten. "As far as the galaxy knows, you're a puppet Iral's trotting out to give his rebellion some legitimacy. You're not essential. Did your people even mourn you?"

"I . . ." I can see him grasping, eyes blinking rapidly as he recalls the newsfeeds he ingested. Of course his people mourned him. Of course they despaired to see their young emperor gunned down.

But I need him doubtful.

"What difference do you make when you sit at that table?" I press, leaning forward to loom over him.

His brows knit. For a brief, optimistic moment I think I've finally gotten through to him. Gotten him to start actually *thinking* about what he's doing.

"Ever since I revealed that signet ring to the galaxy, I've had a little voice in the back of my head," Ettian mutters. "It whispers all my worst thoughts. It only ever tells me that I'm doing this all wrong, and it never actually helps me figure out how to do it right."

His eyes slip over to mine, and my chest tightens in anticipation. "You always say the same things."

His gaze pins me like a vibrosword through the chest. I can hear my own little voice—my mother's voice—daring me to stand my ground. *Don't give him an inch,* she urges me. *He should have seen through you ages ago, and the fact that he didn't means he was never a fit ruler.* He gave me nothing to fight back with, and I figured out a way to fight back anyway. Deidra con-Silon clocked me from the get-go, and he never listened to her. I'm an enemy prisoner. My goals were never his. It's his own damn fault he never saw it.

And yet the words "I'm sorry" linger in the back of my throat, burning with acidity. But I don't let them out because I know—know all too well—what I'd get in return.

What I get anyway.

"No apologies, huh?" Ettian says coldly.

"Look—" I start.

"There's no line, is there? Between you looking out for me and you manipulating me?"

"That's ruttin' rich, coming from the guy who literally took me prisoner to save my life."

Ettian shoves himself upright, his robe slipping drunkenly from one shoulder. The move looked painful, but I think he's too enraged to feel it. His eyes smolder like starship engines on the verge of a hard burn. He's wounded and fierce and furious, and a part of me is loath to admit it's the most imperial he's ever looked. He heaves, pivoting himself off the edge of the bed as he clutches his bandages with one hand. Ettian lets out a long, shaky breath as he settles onto his feet, but his hand snaps out in a flash when I take a step forward. "If you try to stop me again, I'll call in the guards and make sure you get a taste of real imprisonment."

"Oh come on," I scoff. Like he's going to start doing anything genuinely effective where I'm concerned. I take another slow step, eyes locked on his. There's a thread pulled taut between us, a dare neither of us will back down from. I've stopped breathing. He's trying desperately to steady his lungs after the effort of getting out of bed.

I extend my hand like I'm reaching out to a street dog, waiting for him to shy away. But Ettian holds still with what seems like enormous effort, his body tensing with every inch that closes between us.

My fingers slip around his robe's errant shoulder. A horrible gut urge pulls me to yank it lower, shove him back—but I have no illusions about how awfully that would go. Instead I slowly pull it up into place, dragging my fingers carefully over the feverish heat of his skin as I smooth the collar down.

Now Ettian has stopped breathing too.

I pull the ties of his robe taut around his stomach, reading only the barest flicker of the pain it causes him in his expression. "Go on," I murmur softly. "Prove me wrong then."

And there it is. That stiff-lipped imperial sneer he could never bring himself to make. That furious purpose burning in his eyes. Ettian may drive himself into the ground plunging recklessly into this war, but at least he'll die an emperor.

It's the only consolation he leaves me with as he shuffles past me out of the room and the last thought I cling to before the panic attack takes over.

CHAPTER 22

THE FLEET MOVES toward its annihilation, and I do nothing.

I should be speaking up. Screaming. Yelling until I get kicked off the bridge again, trying to get it through *someone's* skull that Archon doesn't have a hope against what's waiting for them at Imre.

But I have no foothold. Once again, I've been shoved back down the stairs to where I started, and this time it's hitting different. Maybe it's the one-two punch of losing my advantage with Wen and then Ettian in such quick succession. Maybe I'm just tired of losing. Maybe there's never been a winning move in the first place, so what's the point of trying? Some combination of that depressing cocktail has turned me into a ghost. The object of my haunting varies from day to day, hour to hour, but I can't stand to be alone while I feel so helpless.

I lurk in the back of the gym, watching Wen furiously swat back the three armored men attempting to take her down. She's swathed in the horrific might of the powersuit, all but consumed by it. I've seen her in it more than out of it in the past couple days. On the one hand, I understand the impulse. Iral gave her the suit with the implicit understanding that she'd take to the field in it, and with the fleet in the process of mobilizing, that day will be soon. She's adept and a fast learner, but she's nowhere near where she'd need to be to survive her first day of combat. But I do nothing—even though as I watch her trainers dogpile her, I can think of several helpful suggestions—because there's no ruttin' point anyway. If she flies combat in that suit, she's dead.

I sit quietly at Ettian's side on the bridge, trying not to visibly react every time I hear him hiss a long, shaky sigh and notice him pressing a hand over his wound out of the corner of my eye. It's clear he can barely concentrate on the orbital maneuvers being plotted out on the bridge's screens, but he's trying his damnedest anyway. I could intervene. I've been sketching out the details myself, practicing holding the data in my head. Our approach to the planet is predicated on several factors, not the least of which is the fact that its orbit has it positioned on the opposite side of the solar system. If we use our superluminal jump to catch them unprepared, we don't have another to get us out again. But if we stay subluminal to get there, they'll have time to prepare. The debate raging across the bridge is exactly how we're going to deploy against the forces our scouts have spotted. Ettian means to pull weight for a conservative approach, sacrificing a single dreadnought to draw fire and then sending the rest in the slow way. Mostly he's just showing off how dark the bags under his eyes can get.

I watch with my heart in my throat as Commodore Esperza presents Wen with what looks like a sawn-off control stick at first glance—until she thumbs a tab on the edge of it and the unmistakable rigid blade of a vibrosword whips out of one end.

Wen weighs it in her hand, her expression frozen in incredulous joy. Esperza's leans more toward a bitter sort of sweetness, and I swear there's a glimmer of a tear welling in one of the ex-pirate's eyes. "The blade itself is a reinforced alloy that can do some serious damage," Esperza says, swallowing back what sounds like a massive lump in her throat. "But the real show is the resonance. If you hit that tab, the blade will start quaking. You've got limited reserves of juice before it goes back to being a hunk of absurdly sharp metal, so make it count."

I've never seen Wen so nervous about something. She adjusts her grip carefully on the sword as if double-checking that she's not about to let it slip and lose a limb. I suppress the urge to shove my hands over my ears. In the dramatizations I've seen, a vibrosword makes a chainsaw snarl, heralding a knight's terrifying approach.

But the noise that rings out when she jams down that trigger is cold and clean—almost musical, like the toll of a bell. Every head in the lab swivels like an electromagnet's been turned on, drawn to the sight of a sword activating in a knight's hand for the first time in a decade. The vibration is only visible in the slight shimmer of the blade's reflection, and I feel myself getting lost in its depths.

I remember the nightmares traded between kids at my pre-military school on Naberrie. No doubt they were inherently distorted by the fact that they were whispered back and forth between a bunch of ten-year-olds, but the lasting fear they left is all too real. There were stories of knights who used their vibroswords to cleave a fighter straight down the middle. Stories where a knight ripped the engines clean off a ship and then rode it through an atmospheric burn, laughing all the way down. The stories about a knight beheading ten babies with a single swat of a vibrosword stretch the limits of believability, but the fact Umber kids were whispering tales like that tells you everything you might need to know about what the suited knights meant to us.

When she donned the powersuit, Wen was just a kid in too-big armor. When she went on her first flight around the *Torrent*, she was a reckless test pilot playing with a new ship. But with the vibrosword singing in her hands—even in plain fatigues—Wen is unquestionably a suited knight.

It's not ruttin' fair. I did everything I possibly could. I fought like hell to save both of them, to get them clear of this incoming debacle, and instead they've both dug in their heels and dragged me headlong into the line of fire.

I've spent so long hiding my emotions behind an indignant mask that all of a sudden it feels like a dam is breaking within me. It must be bad, because Wen immediately clocks it. The vibrosword stills in her hands, and she withdraws it into its hilt, taking an anxious step toward me.

I take a step back.

I see another first flicker across her face—the first time she realizes that being a knight might not be a universally good thing the way everyone around her has been framing it. She sees the raw fear and hatred I've finally stopped bothering to hide and realizes she's not a hero. That's she's only a hero from a certain point of view.

Now I wait to see if she decides that makes me her enemy. It's always been a strange balance between us. Wen's never been one of the pure-of-heart Archon faithful. Hells, the Archon folks themselves have been all too happy to reject her up until the point when she slid into Torrance con-Rafe's powersuit. She's always held herself close enough to the fringes that I hoped I could swing her to my side.

I can't ally with a suited knight. I can't condone another one of those monsters taking the field.

But there's something about seeing her like this—seeing her fierce and horrifying and awesome, a sword that can cleave hullmetal in her hand—that lights a spark in me. Envy kindles it, vicious envy that she started with nothing but a half-burnt face and a stolen ship and now she's risen to *this*. I have more. I have always had more. What right does she have to fly so high?

I've been knocked down, but it's not enough to make me doubt the blood in my veins. The blood that shapes my destiny and etches my name in the stars. If I have to start from scratch, so be it. I'll do it again. Do it until it works.

So I whirl on one heel and march out of the lab, trusting—*knowing*—she has no choice but to follow me.

Wen chases me all the way back to our quarters. She quits trying to catch up to me when she realizes where we're going, instead trailing a few feet back. It gives me the space I need to figure out exactly how to approach this conversation.

It also gives my palms time to build up a decent sweat.

When I blow into the entry room, she closes the door wordlessly behind us. The safety of our room's lack of surveillance should comfort me, but instead I feel my panic worsen the moment I turn around and spot the vibrosword clipped casually to her belt.

"Spit it out," Wen says, resting one hand on it like it already unquestionably belongs there.

"Remember what I told you that night you pulled me out of the vents?" I ask, my eyes slipping to the floor in a way that I hope makes me look distraught but still in control of myself.

"Jog my memory, why don't you?" she replies. She's clearly impatient to get back to her training. This might be the longest break she's taken in days.

"I told you *this*"—I gesture up and down at her—"was only going to get you killed."

"And I told *you* that nothing's killed me yet."

"And you expect that to hold up when we strike Imre and all of Tosa's amassed forces? You expect you're going to come out of that intact just because Iral gave you a fancy powersuit and put a ruttin' *sword* in your hand?"

I wait until I'm *certain* that's doubt I see flickering in her eyes.

"Because it's not gonna."

Pause for effect.

"Not unless you have me too."

She laughs, as I knew she would. I wait for the humor to pass her by, for her to grasp that this is a demand I'm deathly serious about. "What . . . do I *need* you for?" she asks, bemused.

"Remember your first flight? When you nearly plowed headlong into the *Torrent* because you didn't grasp how fast you were going? How often do you think something like that's going to happen when you're so new to the powersuit?"

Gears turn in her head. Her grip on the hilt tightens.

"Look, I was never much of a pilot. I was always better at talking to people. Think about every time you've run an active field with me on comms. Think about how badly you need that when you're about to go to war in a rig you've only had a couple days to get a feel for."

She's thinking. I'm almost there.

"And you heard those drums. You've seen the way the people on this ship worship those poor, martyred knights. I've been watching the way they train with you—like it's a dream come true. They let you get sloppy, because they don't dare infringe on a precious knight's process. I've seen the openings where they should have struck. The moves they didn't take. I wouldn't let one of those people in the same *room* as the channel that's supposed to feed me the information that keeps me alive. They love the idea of you, but they're too starstruck to ground themselves in the reality of what running those comms entails. All they'd do is turn you into another martyr. You need someone on comms who cares more about keeping you alive than watching a ruttin' knight do some fancy tricks. There's only one other person in the galaxy you could trust to watch your back like that, and he definitely doesn't have time to run your comms."

Wen nods—once like she's trying to convince herself, then again to make it clear it's a yes. But before I can lock that yes in, her eyes narrow. "The commodore won't clear it."

"The commodore was in the cockpit with me when I stopped you from splatting yourself on the *Torrent*."

"So?"

"So she saw how useful I can be. She knows we work well together, and at an hour this dire, she wouldn't be half the strategist I know she is if she wasted this opportunity."

"She also wouldn't be half the strategist *I* know she is if she let you onto the bridge during an engagement. Or did you forget that's why you got booted the last time you tried to 'help' me in a battle?"

I shake my head. "This time will be different. We'll get that clearance before, not during or after. She'll clear it if you ask."

Wen makes an incredulous little scoff. "Why?"

I jab a finger at the vibrosword on her belt. I don't need to do anything more than that. Esperza's entrusted Wen with the legacy of the suited knights—the legacy of the friend who dragged her into the war in the first place. She's handed over a piece of technology so precious that it hasn't seen battle in a decade. If Wen Iffan asks, the commodore will set the fleet in orbit around her. She'll give the Flame Knight whatever clearance she needs.

And Silon's going to throw a ruttin' fit—I'm so goddamn excited to see her face when she has to sign off on the commodore's order. If that's the one bright spot in all of this, I'll take it.

Wen's lips settle into a grim, decisive line. "If you're right about this, we need to start training together stat," she says. "From the rumblings I've heard, we're shipping out at any second."

The notion is chilling, but maybe a bit less so than it was a minute ago. Sure, I'll be flung into battle, trapped on the wrong side as the Archon forces fight like hell to beat Berr sys-Tosa out of his stronghold.

But if a suited knight tries to take the field, I'm going to be the only voice in her ear.

CHAPTER 23

THE HOURS BEFORE battle are a series of tense goodbyes that start with the majestic and trickle down to the minute.

Well, maybe majestic is giving it too much credit. I find the whole spectacle around General Iral's departure for the flagship dreadnought gaudy, but I see the necessity of it. The whole affair has overtaken one of the *Torrent*'s outer decks, flooding it with lines of neatly dressed officers, blocks of tightly packed soldiers, and the noise of a hundred skin drums pounding a call to arms.

Iral and his staff process through the middle of the grandeur down the aisle that's been cleared between the entrance to the docks and the massive ramp deployed from his flagship. The general's braids are bound back, his expression set in a serious mask. He's the picture of perfect focus, a far cry from the scattered, frenetic thoughts racing through my head as the battle for the Tosa System inches closer and closer.

I shift my weight from foot to foot uneasily, trying to muster a similar outward calm. I stand at Wen's right in the row of officers positioned between Iral and his ship, doing my best to keep my eyes pinned on the approaching general instead of Ettian, who's planted himself a few paces ahead of us. At this point, I don't think anyone in the administration cares too much about the amount of attention I pay the emperor, but this is for my own edification. If I let myself think too much about how difficult it is for Ettian to keep himself upright, it'll block out everything else, and I can't afford that.

But when Iral reaches Ettian, I lose all ability to differentiate between what I should be paying attention to and what's a distraction. All I can think about is how small the emperor looks against his general. How frail his stature is, framed against Iral's broad shoulders. I have to keep reminding myself that this isn't like when we fought for Ellit, when Ettian was striving desperately to prove himself against Iral's reputation. Ellit earned the emperor respect—not just for his bloodright, but for his prowess. I can see that respect in the way Iral regards his emperor now.

In fact, the reason we're all here, doing this nonsense procession, is so that the rest of the Archon administration gets a firm reminder of who's really in charge. Iral is about to lead the assault on Imre, while Ettian remains aboard the *Torrent* with the rear guard that will sweep in once it's safe to do so. If Iral is victorious—if he reclaims the Tosa System for Archon—the general has an opening to make a play for the reins of the rebellion, and Ettian needs to cut that shit off at the root.

So Ettian stands between Iral and his flagship, head held high, wearing a fine crown of twisted platinum branches that wind around emeralds the size of goose eggs. His shoulders are weighted by platinum bars, his load far heavier than the one that decorates Iral's uniform. He's the very picture of imperial majesty, the clear gravitational center of the room, and I look at him praying to any god who'll listen that no one notices he's about to topple under the weight.

But instead it's General Iral who goes down, sinking to one knee before Ettian like he did five months ago when the young usurper stormed the court with no rational thought in his head beyond freeing me from the general's clutches. The rest of the deck follows suit, bending at the waist until Ettian and I are the only ones left standing.

He glances back over his shoulder, and for a moment I worry that he's going to pull some nonsense he thinks he can get away with because people are too busy falling over themselves to show him deference. Smirk or wink or point at the ground like he expects me to drop for him.

Ettian only gives me a grim look and a firm nod. Months ago, I would have countered it with some nonsense of my own—anything to knock him down in a public forum where I'm not being recorded—but I realize with a horrible pinch that I'm far too committed to keeping him upright. Far too steeped in the seriousness of the general's departure. Far too invested in everything happening here, on the wrong side of the war.

So all I give him is hollowness, and the general rises, and his attention swings back around, and the Archon mobilization marches on.

An hour after the general is safely away, I trail Wen through the grand mess of the *Torrent*'s outer deck, swept up in the tide of pilots exchanging slaps on the back as their superiors trade salutes and soft smiles. There's a goodbye ahead of us that matters to her—so much so that I feel guilty hovering on the fringes of it. A trim shuttle at the far end of the deck is being prepped for departure, and outside it stands Commodore Esperza and her entire retinue of staffers. While the *Torrent* has served her well as a flagship, she's taking her command to a smaller cruiser that will serve as a pivot point somewhere midway between Ellit and Imre—a place where she can minimize communications delay between both the spearhead of the Archon attack and the reserves.

The hope—the wild, reckless hope—is that Wen will see her on the other side.

The reality, I fear, is not so optimistic. I didn't want to taint with my presence what is, in all likelihood, the last time these two ever speak, but Wen insisted that I stick with her. As we approach, I slow my steps, letting Wen go on ahead to greet her commodore.

"Iffan," Esperza says, accepting Wen's salute, then stepping back to look her up and down. She's dressed in her padded undersuit, ready to lock and load in her armor at a moment's notice. Esperza, on the other hand, is kitted out in regalia, her commodore's platinum glimmering in the bright lights of the loading zone. If Iral hadn't stuffed Wen in the powersuit, she'd be dressed similarly and shipping out at the commodore's side.

Both of them seem to be thinking about that; Wen's eyes flick nervously to Esperza's other subordinates and Esperza clocks it with a slight smirk. "You would have been a valuable addition to my team, in time," the commodore says gently. "But I'd wager you always would have ended up here. I do my best work quietly, and I've got this sneaking suspicion quiet is never going to be your style."

"It was an honor to learn from you," Wen offers, a burble of emotion nearly strangling her voice.

Esperza chuckles, then steps forward to lay a steady hand on the Flame Knight's shoulder. "It was an honor to teach you. From the start, you had a spark in you that ruttin' scared me—because I knew how brightly you'd burn one day. You're going to be unstoppable out there. I can't wait to see it."

I swallow the impulse to object. Wen looks like she's about to try to deflect Esperza's praise, but before she can get the words out, the commodore yanks her forward and wraps her in a firm hug. Wen hesitates, no doubt running some fast numbers on chains of command before deciding *rut it* and hugging Esperza back.

Some of the aides behind her barely conceal their shock at their boss so openly displaying affection. Others look jealous—an emotion I find surprisingly sympathetic. War strips our softness. It aches to watch someone reclaim theirs.

But for my part, I try my best not to look sick to my stomach. Esperza's validating every choice that put Wen in that monstrous suit and framing it as all but inevitable. Of course she'd never claim responsibility for turning Wen into a suited knight, but I want *something*—some acknowledgment that thanks to her, Wen's probably about to lose her life.

Instead, Esperza claps her gently on the shoulder and steps back with pride glowing in her eyes alongside hopeless, reckless confidence that she's done right by her protégée.

And then, even worse, her eyes land on me.

"Umber," she says, with far more civility than I would have given her credit for. "I don't like you. I don't trust you. Unfortunately, despite all that, I've gotten to know you. I know that you can never be trusted to do right by Archon. But I'd have to be a complete fool to discount how much you've helped our girl. Thank you—seriously, I mean it," she says around a laugh as I hitch backward in surprise. "Sometimes the advancement of the enemy is in the empire's best interest. I couldn't have taught Iffan half as well as I did without your assistance. And I couldn't leave her side for this battle if I didn't know she's in the hands of someone who's gonna do right by her."

Esperza settles her hands primly behind her back and straightens, a move that looks so profoundly like one out of Deidra con-Silon's playbook that I nearly laugh. "All the same, I'll tell you this: let Iffan down in any way and I'll come up with a manner of public execution that'll make even your mother shudder."

"Understood, Adela," I say with the cockiest, most sarcastic salute I can manage.

Esperza nods like she expected nothing else, and there's something in the gesture that veers dangerously close to approval. With one last crooked pirate's smile and a wink at Wen, she turns her back on us and summons her people with a wave of one hand and a quick beat of her other against her thigh.

Wen watches her go for a long moment I don't like at all. I tap her on the elbow, and she startles, shaking her head. "Any other goodbyes before you load out?"

"One," she says, "but we'll meet him at the lock."

It's not a far walk from this deck. Not far enough for me to brace myself for the sight of the powersuit waiting to swallow her when we enter the staging zone. Wen sinks into its clutches eagerly—too eagerly. The metal wraps around her perversely with so much ease that she doesn't even need a technician to check its fusings. Her helmet remains cocked back, leaving her head the only part of her free from the powersuit's snare. Knight and suit move as one off its mounts, crossing the staging zone to pick up her vibrosword from its stand. She clips it to a magnetic release on the suit's exterior, then lets out a long, steady breath.

Somewhere deeper within the *Torrent*, drums are starting to pound.

I try my damnedest to tune them out. "Right, we need to do a comms check here, then another one at the bridge, and then—"

"Gal."

I don't understand how her voice is so steady. Wen's smarter than I am—of that I'm reasonably certain, even if her self-preservation instinct is a little skewed. She's been clever enough to avoid danger most of her life, escaping with nothing worse than a half-burnt face. But even the smartest person I know—Rhodes Tsampa, a member of Hanji's cohort, for the record—would be aware of the danger she's trying to throw herself into.

Then again, Rhodes was never much of a pilot. But Wen's the one who flew me through the fall of Rana in a souped-up Beamer. I'd never say it to Ettian's face, but I don't think even *he* could have gotten me through that mess.

Don't, I want to beg her. *Don't make me believe you might survive this.* I should be pleading for the exact inverse of that. I want her to live. But I want her to never go out there in the first place.

"Gal," she repeats. "You're clearly freaking out about this."

"You're clearly not freaking out *enough* about this." My eyes fix on the airlock, and I feel my entire body go rigid as if braced for it to blow out at any second. On the other side of those doors is nothing but the void she'll hurl herself into and never come back from. "Wen, I . . . I know I said if you had me, you'd live. And I stand by that, but I need you to listen to me."

After a beat of silence, she startles. "Oh—yeah, I'm listening to you."

I sigh through my teeth. "No, not like that. I mean when I'm in your ear, I need you to take orders. Like, the way Silon takes this ship into battle. I'm Silon. You're the *Torrent*. I'm . . . *scared* that nothing less than that degree of seamlessness will keep you alive."

"Thought you hated Silon," Wen notes, picking absently at one of her greaves.

"She's done her fair share in ruining my life, but gods, you've seen her work."

That admiring note reflects right back at me in the shine of Wen's eyes. Esperza may have done her damage, but she's also shown me all the easy ways to catch Wen's attention, ways I'll deploy mercilessly if it's what it takes to keep her alive. Flash someone else's talent in front of her eyes and imply she might live up to it, and Wen's as good as gone.

And not a moment too soon, because seconds later, I hear the door at our backs slide open and know without looking that my escort has arrived.

"Ettian," I say without turning around. He's come with no others. There are no techs to support Wen's deployment. I'm alone as always. It could be the last time the three of us are alone together, and for a moment it dizzies me how far we've come from that night we slept side by side on the rooftops of Isla. Ettian wears a crown. Wen is resplendent in that monstrous armor. And I'm in platinum cuffs.

I pivot to face him, and the sight hits me worse than the powersuit. He carries himself stiffly, one hand subtly pressed against his still-healing wounds. The day's activity has clearly already taken its toll on him, and the day's barely begun. He's still kitted out in the regalia he wore to Iral's departure, the twisted crown and the platinum bars gleaming against the lock's harsh lights. His eyes are harder than both of them, ready for the fight ahead.

"You should be in a wheelchair," Wen says, nodding at the injury Ettian's doing his best to conceal. "Did you even ask the ward for one?"

"I just gotta make it to the bridge," he mutters sheepishly. "If I keel over, Gal will drag me there by my ankles."

"I dunno if I can with all that metal on you," I fire back. "You're better off with Little Miss Tin Can here."

He takes her in, the steel of his eyes going soft. I know he must have seen her in the suit before, but never without the rest of the *Torrent* bustling around them. With us, Ettian doesn't have to hold himself as an emperor. He can let loose a boyish grin as Wen jokingly flexes her metallic casings, posing like a bodybuilder. His free hand comes up to cover his mouth before he does anything more undignified with it, but it barely muffles the joyful little hum that escapes him.

It feels so wrong that I can't stop myself from letting out a snort. Both of them glare at me, and I hold up my hands. "You already know my opinion on the matter, and it ain't changing. Can't help that both of you are trying to kill yourselves—just gonna do my best to keep you alive despite that."

Ettian looks momentarily perturbed, his eyes flicking to Wen. I sense an opening. I could lean hard on his doubts, make him realize he needs to protect her from what's about to happen if she steps out on the field. But he's already wise to that act, and there's no stupider way to blow the trust I need from Wen right now. All I can do is hope he draws the conclusion on his own. I wait with bated breath.

Wen must sense the change in the winds, because she claps her hands together, her armored fingers clacking like a gunshot. "Remember when *you* used to be the dire one, Ettian?" she says with a smirk.

He nods, looking a little bit sadder and a little bit softer than he should on the verge of a battle. "I miss when I was allowed to be dire. Now Gal just says all my dire thoughts out loud."

It's my turn to glance nervously between them. Has he told her about our last interaction? Primed her to be wary of every word that comes out of my mouth? If she's already wise to my act, I might not be able to pull this off. But I don't have time to untangle what she does know and what she doesn't. The distant drums echoing through the halls have shifted to a new rhythm, summoning us to our stations.

Ettian straightens when he hears them, taking a sudden step toward Wen. She catches him by the shoulders, looking him steadily in the eye. With the powersuit, she's gained the inches she needs to lord over him, lending to the weight in her voice as she says firmly, "Don't make it goodbye. It's not. It won't be. Go do your job, and I'll do mine."

He gives her a stiff nod, believing her as easily as he always does. "Keep flying," he murmurs, catching her forearm and squeezing it gently. "No matter what, keep flying."

Bitterness curdles in the back of my mouth, but I swallow it as Wen releases Ettian and shifts her focus to me. "We're a weird team, Gal, but I think it's gonna work."

"Whatever you say, firecracker," I reply, taking the hand she offers and giving it a firm shake.

"Hey, Iwam's the only one who gets to call me that."

Ettian grimaces as his hand drifts back to his wound. "Well, if this isn't a goodbye, no point in dallying."

It is a goodbye. It very much is. I feel it hit in my gut as my fingers slip from Wen's for the last time. A fear, verging on a certainty that I won't be able to keep her alive. That we're all doomed to die at the hands of Berr sys-Tosa's fleet—and if not his, then my mother's, when the Imperial Fleet strafes this system. I don't believe in Archon. Not the way these two seem to.

But I do believe it's worth it to try my best to keep them alive. That much I can say for sure.

Ettian and I turn away from her together and set off for the bridge with me a half-step behind him. There will be no goodbye for us. No matter how this goes, we're stuck together till the end.

CHAPTER 24

"EMPEROR ON DECK!" Communications calls over the low, rolling thunder of the war drums.

I toss her a sunny smile and mouth *Thanks,* just to watch her expression pucker in distaste. Ettian has to stop himself from rolling his eyes. I smirk. I'm feeling a little more certain of myself now that the ceremony of Iral's departure has passed, and if today is the last I get, I'm going to die as I lived—insufferable to the end.

We settle down at our stations, Ettian immediately swallowed by a deluge of clearance requests and me kicking back, folding my arms behind my head, and letting the atmosphere of the bridge wash over me. It's not nearly as frantic as the previous times the *Torrent* has ridden into battle, which in itself is a little disturbing. Though maybe it shouldn't be surprising. The first battle I weathered on this ship was a surprise attack. The second I only experienced from a distance, shipped off with Ettian to wait it out. I've never seen a planned engagement from this position, but it's the kind these soldiers have been training for their entire lives. Everyone is on task. Everyone's steadfast. And everyone but me crews their stations with utmost confidence that we're going to make it through this.

"Communications pivot is in position," the tech I grinned at calls across the bridge, and at the room's core, Silon's head jerks up. Commodore Esperza's ship has reached the midpoint between here and Imre, ready to conduct both waves of the attack. Now that she's ready, the assault will launch at any moment.

Ettian rises out of his seat next to me, doing his damnedest to make it look like the motion doesn't hurt at all. "*Torrent* bridge," he announces. "The last time I droned on for too long, someone shot me through the gut, so I'll do my best to make this brief."

It nets a few laughs, a few more tight smiles, and a long, exasperated sigh from me.

"We've fought like hell for this moment. We've lost, suffered, and bled just to stand here on the precipice of reclaiming the Archon Core." Ettian pauses. I wonder if anyone else picks up on how much he desperately wants to collapse back in his chair. Finally, he gives his audience a grim little nod. "And I don't know about you all, but I think I could stand to bleed a little more."

The bridge swells with applause as the emperor takes his seat again. The noise of it covers the shaky breath he lets out. I'm torn between concern for his pain and sheer confusion over how effective those lines were at pumping up his people. "Bleeding a little more" isn't something *any* leader should aspire to. We have people devoted to bleeding for us. If a leader is bleeding, shit's gone *far* sideways.

But there's no time to parse the strangeness of Archon thought processes—not when Silon's already throwing telemetry from Esperza up on the screens at the core of the room. Two clocks run in tandem at the bottom of it. The first shows the time Esperza's signal was sent and the second shows the current time, roughly nine minutes later. Interplanetary warfare relies on constant awareness of how much can change in those nine minutes of delay. The *Torrent*'s efficacy will hinge on Silon's ability to weigh the information and orders Esperza can relay against the information the commodore doesn't have yet. From what I've seen so far, she's more than up to the task.

Eyes on your own paper, Umber, I can all but hear Esperza chiding me. I run my fingers through the familiar paces of setting up my station, balancing where my feeds are coming from and double-checking my connection to the bay where we left Wen. I bring up the controls of the airlock doors down there on one side of my screen, then pull Wen's line up on the other.

"*Torrent* bridge to Flame Knight, Flame Knight do you copy?"

"Hi, Gal."

"I think you mean something like 'Flame Knight to *Torrent* bridge—' "

"Rust that—half the reason I chose you to run my comms was 'cause I knew you wouldn't try to pull that formal bullshit on me."

"Bold assumption," I fire back with a chuckle. "You forget that I've been stripped of a formal rank for months now. It's shaken me to my core. I need the validation."

"Of being called '*Torrent* bridge'?"

"I'll take what I can get. I'm about to run a test on the permissions for the airlock controls."

"Fire away, *Torrent* bridge," she replies. I draw up the video feed from her loading zone just to confirm how pleased with herself she looks.

"Testing the inner door . . . *now*. There should be a light confirming it's unlocked. Do you see it?"

"Light's on."

"Perfect. Now the outer lock. First I'm locking down the inner door . . . *now*. Can you confirm the previous light is off?"

"Light's off."

"Good." There's a failsafe built into the ship's systems that prevents the inner and outer doors from being opened at the same time. If the inner door is unlocked, the outer door will be impossible to open. "Unlocking the outer door now. If you look in the chamber, do you see the outer door's light on?"

On the camera, I watch Wen peer through the airlock's porthole window. "Yep, it's unlocked. And now it's locked. Unlocked. Locked. Having fun up there?"

"Someone's gotta," I reply, sitting back in my chair. Ettian casts me a sidelong glance. He's noticed I look a little too happy to be here—and he's right to worry. I should probably tone it down, lest he suspect the real reason I've wheedled myself into this chair. I tap my temple and point at his workstation in the most condescending *eyes front* gesture I can manage.

Which, all things considered, he *needs*. If he fought like hell to sit on this bridge for the battle, the least he can do is keep his focus on it. And to his credit, Ettian takes less offense than I would have expected. He smirks slightly, then turns his attention back to his own work.

Now I'm a little offended myself. "What's that for?" I ask.

"What's what for?"

"You're smiling. About *me*. Something's wrong."

"Always thought it would do you some good to hang out with Wen. Didn't realize it'd get you here at my side for the fight to decide the fate of this system, elsewise I would have straight-up handcuffed the two of you together. And it looks like you're having fun with it too."

I glare. "This isn't *fun*. None of this is fun. You're about to tear the roots out of a stable system, probably triggering several more copycat rebellions that'll lead to other systems collapsing in the process. The damage you do today will be felt for centuries."

"And you're right at my side, helping me do it. Just like I always hoped."

My nose wrinkles of its own accord, even before my brain finishes processing the bullshit. "No," I say. "*No,*" I repeat more firmly when he has the audacity to smile at the first one. "I'm . . . that's not how this works. That's not what's happening here, you vast, void-headed *fool*. There's an *empire* of distance between me sitting here because I'm on your side and me sitting here trying to save someone's ruttin' life—whether it's you or Wen or both depends on how much the gods like me."

Ettian shrugs, still not nearly serious enough for my liking. "Looks the same to me."

The words fall like a hammer to the head, leaving me stunned and slumped in my chair, my hands frozen hovering over my station. Across the bridge, Communications calls that the first wave has made the leap to Imre, but it barely registers. I'm on their side. I'm not out for my own ends. Not doing all this as an elaborate ruse to wait for them to get sloppy and escape. That hasn't been driving me since . . . Well, since Ettian got shot through the gut.

Ruttin' Hanji Iwam. She came to break me out, and instead she locked me in.

But doing it is one thing. *Thinking* about why I'm doing it is terrifying, and it's the thought that has me pinned in my chair, unable to process the sounds of the war drums intensifying as the battle goes hot at Imre. Thinking about it makes it a choice. And am I really choosing this?

It's maybe the worst possible moment to decide.

I had a plan for this battle. A plan I could still enact without drawing a hard line on my stance. But if I ride through the fight without doing anything but sitting primly at the emperor's side, isn't my stance clear enough already?

No, I want to say—out loud, again. Wanting to keep Ettian and Wen alive is related to the survival of the Archon rebellion, but it's different. It has to be different. I'm not doing it for the empire attempting to usurp my territory.

I'm doing it for *him*.

Oh gods of all systems. Rut me ruttin' sideways.

But before my internal crisis can come to its peak, the crisis going on outside the walls of my skull boils over. All at once, I realize the drums have shifted their rudiment to a frenzied tempo that spears panic through me. The first broadcast from Esperza's pivot point has hit. And the scene of the battlefield is . . .

Well, at first it's difficult to untangle. I wipe my station clear and blow the field's telemetry as large as it'll go, trying to make sense of what I'm seeing. Imre was ringed by six of Tosa's dreadnoughts, according to the scouting from this morning. According to what the advance forces are relaying, only two remain. But from the massive heat signatures still eddying against Imre's outer atmosphere, the rest of them were there up until just minutes ago. They've gone superluminal, leaving only a rear guard to defend the planet.

Where exactly they set their vectors for only remains a mystery for a minute more. "Dasun!" Telemetry calls. "Their vectors are all pointed at the Dasun Yards."

"The commodore's sent a scouting shuttle after them," Silon says, and a hush falls over the bridge. Even the drums slow to a steady, mournful beat, recognizing the inescapable fact that Esperza's just committed that shuttle to a suicide mission. Once it uses its superluminal jump to skip to Dasun, there will be nothing left to get it home. Those soldiers will die in the shadow of the massive gas giant and the shipyards built in its icy moons.

In twenty minutes, when the signal reaches us, we'll find out what they died for.

If, in those twenty minutes, we haven't decided to follow them into the maw. There's a strong argument to be made for it. All of those ships that were just guarding Imre have now wasted their superluminal leap to take us by surprise with their escape to Dasun. If we chase them down by a superluminal advance, we could catch them before their drives cool and ensure they can't escape us again. It might be all it would take to stamp the governor's forces out of the system entirely.

Or it could be a trap we're meant to walk right into. My thoughts stray to the Imperial Fleet. Is this the moment my mother has chosen for her grand entrance? If we stake our remaining dreadnoughts on Dasun without knowing what awaits us, there's a nonzero chance we end up impaled on the tip of her spear. Years of academy training rise to the tip of my tongue, daring me to blurt out the possibility.

On the other hand, if only two dreadnoughts hold Imre, we can take it easily. And it seems to be there for the taking—abandoned, just like Rana was months ago, when Berr sys-Tosa sacrificed my identity and fled to regroup. Which probably means that's a trap too. I catch Ettian's eye, noting the deep furrow in his brow. He's stuck in the same loop as me—no surprise, since we were both raised in the same military strategy classes. "If we hold the capital, we've as good as won," he says out loud.

"But it makes no sense for the governor to relinquish it that easily," I counter. "Why'd he leave two dreadnoughts behind if he meant to abandon it entirely?"

"Because he wants our noses to be pointed at them when the rest of his fleet comes swooping back in," Ettian offers. Guess he wasn't sleeping through as many lectures as me—the thought is a little more rankling than I'd like to admit.

"If that's it," I start, heavy on the *if*, "then the trap is obvious. And is this the kind of army that barrels headfirst into an obvious trap?"

"Or the kind of army that barrels headfirst into the less obvious trap?" he replies, fingers fidgeting anxiously over the information spilling across his workstation. "Because now that they know we've clocked them at Dasun, they must have a contingency in place for the off chance our entire rear guard drops out of superluminal there, guns blazing."

I'm doing some nervous calculations of my own, pulling up the system map and sketching hypothetical vectors between Ellit and Dasun, Ellit and Imre, and the possible ways we could arrive there. If we start accelerating for Dasun, it'll be hell to retarget our vector to Imre no matter the speed, and *days* to reach the outer gas giant. If we hop to Dasun, we guarantee we can't come to the advance team's aid at Imre in a timely manner. And if we go superluminal pointed at Imre, that springs the aforementioned trap.

There's an additional factor making all of this light-years more complicated: the chain of command. If Esperza issues an order, it's eight minutes away. Iral is on the advance team, even farther from us. The only way we can act outside their command is if Ettian himself makes the call.

So Ettian has to make the right call.

Or, more accurately, I have to talk him into the right call, because otherwise what the rut am I here for?

Dasun or Imre? Use our speed now, or save it for when it's needed.

Wait on the commodore's word? The general's? The poor, doomed advance shuttle? And above all, whose side am I on when I make that decision? The nauseating head spin of my earlier crisis is doubling down with a vengeance.

Cut through it, Umber, I tell myself. I'm an imperial, born to rule and raised to lead. I can't doubt my judgment. It's gotten me this far.

"We hold," I tell Ettian firmly, fixing him with a stare he can't evade. "But when we hear from Dasun, we move like hell. Tell them to have the reactors hot and ready to get this thing on its vector and the superluminal drives ready to fire."

He nods, steady and sure in what I've said. Under other circumstances, I might immediately tear into him for taking his most critical mission's strategy from a captured enemy, but we're *well* past that. Even with his bridge staff throwing us anxious looks—even with *Silon* looking like she's about to hop off her saddle and come physically throw me off the bridge herself—Ettian knows better than to ignore my advice.

So with shallow breaths and the war drums softened to a low patter that matches our racing hearts, we wait for that shuttle to die.

When the transmission comes through, even the drums go quiet. Silon throws all the data we get onto the bridge screens, and my stomach sinks from here clear to Ellit as I watch the scouting shuttle's final moments play out. They make a valiant effort, and I applaud the comms techs especially for doing their damnedest, in their final moments, to give us the clearest possible picture of what we're up against. But less than two minutes after they drop from superluminal and start broadcasting back to us, the combined might of four dreadnoughts reduces them to nothing but atoms and the echoes of their final messages racing across the void.

Four dreadnoughts at Dasun. Two at Imre. I meet Ettian's eyes.

"Dasun," he says.

"Dasun," I agree.

We can take them. According to the data from the scouts, they haven't even deployed the ships on board. Their launch tubes are sealed. If we hit them from a superluminal arrival, they'll be scrambling to roll out their more maneuverable forces as we come screaming in to raze their batteries hard and fast. They've put their backs to the gas giant, flirting with the edges of its gravitational pull as if they mean to cut off one of our approaches, but it's as good as lining themselves up for a firing squad.

Ettian straightens, leaning forward over his station as his eyes lock on Silon. "Set a course for Dasun. All superluminal-capable reserves form up on the *Torrent*."

Silon rears back in her saddle, eyes wide with alarm. "Your Majesty, we're still waiting on the commodore's assessment. We'll have her broadcast within the minute."

He grits his teeth. "You saw that field. Their doors are down. We have an opening."

The captain looks like she's doing her damnedest to maintain her prim calm. "I just feel we ought to consider the commodore's opinion—"

"I feel that you ought to consider where this order is coming from," Ettian replies levelly, his crown glimmering obviously in the bridge's bright lights. "Get us on that vector. Inform the remainder of the rear. Iral will handle the front at Imre. We hunt at Dasun."

Silon purses her lips, but the next thing that comes out of them is a clipped, "As you wish, Your Majesty."

An almost pilot-like glee floods my system alongside a heady rush of adrenaline as the bridge collapses into preparation for the superluminal jump. Engineering fires the *Torrent*'s massive boosters, heaving our nose around to settle onto our vector. Even with the ship's internal dampeners working their hardest to cancel out the force, I can feel its gentle weight bearing down on me.

Or maybe that's just the pressure of what we're about to commit to. We're hurling ourselves at a waiting armada, hoping desperately that we're about to catch them unawares. We're about to confront Berr sys-Tosa himself head-on. The man who threw me into this mess when he told General Iral exactly who I was.

Despite the larger implications, I think I might enjoy watching the Archon rebellion shred him.

"All ships are aligned with their vectors," Communications announces, flitting between addressing Silon and Ettian with ricocheting nervous glances.

"Ready for the jump to superluminal at your mark," Engineering confirms.

Ettian draws a deep breath, but before he can call it, Silon throws a new communication up on the bridge screens.

A distress call.

From the communications pivot.

"Looks like they traced the scout shuttle's signal," Silon says grimly. "But Esperza's pivot ship had an evac shuttle with superluminal capacity. They should have . . ."

They should have run. They should have rutted right back off to us, abandoning the scouting intel and saving their own skins. Esperza is commodore of Archon's dreadnought fleet and the woman single-handedly—horrible moment to make that joke—responsible for commandeering so many dreadnoughts in the first place. Her command should supersede any mission prerogative.

But when's the last time that piratical asshole did anything she was supposed to do?

Esperza held. She made sure the signal came through clearly for both us and the advance team about to engage at Imre. And now . . .

"She's not dead," Silon says. For a moment, I think it's denial. Of course Esperza's dead. Everyone on that ship is dead—the data's clear that they were boarded and their drives were cut, leaving them nowhere to go. But then I realize the captain is telling the truth. Part of the pivot ship's final signal is a stream from their bridge's security cameras.

We watch as Umber marines storm the bridge. The sight of the brass striping their tac armor makes something ache inside me. They plow through her subordinates, cutting them down in a swath around their commanding officer. Adela Esperza greets them with a hand and a stump in the air, her prosthetic limp and nonthreatening on the station in front of her.

They wrench her arms behind her back and cuff her above the

elbows. But her peaceful surrender has bought her enough time for one last message. As they muscle her off the bridge, her eyes fix on the camera, her mouth shaping itself around one final, silent order.

It's Silon who voices it, the sound choked with a degree of emotion that makes me realize I might not have been paying enough attention to the relationship between the captain and the commodore. One final directive, ringing against the mournful quiet of the *Torrent*'s bridge.

"Give them hell at Dasun."

CHAPTER 25

THE SILENCE HOLDS for three thunderous beats of a heart.

Then Ettian stands, his eyes moving steadily from Communications to Engineering to Silon herself. "On my mark."

The whole bridge sits up straighter, an orchestra waiting for the conductor's baton to drop.

"Three. Two. One. Mark."

We catapult across the Tosa System with our breaths frozen in our lungs. The moment we drop to sublight, a harsh drumroll starts up, bolstered by a new voice at every four-count. Silon drops down in her saddle, swallowed by the dreadnought's operations. Ettian bends low over his station, fingers flying. Everyone's moving with utmost purpose, like their entire lives have been leading to this moment.

My focus falls to my own screens. To the task I've been assigned. A task Commodore Esperza just *had* to go and make ten times more complicated.

"Wen," I murmur, trusting my mic to pick up the sound over the bridge's commotion. "You still with me?"

"What's going on up there?" Her voice is hard with suspicion. "We just jumped. Have we been called in at Imre?"

"About that." Gods, how to explain this succinctly?

"Gal?" she asks, her voice a vibrosword snarl.

"Change of plans. Tosa's withdrawn to Dasun with most of his fleet. We've taken the rear to them."

"Dasun? That's clear on the other side of the system. How's Esperza's pivot going to coordinate both fronts from her position?"

"Wen, Esperza . . ."

Shit. I shouldn't be saying anything. In all the tumult, I forgot my original plan. I pull up the airlock controls and cameras from Wen's loading zone—another mistake, because she's staring right at the lens, her expression stony and her hand resting on the hilt of her sword. In the monstrous metal of the powersuit, she looks like she could lunge right through the screen and rip the answers she wants from my mouth.

Just the sight of her like that jars them loose anyway. "We got a communication from Esperza, just before the jump. An Umber strike team traced her signal. They took her alive."

The words hit heavy enough to sway her, even in the armor. There's a horrible truth inherent in what we just witnessed: it would have been better if Esperza died fighting. Wen's still new to the history of the conflict between Umber and Archon, but she knows exactly what we do to our high-caliber prisoners. Maxo Iral's twin brother was hung on an electrified crucifix. My mother beheaded Ettian's parents at the Imperial Seat. And now she's gotten her hands on the Archon rebellion's wily pirate commodore. Whatever happens next, it will be public, it will be spectacular, and the empress will make sure it hurts like hell to watch.

Wen's grip on her vibrosword tightens. She whirls to face the airlock doors, her shoulders squared like she's about to charge right through them. "Let me at 'em," she says, low and level.

"Wen, Esperza's gone. They got her at the pivot point—you can't do anything for her. And there's a battle going hot on the other side of those doors."

"Like I said," she snarls. "Let me at 'em."

This is exactly what I was afraid of. Exactly why I took my seat on this bridge. In the original strategy, the *Torrent* was supposed to sweep in and pick up the pieces when the general had finished mopping up at Imre—once it was *safe*. And in that pocket of safety, Wen was supposed to emerge, a suited knight triumphant, cementing the resurrection of the Archon Empire as Ettian locked his grasp on the Tosa System. Any Archon soldier would unleash her on the field now, letting her harness that simmering wrath and smash herself against the Umber army waiting in the void beyond.

I open the first airlock door. The second the light flashes on, Wen wrenches it open and steps in, slamming it forcefully behind her. The powersuit's helmet snaps down over her head. "Confirmed seal," she says, her voice muffled in the enclosed barrel of her armor's chest piece. "Open the outer door."

I do nothing.

"Gal, I said open the outer door."

I don't. Won't. In fact, I keep my finger jammed firmly down on the button keeping the inner door unlocked. Wen's not the only one who's spent some time poring over the intricacies of dreadnought systems. One of the most essential failsafes built into a ship of this scale is the fact that there must always be at least one locked door between you and the void.

As long as the inner door is unlocked, Wen can't open the outer one, and there's no way in any system's hell I'm unlocking it for her.

"Gal, you rustin' asshole," Wen growls between gritted teeth.

"Do you know what's on the other side of that door?" I hiss, pulling the battle maps up onto my station. The *Torrent*'s bays are hemorrhaging every craft in our holds, sending them streaking for the four dreadnoughts holding the line against the murderous red bulk of Dasun's stormy clouds. We've got them pinned down, flirting with the edge of the planet's gravitational pull. Already, Telemetry is reporting their guns are starting to target.

But they aren't moving, even as more and more of our ships drop from superluminal to fill out the field. Ettian sees it too—he spares me a worried glance amid his frantic processing of clearances and orders and responsibilities. "They're pinned if they stay there. Why . . ." he mutters.

I almost wish he hadn't asked. Because mere seconds after the words leave his mouth, Telemetry shouts, "I've got movement in the clouds!"

Gods of all systems. I immediately pull up the feeds from that sector, trying to pick out what we're seeing. Something is stirring deep within the gas giant's mass, cloaked by the denser gases that wash the world in a bloody pallor.

Many somethings.

"Shit," I hiss. "They're fully deployed."

In the time since the scouts lost their lives, Berr sys-Tosa has been busy. The full might of the governor's fleet emerges from Dasun's cover, shedding red gas like the parting of a gossamer curtain. No more dreadnoughts, no sign of the Imperial Fleet I feared might be lying in wait, but the sheer scale of the deployment barely comforts that mercy. Every ship that can hold its own against Dasun's gravity has been lying in wait for us.

They enter the field with their guns already hot, their engines burning hard, and their vectors woven like a net.

The Archon strategy shifts in an instant, and not in a good way. The vicious pace of our deployment stumbles into a frantic rush to meet the Umber forces on the field. The war drums have shifted too, but my Umber-raised brain can't translate the message they're sending any more beyond *not good not good not good*.

And Wen is still in my ear, spitting mad that I won't let her out to die in that mess.

"Wen, it's a disaster out there," I tell her, the words thick in my throat. "It's . . . The odds aren't good for us. They baited a trap and we walked right into it."

"Then let me get out there and change the odds," she pleads, turning to the camera to implore me directly. "All I've ever wanted, all I've been trying to do, is make myself useful to this empire. I want to be whatever it needs me to be."

"Wen." I sigh. "You chose this. You had a position on the bridge, a direct line to start calling your own shots, and what did you do? You let Iral stuff you in that ruttin' tin can and decide where and when he'd point you."

"You have the emperor *sitting next to you,*" Wen seethes. "He can probably hear me through the comm. Ask *him* what my marching orders are, if you're so determined to tie me down with the chain of command."

I glance at Ettian to confirm that he can, in fact, hear Wen shouting. I mute my mic and say, "She wants to go out there. What do you say?"

I can feel him sizing me up, settling himself in the knowledge that it was my plan all along to pin Wen in an airlock and keep her out of the fight. Realizing, perhaps, that I'm just as invested in keeping her alive as he is. Ettian's dark, gorgeous eyes speak the truth before he does, the truth I knew before he even understood it.

He can't let her go. He's lost too much already.

I pull out my mic and hand it over to him.

"Wen," Ettian emp-Archon says, damning himself with just that word and its tone. "You're to stay put."

I click off the comm before she has a chance to argue, but I see the betrayal hit her like boltfire on the airlock camera. She even reaches up and presses her chest as she bends low, the gesture so similar to the way Ettian bent on Ellit that it knocks a similar amount of wind out of me. But this isn't the moment to spare her feelings. Not when every system's hell has unleashed itself outside the *Torrent*'s hull.

The battle exists on a scale I can barely comprehend. This was the shit I was supposed to be training for at the academy—to manage an engagement of this scale with the same cool head Silon uses to conduct the *Torrent*. But I was supposed to have *years* before I was ever expected to. For now, I focus on tracing a single ship, trying to decipher its place in the greater strategy.

At least until a direct hit from a dreadnought's main battery reduces it to ash.

"We need to start thinking about evac," I mutter to Ettian. There are superluminal-capable shuttles in reserve for that exact purpose. It's part of a dreadnought's design, ensuring that the most essential people can escape even if the ship itself goes down.

But one look at Ettian tells me that Archon leaders aren't supposed to think like that. Even if he desperately wishes it were otherwise, everyone on this bridge expects to go down with this ship.

I'm weighing my options for how best to drag him to the shuttles when someone in the outer rings of the bridge screams "Hull breach on deck 42!"

"Rut me sideways," I mutter, bending low over my workstation. That's Wen's deck. That's—

"What is it?" Ettian asks when he realizes I've gone still.

I pull up the airlock cameras to confirm it, then release my hold on the inner door's locking mechanism, quieting the breach alarm in an instant. A hit didn't put a hole in the ship. The outer door of the airlock has been hacked to messy pieces with a lethally sharp edge, leaving a gaping hole in the *Torrent*'s hull that's roughly the size of a suited knight.

"She's loose."

CHAPTER 26

WEN STREAKS FOR the thick of the fighting like boltfire unleashed. I fumble as I pull up her suit's data, which only confirms that she's maxing out the burn on her boot thrusters. "Wen," I beg her through the mic. "Get back here right now, before someone sees you."

She ignores me. Ruttin' typical.

I spin up her suit's sensors, mapping them against the battlefield layout I've pulled down from the *Torrent*'s information. So far, nothing's deviated from its flight path to meet her, but it's only a matter of time before someone notices the small, human-shaped bogey flinging herself headlong into the fray.

"Patch me through to her," Ettian says, his fingers flying through similar motions a half second slower than mine.

"Like that's going to do anything," I snap. "She ignored you the first time. What's going to make now any—"

"She's going to need all the help she can get," he retorts.

Which I don't understand for a second. But then my attention snags on an Umber gunship veering suddenly off its course chasing a pack of our Cygnets—an action that would be welcome in any other circumstance but spells certain calamity when its vector abruptly pivots to sight Wen's infinitesimally small form.

She's spotted.

And she doesn't know it yet.

"Wen, above and behind on your left," I mutter. Watch as her helmet cams swing around to clock her new friend. Hiss through my teeth as she fires her palm thrusters, sending her spiraling not away from the gunship but straight toward it. So much for subtlety.

"Patch me *through,*" Ettian snaps.

"All right, all right." I do it with a flick of my fingers, then shift my full attention back to the inevitable collision of Wen and the gunship. They're still several miles away from each other but traveling at speeds making them basically negligible.

"Wen," Ettian whispers.

"Don't you do it. Don't you tell me to stop," she pleads. I spare a glance to note the servos in her hands tightening on her vibrosword's grip.

He shakes his head. "I've only got one thing to say. If you're going to make me watch this, you'd better make it worth my while."

On Wen's end, there's a short pulse of breath that carries with it the shape of a smile. She brings her vibrosword up, poised to strike, and holds a pose I've seen in so much wartime propaganda that the sight of it feels like she's just taken that goddamn sword and run me through.

The tide of the battle has suddenly shifted, but not in Archon's favor. The sight of Wen charging the gunship sends ripples through the field as the Umber craft loops its fellows in on the fascinating new development in Archon strategy. *Oh look,* I can almost imagine every captain saying, *Archon's sent out a suited knight for us to kill.*

But they're not the only ones who've realized that the Flame Knight has joined the party. A familiar rudiment has slipped into the war drums' cadences—the same pattern they beat when we took Wen out for her first spin in a powersuit. News spreads across the field like wildfire, buoyed by the drums' chaotic clamor. For the first time in a decade, a knight has come to call.

Next to me, Ettian is marshaling Archon's answer. "I need a fast roster of all captains who've flown knight escort before," he murmurs urgently into his mic. On his screen, he organizes the affirmative hails by proximity to Wen's location on the battlefield, then handpicks a squad of the most agile ships. The competency does something for me, I'm loath to admit, but I can't spare the distraction when the gunship's weapons are starting to lock onto their target.

"Evasive," I bark into the comm, and Wen obliges with a flip of one wrist, the pulse of her thruster throwing her into a corkscrew. Boltfire follows her like a magnet, and she dodges it by hairbreadths. I'd be shitting myself after a maneuver like that, but Wen's vitals are pilot-steady as she continues to weave through the fire, her movements just unpredictable enough to keep them from anticipating her with a deadly shot.

Agility can only get her so far with her distance to target closing. My palms are slick on my screens as I do my damnedest to track the threats converging on her. It's the most alive I've felt in months.

Three seconds to impact.

Two.

On one, she throws down her boots, swerving abruptly up from her former vector and arcing over the gunship's bulk. Her vibrosword flashes out, fully extended, glimmering red against Dasun's murderous glare. It dips down to carve across the ship's main turret like a gentle caress.

The turret cleaves into an explosion of untargeted boltfire in her wake.

"Yes!" I yelp, just as Ettian throws a fist in the air. The drums triple in intensity. The gunship sails on, belching flares of escaping plasma, trying to swivel its rear mounts around for a strike as Wen swings wide around it, too flushed with victory to realize she's about to get backhanded into atomic dust.

My stomach drops.

But before the rear guns can get a shot off, a barrage of boltfire puts the gunship out of its misery. Wen flips onto her back and retargets her cameras, letting out a surprised scoff, to find the reckoning Ettian's marshaled for her forming up on her tail.

They're a tight squad of ten, all of them fast enough to keep pace with a suited knight and all of them helmed by a veteran of the War of Expansion—someone who's flown with a knight before and knows exactly how to cover her. They let her take the point of a comfortably compact arrowhead, adjusting their vectors to match hers and waiting to see where she leads them next.

"Wen, Flame Squadron. Flame Squadron, your knight," Ettian says through a savage, triumphant grin.

I'm a little bit less surprised than I should be to find myself matching it. There's no time to bury myself in a spiral of conflicting emotions. There's only time to enjoy the unparalleled sight of Wen veering onto a new vector straight for a battle cruiser doing its damnedest to defang one of Archon's dreadnoughts. Flame Squadron follows like a loyal pack.

"Form up on the knight in a Dijkstra shield," Ettian says, a boyish sparkle in his eyes. The ships on my readouts shift effortlessly from an arrowhead into a sphere, some of them pulling ahead of Wen to place her squarely at their center. They hold the formation even as some of them spin their gyros to shift their guns to the most effective defensive position.

Not a second too soon. "Vipers, inbound, headed for your belly," I snap. Wen glances down, clocks them, and shifts her flight path to put a Flame Squadron ship between her and the incoming fire. The ships on the opposite side of her shell pivot what guns they have to lend their support as the void between the two squadrons comes alive with boltfire.

Wen holds her vector through the hellish barrage. She wants that cruiser—which, like most Umber ships on the field, has decided that the glory of taking out a suited knight is more important than the entire remainder of the Archon forces. Horror floods me as I watch it wrench itself off the vector it had been sailing on to strafe our dreadnought and swing its glorious bulk around to face Wen with the full coverage of its massive forward batteries.

"Ettian, we've got a big fellow out here looking like he wants a bite."

"I see him," the emperor growls between gritted teeth. Flame Squadron's doing its best to beat back the Viper flock, twisting in a defensive net, but the fighters are fast, persistent, and determined as hell to sneak a shot at Wen. Ettian's not quite as steady on the comm as I'd prefer, but now's not the time for criticism, and I certainly couldn't step into his shoes even if I tried. Where he fumbles for speed, he makes up for it with the unwavering trust for the soldiers he marshals and an encyclopedic knowledge of knight-based squad maneuvers I've never even heard of.

Something about the brightness in his eyes and the way he seems to have forgotten his injury entirely tells me he's been dreaming of calling these commands his entire life.

The brightness dims, but only by a hair, when we lose the first member of Flame Squadron to a direct hit from the cruiser. The silent burst is barely visible out of the corner of Wen's cameras, but her reaction tells me the rest. She veers abruptly sideways, her vector thrown into an unsteady squiggle as she tries to master herself again. "Rust, that was close," she hisses.

"Focus," I remind her, and in her interior helmet cam I catch her lips pursing with grim determination. "You're faster than them. More agile. Now, go show the big fellow what happens when he messes with your friends."

She obliges with an extra burst to her boot thrusters, ducking her head as if she's in atmo and trying to squeeze herself into the most aerodynamic shape possible. Girl and missile and throwing knife all at once, she sets her sights on the cruiser's main battery and lifts her sword.

And when she strikes true, I feel something inside me start to beat steady as an Archon drum. The sight of a knight tearing into a massive gun, rendering it useless with just a few hacks of her vibrosword, is supposed to fill me with terror. Or horror. Or nausea. The sight of *Wen* doing it should make me dread what she's become. Instead I'm wracked by an emotion so unfamiliar, so absent from my captivity, that it takes me a few seconds to figure out exactly what it is.

It's pride. Fierce, joyous pride as I watch her vault herself over to the next battery and plunge the furious heat of her boots against its side. Pride that I'm here in the *Torrent*'s bridge, running her comms. That I'm sitting next to Ettian, who's marshaling an ever-expanding guard of ships escorting her streak of wrath across the battlefield, keeping her fire alive despite Umber's desperate attempts to smother it.

It's been a long time since I've felt like I'm right where I'm supposed to be.

Wen barely needs any guidance from me to take on the cruiser. She all but skips across its surface, warding off fire from the rest of the Umber forces with her proximity to the cruiser's critical functions. And by operating within the cruiser's firing radius herself, she's invincible.

Worse, she knows exactly what she's doing. Wen did most of her growing up in a mob boss's chop shop, and she fearlessly applies her deep well of mechanical knowledge to terrifying effect against a ship that's literally millions of times her size. Every time her sword comes down, the ship loses a function. She's cutting her way back toward the engines with nothing to stand in her way.

"It's not enough," Ettian mutters next to me, shocking me from the glee of watching Wen wreck shit. I've drawn the easy lot, keeping an eye out for threats to Wen and Wen alone. In doing so, I've lost the scope of the battle, forgetting that we've been scrambling to match Umber's already-deployed forces. And even though fielding a knight created a mad dash to kill her that wrenched a good portion of the Umber forces off their vectors, Archon's still fighting to reclaim ground.

"Got a gun going hot on the *Fulcrum*!" Telemetry shouts from the other side of the room. "Targeting . . . that can't be right."

I glance down. Too late, I see it.

"Wen, *run*!" I bark into the comm.

And watch, helpless, as the dreadnought's boltfire slams into the cruiser's rear. The noise of the bridge is equal parts joy, confusion, and horror, but the only noise I care about is the gentle push-pull of

Wen's breath in the comm, telling me she made it clear of the shot. "Gods of all systems," I mutter, clutching my chest.

"They fired on their own people," Ettian murmurs, horrified.

"Of course he did," I snap, pointing at the command hierarchy we've scraped from the *Fulcrum*'s communications. Berr sys-Tosa himself is at the helm. Of course the system governor, paragon of Umber philosophy, would carve out an entire ship full of lesser people just to destroy a suited knight. The damage Wen could do to his army far outweighs the cost of the cruiser. The decision would be instantaneous, and the weight of his bloodright ensured it was carried out in the same breath. "As long as Tosa helms the *Fulcrum*, he'll dash as many people as he has to on the rocks until he's got a safe path to trample us."

There's a sharp hiss in my ear, the sound of Wen catching her breath all at once. I pull up her vitals. She's rattled, but coming back down from the shock, and she's secured herself safely to the exterior of one of her Flame Squadron ships, the motors in her suit's arm locked to spare her muscles the effort of maintaining her grip as it sets itself on an evasive vector. Through her helmet's cameras, I spot the mangled wreckage of the cruiser. What's left of it could barely be salvaged into enough scrap for a single Beamer. All that, just to kill her—but she didn't die.

Wen's cameras shift from the cruiser to the *Fulcrum*.

"Makes sense," she mutters to herself. "Cut off the head, the rest goes to chaos. They took Esperza and look at us now."

"Wen," I caution. I know where this line of thought goes. I know why her cameras are staying fixed on the *Fulcrum*, no matter how the craft she's latched onto twists and turns.

"Cut off the head," she repeats.

"It's a ruttin' *dreadnought*, Wen."

Next to me, Ettian stiffens. He's caught on too.

"You dodged *one hit*," I mutter urgently. "You're not immune to boltfire. None of these people we've marshaled can protect you, and all of them will die trying."

I wish I could control her suit from out here. Wish I could lock her fingers permanently to that ship and force her to ride out the rest of the battle clinging to its safe harbor. All my life, my voice has been my greatest weapon. I've been *notorious* for being able to talk anyone into anything. But against the immovable object of Wen's iron will, I'm helpless.

Helpless as I watch her fingers slowly uncurl, as I watch her kick her boot thrusters as hot as they'll go and catapult herself onto a direct vector bound for the *Fulcrum*. The bridge's noise goes distant around me. Ettian frantically coordinating Flame Squadron to fly defense for a knight who certainly isn't waiting up for them. The now-familiar rhythm of the knight herald doubling in intensity as the rest of the bridge realizes what Wen's doing. Even Deidra con-Silon's sharp, decisive voice, trying to marshal the *Torrent* as part of the knight's defense.

My universe has narrowed to Wen and Wen alone, to the inbound vectors of dozens of Umber ships coming to kill her, to the way her heart rate still hasn't settled. Nothing I could possibly say can get her to act rationally right now, and nothing I could do will be enough to keep her alive. I told *everyone* this would happen, and it was all for nothing.

The maelstrom of the battle whips furiously around her, and Wen flies on in the stillness of its eye. I numbly call the guns targeting her, and she responds to that, at least, without complaint, weaving through the fire until one of her guard has a chance to drive the aggressor off her. In her helmet's cameras, the *Fulcrum* looms ever larger.

Tosa's flagship is a brute of a beast, twenty miles from tip to tail. The sight of it catapults me back to the first time Ettian and I squared off against it, side by side in the *Ruttin' Hell,* the Beamer we'd just stolen as we made our haphazard escape from the academy. It was the first time I'd ever looked at a dreadnought and felt anything other than vicious pride in the power a single ship could wield. The *Fulcrum* is a monster among monsters, and we only managed to escape it by fleeing to a foreign empire.

And Wen is offering herself wholeheartedly to its inevitability.

In perhaps the smallest mercy I've ever experienced, she's being strategic about her approach, swinging wide around the dreadnought's flank to avoid the *Fulcrum*'s forward battery. Most of the dreadnought's guns move too slow to target her on her approach, but the ones at the fore are so massive that targeting hardly matters. And it would seem Tosa knows this too—because, slowly but surely, the dreadnought is starting to turn, trying to bring her into the sights of those devastating guns. Every degree the ship's nose turns twists around my stomach in a viselike grip. Wen dances on the edge of their firing radius, dragging behind her what seems like the entire Umber host.

But right when I think she's about to go in for the kill, she doubles back, brandishing her vibrosword as she sets her sights on one of the Vipers dogging her. I inhale sharply, ready to warn her of the starboard battery locking on, then save my breath when I realize she's counting on it. My throat goes dry watching the maneuver—watching her basically *sidestep* a ruttin' Viper and run the fighter cleanly into the *Fulcrum*'s shot.

Don't, I find myself wishing I could beg her once again. *Don't make me believe.*

The *Fulcrum*'s still turning. Inexorably closer to making the shot that will destroy her. Wen's just barely fast enough to outpace its rotation, an effort that isn't helped by her attempts to double back and swat down some of her pursuit—either with vicious strikes of her vibrosword or else by baiting the ships into the dogged fire still valiantly attempting to strike her from the *Fulcrum*'s starboard batteries. On my left, Ettian's bent low over his station, trying his damnedest to keep his head up even as his ragtag squadron starts to dwindle in number.

She's supposed to be targeting the *Fulcrum*. Why is she dragging this out? People are *dying*.

And then, it seems, she decides it's time. She vaults backward off another cruiser's skin, feints around a fighter trying to dance with her, and streaks straight for the *Fulcrum*'s surface. A few Vipers try to follow her, and I can't help but respect their courage. One she tricks into the line of fire. Another makes the wise choice and peels off before the same happens to them.

The third follows her right to the bitter end, attempting to veer up to match her when she levels out her dive to fly parallel to the dreadnought's skin. It isn't so lucky. The Viper dies in a quiet streak of flame, pancaked against the *Fulcrum*'s hull.

Wen flies on alone, skimming along the hullmetal. The ship is still tilting underneath her, caught up in the momentum of its attempt to get its guns on her. Now she weaves through fire from the other Umber ships trying to scrape her away from the *Fulcrum*'s hull, running like hell for the dreadnought's rear.

The dreadnought's rear, which is now pointed squarely away from Dasun.

I think Ettian realizes her game at the same moment I do. He tears himself away from his other comms, eyes blown wide with panic as he gestures for me to patch him through to her. I do it with no objections. If there's anyone on this bridge who can talk her out of what she's about to do, it's him.

"Wen," he rasps, his voice hoarse from the near-constant demands of marshaling Flame Squadron. "Please. Don't—I said not to make me watch—"

And if I thought I was being torn in half before, I now know that was nowhere close to my limit. Because just listening to the raw fear in Ettian's voice as he watches Wen flying toward oblivion, just watching *Wen ruttin' flying toward oblivion,* is creating a physical ache in my chest that has me almost pleading for the mercy of dreadnought boltfire.

I love them.

I love them both, each in their own way, and I fought like hell to stop them from destroying themselves.

And now, as always, I can only watch as Wen rounds out around the *Fulcrum*'s rear, around those powerful reactor-fed thrusters. Right now, they're inert, the ship relying on other mechanics to execute its turn. Cold, empty, gaping.

"*Wen,*" Ettian pleads.

She throws herself into their abyss, and I flash back to the first attack we weathered in the *Torrent*'s reactor. *The safest place on the ship,* she'd called it.

The only way to get to it is through the engines themselves.

The comms line crackles with a ragged breath, and Ettian lets out a faint groan. "Hope this is enough," Wen whispers.

And on my readouts, the *Fulcrum*'s engines ignite.

CHAPTER 27

I FEEL WORLDS end inside me. The kind of devastation that's only survivable on a planetary scale. Wen Iffan, the Flame Knight, ever the mechanic, has figured out a new way to take down a dreadnought—and sacrificed herself to its necessity.

I watch the slow inevitability of it. The momentum of the *Fulcrum*'s engines firing uncontrollably and the way it forces the ship forward, forward, forward into Dasun's grasp. The dreadnought's engineers are fighting like hell to counter it with every ancillary thruster aboard, but once twenty miles of starship get moving, they're all but impossible to stop.

Next to me, Ettian is gut-shot again, bent in half, the rest of the battle lost to him as his world narrows to the *loss of signal* error pulsing across my readouts. He hunches over the console like the empty husk of Rafe's armor, like his bones have been vaporized by the blast from the *Fulcrum*'s engines.

She's not gone. She can't be. Nothing's killed her yet, and nothing ever will. But the data is undeniable. *Loss of signal.*

The other data should be heartening. The *Fulcrum*'s valiant attempts to reorient are failing. Escape craft are jettisoning from its hull in droves. The ones with guns dive right back into the thick of the fighting. The ones without—well, they dive right back in too, turning the craft themselves into missiles that they hurl into whatever Archon ship they can lock their vectors onto. No quarter. No surrender.

With their leadership cut off, the rest of the Umber warships are scattering without any sort of coordination. I have no doubt that the captains of the remaining three dreadnoughts are jockeying for command of the vacuum Berr sys-Tosa's about to leave in their hierarchy. The Archon fleet carves through the confusion like a sharp blade through flesh, leaving silent explosions bleeding in their wake.

And in the midst of the triumph, Ettian emp-Archon is falling apart. He hasn't blinked, his eyes still fixed on the *loss of signal* message as if staring at it long enough will make it change.

"Your Majesty," one of the techs from Telemetry calls. Ettian's jaw pulses, his impulse to snap at the man building, but before it can break free, the tech says, "I'm getting something. Whatever it is isn't transmitting, but there's . . . debris, maybe. Or—"

Ettian snaps upright, clutching his side as he shoves himself out of his seat and strides over to the tech's station. A second later, I'm behind him, peering over his shoulder with my heart in my throat. Like the tech said, there's . . . something.

It only takes half a heartbeat for the bridge to erupt into chaos. The drums cascade into rhythms too fast for my Umber ears to parse, Silon's shouting something to her staff, and Ettian's own aides have swarmed to his side, shoving me bodily away from him. Even though the sound is lost in the clamor, I know exactly what he's saying.

Damn the danger.

Damn the protocol.

Get me to her.

The signal the techs are picking up is faint, but it's *there,* and it's roughly the size and shape of a single powersuited body, floating motionless in the void, a blip against the spectacle of the *Fulcrum*'s destruction. Tosa's flagship is beyond hope now, the atmosphere shearing its skin off in fiery flakes as the last and bravest of those attempting to abandon ship leap desperately from its sides. The Flame Knight drifts above it all, above everything she started—or, more accurately, everything she finished.

The day is won.

On one of Silon's screens at the core of the bridge, Berr sys-Tosa is delivering a solemn speech from the *Fulcrum*'s command core. It would seem that the governor has, for the first and final time, elected to do the honorable thing and go down with his ship. Or maybe he's just doing what comes naturally—abandoning his duty and surrendering to the Archon rebellion.

The Tosa System is Ettian's. The Archon Core has been reclaimed.

And the emperor doesn't give a shit about any of it. His eyes are wild, his brow damp with sweat as he shoves his way through the knot of staffers and aides and bridge techs, past anyone who has a chance of talking him out of this. I trail in his wake, invisible as usual, swept up in the crush of people trying to tag along as he storms the intership deck and commandeers a shuttle to the *Torrent*'s outer hull, where a recovery mission is already staging.

The clamor grows louder when the soldiers on deck realize the emperor himself is hijacking their mission. An hour ago, I would have gloated over the amount of pushback Ettian's facing from his infantry—more evidence that his rule is already doomed. But now—

Now—

"*Everyone, shut the rut up,*" Ettian roars suddenly, and the whole deck plunges into the closest thing to silence it can manage. "Who's the pilot?"

"I am, Your Majesty," a stout older woman in a flight suit announces, folding her arms as she steps in front of the rest of her crew.

"I'm overriding this mission's schedule. Get that shuttle prepped for immediate launch."

"With respect, Your Majesty, the field is still active. Our crew isn't cleared to fly combat."

Ettian clutches his head, pressing his circlet so deep into his skin that it leaves a bruised-looking impression. "Either you fly that shuttle out of here or *I* fly it out of here. We can't wait for the field to quiet."

No one wants to tell him the obvious. To tell him that power-suited shape we sighted out on the field isn't showing any signs of life. It likely won't matter whether we get to her now or later, but we all know he won't hear it.

The pilot glances back at her crew, something molten in her gaze. She's an old-timer—the kind who must have fought alongside suited knights ten years ago. "We can make the run, if your explicit wish is to override our protocols and endanger these fine soldiers."

"They knew what they signed up for when they enlisted," I blurt, and every resentful eye in the knot of people gathered here snaps to me. My eyes are only for Ettian, for the grateful look he passes to me that says he understands.

I spoke the words they wouldn't want to hear from him.

"The Flame Knight needs us," Ettian says softly, and for a second he's not an emperor at all—just a boy who's lost enough already. And I think that's the thing that finally pushes them over the edge, because the pilot turns to her crew, flashing hand signals that send them scrambling across the deck. Ettian charges after them, and I follow, braced for a hand to come down on my collar and yank me back.

It never does.

We sit side by side on a bench outside the hold, both of us staring into our hands as the shuttle's bays open and the void rushes in. The grumble of the door machinery wars with the eerie quiet in a way that makes me miss the Archon drums we left behind on the *Torrent*.

There are no windows looking into the hold behind us. The

pilot-turned-mission-lead explained to us that she'll have a live feed from the spacewalking crew that can stream to a datapad, but apparently Ettian's not in the mood to watch it and I didn't dare ask for it myself.

Instead, I stare out one of the windows built into the side of this corridor. From our position, I can't see the recovery mission, but I can see the flashes of light from the battle's scattered remnants against the majesty of Dasun's clouds. Boltfire rains down on the Umber craft making their last stand against the destruction of the *Fulcrum*. There's something poetic about the dreadnought's dramatic end, so close to the shipyards that birthed it. So many Umber war machines were built from the metallic asteroids that once stabilized in the Dasun–Tosa libration points. Now that metal returns to the void we stripped when we overtook this system.

The thought strikes me—we're fighting and dying, all of us, for territory that's already been chewed up and spat out. All this chaos and strife for a few rocky worlds that won't grow much and the empty husks of shipyards that have long since served their purpose. What *point* is there to all of this? Why are we holding on so tightly? With every brilliant flash, I lose more of my army. More of my people. More of the ones who stand a chance of rescuing me. My thoughts flicker to the academy students who must be among the *Fulcrum*'s fleeing crew. Hanji said they'd all been pressed into service.

Another flash. Could be Ollins.

Another flash. Could be Rhodes.

Another flash. Could be Rin.

Even though Tosa's surrendered, every commander on the field beneath him fights with no quarter. They know a worse fate awaits them if they escape with their lives only to explain their loss to our empress. I force myself to keep watching, even though the boltfire sears my vision, even though the spirals of the gas giant's storms are starting to make me feel nauseous. I don't want to be the kind of leader who looks away from all of this. None of my people are here to witness me doing this, but I can feel the truth of it in the chambers of my heart. I won't be able to live with myself if I'm capable of blocking this out.

An intercom overhead crackles to life, the mission lead's voice coming through. "We have contact. The suit is still unresponsive. Bringing it back to the hold now."

I turn around just in time to catch Ettian rocketing to his feet so quickly that his circlet gets knocked askew. He doesn't bother fixing it—and doesn't clutch his wound like I expected him to. He turns in a circle, his hands faltering on the hold door when he realizes that it's sealed tight with nothing but the void beyond it. His wild eyes find mine. He looks like he's on the verge of saying something, but before the words get past his lips, a thud echoes through the ship as the floor beneath our feet shudders. I clutch for the bulkhead, bracing for another impact, my eyes whirling back to the window to find whoever shot at us, but then the intercom announces, "Suit's in the hold. Clear to seal the rear doors and repressurize."

Ettian's at the door in two quick strides, one hand braced against the frame, the other on the handle. I'm at his side a half-second later. "Please, gods, anyone, please," he mutters under his breath.

Hesitantly, I slip a hand onto his shoulder. He should tense at that, but instead I feel his muscles go slack beneath the pads of his suit. I close my eyes, resisting the urge to shake my head. He really is going to get himself killed one day if these are his instincts.

Within a minute, the hold is repressurized. When the door flashes its ready signal, Ettian rips it open and charges through. I lurch after him, nearly knocking him over when he draws up short at the scene inside.

The powersuit lies sprawled on the floor, its limbs locked at rigid angles. The pair of soldiers who recovered it are still in their breach suits and EVA packs, any thought of themselves abandoned as they pry frantically at the casing around the shoulders and helmet. Against the frenzy of their efforts, the suit is horrifically still.

Then they pop the helmet off, and a soft, choking gasp echoes through the hold.

Wen Iffan shimmies free from the suit, her breathing coming in unsteady hitches and every limb shaking like a newborn colt.

She's barely off the ground before Ettian takes her back down, folding her into a hug so vicious that it knocks both of them off their unsteady legs and sends his crown skittering across the floor. They collapse in a heap, Wen laughing, Ettian sobbing—though it's really a mix of the two on both counts. She snares her arms around his torso like she's back in the void and he's her only tether. He buries his face in her neck like he'd rather be lost in the dark of it forever.

It takes a while to parse the muffled, tear-choked words Ettian's muttering. "The suit was . . . No signs of life . . . I thought you . . . I thought you *burned*."

Wen pries him away from her with gentle hands on either side of his head. She wrenches one of his hands up, laying his palm against the rough ruin of her burn scar. "This much," she tells him fiercely. "No more."

The intimacy, the softness between them, the way she lets him touch the part of her she protects the most—it should kindle a jealous ache in me. Instead I'm left with nothing but relief. Relief that she's alive. Relief that despite the carnage below our feet, there's room for soft things in this galaxy still, even if one of those soft things is the giddy, slightly-singed girl who sparked the devastating, decisive blow of this battle. Relief that while Umber commanders are throwing away the lives of their troops with abandon, Ettian emp-Archon threw himself into an active field for a chance to rescue a single person.

And suddenly it hits me like a gut shot—though Ettian would probably try to strangle me for that metaphor—I know what I have to do. What should have been stupidly clear to me from the start, ever since I realized that Ettian's imperial upbringing was full of gaps that would likely get him killed. There *is* a point to all of this, and it's sprawled on the floor in a messy tangle in front of me. My place isn't at the Umber Seat, taking up my mother's bloody standard. It's here at his side, keeping him and everything he loves alive.

His crown lies on the floor at my feet, completely forgotten. I bend and pick it up, a little surprised by the searing warmth he's left behind in it. It's an elegant thing, born of a design sense that's completely foreign to me. I run a fingertip over one of the platinum spirals, pressing it so that it bends slightly.

Months ago, I would have snapped the thing in half over my knee the second I got my hands on it, or else twisted it into a warped knot, not caring if the metal pinched me or the emeralds ground against my bones. I can feel the ghost of that impulse humming through my hands, the faintest whisper of my mother's voice in my head ordering me to do it.

Instead I cradle it carefully and step up beside the Ettian-and-Wen heap still piled on the floor of the hold. I catch a sharp, wary motion from one of the two spacewalking soldiers, but I think she registers my intention just as quickly and stops herself. It's enough to startle Ettian from the moment of relief he's locked in. He pulls back a little more from Wen, but keeps one hand rooted on the solidity of her shoulder. I doubt I'll be able to get an inch between them for at least another hour.

His eyes find mine, and a sheepish expression tugs at his lips. I know he's expecting me to start ranting about how emperors are *supposed* to behave, which is just as well, because I want to surprise him so ruttin' badly.

And I do, bending down and carefully setting the platinum crown back on his skull.

CHAPTER 28

IT DOESN'T FEEL like it's really over. I keep setting up milestones, then watching as they pass and realizing I'm still braced for the floor to drop out from underneath me or another assassin to come crawling out of the vents or the entire Imperial Fleet to drop from superluminal. We take down the last dreadnoughts. We get word from Imre, where General Iral has secured a hard-won victory with his advance forces—a victory that seems almost inconsequential against the spectacle of the battle at Dasun. We stay aboard the fortress of the *Torrent*'s safety, supervising the exodus of Umber-loyal people fleeing the system.

None of it makes anything feel *done*.

Maybe it's because there's so much missing. We took heavy losses in the battles, losses that feel callously outweighed in scope by the empty station on the bridge where Esperza used to sit. I didn't think I'd miss her this badly, but without the commodore, the *Torrent* feels like someone's knocked out a wall. Deidra con-Silon's prim, unbothered ease at the helm has dissolved into a distracted unsteadiness that has more than a few whispers flying around the bridge. It appears the captain is *lost* without the casual needling that seemed to have made up a good portion of her interactions with the commodore.

Wen's all but disappeared. I've tailed her for long enough to know that Esperza was the model she was building all her hopes and dreams around, and the commodore's capture seems to have rent something unfixable inside her. In want of a project—or maybe of something that makes her feel in control again—she's thrown herself into repairing the powersuit. It's only partially operational, last I heard, and who could blame it? The thing may be a nightmarish relic of Archon tech, but it took a fair amount of heat in the *Fulcrum*'s reactor and I'm astonished everyone seems to consider it salvageable. Wen spends every cycle of the *Torrent*'s day in the lab with the techs, puzzling out the last few things she needs to get it up and running again.

I shudder to think what she'll do with it once it's operational. The derisive mutters about the Flame Knight have died in the atmospheric burn that consumed the *Fulcrum*. In the span of a few months, Wen Iffan has gone from Ettian's notorious rogue operative to another one of those Umber stories told in hushed tones. I can picture kids in academies across the empire whispering after lights-out, *I heard the Flame Knight once took out a dreadnought single-handedly*. Honestly I can't think of a feat more impressive, and it scares me how certain I am that Wen will be able to.

But since she's in the lab at all hours, I find myself completely unaccompanied—and completely at peace with that for the first time since I boarded the *Torrent*. I've managed to secure a datapad, and I spend most of my waking moments in my quarters, hanging backward off the bed with my feet propped against the wall, scrolling through the broadcasts we've picked up. I watch the reporting on the power transition on Imre, which is done mostly in quiet back rooms rather than through another grand, disastrous triumph ceremony. Ettian stays absent from most of it, recovering from the strain the battle put on his still-healing body, but he makes a broadcast appearance to announce his appointment for the new system governor.

I scrawl notes nonstop through his speech, trying to untangle the genuinely useful feedback from my uncontrollable urge to force an Umber mindset on his governance. I have to keep reminding myself that gracious sharing of power plays well to Archon crowds—that it's not a sign of weakness. It's an entirely different philosophy of leadership from the one I grew up with, but this time, I'm trying my best to understand it.

Roughly a week after the battle at Dasun, I get a message on my datapad summoning me to the nearest shuttle deck in the *Torrent*'s command core. I consider swinging by the lab and asking Wen to escort me, but there's a part of me that wants to do it all on my own, just to prove I can.

So I do, and it turns out I was right.

When I find my way to the correct deck, I'm greeted by a surprising degree of emptiness and two familiar sights.

The first is Ettian emp-Archon, dressed in a fine suit and a simple platinum circlet, looking far more at ease on his feet than the last time I saw him.

The second is the *Ruttin' Hell*.

Ettian grins at the surprise on my face, keeping a respectful distance as I step up to the Beamer's hull and run my hand wondrously over its heat shield. My fingertips are drawn almost magnetically to the juncture between the ship's body and one of the rotary thrusters' branches, where its unofficial designation has been sketched onto the hull in brassy paint.

I press my index finger against the faint blob of a fingerprint. A second later, Ettian covers the one next to it.

"Been a minute, huh?" he says with a breathy laugh.

"Thought they would have scrapped this thing ages ago," I reply. I trace my gaze along the brass stripes scoring its hull—anything to keep from looking at him directly.

"They wanted to," Ettian says, knocking his knuckles lovingly against the heat shield. "Even after all the modding Esperza did to make it flyable, the fact remains that . . . well, it's a Beamer. We have better shuttles."

"But do we, though?"

"Exactly," Ettian says. His breath catches like he's about to say something more, and I finally make the mistake of looking at him for real.

I can feel the empty space where my revulsion is supposed to be, so recently vacated. I'm supposed to hate him on sight. The platinum on his brow alone should repel me.

Instead I find myself leaning forward.

"It's yours," Ettian blurts.

That's enough to bring me to a screeching halt. "It's . . . What?"

"Look," he says, scrubbing one hand anxiously over the back of his neck, "I should have done this the second someone tried to kill you under my care. I can't keep you safe here. I'm using you as a human shield, dragging you into the worst parts of the war, and then I went and got myself shot and Wen got herself suited and . . . We can't protect you anymore. Not with so much on our shoulders. It's not possible for me. It's not fair to her."

"So, what?" I ask, trying to hold back the incredulous laugh building in my throat.

"So take the *Ruttin' Hell* and go."

"Ettian—"

"The ship is yours. The *Torrent*'s cleared it to fly an exit run from this deck through the outer hull. The fleet's been instructed to give it safe passage, and you have a window to go superluminal. By the time anyone questions it, you'll be well on your way to the Imperial Seat."

I scoff. "Iral will find out soon enough, and he's gonna *eviscerate* you when he does."

Ettian's hand folds protectively over his stomach, and he smiles bitterly. "I've survived it once."

I throw my hands up, taking two quick strides away from the hull as I try to calm my breathing. "See, this? This is why I'm not going anywhere," I snap, whirling on him and pointing an accusing finger at his face. "I leave you alone for a *week* and you get stupid ideas like this."

"You're what?"

"You heard me, dipshit," I snarl, closing the distance between us and jabbing him in the chest. "I swear on the gods of all systems, if I actually got in this ship and rutted off to the other end of the galaxy, you'd be dead within the week."

"But you—"

"Oh, don't give me that self-sacrificing Archon bullshit. Your empire depends on you being a *fixed point,* not capitulating to the safety of your *enemy*."

"My enemy, who is—"

"This is why I made notes on the last speech. We can go over them as soon as you're done covering up whatever it is you've done here to get the clearances—"

"Gal!" he snaps, clutching me by my forearms and jolting me out of the fury that's overtaken me. "Are you . . . Are you seriously turning this down? I thought this was everything you ever wanted?"

Safe passage home. A direct line from here to my crown. It's all we set out to do all those months ago when we escaped the academy together. It's everything I thought I was fighting for during my time in chains.

But I think that time is over. I glance down at the platinum cuffs on my wrists, so familiar to me by now that I sometimes forget I'm wearing them. Taking them off feels . . . wrong, somehow. And I know I *really* shouldn't be this far gone, but after the crucible of the battle at Dasun, I'm . . .

I've changed.

Ettian's hands slip down my arms until he cups the cuffs. His fingers ply carefully at the fasteners, his brow furrowing as he realizes it's a bit more difficult than it looks. My breath feels lodged in my throat until the moment he loosens them completely and lets them fall to the floor between us.

"You're free," Ettian urges. "Leave, Gal—while there's still a window."

I take an unsteady half-step backward, glancing over my shoulder to confirm that the *Ruttin' Hell*'s ramp is fully deployed. I feel unbalanced without the familiar weight of the platinum at my wrists, and I'm placing the blame solidly on that for why it's taking me so long to find the right words.

"You know the nice thing about freedom?" I ask after a long pause.

"Hmm?"

"I don't have to do a goddamn thing you say."

I have him by the collar before any more excuses can tumble out of his mouth. The motion takes me back, back, back to a riverside on Delos, when there was sand between our toes and a galaxy of secrets still between us. Back when I tried to kiss him—after he'd just tried to kiss me—and he held me back and told me we couldn't. Shouldn't. For the sake of my empire. Because we could never really be together—something we both knew and chose to ignore.

Like last time, this is a leap of faith. A question waiting for an answer.

Unlike last time, he doesn't stop me before my lips reach his.

For once, kissing him is simple—if only because I've decided every single consequence of it can rut right off. I don't exist in the fallout of this action. I just exist in the moment of it, in the way he breaks the kiss on a gasp, then dives back in for more, the way my hands fit gently on his sides, pressing him against the *Ruttin' Hell*'s hull. There's a terrifying part of me that wants to make this moment my entire existence, forever, but that part gets shocked back to reality the second I press just a little too hard and Ettian breaks away, seething through his teeth as he clutches the wound on his stomach.

His eyes meet mine, and I expect an accusation. Something about trying to kill him again, about how I must be manipulating him now, about—

"You took notes on my speech?" he asks—not drily, sarcastically, but with so much hope and incredulity that it feels like it might rip me in half.

I offer a sheepish shrug, one hand still firmly anchored on the back of his neck. "I wouldn't trust it either. Both because it's *me* we're talking about and because it's your job as an emperor to be on guard for shit from people like me. But . . . Look, in the battle, there was a lot going on. A lot to process. And something clicked in the midst of trying to keep Wen alive. Something I really, *really* hate having to say to your face." I groan, which only makes Ettian's grin grow wider.

"Go on," he says with a beatific imperial nod.

"Oh rut off with that," I fire back, resisting the urge to jab him where he's sore. "The whole time after you found out who I was but before I knew who you were—it sucked, it was scary as hell, but it was the happiest I'd ever been. Because it was us together against the galaxy. And when the two of us were coordinating to keep Wen alive, I felt it again. I realized how much I missed it. I realized . . ."

This time, Ettian doesn't dare try any sort of smug gesture. He waits with bated breath for what I'm going to say next.

"I realized it's the most important thing to me. I realized I could have the throne, have the entire galaxy laid at my feet, but . . . No empire is worth it if I don't have you too."

He smirks. "Heard that one before."

I scowl. "Didn't have all the information last time I said it. Now I do. And I ruttin' mean it, Archon."

His eyes go wide. I've never called him anything but mocking honorifics and his first name. Addressing him by his territory is a confession all in its own, acknowledging his legitimacy as its bloodright-granted heir. I think that, more than any other word of my haphazard speech, convinces him I'm telling the truth.

"Gods, they're all going to wish Hanji had killed me," he murmurs just before he leans in and sweetly, gently presses his lips to mine.

I've barely gotten used to the sensation when he jerks back abruptly, panic sparking in his eyes. "Shit, Silon, there was a meeting—I'm supposed to be . . ." He glances down, smoothing frantically at his rumpled suit, then back up at me with an anxious smile.

"Go," I tell him, tucking his collar back in place as I reluctantly slip my hand from his neck. "We'll have plenty of time to talk this through later. And go over those notes I took. And—"

"Till then," Ettian whispers, then pecks my forehead and rushes off to the hangar's exit as quickly as his injury will allow him to go. I watch him until he's out of sight, then grin wide, draw back my foot, and punt one of my discarded platinum cuffs clear across the deck.

The magnitude of what I've just done doesn't hit until I'm back in my rooms. I just threw away the purpose I was *born* for and, for the first time in my life, chose something purely because it felt right. My heart's hammering like I just told my mother to her face to go rut herself, but I can't find it in me to fear that like I should.

I'm still giddy, still rubbing one hand disbelievingly over my lips, when the door to my quarters blasts off its track and goes flying end over end across the room.

A figure in a powersuit saunters in. "Oh," Hanji Iwam's voice echoes from within its impenetrable armored shell. "I could get used to this."

CHAPTER 29

THE POWERSUIT WAS DISABLED. Wen *said* it was disabled.

The sheer confusion renders me motionless, but my senses return as Hanji starts toward me. "Now, hold on one second," I stammer, shrinking back against the couch. "I'm your emperor, right? You're loyal to the Umber Crown. Hanji. Hanji, stop. Hanji!" I yelp as she grabs the arm I've flung out in a pointless attempt to ward her off. With her other, she grabs me by the waist and hoists me over her shoulder like I weigh no more than a towel. "I *order* you to stop," I choke.

"Sorry, Highness," she says as she turns back to the ruins of the door and takes off at a jog. "I've got orders from a little higher up."

And oh, there's the shock. My blood feels like I've been tossed into the void, like it's boiling and freezing simultaneously. This is my mother's reckoning. It starts with my safe return to the Umber Core and ends with the annihilation of the Archon fleet and everything Ettian's rebellion has built. With license to hold nothing back, the Imperial Fleet will sweep clean through this system until nothing Archon remains.

I convulse violently against Hanji's armored grip, trying to worm free. My presence is the only thing protecting Ettian from annihilation. He needs me now more than ever. I still have the taste of him on my lips.

"Help!" I shout, but as usual, there's none to be had. Nothing's changed in the months since the last time someone burst into my quarters and assaulted me. I should be thanking every god that this particular person wants to abduct me, not kill me, but right now I just need somebody, *anybody*—

We round a corner into one of the *Torrent*'s service halls and Hanji stops dead in her tracks. I squirm, twisting my head as I try to see what's frozen her, and my heart lifts like the gravity generators have failed.

Wen Iffan stands in the middle of the corridor, one hand on the hilt of her vibrosword.

I let out a short laugh that blasts through my panic. Hanji might fancy herself unstoppable in the powersuit, but I'd like to see her try to get past the girl who took down the *Fulcrum* single-handedly. If Wen's standing between her and the exit, Hanji goes this far and no farther.

"Firecracker," Hanji says, nonchalant.

"Longshot," Wen replies. Her hand stays anchored on her vibrosword. No need to draw it just yet, apparently. Her eyes meet mine, and she nods.

I jerk my head, desperately hoping it reads as a nod in return.

Then her eyes shift back to Hanji. "This corridor should be clear all the way to the airlocks," she says, then pulls a comms clip off her belt and tosses it. Hanji snatches it out of the air with her free hand.

Wait.

No.

"No," I blurt out loud. "Wen, *help*. She's abducting me." I beat uselessly against Hanji's grip as she strides toward Wen, who steps aside easily, her sword still infuriatingly sheathed. Just as we're about to move past her, Wen reaches up to lay a hand on Hanji's plated shoulder. "I've done my part," she says, low and level. "I'm giving you three months to do yours."

Esperza's voice echoes wryly in my head. *Sometimes the advancement of the enemy is in the empire's best interest.*

"Three months?" Hanji replies, an unmistakable grin in her voice. "I'll do it in two."

"Wen!" I yelp, trying to squirm free and grab her simultaneously as we pass. She takes a steady step back, folding her arms behind her. "*Why?*" I seethe.

Her gaze flicks away, her lips going tight.

"What do you think my mother's gonna do to this fleet once I'm not in it?" I ask.

Wen's hand clenches on the vibrosword hilt. I don't understand. She's done all this—taking Rafe's armor, running the gauntlet of the battle at Dasun, nearly immolating herself in the *Fulcrum*—to protect Ettian, and now she's letting Hanji Iwam saunter out the door with his most effective shield slung over her shoulder. While wearing *her* most effective shield, for that matter. "Are you just gonna let her steal your goddamn suit?" I holler as Hanji rounds the corner.

Wen doesn't come after us.

Hanji finally loosens her grip on me once we're sealed in an airlock—which of course opens and closes to admit us without complaint, no thanks to Wen and whatever games she thinks she's playing. I immediately flounder down from her shoulder and try to lunge for the door, but she grabs me by the collar like a stray kitten, laughing as she lifts Wen's comm to her chest. "This is Wraith One. I've got him. Drop in five."

Wraith? Oh gods. No, no, no. Not again. I strain against Hanji's grip, practically choking myself as I try to reach the door controls. Wraith Squadron is the designation twenty people once used to try to kill me. No way in *any system's*—

Hanji jerks me back, cackling into the comm. "Nothing, Gal's just freaking out," she tells whoever's on the other end then clicks it off. "It's fine, Your Highness. Just a bit of fun. We've been calling ourselves that for a while now. Seemed a shame to stop."

I think I've miscalculated in nearly strangling myself. Not enough oxygen's getting to my brain—I can't make sense of half of the things Hanji's just said. "So you decided to give me a *heart attack* instead?" I wheeze, whirling on her.

"Yeah, well . . . okay, I get it, it was mean. But seriously—Wraith Squadron has your back."

"If you really had my back, you wouldn't be—"

"I'm popping the outside hatch in a minute," Hanji interrupts, dragging open a bin full of emergency breach suits. "You might survive the exposure by the time our ride arrives, but I wouldn't gamble on it. Suit up." Hanji pitches one at me.

I have a few suggestions where she can stuff it, but instead I bite my tongue and jam my feet into the leg holes. Hanji and the void scare me in equal measure, and if one's going to have her way with me, I'm sure as hell not going to let the other one touch me.

When I grab a breach helmet and seal it over my head, Hanji nods in approval. "Well, here goes nothing," she says, and yanks up the mechanical release for the void-side door.

"What do you mean 'Here goes—' "

The whumph of escaping air shocks me to silence as I instinctively haul in what could be my last breath. The perfect quiet of the void has rushed in to replace all of the airlock's atmosphere, rendering Hanji mercifully and terrifyingly silent. She reaches out and grabs my wrist, and I do my damnedest to dig in my heels, despite it being a lost cause. She yanks me forward, toppling us out of the *Torrent* core's gravitational field and into that sideways-swimming-pool-dive sensation of slipping into zero g.

I go from struggling to worm out of her grip to holding on for dear life in the space of a blink as the void truly takes hold of me. The powersuit's propulsion is the only thing that's going to save us from drifting hopelessly in the blackness of the dreadnought's hollow inner space until our air runs out, and I very clearly remember what happened to Wen the first time she tried it out.

After a minute, it becomes clear that Hanji hasn't even gotten to that step yet. "Do you even know how to turn it on?" I yell pointlessly into my helmet. "Did you seriously just toss us out into the void with no idea how to operate the ruttin' suit? ARE YOU. COMPLETELY. BRAINLESS?" I punctuate each word with a smash of my fist against the powersuit's helmet, which, while ineffective, does genuinely make me feel better about our predicament.

Hanji seems unbothered. At first I think it's just because she can't hear me, but the more I smack her, the more I realize she's *glowing* against the darkness of the *Torrent*'s interior. Something has a light on us.

I stop trying to beat through a tactical weave and twist, squinting against the blinding beams.

"You've gotta be ruttin' kidding me," I groan.

The familiar outline of the *Ruttin' Hell* flashes its lights.

The second the cargo-hold door seals behind us, I start pounding on the floor. The sound's deadened by the void, but as air trickles back into the hold, the volume starts to reach my ears. As soon as it levels off, I tear off my breach suit's helmet and let out a long, wordless yell that rattles the walls of the hold around me.

I'm about to turn on Hanji and see if I can't find a way to crack that powersuit open and start beating her face in again when the door above me slams open and Ollins Cordello all but jumps on top of me.

"Holy ruttin' shit, it *worked*!" he crows, clapping me on the back obliviously and then bouncing over to all but run circles around Hanji's powersuited bulk. "Holy shit! We got the prince. We got the suit. We got *you*. Wait, it is *you* in there, right?" he asks, slapping his hands excitedly against the suit's chest.

"Yeah, it's me, and *stop that*—it's so loud in here," Hanji gripes. She grapples uncertainly with the powersuit's helmet. "Okay, how do I—"

"*Gal?*"

I whirl to find Rhodes Tsampa picking his way cautiously down the ladder into the hold. His disbelieving grin is stark-white against his deeply dark skin, and I swear I catch a glint of tears in his eyes as he steps off the ladder and pulls me into a hug that I don't return. Before he can process the fact that I don't look particularly thrilled to be here, Hanji yells, "Hey galaxy brain, get over here. I can't figure out how to get out of this thing."

Rhodes easily abandons me for the more interesting problem. "How'd you get into it in the first place?" he asks, pacing around her as he peers curiously at the powersuit's joints.

"I dunno, Iffan had it all figured out."

"And she didn't tell you how to open the suit back up?"

"We were in a bit of a rush," Hanji snaps, prying impatiently at her shoulder plating.

"Okay, well, bend over and let me see if I can get inside—"

"*Gods,* Tsampa, buy me a drink first."

"Do you want me to leave you in there? Because I will leave you in there."

I startle when a gentle hand slips onto my shoulder, nearly elbowing Rin Atsana in the face when I whirl on her. "Welcome back," she says softly, a wry smirk tucked in the corner of her lips. "Did you miss this?"

I blink.

Because there's a truth there. I did. I spent months in captivity yearning for their company, longing to be surrounded by people on *my* side. I missed their simple chaos so goddamn much, and watching Ollins dance circles around Rhodes and Hanji as the former tries his damnedest to yank the latter's helmet off, I'm tempted to breathe deep and soak it all in again.

But then there's the fact that they're dragging me bodily away from everything I've chosen.

And—

Wait.

"The four of you?" I ask, both to stave off answering Rin's question for real and because I have a concern.

"The four of us," Ollins says, sidling up to my other side and throwing an arm around my neck.

"Then who's flying the ship?"

There's a brief beat.

"*Shit!*" Rin yelps, and darts for the ladder.

The four of them, I think with an exasperated roll of my eyes. Float me out the airlock, this is gonna be a long trip. I've probably got better odds of survival stuffing the breach-suit helmet back over my head and hopping out the rear door. I glance right to find Ollins grinning at me.

"Weren't you taller?" he asks.

I shrug him off me and clamber up the ladder after Rin.

Credit where credit's due. Somehow those four dipshits busted me out of there. Well, those four dipshits and Wen, whose turn I still don't completely understand. I thought she'd finally done what she set out to do. She'd carved a place for herself in the Archon administration and proved her worth unquestionably with her run at the *Fulcrum*. And, what? She just threw all that goodwill she spent *months* fighting for away?

I guess that's assuming she gets caught. Which might be a tall order, given how hectic things are now that the entire Tosa System has been claimed in the name of the Archon restoration. With her intimate knowledge of the *Torrent*'s workings, it's entirely likely that she managed to frame Wraith Squadron—which I still can't *believe* they've called themselves—as the sole perpetrators of my abduction.

I move through the *Ruttin' Hell*'s corridor like a ghost, haunting the familiar darkness. The kitchenette and bathroom on one side. The bunks on the other—the ones where Ettian and I curled up together with Wen overhead the last time I was aboard. At my back, there's a sudden gleeful shout that must mean progress has been made in getting Hanji out of the powersuit.

And ahead, the cockpit. Rin's taken the pilot's chair, and I drop into the copilot's with a sigh of resignation, my hands automatically flying to their usual places on the communication screens before realizing that Rin has done the smart thing and disabled them completely. She shoots me a worried look, her tongue poking between her teeth as she steers us onto a vector bound for the same outer-hull hatch I entered the *Torrent* through all those months ago.

"You seem . . . less than thrilled about all of this," she hazards.

"Perceptive," I grant her with a snap-point motion that used to make me feel so imperial. Now it feels like some kind of cosmic joke.

The feeling deepens when the massive hatch starts to slowly winch open, letting in a sliver of the starlight beyond the *Torrent*'s hull. Like Ettian said, the dreadnought's been instructed to let the *Ruttin' Hell* go. Our departure is by the mandate of the emperor himself.

What's he going to think when he discovers me gone? Horror starts to rise inside my gut as I realize exactly what he *could* think. Maybe he'll guess that I was planning on leaving all along, that I only told him I'd stay so that I could devastate him the way he devastated me. I've spent the past months manipulating him—why wouldn't I turn him throwing the door open for me into one last chance to tear his heart out?

The *Torrent* disgorges us into the stars, and I slump deeper into my seat, throwing my feet up onto the inert dashboard. Back to square one again. At this point, the sensation is so familiar that it's almost comforting.

In fact . . .

Well, the thing is I've been here before. Over and over, I've been kicked back down to nothing, my resources stripped away, the careful plans I built shattering around me. And if I've learned anything, it's that I always have more than I thought. Sure, they've torn me off the *Torrent,* away from Ettian, away from the choice I thought I'd made and the sureness I thought I'd instilled in his heart. Sure, it hurts like a dreadnought's hit me at superluminal, like something has torn through my essential matter.

My eyes slip sideways to Rin Atsana. Clever Rin, who can build almost any piece of weaponry if you just slide her the schematics. In the hold, I have Rhodes Tsampa, who could find those schematics if they exist and whip them up if they don't. I have Ollins Cordello, the ever-faithful witless muscle who's cheerfully borne the brunt of so many ill-advised plans—and holds the dubious honor of being the only academy student in history to streak the officer quarters all the way to the head's door and back.

And I have Hanji Iwam, the devilishly smart tower tech turned soldier of fortune, the only person to come close to killing Ettian emp-Archon since he took his throne, and my long-lost academy co-conspirator. She may be the trickiest asset to manage, but she's an asset all the same.

It's a week to Lucia from here. I don't need them beating Archon triumph rhythms by the end of it—I just need them more loyal to me than to my mother. It'll take a lot of talking, but if I don't have the bones of something by the time we reach the Imperial Seat, I never deserved a crown in the first place.

I wait with bated breath as Rin takes the *Ruttin' Hell* superluminal.

When the black around us settles into gray, I catch her eye, open my mouth, and go to work.

EPILOGUE

THERE ARE THREE versions of myself in the mirror.

The first is a photograph of me on the day I crowned Ettian. I look exhausted and betrayed, my wrists locked in platinum cuffs and my hair slicked back to expose my face to the galaxy. The image has been pulled up on one of the screens by the makeup chair for reference.

The second version is a doctored picture of a headshot taken a few weeks ago, which has been painted over with the stylists' vision of the man they're trying to shape me into. My skin has been smoothed over with makeup, my cheekbones have been shadowed, and the dark spots under my eyes have been brightened. My curls have been artfully tousled. I look bright, polished, and unquestionably Iva emp-Umber's. The artists have done everything in their power to distinguish me from the boy the galaxy met in chains.

In between the two sits my face as it stands right now, desperately being yanked toward the man on the right.

It's not going well. In theory, everything should be in place. My makeup matches the picture exactly, my hair falling in the same wavy swoops carefully placed to look careless. But there's nothing the artists can do for the emptiness in my eyes. I try to set my expression to match their rendering, but all I feel when I mimic it is how distant I am from the way I should be feeling right now.

This was supposed to be the most important day of my life. A spare few months ago, this moment was all I ever wanted—everything I had been born for. Now my heart is tied to a man on the other end of the galaxy, who's just lost the most effective shield he had against the reckoning coming for him. The last thing I want is to be a part of the force that's out to destroy Ettian emp-Archon.

But there's still a chance I can help him. A chance I can sway the course of his reckoning enough for him to escape it. The thought of the careful web I've been weaving lights a determined glint in my eyes, and suddenly I find my reflection twinning with the one on the right, the one that paints me with my mother's features and her raw ambition.

Behind me, there's a knock on the door. "Showtime, boss man," Hanji calls through it. I rise from the chair, nodding gratefully to the pair of stylists as they bow and mumble what might be the last "Your Highness" I'll ever hear.

Hanji greets me in the corridor, looking smart as hell in a slim-cut suit and a brand-new pair of glasses. Since my return to the capital, she and the Wraiths have slid effortlessly into my shadow—though to my chagrin, the four of them are nowhere near as effective in the role of "unofficial operative" as Wen was in Trost.

Maybe I should be thankful for that. Wen caused a *lot* of trouble in Trost.

I want to hate Hanji—I *do* hate her—for what she did to me, but in my current sketch of a plan, I need her too badly to hate her properly. She and the rest of the Wraiths have been indispensable since my return to the Umber Core, and not just for my machinations. Gods of all systems, I missed having drinking buddies, and one of the easiest ways to make people write you off as a dipshit is to surround yourself with the biggest gang of dipshits you know. What's a kidnapping between friends, anyway? I do occasionally look at Hanji and fantasize about breaking my hands on her face again, but we've got a common goal now—one too important to jeopardize with a grudge.

"Any news?" I murmur, bending close so the rest of my escort won't pick up the words.

"Still no schedule for the execution," Hanji replies. "But I'm keeping an eye on her condition—seems like the detention facility's not giving her too much of a problem. Swapped her arm out with a less troublesome prosthetic though, which she's clearly not happy about. Believe her exact words were, 'If I wanted a floppy wad of silicone, I'd—' "

"I get the picture. See if we can't do something about that. Have it ready for when . . ."

She nods knowingly. "I'll get Rhodes and Rin to dig up where we're keeping it."

As we move down the long hallway of the hypocaust, she falls into an uneasy silence. I never like Hanji's silences—it's usually when the bad ideas get time to percolate. Or the jokes. Not sure which is going to be worse in this moment.

So it startles me when the next thing out of her mouth is "You ready?"

We've emerged into another subbasement room, where a massive round platform waits—and once I step onto that thing, I won't be able to stop what's set in motion. It's my last chance to run. I meet Hanji's gaze, my mouth going dry at the magnitude of what I'm about to do.

"No," I tell her, shrugging. "But when has that ever stopped us?"

Hanji's vicious smile is the fuel in my engines, pushing me that final step up onto the platform. I drop my chin against my chest, tangling my sweaty fingers together as the mechanism shudders beneath me. It lifts me up through the aperture that swivels open in the ceiling, up through the dark channel of the citadel's innards, and out into the blinding light of day, the sight of my people, and the swell of thunderous noise that greets my arrival.

I realize with a sharp, twisting pain that I miss the Archon drums.

The glory of the Umber Imperial Seat splays before me. Towering, angular skyscrapers rake the sky like the points of a crown along the wide expanse of Triumph Way. On any other day, the road's brass-woven concrete would light up like molten gold in the late-afternoon sun, but today a swell of humanity pours over it, dressed in their glimmering black finest. At my back, the monstrous ziggurat of the citadel looms, its brass edges reflecting lethal blades of sunlight that force everyone's gaze to bow down to the twin pavilions and the raised path stretching between them that crown the steps up from the Way.

I spent ten years buried beneath this grandeur. Today is the first time I walk in the light above my home.

As I step out into the open-air pavilion with a beatific wave to the crowd, I glance along the raised walkway that stretches before me to the pavilion on the opposing end of the citadel steps. Two familiar silhouettes await there, and the sight of them sends guilt boiling through me.

I can barely see the glint of the sharp-edged brass crown waiting in my mother's hands.

I still don't know what to think of her. After months in Archon hands, I got so used to seeing her image painted with such a vicious brush that I was terrified I wouldn't recognize her when I arrived in the citadel.

But I did. She was on the landing pad when Rin brought the *Ruttin' Hell* screaming into one of the citadel's subterranean hangars, and I knew her in an instant, even blacked out in tac armor to disguise her among her retinue. My eyes locked on her magnetically, and I set my vector for her the moment the ramp hit the ground.

I waited to bow until she lifted her helmet off and met my eyes. They're hooded and richly brown, exactly the same as mine, and they shone with a wry spark of humor when she realized exactly why I'd held back. Only when I knew for certain I was looking into the face of someone with equal claim to the throne did I drop my chin in deference to the woman who carried and birthed me.

And I let her set a hand on my shoulder and turn my jaw this way and that, let her trail her nails carefully through my hair as she inspected me, and with that look decided that I passed some sort of muster. I could see it in her eyes—she'd worried that I'd been broken, that I'd been stained, that I wouldn't be the perfect heir she needed. And I inspected her in turn, confirming all the ways we intersected, all the ways our blood linked us inextricably. I could feel myself tumbling back into myself, or at least one of my selves that had so desperately wanted to be worthy in her eyes. I could look at this woman, remember her brutality wholeheartedly, and still want that.

I barely remember the particulars of our conversation, but there was a tacit assumption running beneath it, an undercurrent I never tried to divert.

That assumption has carried me all the way to this moment. All the way to the slow, steady steps I take as I cross to the middle of the walkway. My mother approaches from the other end, my father a few steps behind her, the noise of the crowd growing and growing and growing as we advance on each other. I'm close enough to meet her eyes, close enough to read the pride she wears openly, the doubt that runs beneath it, and the ruthless acceptance that suffuses it all.

Iva emp-Umber is dressed in a midnight gown that prickles with shards of rough-cut obsidian, woven through with clean brass bars that cut uncompromising edges around her figure. She's every inch a woman who broke an empire over her knee.

And every inch my mother, who raised me and cherished me and fought for me to have everything she'd built. As we reach the midpoint of the walkway and the crowd's noise winches to its apex, I settle into the resolution I feel like my entire captivity has been preparing me for. I spent months weaving a careful web of deception that—if I had seen it through, if my heart hadn't given out halfway to the finish line—could have destabilized an entire empire.

So I'll harden my heart and I'll do it again. Right this time.

I greet my mother at the midpoint with a soft smile, a gentle nod. She nods back, a pleased sparkle in her eyes. I drop to my knees in the spot she once bent, in the spot her sister once bent, her father once bent, and his mother before, and *her* sister before, and *her* mother before. Generations of Umber rulers have knelt in this spot to claim their bloodright, with the crowds chanting their names.

"Gal emp-Umber," they scream now. Long may he reign.

Well, we'll see about that, I think as my mother sets the crown on my head.

ACKNOWLEDGMENTS

This is my fifth published book but my first “middle book”—a notorious tough hill to climb for many authors. Add to that the fact that a good portion of that hill was climbed in the context of a global pandemic, and it’s honestly a miracle we made it here in the first place. For that, I have so many people to thank.

Thanks to my outstanding editor, Sarah Peed, and the entire team at Del Rey, for their continued dedication to the Bloodright Trilogy. To Cindy Berman and Sarah Feightner in production, Jordan Pace and David Moench in publicity, Ashleigh Heaton and Julie Leung in marketing, and Scott Shannon, Keith Clayton, and Tricia Narwani in publishing—thank you all for your magnificent work. Thank you to Charles Chaisson for the gorgeous cover illustration and to Ella Laytham for the keen-eyed design. I also didn’t get to thank Merilliza Chan for her lovely illustration on the first book’s cover in the acknowledgments of *Bonds of Brass,* so here is my belated and profound gratitude for the cover that took FinnPoe Twitter by storm. Thank you to the authenticity readers who have lent their insights to the series, in particular Cesar Guadamuz. Any mistakes and missteps that may remain are my own.

Even with five books under my belt, I remain unable to put into words how grateful I am for Thao Le, my agent and fiercest advocate. Thank you to the entire Sandra Dijkstra Literary Agency team, especially Andrea Cavallaro and Jennifer Kim, for their continued hard work and support.

Thank you to my critique partners, Tara Sim and Traci Chee, for being there for the best and worst of all of it. Tara, thank you for fielding every unfiltered scrap of nonsense I fling your way—I wouldn't be anywhere if I wasn't trying to entertain you. Traci, I aspire to have a heart as big as yours, and I'm so grateful for my place in it. Thank you to the Cobbler Club team—Alexa Donne, Gretchen Schreiber, and Alyssa Colman—for every necessary drunken vent session. I hope by the time these words are printed, we'll be doing them in person again.

Publishing is impossible without a life outside it, and none of this would exist without the people in my life who only vaguely understand terms like "print run" or "advance against royalties." Thank you to my day job cohort, for making earning my living so damn fun. To Wop House for every multi-time-zone hangout session, and for the epic adventures we'll have when we can see each other again. Thank you, Mom and Dad—I swear one of these days I'll write a book where the science passes muster, but in the meantime I'm grateful for your patience. Sarah, you're on your way—thank you for bringing a few of my wildest dreams to life with your art. And to Mariano, here's another *no u*.

Thank you to the librarians, booksellers, booktubers, bookstagrammers, and everyone who's done anything, small or large, to put my work in other people's hands. I would be nowhere without your support.

And to you, the reader, whoever you are. Thank you for joining me on yet another roller-coaster ride—now on to the grand finale. I'd promise not to do another diabolical rug pull, but at this point you should know what you signed up for.

Read on for a sneak peek at

VOWS OF EMPIRE

by Emily Skrutskie

Two young princes on opposite sides
of a galactic war must decide between loyalty and love
in this exhilarating finale to the Bloodright Trilogy.

CHAPTER 1

ETTIAN

MY STOMACH DROPS with the shuttle.

"Ruttin' hell," I mutter, one hand flying to catch the overhead straps, the other snapping to my forehead to keep my circlet from tipping off. It's a gusty day over Ichano, and the pilot isn't doing us any favors. My eyes catch Wen's across the hold.

She gives me the subtlest shake of her head, a wry smile twisting her lips. I know she wants to storm the cockpit as badly as me. The pilot couldn't stop either of us if we demanded he hand over the controls.

But both of us have higher duties than shouldering through turbulence.

So I grit my teeth through the *utterly avoidable* rattling and try to bend my focus back to my responsibilities for today. Beneath my feet sprawls Ichano, a newly liberated Archon city and the capital of Osar, a newly liberated Archon system. We've strung the second jewel in our belt after a month of fighting like hell—and all my thoughts keep circling back to is that it's been a month since Gal slipped past our fleet and disappeared into the black.

Because you let him, an ugly voice in my head reminds me. *Because you gave him the* Ruttin' Hell *and told the fleet to let it go.*

And then Gal refused, kissed me breathless against its hull, and told me he wasn't doing a damn thing I said. I took him at his word. I wanted so badly for it to be real. For him to be choosing me, siding with me, throwing off the shackles of his bloodright to fight this war at my side.

It was the happiest I'd been in months. I practically floated out of that hangar.

As far as I can tell from the tattered scraps of the security logs, the moment I left was the moment Gal got to work. He hadn't meant a word of it. All along, he'd been biding his time, waiting for his opening. From the holes in the camera footage and the drugged guards we discovered left in their wake, it seems his team sprang Hanji from her cell, rendezvoused with Gal, stole the powersuit, and flew the *Ruttin' Hell* free from the *Torrent*'s core without a single person lifting a finger to stop them.

If it hadn't torn my heart out, I'd almost be impressed.

Another gust of wind shakes the shuttle, and I let out a soft groan. No weather's ever been enough to put a fear of flying in me—and I've flown through a hell of a lot worse—but the grating on my nerves is the last thing I need ahead of today's event. "Five minutes to the drop," the horrible pilot announces over the intercom.

Wen rises from her bench, resplendent in platinum-trimmed tac armor that almost makes up for the fact that she *should* be wearing that powersuit. Her feet are encased in a pair of boot prototypes welded to a carbon fiber exoskeleton that frames her hips—a poor substitute, but enough to get her airborne. Her vibrosword hilt is latched to the magnetic sling on her waist, a reminder that powersuited or not, she's still the Flame Knight. To top off the look, her shoulders are mantled by a fine emerald cape that's been cut with vents.

It takes the breath out of me a little to see her like this—though certainly some of that comes from the wound Hanji bored through my gut two months ago. Wen Iffan's come a long way from the chaotic little troublemaker I found on the streets of Isla. I had no way of knowing the girl dressed in rags trying to sell me a skipship with no engines would one day singlehandedly win the battle for my birth system by taking out a dreadnought with nothing more than a powersuit and her sheer force of will, but there was a little voice in my head that day telling me to bet on her—a little voice that's never steered me wrong.

"You're staring," she says, checking over the straps of her armor. "Again."

"Can you blame me?"

When her eyes catch mine, my smile falters. No happiness of mine can stand up under scrutiny—especially not hers. I've tried to keep the effect Gal's abandonment has had on me concealed, throwing myself headlong into the war effort. I've been burning myself out on strategy meetings and resourcing meetings and gods-of-all-systems-know-whatever-else I can involve myself in, praying that somewhere in the middle of all of it, I'll shovel enough into the hole Gal left inside me to patch it over.

Wen hasn't been faring much better. I've seen a darkness eating at her ever since the battle that claimed the Tosa System and cost us her mentor, Commodore Adela Esperza, in the process. After Esperza's capture, Wen threw herself into repairing the damage her powersuit sustained at the Battle of Dasun. When Gal and his operatives stole it, she dug up the boot prototypes and all but stormed the battlefield. I feared for her, but she held her promise—the Flame Knight has burned enough for one lifetime. Even without the protection of the powersuit, even with Umber armies throwing everything they have at her, Wen Iffan is untouchable.

Within a month, we'd liberated a new Archon system, so . . . at least there's that.

"C'mon," Wen says, crossing the hold and laying her hands on my shoulders. "For the people, right?"

"For the people," I echo numbly. The past month has ground me down to dust for the people. I'm their emperor; I was born to serve them, and it's eating me alive. I pitch forward, letting my forehead rest against the cool shell of the armor plating her stomach. It grinds the circlet into my skin, but at least that wakes me up a little.

Above me, Wen huffs a sigh, barely audible over the rumble of the shuttle's engines. "Look, I think there's something I need to tell you." Her grip on my shoulders tightens. "I can't take watching you mope around like this anymore and if this . . . Okay, I'm just going to say it."

Then she doesn't.

"Wen?" I ask after the silence stretches on for an uncomfortable minute.

"I arranged Gal's escape."

The pilot's flying steady, but I feel like the shuttle's just been shot out of the sky. "You . . . No," I choke as my body locks rigid, braced for a spinout that's only happening in my head. *"No,"* I repeat louder. I try to wrench back from her, but she locks one hand around the back of my head, keeping me from looking her in the eyes.

"I had to. I'm sorry—I *had to*. I struck a bargain, and when you filed the clearance for the *Ruttin' Hell* to leave, I knew it was an opportunity I couldn't miss."

"You struck a bargain with Gal?" I seethe against her plating. The circlet digging into my forehead is the only pain that makes sense anymore, so I lean into it. "What could he possibly have offered—"

"I struck a bargain with Hanji Iwam."

My stomach convulses involuntarily at the mention of her name, the scar burned across it twinging. Modern medicine has worked its miracles for my gut wound, but it can't take away the memory that bullet seared into me. "I don't understand," I grind out, and Wen's grip on me softens enough that I'm finally able to pull back and tip my head up to search her face for answers.

I regret it instantly. I can't handle the way she's looking at me—the way this is tearing her apart just as much. She's trusted me so absolutely, and I thought I could trust her the same. "*You* told me you were going to set him free," she says, her eyes glimmering in the hold's low light. Another burble of turbulence hits the shuttle, forcing her to tighten her grip on me to keep upright. "*You* told me that we couldn't protect him anymore."

"And he *chose to stay.*"

If I thought she was torn before, it's nothing compared to the way her expression breaks now. "He did," she says, her voice choking on a sob she's desperately trying to suppress. The confirmation tears through me like she's just speared me on the end of her vibrosword. "He fought. He didn't want to go, but . . . It never would have worked. I know you wanted to believe—"

"I am *emperor.* I don't need to believe. I can make it happen. I could have—"

"Ettian," she murmurs, and even in the wake of a betrayal that should render us blasted apart, I still can't stand to see the tears spilling haphazardly out of her eyes. I reach up and catch her scarred cheek, my heart seizing as she leans into the touch like she always does. "Tell me we would still be here, right now, above a liberated city on a liberated planet in a liberated system, if Gal was working freely at your side. Tell me you could have negotiated your way through the infighting on your advisory. Tell me you could have held up your legitimacy against Iral's shadow."

Her words saw their way to bone. Letting Gal stay was what I wanted, but it wasn't in the empire's best interests, and the bloodright in my veins is nothing if I lose sight of the fact that I was born to serve the people. I shouldn't need her to remind me. *No empire . . .* a little voice in the back of my head starts, but I grab it by the throat. "I wouldn't have just had him by my side," I reply. "I'd have the Flame Knight too."

The flattery earns me a soft, sad smile that forces another spill of tears down her cheeks. They sear along my thumb as I brush them away. "Don't make me throw myself into another dreadnought engine trying to be enough for you."

She may as well have kicked me in the gut for the way it knocks the air out of me. "Wen . . ." I breathe, not knowing what I could possibly follow it with. Has she felt like this all along? Have I been letting her give herself to my rebellion, not realizing that she saw it as taking? I've already lost Gal—now I realize that I may have lost her as well.

The intercom crackles overhead like a slap to the face. "One minute to the drop," the pilot announces.

"I did what I had to," Wen murmurs, stepping back out of my reach. "What I always do. I did what it's going to take to win this rusting war."

Without her locking me in place, a sensation of weightless nausea envelops me. I haven't felt this fragile in the air since my earliest days at the academy. "What was the bargain?" I ask numbly. What price could possibly be worth all of this? What did she pay to bring me a month of suffering, thinking that Gal had deliberately abandoned me?

"I proposed a trade. I gave them their prince, and they have three months to pay me back with Commodore Esperza's freedom."

My gut reaction is fury. Gal wasn't just a prisoner—he was a guarantee. The most effective shield we had against the wrath of Iva emp-Umber was the knowledge that she couldn't risk eliminating her own heir in her effort to reduce us to dust and ash. Commodore Esperza was Wen's mentor and a critical part of my advisory, but there's no way her value matches Gal's.

But as the shuttle ramp comes down and the hold floods with furious daylight, I feel my own perspective burn away until all I'm left with is what Wen so clearly sees. Esperza was a cornerstone, one that's been knocked out from under my administration's foundations. Ever since her capture, I've had to fight twice as hard to balance out General Iral's attempts to wrest power from me—a tall order when I was still recovering from a hole in the gut. I need her moderation, and after all she's done for me, I owe her whatever chance we have at saving her life.

My anger shifts its target. How could I have abandoned the commodore to Iva emp-Umber's clutches? Over the past month, I've barely thought of her capture as I found myself pulled aside by the Osar campaign and the thousand other responsibilities hooked into my shoulders. It never even crossed my mind that we might have a chance to rescue her, to spare her the fate of my parents. What does that say about my ability to serve my people?

Wen swings her way to the shuttle ramp by the handholds overhead, reaching down and pulling a set of darkened goggles from her neck up over her eyes. Her cape flaps frantically against the wind as she squares her shoulders. Her hand drops to the sword hilt magnetized to her hip.

My heart aches at the sight of her against the city skyline—proud, unflinching even before a terrifying drop, and so willing to do what's necessary that she'll rip me in two to make sure we win. There's a solidity to Wen that defies the rocking of the shuttle, a confidence that the universe will stabilize around her will. I've tried to learn that confidence from her, but I've never been able to pin it down. The rug's been pulled out from beneath me one time too many.

And speaking of my traitorous, doubting heart—

"If you just gave them Gal, what's to guarantee they'll return Esperza?" I holler over the scream of the shuttle's engines as it wheels into position over the arena. "What's holding them to that promise?"

Wen turns around, pulling her vibrosword from her belt as her lips twist in a smile that's a thousand times more menacing with her eyes blacked out behind the goggles.

"Me," she says, then extends the sword with an electric snarl and topples backward out of the hold as below the crowd begins to roar.

PHOTO: © MARIANO MERCHANTE

EMILY SKRUTSKIE was born in Massachusetts, raised in Virginia, and forged in the mountains above Boulder, Colorado. She attended Cornell University and now lives and works in Los Angeles. Skrutskie is the author of *Bonds of Brass, Hullmetal Girls, The Abyss Surrounds Us,* and *The Edge of the Abyss.*

skrutskie.com

Twitter: @skrutskie

Instagram: @skrutskie

ABOUT THE TYPE

This book was set in Sabon, a typeface designed by the well-known German typographer Jan Tschichold (1902–74). Sabon's design is based upon the original letter forms of sixteenth-century French type designer Claude Garamond and was created specifically to be used for three sources: foundry type for hand composition, Linotype, and Monotype. Tschichold named his typeface for the famous Frankfurt typefounder Jacques Sabon (c. 1520–80).